UNEXPECTED RICHES

C. S. Boyll

Unexpected Riches is dedicated to family members and friends
who heard me discuss this story for years.
You know who you are, and I love you.

An extra shout out for their encouragement goes to
Chuck Boyll and Helen Schaible. Thank you.

Chapter 1

Boston, April 1666

It snowed outside the smoky tavern window, the kind of snow that gently touched passersby, ornamenting their dark, woolen clothing as they bobbed along Boston's cobbled streets.

From her upstairs window Elisabeth marveled at such bustle in the frosty chill. She wrapped her deep blue cloak more tightly around her. Never could she imagine missing the intense tropical sun of St. Paola, and yet there it was. Her mixed feelings of making it to Boston surprised her. After so many months of struggling to get here, she finally had arrived! Soon, she would be reunited with her David. Yet, what was this tightness in her chest?

She chastised herself: *Foolish woman, your heart should be over-flowing with anticipation.* But she could not rally such affection; weariness clung to her like snow. The dismal gray sky matched her melancholy; damp cold seeped into her bones.

In the room beneath, Elisabeth heard deep laughter and an occasional woman's bawdy protests.

"Such a fibber ye are! That she devil could not be as big as ye say."

A gravelly voice interrupted, "I swear it, on my mother's grave!

She towered over our ship and attacked, as if commanded by King Neptune himself. Dark she was, with teeth sharp as a hundred blades. But, saints be praised! We brought her down! Aye, we did."

During the long pause Elisabeth pictured the seaman wiping his foamy mouth on a hairy arm. "But, that was not the end of the matter. I ask ye, how were we to know that such an ugly beast would have her mate nearby? A little more ale, gentle Anne, and I best be telling ye the rest of the story."

Up from the floor below came a constant shuffling of benches, pewter bowls and tankards, joined by loud voices, restless bodies, and barking dogs. Elisabeth left the window and sat on her stale bed. She wanted to believe everything would be all right. She must keep faith. She and her husband had been separated far too long. Of course, reunion was what she desired. She sensed with all her being David knew she lived, just as she knew he still breathed. This instinctive connection and her marital covenant had been her compass to reunite with him. God's will remained clear on the matter.

But then, for better or worse, Mr. Colin Richardson existed in her life. If thoughts were sins, she had fallen more than once.

Panic rose within her. She forced it down with a deep breath. When fear roiled again, she stood and tried to shake it off by pacing the floor. Finally, she crawled into bed. She needed strength. The tavern bedding smelled moldy, its collective scent the signature of many strangers and old hay. Could she even remember the comfort of a decent English bed?

Elisabeth closed her eyes and thought back to David's and her stay in London before they boarded the *Sea Venture*. She remembered peering out a bedroom window from a home built on the London Bridge. There, too, she had heard numerous voices below. She had looked out on a bustling wharf where the great and small trading ships anchored. One of them would take her away from family and friends and carry her to a new colony near Boston.

Could her numb mind remember those feelings? That day, viewing the River Thames had sparked in her a desire to reach out to the adventure that lay beyond the Atlantic Ocean. But another part of her had wanted to recoil like a starfish out of water.

She was a country gentleman's daughter, a midwife, and newly wed to David Allerton. Her simple life had been enough. She thanked God she had not known then what she would endure to get to Boston. How would she soon explain all of it to her husband? Would David believe her? She closed her eyes to remember, to order her thoughts before she reunited with her husband.

Chapter 2

London, July 1665

David Allerton joined his wife at the window overlooking London's Thames River. He wrapped his arm around her waist. "We're going to do well, God willing, Elisabeth," he reassured. She quickly whisked her hand across a teary eye.

"Oh yes, David, I know that to be true, but it is so final, leaving the only place we have ever known." Elisabeth reached up for the comfort of holding her tall husband. He hugged her briefly, kissed the top of her head, and gently squeezed her shoulders.

"The sooner we go, the better you will feel. I am certain. There are, however, some final preparations to be handled. I must speak to Captain Briggs about our living arrangements aboard ship. Like it or not, the *Sea Venture* surely harbors wretched seamen who suffer the devil's business."

Elisabeth noticed her husband's edginess as he continued. "Once on shore, such men have reputations as alehouse haunters and whore masters, consumed by carding, dicing, and gaming. We must assure that even before this voyage begins there are no misunderstandings between crew and passengers. A solid line must be drawn. I am certain the captain and I will come to an understanding."

David Allerton, Oxford-educated and son of a country squire, was a capable man of twenty-six. His confidence and organizational skills were qualities admired and needed by the Puritan fellowship. He particularly was apt with horses, and their ship would carry two of his prized animals to the New World. Like other Puritans of their time the Allertons were leaving behind family and friends. Many from the previous generation had already headed to the New World and successfully established communities.

The Allertons knew the risks of sickness and shipwreck, but they also relished the fact that their unpredictable monarch King Charles II would be an ocean away. In the Massachusetts Bay Colony they would worship more freely, enjoy a community of kindred spirits, and make a promising living. The papist rumors of this king would not so easily meddle into their affairs.

The Allertons were indeed fortunate. They would join David's Uncle Tobias and Aunt Sarah, who had already established a profitable codfish business at Dorchester, six miles south of Boston. In London, the newlyweds also had comfortable lodging with David's cousin, John Allerton and his wife Katie, a German Lutheran immigrant from the District of Lippe.

Elisabeth smiled as she looked down at the walnut medicine chest she and David had acquired at a nearby apothecary shop. The shop's entrance displayed a glowing green "show globe." The alchemist's signature light beckoned Elisabeth, and David indulged her.

Once the Allertons entered the cluttered shop, Elisabeth and her enthusiasm for medical knowledge greatly impressed the chubby, chatty proprietor. "You say your mother was a midwife acquainted with Dr. Nicholas Culpeper?"

He lowered his voice as if someone else would hear. "A fine man, very knowledgeable, no matter what the Academy says. I fear his work suffers at the hands of his widow."

Elisabeth vigorously nodded. The materials Widow Culpeper published bore little resemblance to what Elisabeth found invaluable in Culpeper's *English Physician*. She felt certain the late doctor's work suffered defilement from greed.

The talkative apothecarist continued. "Mrs. Allerton, are you acquainted with Dr. Thomas Syndeham and his laudanum—tincture of opium some call it? Amazing medicine! It greatly eases pain and helps the ailing to sleep."

"No, sir. Would you please tell me more of its benefits?"

Their agreeable banter led to the purchase of the medicine chest at a good price. The generous man also gave Elisabeth a pewter vial of laudanum as well as dried herbs, powders, ointments, and other distilled liquids. He elaborately explained how to use them for many treatments.

This chest was David's special gift to her. How she loved him for supporting her keen interest in medicine. Not many men would encourage their wives in this way. Her father, too, had supported her mother and her in midwifery and nursing duties for their community as well as strangers who knocked on their door.

Thinking of her father prompted Elisabeth to reach atop her travel trunk for his letter. It had arrived yesterday from Bromsgrove, Worcestershire. She held it to the window.

My dearest daughter Elisabeth,

This is my last letter to you before you board the Sea Venture. Without any more trepidations, daughter, I desire for you to rest assured your family supports your decision to move to New England. You and David are in our daily prayers. I also want you to know that your father could never let you go if he did not believe you were seeking God's will with all your heart, mind, soul, and strength. Although apart by distance, we can readily pray in unison, 'Father, thy will be done on earth as it is in heaven.'

When we said our goodbyes there was so much I wanted to say that went unspoken. You must understand how sorrow bounded me. Like John Bunyan, imprisoned and apart from his family, my pain felt like the pulling of flesh from bone.

But do not be anxious about your father. I am greatly recovered and resolve to trust God in this matter. Still, there is unfinished counsel I desire to give you, even if it must be written rather than spoken.

Since the death of your dear mother, I have been pleased to witness how your trust in God's grace grew more and more through both trials and joys. Dear Elisabeth, you are so much like your mother. Your strong faith has brought me much comfort. I have full confidence that your patient and noble heart, your desire to do what is good and proper, and your love for David and others will bless all you meet.

As your father, I charge you to apply diligently the gifts God has given you. Out of his bounty, grace, and mercy he not only provides salvation for our needy souls, but he also has supplied all we need to fulfill his will during our lives. All these gifts we accept by the steady hand of faith, and it is in thankful obedience we use them.

What you will discover, beloved daughter, is that when you are obedient to God's will, unexpected riches follow. Admittedly, you will not escape the troubles and despair that are the condition of this world. These afflictions can make it difficult to discern God's will and tempt the flesh. But remember, dear one, when you find yourself in such trials, do not hesitate to do good, no matter what the cost. Surely, this is the Lord's pattern for us....

There was more her father wrote—how her stepmother missed her sweet conference, how her brother Adam fell from the apple tree, and how Paul ungrudgingly did his brother's chores. Finally, her father concluded:

Dear Elisabeth, remember the Lord Jesus will never leave you nor forsake you. May his face shine upon you and grant you peace. We look forward to a letter from you and David when you arrive safely in the New World. Until then, with the gentlest kiss and pure embracing of my kindest affection, I rest.

Your father,

John Compton

Elisabeth held the letter tightly for a while and closed her eyes, taking in a few deep breaths and trying to conjure up her father's familiar woodsy scent. Choosing to leave her family was the hardest decision she had ever made. When she married David just six months earlier, she had no idea this would be her destiny. But David's Uncle Tobias and Aunt Sarah in Dorchester, Massachusetts, extended an enticing invitation. Then she and David heard of a fellowship of Puritans making plans for the overseas journey.

Soon, in a whirlwind of decision-making, the voyage became more than a dream. Elisabeth tucked the letter in the leather journal her father had given her and placed it in her trunk. Her hand lovingly touched the medicine chest before she joined David's relatives downstairs in the kitchen.

Chapter 3

Going Aboard

Elisabeth groggily opened her eyes when David shook her shoulder. In her dreams she had been back home in Bromsgrove. David's voice rose with excitement.

"Praise God, Elisabeth, this is the day! The weather is clear, and the tide is in. Captain Briggs has given us permission to board. Cousin John has already sent out a servant to hire us a carriage."

Elisabeth threw off the cover, shaking from the unknown. Quickly, she used the chamber pot and dressed. Her boar bristle brush bumped through her wild red hair, nimble fingers quickly braiding. Crowning her head was a white cap. One finger dipped into a salt tin and then swiped across her teeth. She took a rag, moistened with water from the pitcher, and wiped her face. She did it again longingly because she knew she would not have good water as a luxury for a long, long time.

David and John carried their trunks downstairs. Then together at board for breakfast, they and their smiling hosts ate pottage and drank their morning draft. By the light of the kitchen hearth, John said to them, "I know you sing only from your Psalter, but Katie has taught me a hymn by Johann J. Schultz we want to sing to you as a blessing."

The couple held hands. As their excellent voices filled the kitchen, Elisabeth felt fear dissolve and peace settle in her soul. She believed and experienced God's healing balm and his presence and power. She silently recommitted to doing her part as her hosts sang:

> Sing praise to God who reigns above,
> The God of all creation.
> The God of power, the God of love,
> The God of our salvation;
> With healing balm, my soul He fills
> And every faithless murmur stills:
> To God all praise and glory.
>
> What God's almighty power hath made,
> His gracious mercy keepeth;
> By morning glow or evening shade,
> His watchful eye ne'er sleepeth,
> Within the Kingdom of His might,
> Lo! All is just and all is right:
> To God all praise and glory.
>
> The Lord is never far away,
> But through all grief distressing
> An ever-present help and stay,
> Our peace and joy and blessing.
> As with a mother's tender hand,
> He leads His own, His chosen band:
> To God all praise and glory.
>
> Thus, all my toilsome way along,
> I sing aloud Thy praises

That men may hear the grateful song.
My voice unwearied raises,
Be joyful in the Lord, my heart,
Both soul and body bear your part:
To God all praise and glory.

"Very thoughtful," said David, already moving to the door.

"Thank you!" Teary-eyed, Elisabeth reached out to hug both of them. "That was beautiful. What an unexpected gift!"

Soon the carriage arrived, and there were more tears and hugs. As Elisabeth and David bounced along the narrow street and peered out the window, Elisabeth realized she had never seen London at this hour.

The carriage's lantern cast long shadows on passing buildings. Elisabeth shivered and leaned into David's arm as they passed a house with a red cross painted on its locked doors. Plague was in that home, and the residents could not come out for forty days. Their fate was left to God and to brave souls who would leave supplies in a roped basket that the poor family lowered from a window.

Father, have mercy on their souls, Elisabeth prayed. She was certain country air, rest, and wholesome food prevented this disease. Her mother had survived an outbreak of the pestilence as a child, and told her of its horrors. A victim's skin would turn black in patches and rot, the tongue would swell, and there would be inflamed buboes, especially under the arms and in the groin area. There would be compulsive spewing, severe headaches, coma, and often death. Elizabeth prayed this outbreak would quickly diminish. Secretly, she was relieved to be leaving the city.

As the day's light grew, it gently touched the sky with pinks and purples. David quickly spotted the *Sea Venture* anchored in the harbor. Its three masts, web of ropes, and solid wooden structure reassured Elisabeth. *Why, it looks like a stalwart old lady,* she thought, approving of the wooden mermaid that ornamented the front of the carrack. Perhaps she would actually see one of these elusive fish people on their voyage.

Already, other passengers were boarding. Elisabeth spotted several familiar faces as they followed First Mate Robert Stone to what would be their home for two months. Elisabeth and most of the other one hundred passengers had never been on a large ship before. The smells of salt, rotted wood, and pitch were strong and barely tolerable.

First Mate Stone had them carry their belongings below deck, down a wooden ladder into moldy darkness. After David assisted her in climbing down, Elisabeth held her sleeve to her mouth to keep from gagging. She could hear one poor soul already retching in the shadows. Stone grabbed a bucket hanging on a peg and dipped it into a barrel filled with water. He pushed it into the heaving passenger's hands.

"Here, you will soon be used to it," he rumbled. "Make claim on a spot for bedding down. It will be your home for a weary season."

Elisabeth choked and tried to swallow, thinking First Mate Stone seriously erred using the word home for this vile cavern.

Everyone shuffled the best they could, claiming space with trunks for boundaries and stringing bed linen for makeshift walls. The hull was dark and dimly lit by a few permitted lanterns hung on posts. They swayed slightly from the ship's gentle bobbing.

First Mate Stone emphasized the chain of command. "With my permission, only a few of you will light candles. Once we sail, forget that comfort. I know for certain you do not want to be on open sea aboard a flaming carriage."

Elisabeth cheered herself with the thought that a dark hull kept her from seeing every roach, beetle, mouse, and rat that roamed hither and yon among the beams and corners. Then she noticed a black shape slithering in the shadows. She found a loose piece of timber along the hull and decided it would stay by her bedding as a vermin weapon. The passengers cooperated with excitement and hope. They flocked together on deck, a jittery crowd of brown, scarlet, and forest green cloaks with black hats donned by the men and white caps by the women.

The sailors scurried around them. Elisabeth had never seen so many barefoot, sinewy men together before. Hot ocean sun and salt water seemed to have molded them into taffy men. Brown-skinned, except for two black men, they moved like actors in some Shakespearean play. Not that she, as a Puritan, had ever witnessed a worldly English play. Nevertheless, she wondered about theater, and it made her smile to imagine the *Sea Venture* as a stage.

She approved that these seamen wore tolerably clean britches and shirts and many had shaved—not usually the sailor's custom, as she had been told. Yet, even scrubbed up, the crew seemed like a different breed of men from any she had known in country manor living. She wondered how many of them were English-born.

Elisabeth noticed some had scars on their arms and faces as well as tattoos of anchors, sail ships, mermaids, and snakes. The younger ones tied their long hair in blue and red ribbons. Some of the men limped as they readied the sails. She could not imagine what experiences produced their marks, nor would she let her curiosity run wild. It was not proper for her to do so. Most of the Puritans stood along the deck watching as David directed the sailors in bringing up his prized horses. This was no easy task, and it had been saved for last.

David put the blindfold on the first horse. "Easy, boy. Easy, Bounty," he whispered into the stallion's ear. The nervous animal started to bolt as several seamen tried quickly to put the ropes around Bounty's belly.

"Be careful, fools," David yelled, irritated the men had not waited for his command. "You will spook him! He certainly will kick if you approach unannounced!"

It was too late. One sailor lingered too close to the horse's hindquarter, and Bounty jerked into the air, his hoof knocking the man backward. He stumbled from the impact, falling on the dock. Elisabeth gasped as she saw a bloody gash on the sailor's forehead.

Quickly, the other sailors swarmed the frightened beast, tying its legs securely and hoisting it into the air. With much wriggling and angry neighing, Bounty swaggered up and onto the deck. Then he was untied and led to an awaiting livestock pen where the ship's cook also kept a cow and some chickens. David's jaw clamped down in anger, and Elisabeth held her breath as her husband held his tongue. Shipmates helped their wounded seaman aboard, and he slumped against a mast post. Instinctively, Elisabeth took off her apron and offered it to the man.

"Here, hold this on the wound," she ordered, using her midwife's commanding voice.

Waving her away with his hand, the seaman muttered, "No! I need no damn nursemaid."

Elisabeth let out an exasperated sigh. The man, dizzy from the horse's blow, obviously did not exhibit proper judgment.

"Are you all right, Colin?" asked a portly, gray-haired sailor. Colin tried to rise, but thought better of it. He held his hand against the bloody head wound.

"Aye, Duff. Damn horse. He must have sensed my dislike. I got the wind knocked out of me, but I will be able to help you in a bit."

Elisabeth knew he needed aid. "I have some salve that will help stop the bleeding," she pressed. "You should lie down and let the ship's doctor tend you."

The seaman squinted up at her. "No!"

Elisabeth surveyed the man and then Duff, trying to measure their attitudes. Duff warned her with a negative shake of his head not to insist. She decided to try anyway. It was the logical course. Hurriedly, she climbed below deck and opened her new medicine box to get out the salve.

She paused. This medicine was precious, and it would have to last a long time. Yet someone needed help, and she knew this salve could heal. Taking one of her clean rags, she scooped out some of her mother's receipt of fat mixed with boiled wild daisies and bundled it. This salve would stop bleeding and aid with faster healing.

She carefully climbed back up the ladder and spotted the sailor Colin with two other mates. They were about to hoist the ropes that were pulling the other horse, Blessing, aboard. The sailor's neck scarf, tied around his wound, was blood-drenched. He looked pale and woozy.

"Here, please take this, Mr. Colin," she insisted, offering the salve as if she were addressing her younger brother Paul. "I promise this will help stop the bleeding."

Colin Richardson scowled at her and heaved spit over the deck's rail before his brown eyes pierced her face. In a quiet voice, he gritted through his teeth, "You glib-gabbety puke stocking, do you not know the meaning of no? Tend to your own kind! Leave me be, and get out of our way."

"Aye, mate!" muttered a nearby comrade.

The wounded seaman ordered, "Forget me. Let's just get this bloody mare aboard." Colin turned his back on Elisabeth, dismissing her like a child.

She stepped back in disbelief, her rag of salve falling at her side. What a wretched man! No one had ever refused her kindness before or cursed her with such hostility. With flushed face that matched her hair, she quickly scurried away. No Puritan seemed to notice their exchange. The passengers were busy watching the frightened Blessing on the wharf, kicking and neighing for her mate. David yelled commands. Elisabeth held in her emotions until she climbed down to the safety of her corner of the hull. She felt shaky but pushed aside her anger.

"Father, forgive that man, that Mr. Colin!" she prayed. A few angry tears dropped on the salve as she pushed it back into the container. After taking some deep breaths, Elisabeth determined to act like this incident never happened. It would do no good to tell David, and it could create bad feelings aboard ship.

She returned to the deck to stand beside her husband, now aboard. He put his arm around her and introduced her to several families from different parishes. He was more relaxed with his prized horses safely aboard.

Soon it was time to hear from their Captain Briggs, who had said very little as they boarded. The passengers tilted their heads upward to hear his speech. He stood a little higher than them by the ship's steering wheel—a straight, thin man, with trimmed mustache and full beard. His dull green eyes seemed washed by too many salty ocean days. His blue uniform, too, was weary from use, but he held a commanding voice.

"First Mate Stone has been acquainting you with the *Sea Venture*. If you have any questions, he is your man. As your captain, I want to assure you that the crew is one of the finest in the kingdom— these sea dogs will get the job done, and God willing, we will have you stepping onto New England's soil in six weeks."

A few cheers went up from the group. Elisabeth wondered if any of his words were chosen because of David's conversation with him. Her question was soon answered.

Captain Briggs looked straight at David and said firmly, "Do as me mates request so they can do their tasks. If you have any complaints, take it up with First Mate Stone. In my experience, I have found that a strict chain of command keeps discipline and gets the work done by all."

Elisabeth glanced at the stout, scowling Stone and was glad she did not have to deal directly with him. She did not even want to imagine how he meted out punishment.

The captain continued, "And now I believe your Reverend Hughes wants to say a few words."

The reverend, with his smooth round face and white, wispy hair, seemed to glow as he spoke, and he inspired hope in his listeners.

"Brothers and sisters, God Almighty, in his most holy and wise providence, has brought us to this time and place. Many days we have been praying and preparing, and now this day is upon us.

"We can rejoice with full confidence that God has brought us safely thus far and will continue to be with us at sea as well as with loved ones we now leave. Across these waters, our new home awaits. There we will find ample opportunity to fulfill each of our callings in covenanting communities. Under the shadow of God's protection, we will find strength, comfort, and courage. With his mercies, new every morning, we will be provided with all that we need. Let us pray."

The thirty restless sailors had gradually eased back into working as soon as their captain finished his speech. They were whispering to one another, loudly coughing and spitting. To Elisabeth, it seemed there was extra noise when Reverend Hughes offered his prayer. How could these men not humbly respect such appropriate petitions to their Maker for all of them?

As the *Sea Venture* navigated slowly out of London's harbor, people on shore and in small boats waved and yelled farewells. Several cannons boomed. Later in the day, the ship lost sight of the shoreline and picked up speed. It now was its own moving island, surrounded by endless open water.

The excited passengers talked of people they mutually knew, inquired where people were headed in the New World, and exchanged information they had of each place. Mostly, everyone affirmed everyone else—of course they were making the right choice to leave their homeland.

Elisabeth did notice, however, some passengers kept looking back toward the shoreline long after it disappeared. She determined only to look forward. Colony life was what David desired, and he thought it was best for them. She longed to please her husband. She must ward off melancholy and honor his leadership.

As for that rude seaman, she only saw him briefly with a dried, blood-soaked scarf tied around his forehead. *Still scowling. Probably has a pounding headache,* she diagnosed with a little satisfaction. Yet he seemed to be working as if his injury were no more troublesome than a buzzing fly. *Fool!* Even though she was aboard a small ship, Elisabeth intended to stay clear of that foul-mouthed man.

Later in the day a young, pregnant woman named Mary Rogers

attached herself to Elisabeth after learning of her midwife skills. "Elisabeth, is your stomach upset yet?"

"No, not a bit." Elisabeth had not given seasickness a thought. Her stomach never bothered her. "What about you, Mary?"

"I am a little queasy, but I will manage. Elisabeth, since you are a midwife, may I ask you if you can tell how my baby is faring?" The eager, young woman looked down at her bulging waistline and turned to the side.

Elisabeth smiled. "If the mother is content in her circumstances, her babe reaps this blessing also. And Mary, you carry well. Perhaps, after this journey your wee one will be especially fond of water, desiring it in abundance!" Elisabeth wanted to encourage the pale woman, who now looked more than a little queasy.

"Maybe you should go below and rest a while," Elisabeth suggested.

"Oh no, I would fare worse down there. The smells are very offensive."

"Yes, I heartily agree they are quite challenging. I would rather stay out here, bobbing to and fro, than deal with the dampness and darkness below. Acquiring our sea legs will take some getting used to, but we must make the best of it."

Mary appeared worried as she stared out across the ocean. Her face became even more despondent as she watched two children chasing a cat among some barrels. Elisabeth tried to lift her spirit.

"Mary, thousands have already crossed the ocean safely to the New World. And, God willing, so shall we."

"Yes, Elisabeth," Mary said in a quiet voice. "But God allowed some to go to a watery grave. We could be traveling above their remains."

Elisabeth had not considered this rather dark thought. She had heard there were very few shipwrecks among Puritan ships. Did Mary know differently?

"It does no good to worry," Elisabeth responded confidently. "Let us trust in the one who is able to keep us from falling."

"Oh, Elisabeth, I just feel so sick."

Elisabeth quickly helped the pregnant woman to the guardrail. They made it just in time. As Mary vomited, Elisabeth thought she heard a seaman chuckling. David was right about these sailors. They were troubling companions.

Chapter 4

First Night Aboard

With the setting of the sun, melancholy descended on the *Sea Venture* passengers. After partaking in a meal of beans, salt pork, bread, and the drinking of ale, most of them decided to bed down early. Elisabeth desired a starry sky for comfort. Instead, there was uncertain darkness and muffled noises of sailors working above.

Sleeping in the pit of a ship felt like a foul dungeon, only this jail jolted forward. Its creaking, timbered walls were all that kept one from drowning in an ocean miles from anywhere. This uneasy thought of so much water pressing inches from their heads made Elisabeth tense as she and David bedded down beside their trunk. Elisabeth touched her vermin board.

For a while the Allertons did not speak, adjusting to the sounds of stranger miseries: belches, flatulence, snores, coughs, and occasional deposits into a bucket. A child wailed, and soon they heard the mother's soothing whispers.

In the darkness, David reached over to caress Elisabeth and whisper in her ear. "How fare thee, Mrs. Allerton?"

"I fare well, husband. And yourself, Mr. Allerton?"

"A little queasy but not bad. The smells are awful!"

"Yes! Do you think your Uncle Tobias' codfish factory will be worse?"

"The Lord forbid it!"

They chuckled, remembering their jokes about the fish smells that awaited them.

"How are Bounty and Blessing doing?" Elisabeth whispered.

"I think they will be fine. They take solace from each other's company. And eager Will and Nathan Norton asked me if they could care for them. They are good lads."

"David, I think there is something crawling up my leg!" David and Elisabeth shook out their blanket and readjusted their bedding. Then they settled close together. There was solace in holding each other, and sleep finally came.

The voice whispered, "Mr. Allerton, Mrs. Allerton."

Elisabeth groggily opened her eyes. Where was she?

"What do you want, man?" It was David speaking gruffly, as he turned toward a lantern's candlelight. Elisabeth propped herself up, startled to realize a seaman hovered over them.

"Beg your pardon, sir," the man whispered. "My name is Duff Richardson. I'm the boatswain on this vessel, and I am come for one of me mates. You know the man who took the horse's kick to the head."

David tried to remain calm, but Elisabeth could feel his back tense in anger. He sputtered impatiently, "Yes, I remember! But boatswain, what does that have to do with us? You know the captain's orders. Take this matter up with First Mate Stone."

"My mate's not well, sir, and I thought maybe Mrs. Allerton—

since she knows something of healing—could give him some medicine, maybe ease his pain."

"What! Mrs. Allerton!" David huffed in a whisper. "Does Captain Briggs know you are down here?"

"No, no, sir." Duff waved his hand dismissively. "Forget I came. It was a mistake. I should have known you Puritans would not help us. Such wind."

The sailor started inching away.

"Boatswain Duff, wait!" Elisabeth whispered. "Why is your ship's doctor not treating your injured mate?"

The seaman turned his light to her. "Drunk, ma'am, his usual posture. Colin made me swear I would never, ever, let Dr. Stillingfleet lay a finger on him. He said I would be good as dead, quartered, and served for shark bait if I would let that limb-cutting leech sucker near him. Colin would do it, too."

David broke in, "Really man, watch your tongue! This is surely no concern of ours. We are just passengers."

The sailor eased away but muttered so they could hear, "No concern! It was your damn horse!"

"Stop, Boatswain Duff!" Elisabeth whispered. "Wait, sir. I will come and do what I can."

"Elisabeth, I cannot allow you to do this!" David protested a little too loudly.

Someone in the dark cried out, "Be still, man! Take your concerns on deck. We finally have sleeping children. And snuff that candle!"

"David, please, let us not be hesitant in charity." Elisabeth put her hand over his heart. "Dear husband, we cannot forsake someone needing our help."

"Elisabeth, really, what can you do?" David was exasperated. "Treating our family is a proper place for your skills. But this is entirely different. You are not a doctor. It is in the middle of the night. We do not even know these men."

"I know, but I cannot go back to sleep. What if this man grows worse, and we do not help? His soul would be on our consciences, David."

Elisabeth could not see his face, but she sensed David's uneasiness.

There was a long pause. Then he exhaled and growled, "All right, all right, but we go together."

Turning to Duff, David ordered, "Leave. We will meet you on deck in a few moments."

"David, the medicine chest. Could you carry it?" Elisabeth whispered as she quickly dressed and grabbed her cloak. "I will gather some rags for bandages."

David sighed. He had hoped they could hang onto their medicines for trading in the colony. But he knew Elisabeth would freely use what they had with anyone needing it. Sometimes, her generosity was just so childish. They stumbled to the hull opening and climbed up to the deck. David huffed in protest as he managed the cumbersome chest. Across the deck, they saw Duff's swaying lantern at another opening in the hull that led to some of the seamen's quarters.

Duff helped David get the chest down the ladder. Then Elisabeth climbed below. Duff held the lantern as Elisabeth's eyes adjusted to the quarters. Most of the scrawny men were in hammocks. A few raised their heads and silently blinked at them while others snored. One man squatted next to the moaning Colin, lying on the floor.

Elisabeth shook off her fear of this place of strange men and masculine smells. Surely it was not that different then being back home where she nursed local peasants in dim, smoky dwellings. She hurriedly handed her cloak to David and rolled up her sleeves.

"Hold the light closer to his head wound," Elisabeth ordered. She peered at Colin's temple, caked with dried blood. She was aware the semi-conscious man was half naked, wearing only breeches. She gingerly took two fingers and touched his hot forehead, keeping her eyes steadily on his shadowed face.

Suddenly, Colin grabbed her arm hard, wide-eyed, and yelled, "Angelique, please, listen to me! You need to know the truth!"

He clawed at his face, showing Elisabeth a zigzag, pink scar that ran across his cheek, concealed partially by a scruffy beard. Elisabeth froze and stared into his delirious eyes. What possessed this man with such desperate passion?

David moved forward and pried Colin's arm off of Elisabeth. "Let go of her! This man is clearly out of his head! We need to take this matter up with Captain Briggs and Dr. Stillingfleet."

"No!" said Duff, and the others murmured agreement.

"Has he purged or fluxed?" Elisabeth asked quickly, wanting to do what she could before David pulled her out of there.

"Aye, some puking," affirmed Duff.

"Any blood present?

"No, I think not."

"Good. I will need water from your barrel," Elisabeth ordered to a nearby sailor. "Boatswain Duff, I need your help. You must remove his headscarf. We need to get a good look at the wound. Perhaps you can get some men to hold him still."

It was not a pleasant job, but Duff and three other men finally got the delirious and flailing Colin in a locked position to remove his bandage. Elisabeth mixed her distilled rose and rhubarb liquid with water and poured it on the wound. Then she covered Colin's temple with Paracelsus' "styptick plaister," courtesy of the generous London apothecary and Dr. Culpeper's excellent receipt.

Her exhausted patient had fallen back and closed his eyes. That could be a good sign. Rest was what the agitated patient needed. Under David sputtering protests, Elisabeth gave more balm to Duff in a rag, to be used as needed.

Under normal conditions, she could have sat by the patient's bedside and treated symptoms as necessary. That was impossible here. She handed Duff a walnut shell and vial. "This is syrup of rose and mints with Bole Armoniack for the flux. Mix this in red wine and have him drink a little at a time. Get him into a hammock and cover him with blankets."

She paused, wanting to do more, but that was really all she could do. Hastily, David ordered a sailor to carry the medical chest back to their quarters. He grabbed Elisabeth's hand and pulled her toward the ladder as Duff's thanks followed them. David muttered, but Elisabeth was glad she could not make out his words. She had never treated a patient so quickly.

Chapter 5

Indebtedness

Colin and Duff finished their duties on deck, satisfied with keeping the sails fully blown and the ropes taunt. Eleven times since they started working, a seaman had turned over a half-hour glass of pulverized seashells, and now he rang the bell ending this six-hour shift. It was Colin and Duff's turn to rest. They stared out at the ocean, hearing the comforting creaks from the masts and feeling the rhythm of forceful waves as the ship pushed along. This day, the *Sea Venture* would make good sail.

It had been four weeks since Elisabeth treated Colin's wound. He grudgingly admitted to himself that she had some kind of healing skills. He only suffered minor headaches when he grew tired, and there was barely a pinkish scar. The other sailors declared his recovery as some kind of miracle. *Pshat and fish bones to that!*

Captain Briggs and First Mate Stone had ordered Duff and Colin to stay clear of the Allertons. Despite these orders, Colin had approached David and asked him to pass on his gratitude to Mrs. Allerton. The pompous Puritan barely nodded and turned away. Colin wondered if Mrs. Allerton ever received the thank-you message. She stayed with the womenfolk and children most of the time and never looked his way. Her prideful husband definitely kept a fishhook in her mouth.

The Allertons' lofty aloofness toward him and the other sailors confirmed what Colin once read about Puritan attitude in a discarded book: "There are two grand sides in the world, to which all belong: there is God's side and those that are his, and there is another side that is Satan's, and those that are his; two kingdoms, two sides, two contrary dispositions, that pursue one another." God and Satan. He scorned this dichotomy, counting himself fortunate he felt no allegiance to either one. He was no slave, neither to God or the Devil, nor to Puritan theology or to pagan practices. By his own lights, he forged his own path.

Colin noticed the Puritan passengers wearing cloaks and blankets against the ocean's sprays. He found this amusing. Nodding in their direction, he exclaimed, "They need a full baptism in the Atlantic, say in March, to leather their delicate skins. Would you not agree, Duff?"

"Aye, Colin, but I think you are too harsh on these poor Christians. They are not a bad lot, as passengers go."

"Duff, you are getting like a weepy, sentimental widow."

"Maybe, nephew, but your calloused heart shows no sign of softening toward matters of faith or those who practice. It really could do you some good to turnabout."

Thoughtfully looking at this man who was like his son, Duff challenged, "Are you still vexing over that Puritan woman saving your ungrateful soul? Feeling some discomfort, are we?"

"In God's name, Duff, let me have peace on that one. Her little bit of nurse-maiding hardly made the difference in my recovery."

"Colin, you do not fool your old uncle. I know you too bloody well. I wager that sooner or later you will have to find some way to repay this debt of healing. That was your father's way, and you cannot help yourself in being like him. You are more pig-headed than he, but I know you through and through. This debt sticks in your craw."

Colin shook his head in denial, but he liked it when Duff compared him to his father. "If there be any truth in what you say, Uncle, then it will not take long to fulfill my obligation. These land lovers need the constant care of a nursemaid for one task or another."

Colin's eyes narrowed on David, who was deep in discussion with several men over the codfish industry that awaited him in America.

"Yes!" Colin could hear Allerton boast, "A hard-working man can turn a profit because the demand for the dried cod is so great in England."

Samuel Norton countered, "Brother David, remember riches have no part with felicity. 'Plentiful provision tempts corruptible flesh.' I have journeyed that road and know I would rather be a miserable saint than a prosperous sinner. Trust my counsel and be watchful of sly greed."

Colin observed David flushed from this exhortation but the wily fox recovered. "Brother Norton, I heartily agree with you! One certainly must flee avarice. But if it is God's call to provide food, like dried cod, for the hungry, I am sure you agree that be a noble calling. And you would not begrudge a diligent man just wages so he could support his family. We spread our nets, but it is God who brings what he wills into them."

Mr. Norton pursed his lips and nodded.

Colin shook his head. This man planned to take much from the sea, but what would he give back to it? "There, Duff, is a man whose heart weighs heavy with greed as well as his so-called pure religion. He serves self uttermost."

Duff shrugged, "Is he not like most men?"

"Duff, are most men so dishonest that they use God to justify greed? He plays his religion with one hand and his selfish designs with the other. How can his wife and the others not see both hands?"

Duff looked into Colin's eyes and softly said, "Aye, sometimes we are blind to what is close to us."

Colin knew Duff was referring to other relationships, but he chose to ignore the subtle reminder of his fractured family.

"Duff, I have no stomach for these pious souls. This voyage will not end too soon for me."

"Nephew, you were good to join me on this one. I vow our next journey shall be aboard a whaling ship. There will be little formal religion to torment you there."

"Uncle, I hold you to it!" Colin spat into the churning waves and studied the water. "Do you think the wind bears ill will?"

"Aye, I do. Mid-afternoon will tell the tale."

As Mary Rogers and Elisabeth sat doing needlepoint on a makeshift bench of board and stools, the pregnant woman suddenly jolted. "Elisabeth, I feel such terrible pain. The baby must be coming soon."

"Where is the pain strongest, Mary?" Elisabeth was not convinced birth was imminent, because she had learned Mrs. Rogers leaned toward exaggeration.

"It hurts here, like someone punched me in my loins." Mary clutched her side. Elisabeth looked closely at her patient's belly. Mary Rogers had carried the baby in low position for weeks. It was difficult to judge if the woman was in early childbirth or simply experiencing false labor. Elisabeth did not want to discredit her claims.

She simply asked, "Would you like to lie down?"

"Oh, yes, I think I shall. You will stay with me, just in case?"

"Certainly I will, as long as you want." Elisabeth reached for Mary's arm. "I do not think we need to alarm the other women yet. Let us give it some time to make good."

The two made their way across the deck and down into the hull.

Elisabeth fussed over the Rogers' bedding, rearranging it as comfortable as possible.

Although pale, Mary appeared calmer. "Do you think the baby will come by dusk, Elisabeth?" Her young face was so hopeful.

"Maybe, but more likely you will have much work to do during the night. That is, if it is God's bidding for this wee one."

Elisabeth held Mary's hand as she squeezed it mercilessly. From the pressure, Elisabeth surmised the baby was either moving downward or Mary had very low pain tolerance.

"I think I had another contraction!" Mary fidgeted.

"Good, that is very good." Elisabeth smiled encouragingly at the fearful face.

"Why did the good Lord have to put such pain on us, Elisabeth? It was not our mouths who bit into the forbidden fruit."

"That is an excellent question. Let us ask the Reverend Hughes next time he expounds on Genesis."

Mary rolled her eyes. "Oh, Reverend Hughes is a learned and godly servant of the Lord, but he is still a man. He will tell us that men bear different burdens that are just as painful."

Elisabeth smiled and studied the younger woman, measuring how she would endure the coming hours. Her face pinched a little from exertion, but she had yet to experience pain that would crush her into submission. How could she prepare her?

"Mary, although the pain will grow greater, you must understand its message. The intensity brings your baby closer to birth. The greater the pain, the sooner the baby will come. You may sweat a lot and get shaky from the effort, but this is how a baby is born. You and your wee one must work together."

Panic crossed Mary's face, but she nodded her head as she grabbed Elisabeth's hand, anticipating the next contraction. "I should have paid more attention when my mother had her babies, but I had no desire then," she said. "How many infants have you seen come into the world, Elisabeth?"

"Oh, I seem to have lost count. But I believe I assisted my mother with twenty deliveries. I was also privileged to aid my mother's friend —Mrs. Jane Sharp, a very skilled midwife—with many births. She is even writing a book on midwifery that I am most desirous to see published."

Mary did not seem comforted, so Elisabeth said firmly, "Mary, do not be consumed with anxiety. My mother and Mrs. Sharp taught me well, and there is no greater joy than bringing a child into the world. It is such a wondrous blessing. You will see."

Elisabeth was relieved Mary did not ask how many childbirth deaths she had witnessed. It was understood, unspoken, that there were always some. Every woman on their ship knew mothers who died in childbirth, and most mothers knew they would eventually "take grief" in losing babies and small children to various afflictions.

As she held Mary's hand, Elisabeth was surprised to discover she felt queasy herself. At the same time, Mary's husband Jonathan came to check on his wife, and he was followed by several concerned women. One of the women, Mrs. Leah Norton, mother of six, gave a knowing nod to Elisabeth. That was all Elisabeth needed to seize her best opportunity for some fresh air. If labor continued, it would be a long day and night.

"Mary, I will be back shortly," Elisabeth said, releasing her cramped hand and patting the expectant mother's shoulder. The women and Jonathan huddled closer, and Mrs. Norton grabbed Mary's hand. A baby's birth would be such good news to break the ship's monotony.

The wind had come up, and the ship's jostling made it difficult for Elisabeth to keep her balance. She barely made it to the side of the deck before she lost her breakfast of beans and hard tack. As she turned from the deck's railing to wipe her mouth on her apron, there was Mr. Colin Richardson smirking at her expense. With strict orders from David, Reverend Hughes, and a sober Dr. Stillingfleet, she had obediently avoided him since that night of treating his wound.

Dr. Stillingfleet's indignant words still seared her memory and made her blush. "The appropriate behavior for a married Puritan woman is not to fraternize with the ship's crew!" the disheveled doctor pontificated as David protested.

Dr. Stillingfleet also made it clear he had no respect for Nicholas Culpeper, someone she considered a mentor. To defend her treatments of Seaman Richardson, she had mentioned Culpeper's *Book of Receipts*. Dr. Stillingfleet scoffed, "That man is a Vicar of St. Fools!"

Now here stood her healed patient, Mr. Richardson, grinning at her discomfort. She must be careful because she knew absolutely that some passengers were watching to make sure she complied with the orders of captain, doctor, reverend, and husband.

"Tummy problems, Mrs. Allerton? Maybe some of your medicine would help you."

"A good day to you, too, Mr. Richardson. I am pleased to see you appear recovered. As for myself, I just needed some fresh air."

She dabbed her mouth again on her apron, remembering how this ungrateful sailor had not even thanked David and her for their help that night. She determined not to dwell on his manners, or lack of them, and to conduct herself in a civil way.

She informed him, "Mrs. Rogers is in labor."

"Is that so?"

Elisabeth thought Colin sounded surprised. His brown eyes bored into hers, as if probing whether she hid some knowledge, a secret. But then he broke contact and looked at the sea.

"You better take a good whiff of this telling wind, Mrs. Allerton. There is a big storm brewing, and it will be a most unpleasant night."

"Oh, that is bad news, Mr. Richardson! What can we do to prepare?"

"Aye, secure everything. Find something to hold on to and try to keep some clothing dry to aid the newborn after the storm has played its worst with us. I am certain First Mate Stone will not tolerate one candle, even for the birthing of a babe in the midst of a storm."

Elisabeth grasped what he meant immediately. "Oh, I understand! Yes, thank you!"

These new concerns made her forget her queasiness as she made her way back to Mary. She had not even realized that she and Mr. Richardson had exchanged their first conversation without insult or anger. The sky threatened rain and the wind picked up. Elisabeth so wished the *Sea Venture* could head away from that dark horizon instead of into it.

Chapter 6

The Storm

Elisabeth did not believe in purgatory, but that night she and the other travelers experienced a seemingly endless ride of terror. Mary Rogers' delivery made matters worse. As the storm's battering grew, Mary's shrieks for deliverance increased. Her sounds punctuated the howling wind and creaking timbers. Elisabeth's patient was completely undone, and there was little the midwife could do.

Early in the storm, as the sailors fought the wind to secure the ship, the Puritans bravely sang their psalms of deliverance. As was their custom, their presenter, Mr. Norton, would lead them in lining out. He'd sing a line of a psalm to a familiar tune. Then the group repeated that line.

Mr. Norton bellowed, "God is our hope and strength."

The huddled group echoed, "God is our hope and strength."

Mr. Norton continued, "and help in troubles, ready to be found."

They repeated, "and help in troubles, ready to be found."

"Therefore, will not we fear," sang Mr. Norton.

"Therefore, will not we fear," his congregation responded.

"Though the earth be moved/and though the mountains fall into the midst of the sea/ though the waters thereof rage and be troubled...."

There was uncertainty in some voices, and sometimes the children wailed and whimpered. As the night wore on, the singing ceased. They all grew exhausted from tumbling into each other. Many pleaded to God for the storm to end. Some wept in fear.

With one hand, Elisabeth gripped the rope David had secured to a beam. Her other hand held on to Mary. Her feet tried to stay planted against the wet and slippery wall. Sometimes Mary's nails would dig into her palm, and Elisabeth tried to loosen her grip, risking the little balance she had secured.

They were all soaked. Thunder and waves roared; lightning flashed. More and more water trickled through the cracks. Elisabeth thought the ship swerved like a giant rocking chair tormented by a demon.

At one point, David angrily yelled to her above the trickling water, thunder, and wind, "I cannot just stay down here and drown! I am going to ask Captain Briggs what we can do. Surely there must be something!"

Before she could protest, he was off. Moments later, dripping in water, he staggered back to report it was worse on top, and they were ordered to stay below.

"Mary, you are doing well," Elisabeth yelled into her ear. "This baby is going to be a fighter, born in a storm like this."

"No, Elisabeth, we are all going to die!" Mary screamed back breathlessly. "I cannot stop shaking...my back...oh the pain that is cutting my back....Elisabeth, you must promise me you will look after my baby!" Her nails were slicing Elisabeth's skin.

"Shhh, none of that talk. Here, turn sideways the best you can. I will press my hand on your back. Pray, dear Mary. Have faith! God will deliver us. He is with you, with all of us! Hold on!"

Because it was completely dark in the hold, except for occasional flashes of lightning, Elisabeth felt Mary's abdomen and hips the best she could to gauge progress. If only Mary could relax, she was certain the birth would be forthcoming. But that was impossible in such conditions. In the middle of the storm, they heard a tremendous boom, louder than any they had heard before. It reminded Elisabeth of the lightning back home in Bromsgrove that splintered one of their tallest oak trees. A crazy thought came to her, but she did not want to ponder its meaning. *Sometimes hearts sink before ships do.*

The ominous noise silenced them. Surely death was near. Even Mary quieted down, clasping Elisabeth's hand so hard the midwife could not feel pain anymore. Then, First Mate Stone and another drenched sailor came down into the hull to speak to the men. Amazingly, Stone held a lit lantern.

"Did we lose a mast?" David yelled over the storm.

"Aye, the center one," Stone shouted back. He was dripping wet but highly excited. His wild eyes looked like sparked coals in the dim light. "Men, we have greater concerns than the mast! The captain asked me to get you. We must pump out rising water in the hold! We could sink fast! Be quick! Hurry!"

Jonathan shuffled over to Mary and kissed her wet forehead. "I will be back. I promise."

To Elisabeth he pleaded, "Please, take care of her. God bless you."

Elisabeth wanted to give David a hug before he left, but his tall form was already following Stone.

She pushed aside her uneasiness. This was no time to muse on affections or lack of them from her husband. Mary needed her. She tried to press the pregnant woman's back while keeping her balance. She tucked a soppy blanket around Mary and tried to keep from shivering herself. She felt the urge to throw up. Finally, she decided it was best just to purge and worry about clean up later — that is, if they survived. *What was such a little mess among so much chaos,* she thought, and for some reason she wanted to laugh out loud at their helpless circumstances. She resolved not to give in to delirium and to concentrate on her duties.

"You are doing well, Mary. Hang on. Oh, God, please, have

mercy on us! Only you can save us!" Elisabeth did not know which words she spoke out loud or which ones she prayed silently. Everything swirled together during the longest night of her life. Her eyes were wet from tears as well as salty water.

Numbness, exhaustion, and shock took their turn by the time the storm's rage lessened and dawn's light illuminated their quarters. Mary had settled down to shallow breaths and whimpering, but then suddenly she cried out in anger, giving one forceful push before falling back on her wet bedding.

The yell brought Elisabeth out of her stupor. "Yes, Mary. That did it! Oh, Mary, look!" Elisabeth could not believe her numb, chilled arms caught the slick, warm boy. She gladly put her cold finger into his warm mouth to clear the passage, and the baby's startled cry filled the air. People around them stirred in exhaustion and joy.

Mrs. Norton and one of her daughters came alive to their duties and worked rapidly to untie the ropes around Elisabeth's trunk. Mrs. Norton then unfolded a dry blanket. Elisabeth quickly wrapped the infant but felt a pang of sorrow that she could do little more for him. Mrs. Norton also handed her knife and rags. With shaking fingers she carefully cut and tied off the umbilical cord.

Mrs. Norton nodded approvingly as she put the little one next to Mary's breast and supported the infant in the mother's trembling arms. Mary could not stop whimpering, whether from terror, relief, or shock.

Elisabeth stood over them, too numb and stiff to move. She was not thinking clearly. A weary Mrs. Norton ordered her to rest, and when she did not move, Mrs. Norton yelled, "Mrs. Allerton! You must rest! We will tend to matters here."

By the time Elisabeth slumped against the wall of the ship, she realized the storm had done its worst. They had survived the night. So far, the men had pumped out enough water to keep the *Sea Venture* afloat. She collapsed against the wall, too exhausted to care what happened next.

Chapter 7

Funeral

"Sister Elisabeth, Sister Elisabeth. Wake up." It was Jonathan Rogers gently shaking her.

"What has happened? Oh, Jonathan. How is Mary? The baby?" Elisabeth staggered to rise, worried about her patients. Her body ached, and her clothes were soggy. How long had she slept? As her eyes adjusted and she looked up toward the hull opening, she could make out blue sky and sunlight. Glorious blue sky!

"Mary is fine, thanks be to the Lord, and to you, Elisabeth. Mrs. Norton is tending to them on deck like a mother hen clucking over her chicks." Jonathan beamed. "Elisabeth, we made it, praise God! Here, let me help you. Come, you will dry out faster on deck."

As Elisabeth got up she felt lightheaded with more nausea. She grabbed Jonathan's arm.

"Where is David? Is he all right?"

"Yes, Elisabeth, he is well. Many of the men are still pumping water out of the hold. Come on. Lean on me. Let me get you to the others."

Jonathan helped her onto the sunny deck where barrels had been piled together to form a shelter.

"Elisabeth!" A smiling Mary waved to her. She reclined against the barrels and held a blanketed bundle. "Come look at our precious babe!"

Elisabeth sank down beside Mary, who lifted up the blanket to reveal a sleeping infant. "This is little Isaac Rogers. Is he not the most beautiful gift from our Lord?"

Elisabeth shook her head in amazement. Mary was thriving after the night's crisis, and the baby contentedly slept.

"Oh, Mary, yes! He is wonderful! And a good name! How are you feeling?"

"Tired, but I am filled with joy. What a horrible night! They say one seaman died when the mast broke. He was trying to keep it secure."

"Who?" Elisabeth was certain the reckless Mr. Richardson would be the one to disregard danger and be in the thick of a mess.

"I heard it was the boatswain, the man they call Duff. He was the uncle of that seaman you treated." Mary hesitated to mention such an embarrassing incident.

"Boatswain Duff? Oh, no! You say he was Mr. Richardson's uncle? I did not know they were related." Elisabeth was surprised by the connection, although it explained Duff's loyalty.

She said out loud, "They did seem very close. Poor Mr. Richardson."

Mary eyed Elisabeth curiously but nodded. "They are going to have a funeral after everyone has breakfast. Here is yours. I am afraid it is not much."

Mary held out a bowl that contained white lumps of soggy biscuits with a few drowned weevils floating on top. "We have to eat to get our strength back. Captain's orders."

"I cannot eat." Elisabeth was too nauseated and exhausted for food.

"At least a little, Elisabeth," Mary persisted, pushing the soggy gruel closer.

Elisabeth stared at her and wondered how their roles had

exchanged so radically. Here she felt hopeless, exhausted, and Mary Rogers glowed, giving her, the midwife, orders!

Elisabeth took the bowl and swallowed a little of the soggy dough. Mary was rambling on about how the cook had already butchered the cow that did not survive, and there would be meat later in the day.

Immediately, Elisabeth regretted her bite as she felt her stomach cramping. She tried to hide the pain. Mary cheerfully spoke of Isaac's delivery and birth. The new mother's version left out her endless shrieks during labor. Elisabeth opened her red, swollen hands to view the night's dents and scratches, but Mary did not even notice.

Elisabeth was relieved when Mrs. Norton popped her head around a barrel and soberly announced, "You must rise, ladies. We are going to have the funeral for Boatswain Duff and hear a report from Captain Briggs."

Elisabeth gave Mary a hug, found strength to get up and offered her arms to hold baby Isaac. What a sweet babe, wrinkled and pink with lovely lashes. She could wish he had a little more weight, but at least Mary and her son were taking to breastfeeding.

Elisabeth spotted David on the other side of their group. She could not reach him before the service, but he nodded to her and gave a tired wave. She handed infant Isaac back to his mother and leaned against a barrel for support.

Prior to the storm, she had found some amusement in observing passengers teetering to maintain balance. Now there was no pleasure in viewing the group's forlorn staggers on deck. Her ragtag companions were a collective casualty of exhaustion and hopelessness. They may be alive, but the storm had swept away future hopes. Many people slumped over; others appeared frozen in distress except for occasional blinks. Elisabeth surveyed the ship for Mr. Richardson, but he was nowhere to be seen.

"God spared us last night," Captain Briggs began, looking drained but stalwart. "That is, all of us except our good mate, Duff Richardson. Our boatswain died trying to save us all, but he could not keep the mast from falling."

Elisabeth surveyed the shattered mast stump as Captain Briggs continued. "We shall not easily forget his bravery in putting others before himself. His self-sacrifice was God honoring, reflecting our Lord's admonition to regard others as more important than ourselves."

Captain Briggs paused for effect. "This day, Boatswain Richardson's struggles cease. He was a baptized Englishman and proud of it. But his other country was always the open sea. He dearly loved it, and into its arms, we release his body."

Captain Briggs motioned to Reverend Hughes. The pastor wearily stepped forward. "Dear ones, I want to read from Psalm 107. May you find solace from God's Word: 'they mounted up to the heavens and went down to the depths; in their peril their courage melted away. They were at their wits' end. Then they cried out to the Lord in their trouble, and he brought them out of their distress. He stilled the storm to a whisper; the waves of the sea were hushed. They were glad when it grew calm, and he guided them to their desired haven....' "

As the Reverend Hughes read on, Elisabeth wondered what Colin Richardson thought. Did he have any faith to give him solace? Where was that nephew of the deceased?

The minister concluded in prayer, "Our gracious and merciful Lord, we thank you that you had mercy on us during this long and terrible night. We do not know why you called home our fellow voyager Boatswain Duff Richardson, but we know his spirit belongs to you, and he is in your loving and merciful care. By the sacrifice of our Lord Jesus Christ, we commit Duff Richardson's soul to you, and to the ocean we commit his body. Amen."

The passengers watched two sailors tilt the plank that held the body of Duff Richardson. The corpse was wrapped tightly in a blanket, tied with rope, and weighted with ballast rocks from the hold. Somber silence enveloped the group as they heard the faint splash. Elisabeth and the others tiptoed to glimpse the body slip beneath the frothy, white waves. In spite of the loss of the central mast, the ship rocked steadily along, albeit choppily and in zigzag fashion.

Elisabeth finally spotted Mr. Richardson standing alone at the bow of the ship, looking out at the waves. She could not help but feel sadness for this lonely, bitter man, and yet she wondered what extra meanness would sprout in him from such a tragedy.

Later, after tallying losses, Captain Briggs reported they had traveled far enough that their supplies should hold until they reached Massachusetts's shore. As a safety precaution, however, they would ration. The captain regrettably reported their maps suffered irreparable water damage, and the ship's compass was broken. They now would rely on the stars as a general compass. He urged them to pray for clear nights.

Captain Briggs assured their plight was not an unbearable hardship. He and his crew had survived many worse situations and lived to tell the tale. He was confident God's course for them was Boston. Meanwhile, they should rally together to get the ship repaired and back to its routine as much as possible.

When strength allowed, everyone spent the day rearranging possessions, throwing damaged goods overboard, and drying out what they could. Each plank and beam was scrubbed with vinegar. The salt water made clothing stiff and scratchy, and they smelled even more like the ocean.

First Mate Stone seemed determined to keep them occupied with more work and less chatter. David approved, whispering to Elisabeth that busy hands prevented wandering minds and deteriorating morale. He was relieved Bounty and Blessing had somehow made it through the night with only bumps and bruises. He and the Norton boys busied themselves with drying out the animals' feed and resettling the horses and a few surviving chickens.

A few days after the storm, Elisabeth noticed Mr. Richardson sitting alone, mending sailcloth. Because of Duff's death, he had been promoted to boatswain. Why had he not assigned this mending task to others?

She hesitated but decided it was appropriate to offer the sailor her condolences. "Mr. Richardson, I am truly sorry about your Uncle Duff."

He looked up, and for a second she held her breath, because she thought he would swear her off as he did before. His pause indicated he weighed that choice and dismissed it. The spark in his eyes dulled, and he shrugged. "Thank you, Mrs. Allerton, but you need not trouble yourself. My uncle lived a life fuller then most, and he died the way he would have handpicked. Seamen know a watery grave is often their fate."

He thoughtfully continued with his mending and added, "It might be best if you place your pity where it can reap the most good. I believe in neither a heaven nor a hell, so I take no solace in the afterlife."

He paused again and then put another stitch in the sailcloth. "Duff's memory holds me," he said with conviction.

"Mr. Richardson, you do not believe in God?" Elisabeth had not thought this man could shock her anymore, but he managed to find a way.

"Oh, I may believe in a God of sorts, Mrs. Allerton, but I do not believe he made a heaven or hell for us. I think he moved on long ago and left us to our own devices."

"So, you do not think God cares for Mr. Duff's soul?" Elisabeth was incredulous.

He shrugged. "Not any more than I care for the grubs in my sea biscuits. There is a Spanish saying, '*Antes Muerto que Mudado.*' It satisfies me."

Seeing Elisabeth's puzzled expression, he translated, "Rather dead than changed."

Elisabeth had never met a man who dismissed God in such outspoken fashion. He invited God's wrath.

She said sadly, "Mr. Richardson, I am sorry you reject God's care. In this world, it comforts me that he is with me always—not because of my goodness but because of his love. Do you not know his love compelled him to pay our sin debt against God? He sacrificed himself on a cross for our offenses? Death could not hold him; he was resurrected. This makes a way for us to live again with him, once we die. There is hope for our miserable souls because of love. I think your Uncle Duff knew this truth. We may die, but we are safe."

Mr. Richardson gave a condescending smile. "Like I said, Mrs. Allerton, you do not have to waste any sermon on me. Instead, you might want to put your attention toward that baby."

Such peculiar advice, but maybe it was because baby Isaac was born shortly after Duff's death. Elisabeth agreed, nodding. "Yes, I am helping Mary Rogers with the baby as much as she allows. I am pleased they seem stronger than most of us."

Colin eyed her carefully. "No, Mrs. Allerton, you misunderstand me. I mean *your* baby."

"What!" Elisabeth face went red as she touched her stomach and backed away. "You should not speak of such! I am not with child!"

Then it struck her that maybe her nausea was more than seasickness. It was quite a revelation, and she saw Colin's satisfaction. He burst out laughing.

"If Duff were in your heaven now, he would be enjoying a good chuckle at that expression on your face. He is the one who was able to look into a woman's eyes and tell if she were with child. He told me some time ago. I thought you, a midwife, knew thy self." He shook his head and laughed some more.

Her face turned as red as her hair. "Excuse me, Mr. Richardson, I think I have been away from Mrs. Rogers and her baby far too long." She swirled about and hurried off.

He yelled merrily after her, "Thank you, Mrs. Allerton, for your condolences. I do feel cheered."

How dare this crude sailor speak so to her about such intimate matters! Every time she was well meaning toward him, he turned the conversation around, making such a fool of her! No longer! For the rest of this journey, no matter how long it would take, she would succeed in avoiding him. Let the Reverend Hughes and Captain

Briggs tussle with his roguish soul. She would keep her mind on David and their baby. Their baby!

This was not bad news at all, yet she chastised herself for not recognizing the early signs, for being too preoccupied with this journey and its passengers. But how should she tell David? She wanted proper timing, but with such distress all around them David was distracted. She decided to hold off on the news. It could wait a little while. She doubted if anyone aboard read eyes like sailor Duff.

Elisabeth found David sitting with some men discussing survival tales of other damaged ships at sea. He beckoned her to him. She sat beside him on a board bench and was comforted, absorbing her good news with silent amazement.

Chapter 8

Encountering the Xavier

Underneath unspoken fears they knew not how they would survive. The *Sea Venture's* passengers became more subdued and lifeless. Sea knot after rolling sea knot produced an endless horizon of water. Many strained their eyes for a miraculous sighting of land. The slightest dark clouds struck them with premature anxiety. No one dared ask the confident Captain Briggs if they were lost. What good would it do? Elisabeth noticed that even David suppressed his impatience, and she loved him for it.

The creaking vessel had an untamed mind. Frustrated sailors guided it as best they could. Each night they consulted with Captain Briggs in hushed voices as they judged their position by the stars. They were grouchy with overcast skies, cursing as they took best guesses.

About a week after the storm Captain Briggs overheard Mr. Norton recall how he had heard about a ship of Pilgrims that, after losing their center mast, improvised one from a farm plow.

"Too bad there is not one of those in the hull," the captain mused out loud, joining their conversation.

Jonathan Rogers perked up excitedly. "But, Captain, I have one! I crated it myself, and I know it survived the storm. It beds below!"

Captain Briggs stared at him incredulously, wondering how they had not come upon this news sooner. He instructed Colin to go with Mr. Rogers and several others and retrieve the plow. Later, Colin came back and announced with a smirk, "It will not be a pretty sight, but I am quite certain it will be better than what we have."

Everyone cheered.

Together, seamen and Puritan craftsmen worked to change the plow into an improvised mast. When it was hoisted and secured into place, the ship's navigation became steadier, and morale lifted. There was hope again. Captain Briggs increased rations for the day. Elisabeth marveled this catastrophe had united them, and she felt reassured of God's sovereignty in their troubles. The ship's unity, however, did not last long.

The day after, David discovered the children huddled around First Mate Stone. He recited an old and well-known English story. The seaman's stern composure, his wild eyes, fly away hair, and arm movements enhanced the tale of two orphans left in the woods to die because of their uncle's greed. Stone's voice grew softer with sorrow, and the wide-eyed children leaned into him as he continued:

He took the children by the hand,
Teares standing in their eye,
And bad them straitwaye follow him,
And look they did not crye:
And two long miles he ledd them on,
While they for bread complaine;
"Staye here," quoth he, "I'll bring you some,
When I come back againe."
These pretty babes, with hand in hand,
Went wandering up and downe;
But never more could see the man

> *Approaching from the town:*
> *Their prettye lippes with black-berries,*
> *Were all besmear'd and dyed,*
> *And when they sawe the darksome night,*
> *They sat them downe and cryed.*
> *Thus wandered these two little babes,*
> *Till deathe did end their grief,*
> *In one another's armes they dyed,*
> *As babes wanting relief:*
> *No burial this pretty pair*
> *Of any man receives,*
> *Till Robin-red-breast painfully*
> *Did cover them with leaves.*

David could not believe his ears. This was not the lesson their children should hear, especially during their plight. He rushed forward and stood between Stone and his audience. "First Mate Stone, stop! We cannot have our children's minds filled with stories that do not exalt God's Word."

The First Mate blustered with surprised. "Surely *Babes in the Wood* is a good English tale, and Christian at that."

"Sir, I beg to differ. This story is not found in Holy Writ. You must stop!"

The children groaned, and Will Norton protested, "But he's almost to the end — the best part."

Hearing David's agitated voice, Elisabeth left her needlework and joined the gathering group. She personally thought the story harmless, and she knew others did, too. Why did David nitpick?

But her husband would not let up. "Reverend Hughes, do you not agree the children would profit more by hearing Bible stories?"

Reverend Hughes desired peace at all cost. He stumbled over his words, saying, "Well, um, yes, Mr. Allerton. I think the children have had enough storytelling for this day. More exercise and scripture memory would provide balance."

First Mate Stone's face puffed with anger, but he restrained himself. Gritting his teeth, he said, "Very well then. I have work to do."

Later as the children played skittles, they stopped to listen as they heard Stone belting out from the crow's nest the ending of "The Children in the Wood." Standing like a preacher in a pulpit, he declared to the ocean:

> *And now the heavy wrathe of God*
> *Upon their uncle fell;*
> *Yea, fearfull fiends did haunt his house,*
> *His conscience felt an hell:*
> *His barnes were fir'd, his goodes consum'd,*
> *His landes were barren made,*
> *His cattle dyed within the field,*
> *And nothing with him stayd.*
> *And in a voyage to Portugal,*
> *Two of his sonnes did dye;*
> *And to conclude, himselfe was brought*
> *To want and miserye:*
> *He pawn'd and mortgaged all his land*
> *Ere seven yeares came about;*
> *And now at length this wicked act*
> *Did by this meanes come out:*
> *The fellowe, that did take in hand*
> *These children for to kill,*
> *Was for a robbery judged to dye,*
> *(Such was God' separats blessed will;)*
> *Who did confess the very truth,*
> *As here hath been display'd:*
> *Their uncle having dyed in gaol,*

> *Where he for debt was layd.*
> *You that executors be made,*
> *And overseers eke,*
> *Of children that be fatherless,*
> *And infants mild and meek;*
> *Take you example by this thing,*
> *And yield to each his right,*
> *Lest God with such like miserye*
> *Your wicked minds requite.*

David ignored the sailor's recitation, sitting on a bench reading from his book. Everyone else kept their opinions low, but the ship's atmosphere again strained.

Elisabeth busied herself by tending to Mary and baby Isaac. Sometimes, she felt guilty and chastised herself for resenting Mary's demands for assistance, especially since the young mother's strength and happiness contrasted so much to her own. It did not help to observe how much Jonathan Rogers doted on his wife and baby.

David seemed oblivious to Elisabeth's occasional nausea. Having positioned himself as Reverend Hughes' right-hand man kept him busy with everyone's concerns except those of his wife's. Elisabeth decided to keep their baby a secret until they had some intimate time to rejoice together. They obviously were not going anywhere fast.

When Elisabeth reflected on her marriage, she consistently came back to a sermon quote she had heard by the great Reverend Richard Baxter: "It is a mercy to have a faithful friend that loves you entirely...to whom you may open your mind and communicate your affairs. And it is a mercy to have so near a friend to be a helper to your soul and to stir up in you the grace of God."

A soul mate to stir her up in God's grace was the part of her marriage she pinned her hopes on. Unfortunately, it had yet to be a reality for

David and her. This voyage to New England preoccupied so much of her husband's time. He was attentive only at bedtime. Still, she believed the bud of lasting friendship and love was there. It just needed time.

As for Mr. Colin Richardson, Elisabeth noticed he stayed away from her as much as she avoided him. No more did she catch him mischievously smirking at her. Instead, he seemed preoccupied with helping the crew sail a broken ship. He spent much time in the crow's nest. Elisabeth thought, *He must get such satisfaction looking down upon us.*

About ten days after the storm, it was Mr. Richardson who yelled from the crow's nest, "Sail Ho! Captain!"

"Can you make out its colors, Boatswain Richardson?" shouted Captain Briggs as he reached for his telescope.

David came rushing to his side. "Captain, we must hail them quickly so they see us. This ship must be God's providence! They can help us and tell us where we are!"

"Patience, Mr. Allerton. Patience. No doubt they can provide some aid, but for what price off our flesh?" Captain Briggs had the ship in his sights.

Half addressing David and half thinking out loud, the captain muttered, "If I were not anchored with a lame vessel I would try to outrun this shark. We do not have that choice."

He continued, turning to David, who sputtered a protest. "Steady, man! Thanks to our continental royals, God only knows whether we are at war with Spain or the Netherlands. There were even rumors as we left port that our Merry Monarch might turn to war against his own cousin, that vain Sun King. I highly doubt it, but one cannot take chances out on these treacherous seas. What would be worse for us, God forbid, Mr. Allerton, is if this be a buccaneer ship trying to trick us! Patience!"

The captain looked anxiously up to the crow's nest. "Boatswain Richardson, do you see the colors yet?"

"Aye, sir. The frigate bears a French flag. They are advancing."

"Good! I will take the French." Captain Briggs retracted his telescope. "Come off the crow's nest to assist in greeting our visitors."

He turned to David. "Well, Mr. Allerton, I would have preferred another English ship, but so be it. I am hopeful we are not hostile with France, and we are fortunate Boatswain Richardson speaks fluent French."

The captain handed his telescope to First Mate Stone and loudly declared, "Expedient precaution and absolute obedience are the orders of the day."

He grabbed David's arm and whispered, "Mr. Allerton, I want you to arm your men. Give them strict instructions that their weapons are only for show unless I give the command. Make that very clear! And let us pray this French captain is benevolent toward a ship full of Puritan pope haters."

Elisabeth moved closer to David. The captain addressed her gently, "Mrs. Allerton, I think it best for you to lead the women and children below and stay as quiet as possible."

Louder, he commanded, "Everybody, show no fear. Steady the course. I must prepare myself for our guests." He rushed to the cabin to grab saber and pistol.

Chapter 9

Friend or Foe

W ide-eyed with anxiety, the women held and shushed their children, whispering nervously about what happened above them. Reverend Hughes' wife clung to her copy of *The Saints Everlasting Rest* and quietly prayed. Finally, encouraged by the others, Elisabeth ventured up the ladder, just high enough to peek.

"What do you see?" the others pleaded in a soft chorus.

"Shhh!" Elisabeth whispered. When they quieted down, she reported their brave men were positioned and ready with weapons in hands. Sailing into view was a formidable French frigate of 26 cannons. Elisabeth caught her breath at its superior size and strength to their dwarfed vessel. Then she noticed the war ship's splintered wood and charred wounds.

Elisabeth excitedly reported, "It is a military ship! And it has been in battle!"

She took notice of the stiff French crew. Although weary and sooty, they stood like statues. It chilled Elisabeth to think how one quick command from their captain could bring bloodshed to them all.

No soul in this world would ever know what happened to us, she thought.

She strained to hear Mr. Richardson's friendly greeting. It was in French, and she could pick out a few words.

"God speed to you, captain, and to your valiant men," Mr. Richardson said.

"And to you," came the reply in French. "I am Captain Pierre Gaspar of the *Xavier,* under the royal command of our blessed King Louis the Fourteenth."

"A pleasure, sir. I am Monsieur Colin Richardson, speaking on behalf of my commander, the honorable Captain John Briggs. We sail on the *Sea Venture,* under the protection of our royal highness, King Charles II."

The captains saluted each other with their swords across the short span of water. Captain Gaspar called out, "Yesterday, we were in a skirmish with some buccaneers who menace these waters. Have you seen them?"

"No, Captain Gaspar, thank God!" replied Colin. "We have seen no one on this voyage until the *Xavier.* As you can observe, we, too, have met with hardship."

"Ah yes, your mast. Your adjustments are clever."

"In our need, Captain Gaspar, your kind assistance would be most appreciated. And perhaps there is something we can offer to benefit you and your brave men?" suggested Colin.

"Yes," he said firmly. "Please, ask your Captain Briggs to send a delegation over to the *Xavier* so we might further discuss how we can be of service to each other.

Colin translated the invitation to Captain Briggs. "Can we trust him, Colin?" the doubtful captain asked, stroking his beard.

Colin shrugged. "I don't know, sir. He needs something from us—just like we need something from him. Otherwise, I think he would have been over the horizon, not taking the trouble to bother with us."

"Aye, Boatswain Richardson, I agree. Unfortunately, I am afraid we have no recourse but to find out. I want you and First Mate Stone to go aboard. You have my permission to bargain as best you can. But most importantly, try to get us the coordinates of our present location and a compass would be a godsend. I do not know what we can offer this war ship—perhaps some of our rations. Do what you must to get what we need."

Colin and Stone rowed over to the *Xavier* accompanied by a couple of well-armed seamen. Once aboard, Colin noticed an officer tightly gripping the guardrail. Fresh blood seeped through his uniform. *Perhaps their strength was not as great as it first appeared*, he thought.

Captain Gaspar did not invite the Englishmen to his cabin. Instead, he ordered several men to bring out two chairs, a small table, goblets, and a bottle of Madeira.

Colin wondered, *Strange to negotiate on deck. What is he hiding in his cabin?*

Captain Gaspar did not miss Colin's quick survey of the crew. He gestured for him to sit and said, "As you see, Monsieur Colin, I have several wounded who need tending. Unfortunately, our surgeon died in our recent battle. Certainly, you must have a doctor in your company?"

Colin sensed Captain Gaspar's anxiety, but he could not discern its source. Sea casualties, from the least to the greatest, were expected. And after a battle, all able-bodied men pitched in to aid the wounded. Why did the captain's demeanor seem to border on desperation?

"I am sorry for your losses, Captain Gaspar. May your enemy's wounds be greater! Certainly our Dr. Stillingfleet could be of some service to you in this hardship." As he made this suggestion, Colin knew he wished on the stars, but he hoped the incompetent doctor could pull himself together enough to be convincing.

"Ah, very good, very good. May I then suggest your Dr. Stillingfleet come aboard immediately?"

"Of course. I will send for him," said Colin, taking a swallow of some very good wine. "We also have medical supplies that may be useful."

Turning to Stone, who grudgingly stood by, Colin ordered in English, "First Mate Stone, please make arrangements for Dr. Stillingfleet to come aboard with as many medical supplies as we can spare."

"Yes, sir." Stone gritted the words through his teeth, and his eyes warned the boatswain to remember this was a break in chain of command. Stone wanted to protest taking orders from his boatswain. Yet he could not, and Colin heard the command given to bring Stillingfleet aboard.

Colin waited expectantly in a long silence. It was Captain Gaspar's move.

Only when Captain Gaspar was convinced Stone's directions were being followed did he say, "Merci, Monsieur Richardson. Tell me, how may we best assist you?"

Colin decided the direct approach was the appropriate tack. He simply stated, "Our greatest needs are an astrolabe, compass, and coordinates."

"Ah, you and your passengers wander as I suspected." The captain knew he had the upper hand.

"Well, good seamen always use the stars." Colin casually took another swallow of wine, holding eye contact. He must keep some leverage.

Captain Gaspar paused a moment and then said, "We can help you with the compass and coordinates, but I am sorry we cannot spare our only astrolabe."

"Any help you offer is a kindness, sir." Colin shrugged, lifting his glass in salute.

The captain instructed another sailor to get the compass. Colin took another sip of his wine, wondering if these negotiations would continue to go so cordially.

"Monsieur Richardson, you speak French very well. How does an Englishman do that without even an accent?"

Colin shrugged. "After my father died, my mother married a Frenchman. He taught me well." Colin hoped the captain did not sense his uneasiness as he winced, remembering his stepfather's brutal chastisement during French lessons.

"Ah, then you have had the best of both worlds, or the worst of both?" The captain fished for information, but Colin was not interested in memoir.

"It has been a mixture like myself," he said, raising his glass and changing the subject. "How did the buccaneer ship fare in your battle?"

Captain Gaspar's jaw tightened and his hand clenched. "The cursed cowards fled into the blinding sun, but I do not think they are far. I am quite certain one of our cannons damaged their hull. God willing, we will overtake these scoundrels before their ship slowly sinks to the ocean's bottom."

Colin realized Captain Gaspar must be pursuing pirate treasure, but that meant the *Sea Venture* was farther south, farther off course, then he or his mates had estimated.

"Ah, you are anxious to pursue, Captain?"

"Very much so, but the wounded come first," said the captain with determination.

"Captain, I agree with that. And now, sir, what are our present coordinates?"

"Monsieur Richardson, you can easily make it to your country's island of Bermuda. You are North 35 degrees, 28 minutes."

This was startling news. Yet it was not hopeless. Quickly, Colin realized the *Sea Venture* could sail to bedraggled Bermuda, trade and re-supply the best they could, and then head north to Boston before winter's worst.

Colin was just about to ask for more of the captain's fine wine when he noticed a rowboat returning from the *Sea Venture* with Dr. Stillingfleet and other passengers. He squinted his eyes. There, sitting alongside Dr. Stillingfleet and First Mate Stone, flashing her white cap and flaming red hair, was Mrs. Allerton! Next to her, sitting proudly with his hand on a sword, was her fool of a husband!

Damn! These ignorant Puritans! Why would Captain Briggs allow this? How could David Allerton lead his wife onto a war vessel! Did that man have any sense at all?

Climbing the rope ladder up the side of the ship took all of Elisabeth's strength, but she was determined. David's support comforted from below. He provided a barrier for her modesty. Elisabeth steadied herself on deck and was quickly greeted with a kiss to her hand by Captain Gaspar.

"Mademoiselle. Welcome," he said in English.

Recovering her surprise and balance, she curtsied and caught the scowl on Mr. Richardson's face. She would not let him thwart her confidence. The wounded needed her.

As Captain Gaspar turned to Dr. Stillingfleet, Colin muttered to the couple, "Do you realize the danger you have placed yourselves in?" And then with a smile, he formally introduced David and Elisabeth.

Elisabeth curtsied again, and while smiling at the captain, she instructed Colin, "Mr. Richardson, please explain to Captain Gaspar that I am a midwife. Dr. Stillingfleet suggested I come, and Captain Briggs agreed. My husband and I are together, so I do not see any reason for your disapproval."

"My wife is correct, Mr. Richardson," David said as he touched the sword and a pistol at his waist. "We are capable of helping in this matter—anything to get our people to Boston."

While Captain Gaspar and Dr. Stillingfleet greeted one another, Colin gritted his teeth and whispered, "Have you considered our doctor's incompetent record? It will not take Captain Gaspar long to realize who can provide the best care? He may not permit you to go back to the *Sea Venture!*"

"That is absurd!" said David, showing less bravado and more uncertainty as he surveyed the sulking crew's faces. Elisabeth was startled to hear any kind of compliment of her skills coming from Mr.

Richardson, but she needed to keep mind on the wounded. She wanted to help if she could.

Captain Gaspar turned his attention to Colin, David, and Elisabeth. In French, he tersely said to Colin, "Yes, the smell of Dr. Stillingfleet's breath tells me you have quite a fine doctor. At least he had enough common sense to bring this midwife. I hope for your sakes, Monsieur Richardson, it is enough."

"What do you mean?" asked Colin.

"Follow me to my quarters," he ordered.

As they moved to Captain Gaspar's cabin, Colin gave Stone the coordinates of their location. Stone shook his head in dismay as he carried the compass to the rowboat. He and his sailors had already unloaded Elisabeth's medicine chest, which she insisted on bringing aboard. Inadvertently, one harried sailor also scooped up her bag containing journal and medical books.

"Where are you going?" David demanded of Stone, not liking the idea of their rowboat leaving so quickly.

Stone savored a silent pause. Finally, he said, "Mr. Allerton, Captain Briggs wants this compass straight away. Do not fret. Have courage, man! We will be rowing back and forth with supplies."

"Of course, I understand," David said, but he was rethinking his decision to board with Elisabeth.

Inside the cabin, a guard stood watch over an unconscious, pale boy lying in the captain's bloodied bed. Elisabeth guessed the lad was ten years old, no bigger than her brother Paul. She surmised this poor child must be part of Captain Gaspar's family to receive such special attention in the captain's quarters.

As she hurried over to hold the boy's hand and touch his head, Colin translated Captain Gaspar's words. "This is my son Remille; he disobeyed orders to stay in the cabin during the skirmish and was wounded from cannon fire."

Dr. Stillingfleet lifted the blanket and viewed the bloodied pant leg showing crushed flesh. "Damn, this is bad," he whistled through his breath. "No doubt. The leg must certainly come off."

Although Elisabeth had little confidence in Dr. Stillingfleet, she knew he was correct: the wound was so severe and the boy so weak. Surely this boy would die if something was not done soon.

Colin translated to Captain Gaspar, who seemed prepared for such an outcome. "Tell them," he said to Colin, but not taking his eyes from Remille, "his mother will never forgive me if I do not bring him home. If God wills for my son to die, then I vow that you also will all die."

Captain Gaspar kissed his son on the forehead. "Ask my master sergeant for whatever you need." Then he quickly walked out of the room.

Colin's translation disconcerted David. "What? He threatens us! This boy is at death's door! We came in good faith. We have been tricked! Dr. Stillingfleet can manage here. Elisabeth and I must get off the ship!"

"Steady, man. Keep your voice down. We need to keep our heads!" said Colin.

"David, please!" Elisabeth grabbed his arm. "We need to help this boy and the other wounded."

"Aye, I agree with that. We are at Captain Gaspar's mercy," said Dr. Stillingfleet. He seemed to have found some professional confidence. "Master Colin, please tell this big French ogre to bring us water and as many clean rags as they can spare. They certainly know the drill for an amputation. We also need boiling black tar, and I would like their surgeon's tools, particularly his saw. I will combine his instruments with mine. Oh, and get me a whetting stone. Meanwhile, I will look into the captain's cabinet for other useful supplies."

Elisabeth could not believe the doctor was thinking of spirits, even at this dangerous time. "Dr. Stillingfleet, you must not!" she pleaded.

"My dear, it will steady me. I am quite undone." He lifted his shaking hands.

She nodded and added, "Doctor, I will treat the boy's other injuries the best I can. He has several powder burns."

"Yes, good plan," Dr. Stillingfleet said, popping the plug off a rum bottle.

Throughout Colin's many voyages, he witnessed amputations on numerous occasions, but he assumed correctly it was Elisabeth's first one. There was some mercy for the half-dead boy and his father. At least the patient was unconscious.

Taking Elisabeth aside, David whispered, "I think I will wait outside and keep a watch on affairs. Are you all right?"

She sensed his intense uneasiness and wanted to encourage him, yet she needed his strength. "Yes, thank you, David. Pray for this boy's recovery. Do not worry, husband. We will be fine. We are together."

She pressed his hand and held it. "David, there is something important I want to tell you. I have been saving it for the proper occasion, but it must wait. When we get back to the *Sea Venture*...."

"It can wait," he said, patting her hand and giving her a brief hug before leaving.

Elisabeth steadied herself with a prayer and was ready to assist Dr. Stillingfleet. The surgery did not take long. Colin and the guard remained in the room to fetch any needed items. When Dr. Stillingfleet presented a mangled, small leg wrapped in some cloth to the guard, Elisabeth fought her nausea by concentrating on Remille. How she wanted the lad to live and be reunited with his mother.

While they were finishing dressing the stub, Colin heard shouting outside. He also felt the shifting of the ship. "I will be back," he told Dr. Stillingfleet and Elisabeth, who seemed too involved with their patient to notice him.

Outside, he found David frantically trying to keep two sailors from hoisting a sail.

"Richardson!" he yelled. "Help me stop them! They want to leave. Do something!"

"What is going on, Captain Gaspar?" Colin demanded from the man looking through his telescope.

"Monsieur Richardson, I am sorry, but we have spotted the

buccaneers. I told you they were not far, but we must make haste. Unfortunately, you will have to travel with us for a while. There is no time to get you back to the *Sea Venture*."

For a second Colin weighed his options and liked none of his choices. He would need his wits to get them out of this mess, especially to calm Mr. Allerton, who tugged on the captain's arm.

"This is an outrage! You cannot kidnap us!" David yelled. "We came aboard in good faith and you, sir, have violated our trust. Your son's operation is done. Go look for yourself. Just let us get off this ship! Sir, I beg of you!"

Captain Gaspar shook free of David's grasp and said to Colin, "You English certainly bear enough idiots. Tell him to be quiet, or I will have him shackled."

Colin pulled David away. "Be still, man. We are at a disadvantage here, and he might throw you into the brig."

David pushed Colin away. "No! I will not let that happen," he said, shakily pulling out his sword and then his pistol.

"Mr. Allerton, stop this craziness! You are outnumbered! Think of your wife's safety, if not your own!"

David waved his pistol and sword as several sailors moved toward him. He reached the guardrail and looked down at the churning water. The soldiers took out their swords and slowly advanced toward him.

It happened so quickly Colin could not be certain if Allerton jumped or lost his balance as the soldiers rushed to grab him.

There was a splash, and from the water a floundering David yelled, "Elisabeth! Elisabeth!"

One soldier announced, "The fool jumped!"

Already, the *Sea Venture*'s rowboat moved toward the splashing escapee. Stone and another sailor's pistols aimed at several of the *Xavier*'s soldiers, whose guns were pointed at David.

Colin took a deep breath. He was conflicted. The *Xavier* moved away from the *Sea Venture* and toward a speck on the horizon. He was an excellent swimmer, and his impulse was to jump and save himself.

Yet, his feet remained stuck to the deck. He wanted to sneer at Mrs. Allerton and report her saintly husband had just abandoned her. But was that truly possible? Could this man be such a coward? It gnawed at Colin that a decent woman like Mrs. Allerton would love such a man so clearly not her equal.

Colin knew if he did not hurry and jump he would be stuck with Mrs. Allerton and the alcoholic Dr. Stillingfleet. Their odds were not good. He felt an anchor held him to the deck. He had to make his decision.

Ah, Duff, you were right. I feel obligated to repay this blasted woman for saving my life. But this is no fair exchange!

Chapter 10

David Allerton's Plight

While David Allerton treaded water and watched the *Xavier* sail away, he mulled over his decision to abandon Elisabeth by jumping overboard.

In crisis, he and Elisabeth had been forced to make decisions too quickly. It was her irresponsible insistence on using medical skills improperly that had pulled them onto the *Xavier*. Surely providence foreknew he could not leave the others on the crippled *Sea Venture*. They needed him. After all, he was a key leader.

Also, it was not just about the passengers. His uncle and aunt in Dorchester were depending on him to run their business while they returned to England. God had laid out this plan so clearly, and David had to follow it.

Yet this was a delicate matter to explain—leaving Elisabeth, losing a wife to the fate of sea wanderers, French papists no less. The drunken Dr. Stillingfleet and sour Colin Richardson would be of little help. His poor, sweet Elisabeth! She could not possibly survive without his care. This was an awful truth to bear. It comforted him that his wife's strong faith would sustain her to the end. He knew her well.

As his clothing pulled him down into the choppy waves, David sputtered and floundered to hold on to his pistol and sword. He had to think of a convincing story. The rescue boat hurried toward him. David knew people would judge him a coward, because they could not appreciate the subtle nuances of difficult decisions. David Allerton believed he was no coward!

Yet, how could he explain his plight so the Puritans would not whisper? Would it not be better to say the soldiers had tussled with him after they drew their swords? Surely that was plausible! He had been cornered. True! He thought he was going to be impaled. True! In those moments when thought moved to action, the fighting resulted in him losing his balance and falling overboard. If he embroidered the circumstances somewhat that would bring clarity to the others. Yes, it could have happened that way. His people were dealing with a broken ship and dispirited hearts. Why add more sorrow then was necessary?

As Stone pulled him into the rowboat and the *Sea Venture* lowered a rope for them to climb aboard, he was truly shaken and grief-stricken. Such pain he had not endured since he had put down the horse that had sired Blessing and Bountiful. It had become lame, and there was nothing else to do. Promising life had been cut short.

David reached for Captain Briggs's arm, pleading loudly, "They have my Elisabeth! We must make chase!"

He knew rescue was impossible, but he had to say it. Once aboard ship, people gathered around him—he observed the sympathy on their faces. They would believe his story and comfort him. He could soldier on to provide leadership and strength through this wretched crisis. This was his destiny.

Chapter 11

Abandoned

Elisabeth and Dr. Stillingfleet felt the ship jolt forward, and they attempted to flee the captain's cabin. The French guard pushed them away from the door and pointed his sword to indicate they sit down. Elisabeth knew she heard David's frantic voice, but she could not make out what he said.

Dr. Stillingfleet saluted the guard and plopped himself into the captain's chair. Elisabeth returned to sit with Remille. Unconsciously, she held the boy's hand and squeezed it. *I must calm myself and wait patiently in prayer.* Her heart raced. Hearing muffled French shouts, she prayed, *Oh, Lord, protect my husband. Let him be safe.*

The French crew, stinging from battle without victory or treasure, was bent on catching this buccaneer ship. Colin wagered it was a vain attempt. The pirate ship had spotted them first and was already using sun and wind to put distance between them once again. The *Xavier* would not catch up with their treasure this day. Colin hesitated to give Stillingfleet and Mrs. Allerton the bad news of David's absence. But he had to rally them. Their success in saving the captain's son was their best bargaining chip in getting out of this mess.

"You mean David is not with us?" Elisabeth stood up stunned. She started twisting her apron as her mind tried to sort out the circumstances.

Colin was uncomfortable with her dismay. He much preferred her lofty confidence.

"I am sorry, Mrs. Allerton. In the scuffle, it appears your husband fell overboard."

"He fell overboard! Do you know if he is all right? Poor David," she whispered, tears clouding her eyes.

"Poor David!" snorted Dr. Stillingfleet. "Albeit dripping wet, he is safe on the *Sea Venture*! We are as good as dead!" The doctor walked over to the captain's liquor cabinet and angrily grabbed a flask.

Colin quickly responded, watching Elisabeth's face. "Guard your tongue, doctor, or I will silence it for you! We are not going to die! Captain Gaspar is no barbarian!"

"But, Mr. Richardson, what happens to us? Where is this ship going?" Elisabeth wanted to stay calm, but she felt nausea coming on.

"One crew member told me the island St. Paola is where the *Xavier* plans to anchor over winter. I assume once Captain Gaspar and his men satisfy their futile pursuit of the buccaneers, the *Xavier* will head for St. Paola. The captain is most anxious to get his son back on shore. I wager that once we reach land, he will turn us over to the St. Paola authorities."

By the look on Elisabeth's face, Colin knew she was not comforted.

"Mrs. Allerton, catching a ship to Boston, even from a French Carib port, is not impossible. There are ways. I know. And the *Sea Venture* is a good ship. It now has coordinates to reach the island of Bermuda and resupply there to complete the journey to Boston. Captain Briggs and his crew will make sure Mr. Allerton and the others arrive safely. I swear it: you will reunite with your husband."

He added softly, "It just may take a little while."

Colin wanted to give Elisabeth hope, even if it were just a flicker. He needed her to keep sane and nurse the boy back to health. Their lives depended on it.

"Aye, Richardson, you sure can spin a web of hope. Who knows what the French will do with us." Dr. Stillingfleet took another swig of rum.

"What do you mean?" Elisabeth's head hurt. She could not believe she was in such a mess.

Dr. Stillingfleet eyes gleamed like a rat's. "Well, Mrs. Allerton, we could become their prisoners on trumped-up charges. We are simply at their mercy unless you have royal connections or your husband can send ransom money to free you. But, hell, he does not even know where you are heading! Trust me, a Carib island is a far journey from Boston."

Elisabeth's hopeless pain made him chortle and take another swallow. She glanced at Mr. Richardson to counter Dr. Stillingfleet's doom and gloom.

Colin would not lie about their plight. "It's true, Mrs. Allerton, we are in a bad way. But hope remains. I will not leave my fate to men who hold us against our wills. This island we are going to—I know it. I have a few mates who might help us."

"Friends? Bah, what kind of friends would someone like you have, Richardson? French? Pirates?" Dr. Stillingfleet waved his hand away and settled into the captain's chair with his bottle.

Colin's patience had run out. He crossed the room and kicked away Stillingfleet's footstool. He grabbed the man's collar. "Let me make it clear, Dr. Stillingfleet. Your miserable, drunken hide means nothing to me, and I do not trust you!"

Then Colin pulled out his knife for effect. "I will be watching you on this voyage. Do not betray my trust, or you will find yourself in the Atlantic as shark bait before the island authorities ever have to deal with you! I owe Mrs. Allerton for saving my life. But you I owe nothing!"

Dr. Stillingfleet withered. "Richardson, please, sir, I am sorry. I overstepped. We are all rattled by this unfortunate affair. Forgive any offense I have made. No harm was meant. Please, might you not put your knife away? Sir, I beg you to take your hands off of me."

To ease the tension, Elisabeth gently pulled on Colin's arm. "Mr. Richardson, I am most grateful for any help you can give me in reuniting with my husband. Do you not think it best, under these circumstances, that we try to work together?"

Colin released his grip on Dr. Stillingfleet but continued to stare at him. "Increase your prayers, Mrs. Allerton. We are going to need all the help we can get."

As Dr. Stillingfleet resumed his drinking and Mrs. Allerton fussed over an unconscious Remille, Colin could not stand the confinement of the cabin any longer. He knew he would go mad with such a heavy dose of these burdening companions reminding him of his plight.

The guard allowed him out on deck. Colin surveyed the weary crew. A helping hand and quick ear could gather much useful information and allow him easier access on the ship. How useful his French was. The sailors gladly accepted him because of it. Their battered ship required many repairs, and Colin was handy at most tasks from carpentry to netting the sails. While sharing their drink and stories, Colin knew he could become very familiar with the *Xavier*.

It was not a bad lot the English had fallen upon. Captain Gaspar held respect by most of his sailors, yet there was tension. Colin quickly sensed the second in command, Lt. Jacques Baptiste, misused his power over others. He had one manner with his captain and another with the crew. Many a man had felt his whip for minor offenses. He was hated and feared.

Whenever Colin offered to help a grateful sailor, the beefy Baptiste seemed to shadow him and chastise his men, "Fools, do not forget this one is English. Do not let your guard down. You cannot trust him nor his French tongue. I have seen his kind many a time!"

Colin knew it would be difficult, but he planned to stay away from Baptiste and his whip. The man was a sadist. Although Captain Gaspar approved of Colin pitching in, Colin knew Gaspar's good will would only stretch so far. Baptiste trumped a kidnapped seaman.

Chapter 12

Changing Clothes

Elisabeth eyed the snoring Stillingfleet slouched over the captain's table, an empty flask beside him. Odd, but she did not despise him as Mr. Richardson did. He seemed too pitiful, reduced to finding comfort in drunkenness and sleep.

Her family had protected her from alcohol's excesses, but she observed its destruction in the lives of local peasant families. She remembered one of their servants, Molly, who occasionally displayed bruises—the aftermath of her drunken husband's rage. Elisabeth's father finally visited that man, and the beatings ended as quickly as they had begun. She always wondered what her gentle father had done to create the change for Molly.

It seemed to Elisabeth that Stillingfleet did not display meanness as much as mere weakness of character when consuming liquor. She sighed and said out loud, "Count that a blessing."

Her young patient slept, but he looked dead. Drained of color, Remille was a withered form, too small for the bed. Fortunately, his chest rose and sank steadily. Her heart ached for him. She dripped a few drops of water into his mouth, placing the moist rag on his brow. She adjusted his blanket. Then it was waiting, praying, waiting.

She felt faint and nauseated. Her clothes were covered in Remille's sticky blood. And worse, her husband was drifting farther and farther away from her.

Oh, husband, what happened to cause you to fall over board? Why were you so close to the guardrail? She kept puzzling over it, having difficulty accepting that she really was without David's support.

Mr. Richardson had told her what he witnessed, but for once his words seemed uncertain. He said David struggled with two soldiers, and when they attempted to grab him, he fell overboard, crying out her name. Yes, she thought she had heard her name being called out. David had not forgotten her when he was in danger!

And Mr. Richardson expressed some hope for their plight: it was not impossible to get a ship to Boston. She must bear that in mind, he said, and then he added begrudgingly that he would help her.

It rattled her to realize her future depended on a pagan sailor who obviously despised her. She felt uncomfortable with his reminder that he did this because of her treatment of his head wound. He would never listen to one word of protest that God was the true healer. She had never witnessed such rapid healing of a wound so severe. It had little to do with her skills.

How she wished for just one godly companion for solace. Why had God flanked her with such unbelievers as Dr. Stillingfleet and Colin Richardson? She was the only woman on a ship of French papists! How was she to make it through her pregnancy without David and the others? She so wished she had told her husband about their baby!

Elisabeth knew Captain Gaspar's protection was all that kept her safe. He had been in the cabin several times, briefly acknowledging his "guests" but concentrating on the wellbeing of his son.

The stoic captain was the helpless father, feebly caressing the boy's head, holding his hand. Yet he also used his position for what he wanted. His emotionless eyes looked like two lifeless brown pebbles when they addressed Elisabeth. Mr. Richardson translated that Captain Gaspar appreciated her help. Yet there was no gratifying warmth from his manner. She knew she was expendable except for her medical skills.

It made Elisabeth uneasy to watch Mr. Richardson transform into a Frenchman as he translated for Captain Gaspar. It made her alienation from him even greater. She could not trust that man.

She was bone tired. She could not think straight nor pray with a clear head. Sitting next to Remille's bed, she closed her eyes a little as the ship rocked forward.

"Here, you might want to put these on." She jumped from her slumber as clothes were tossed into her lap. Mr. Richardson stood near her.

"What are these?" She was embarrassed he had so easily crept up on her.

"The captain said you might need them as well as some water for washing. Elisabeth saw a leering sailor behind Colin putting down a small barrel. His lopsided toothy grin made her uneasy. Dr. Stillingfleet may have rightly labeled him an ogre.

"Captain Gaspar expects me to put on seaman's clothes?" Elisabeth touched the coarse fabric trying to comprehend such a request.

"Mrs. Allerton, you need to wear something while your bloody clothes dry out. Captain Gaspar is just a practical man."

Colin could not help but find amusement at the thought of this Puritan woman dressing like a seaman. He had known a different kind of woman, his Angelique, who relished wearing breeches. But Mrs. Allerton was no Angelique!

Elisabeth quickly shook off her grogginess. Examining her bloody garment, she faltered. "Oh, yes, I see why this is necessary. Please tell Captain Gaspar thank you."

Still smirking, Mr. Richardson and the hulking sailor left.

Elisabeth eyed the doctor sprawled out on the captain's chair. He still snored deeply. She knew the captain might return any time. She sorted out the clothes. She recalled some holy scripture forbidding women from wearing men's clothing. Were there exceptions to this command? She could imagine David's protests. Yet, she was in a difficult position, and she could think of no alternative without further embarrassment.

She moved as far away from Dr. Stillingfleet's vision as she could, ever watching him. She slowly untied her bloodied apron, waistcoat, and blouse.

Elisabeth gingerly touched the borrowed seaman's garments. She pushed away thoughts of who might have been the former owner. At least the musty clothing seemed generally clean.

Dr. Stillingfleet snorted and that made her hurry. She pulled the seaman shirt over her thin blouse; she pulled dungarees under her other petticoat. They covered up her stockings and garters and provided warmth.

Then she threw her bloody clothes into the barrel of water. She winced at the thought of how stiff the salt water would make them. She had never considered her family's well of water such a blessing. How could she have taken such comforts for granted?

Oh, for a warm hearth and a big black kettle of water that did not smell like the sea! After checking on Remille, she scrubbed her clothes as efficiently as possible. The sooner she could get back into them, the better, she reasoned.

"You know our odds of survival are not good, Mrs. Allerton." She looked up from hanging her garments on some pegs. A rumbled Dr. Stillingfleet stood and stretched his arms. He did not even seem to notice her odd attire.

"Sir, you have spoken plainly on that matter, but I choose to believe our fate is in God's hands." She shook out her waistcoat with an extra flap before hanging it.

"Good Puritan answer, Mrs. Allerton, but it gives me little comfort in our present condition. Before journey's end, you may desire a more accessible companion." He tapped his empty jug. She shook her head and checked on Remille.

Doctor Stillingfleet slowly ambled to his patient, lifting the blanket. From the bed, the child moaned. "Aye, the wound looks better than most I have tended. I wager he will live, which is indeed fortunate for us. The turning point will come when his fever breaks."

"Dr. Stillingfleet, do you think there is any possibility Captain Gaspar would just release us when we reach shore?"

"Very unlikely, Mrs. Allerton. On that score, Mr. Richardson and I agree. The good captain will turn us over to the viceroy of St. Paola as soon as he has Remille in the hands of a French doctor."

"I do not know how to prepare for what lies ahead. Everything is unknown," she said feebly.

"My dear, these kind of island authorities usually come from the same cloth. I suspect Viceroy Philippe de la Roche will treat you like a guest, albeit a captured one. You will have some level of comfort. I have met de la Roche once in France. He has a charming daughter. Isabelle, I recall, is her name. And de la Roche struck me as above par as island governors go. He probably will send a letter to Boston and see if your husband will pay for your release."

Elisabeth's eyes widened. "Ransom money! That could take months to sort out!"

"Mrs. Allerton, once we harbor for the winter, we will have months on that blasted French island. Only ships of fools venture forth during winter."

For the first time, it dawned on Elisabeth that she was going to have David's and her baby alone in an unimaginable place with no family or friends to help her.

She feebly asked, "Doctor Stillingfleet, what will they do with you and Mr. Richardson?"

"I do not think we will fare as well, my dear, unless we can think of some way to make ourselves more valuable. I am afraid our fate will be servitude on some other French ship. I do not relish that thought. You can be certain Mr. Richardson does not either. We will do what we must to break free."

Elisabeth needed to think, but she was still too tired. "I think I better rest a little."

"Oh yes, of course. I will keep vigil over our patient."

It did not take long for Elisabeth to fall asleep. Dr. Stillingfleet considered her and his empty flask. The boy slept. There was nothing for him to do, and he was restless. He decided to go outside and stretch his legs. Perhaps he could earn some goodwill among these French.

Chapter 13

Attacked

When Elisabeth opened her eyes, the leering ogre, who earlier had brought the water barrel, hovered over her. She was about to scream when he covered her mouth with his big grimy hand.

She felt a knife pressing her side. He whispered in French, breathing heavily. As he thrust the knife more painfully into her, he removed his hand. Terrified, she could not scream or move. Where were Dr. Stillingfleet and Mr. Richardson?

The ogre lifted her up and pushed her roughly to the floor. He started lifting her petticoat and chuckled when he saw the breeches underneath. Elisabeth shook her head no and pleaded with her eyes. For a few seconds, he relaxed the knife and moved his hand lustfully over the trousers. His breath smelled like rotten eggs.

Thoughts of her baby suddenly sent a wave of survival strength that Elisabeth did not know she possessed. With as much force as she could, she grabbed the hand with the knife and bit this monster. Startled, he yelped and dropped the knife.

The ogre swore softly in French and struck Elisabeth across the face.

"No!" she finally yelled. "No!"

He tried to cover her mouth and press his body down on her. As she frantically flailed around, her hand grasped the knife. She thrust it into his flabby side and pulled it out. She felt him stiffen in pain as a surprised look crossed his troll-like face.

She pushed him hard and rolled away, scrambling to get around the map table. She clutched the knife for protection. The ogre wiped his bloody hand on his clothing, shaking his head and chuckling a curse. Then, he clenched his fists and charged. Elisabeth prepared for impact. But in that dim cabin, the ogre tripped over Elisabeth's medicine chest and fell across the table.

Elisabeth's reaction was instinctive. She brought the knife down on her attacker, landing a lucky stab to the back of the neck. There was only one slight groan, and his body went motionless.

"Oh, Lord, what have I done?" she whispered in shock. Surely, he could not be dead so easily?

Elisabeth was too frightened to touch him. She could not believe she had survived this huge man's attack. Her bruised mouth still had the lingering taste of his filthy, bloody hand. She quickly cupped water from the barrel, slurped it, and spit it out. She shuddered as she looked at the corpse and backed away to sit next to Remille.

Colin had not seen the seaman enter the cabin with a food tray. He had succumbed to sleep against a barrel on deck. He assumed Dr. Stillingfleet's presence was some protection for Mrs. Allerton. But he awoke, sensing something was wrong. He saw Dr. Stillingfleet's silhouette standing at the ship's rail next to a seaman. Mr. Richardson cursed the drunken doctor and quickly dashed through the cabin door.

He found Mrs. Allerton sitting next to Remille. She lamely pointed to the sprawling bulk across the table. He touched the sailor and pulled out the knife.

"He is dead! How did you manage? Did he harm you, Mrs. Allerton?"

She whispered, "No. No. I did not mean to kill him. He attacked me; he tripped. It happened so quickly."

Several sailors entered the cabin. They saw their dead comrade and the knife in Colin's hand. They grabbed Colin and started beating him.

Elisabeth yelled, "No! Please stop! You do not understand!"

Dr. Stillingfleet and Captain Gaspar came rushing in with more men. The captain took one look at Elisabeth's bruised face and ordered his men to attention. Baptiste cracked his whip in the air.

In French, Colin yelled, "Your dead dog here attempted to defile Mrs. Allerton. She defended herself! Is this how you repay someone who is helping your son?"

Captain Gaspar understood the situation, but he had a dead French sailor. His men would not so easily be appeased.

He shouted, "Silence! I am no fool! This is an outrage in my cabin, with my son at death's door! Take Monsieur Richardson down below and shackle him for the rest of the night. I will question him later."

This order satisfied Gaspar's men. As they dragged Colin away, he yelled, "Stillingfleet, you damn well better make sure Mrs. Allerton is protected or you will soon find yourself overboard with the rest of the flotsam."

Rushing to check on unconscious Remille, Captain Gaspar ordered the ogre's body removed. Then his blazing eyes turned on Elisabeth.

"Please sir, I was attacked. I did not mean to kill your man. Mr. Richardson was not even in the cabin when it happened." Elisabeth hoped he could understand her through her sobs.

The captain nodded his head and pointed to her bruised face, simply saying, "Madame, I am sorry." He bowed and left Dr. Stillingfleet and Elisabeth alone with Remille.

Elisabeth sank to the floor. She could not stop shaking. Dr. Stillingfleet tried to comfort her by putting a fatherly hand on her shoulder.

"My dear, I am so sorry I left you unattended. I thought it was safe to leave for just a little while. My, how did you ever handle such a brute of a man?"

"Do not touch me!" she quietly said, not bothering to look at him.

Elisabeth slowly got up and checked her clothing. Only her seaman shirt was torn, and she had a long knife scratch on her left arm. She took out some salve from her medicine chest and with shaking fingers dabbed the cut, as well as the welt on her swollen face.

Ignoring the rambling of Dr. Stillingfleet's voice, she moved to Remille's bedside. Laying her head on the bed, she softly sobbed, trying to shut out the nightmare of that man's fowl breath, violent hands, and evil intentions. What would her beloved David think?

She had killed a man, and she did not even know how that was possible. Yes, he had attacked her, but how had that knife fatally found his neck? Did Captain Gaspar even believe her? What if the medicine chest had not been on the floor? It felt like a nightmare, and she had trouble making the sequence of events fit together. She should have yelled for help. If this was God's protection for her, it had come at great cost to her soul.

She silently cried out a psalm she had memorized from childhood:

> "Oh, that I had wings like a dove:
> Then would I fly away and rest.
> Behold I would take my flight far off,
> and lodge in the wilderness.
> He would make haste for my deliverance
> from the stormy wind and tempest."
> Psalm 55:6-8

Dr. Stillingfleet brought Elisabeth a blanket and laid it on the bed beside her. He shrugged and sampled the hardtack and stew the ogre had brought. He looked around the room. There, on the floor he spied a flask, probably belonged to the dead man. What luck! It was half full.

Chapter 14

Escape Plan

Elisabeth had fallen asleep across the bed of her patient with her arms cradled under her. She felt a slight tug on her sleeve. Groggily, she opened her eyes and saw pleading eyes.

"Remille, you are awake!" she said half to herself and half to the boy who whispered, "Poppa?"

"Oh, yes, Captain Gaspar! I will get him."

Elisabeth got up and winced from her body's aches, the aftermath of the night's horrible ordeal. She staggered to the cabin's door and instructed the guard posted outside, "Tell Captain Gaspar, his son, Remille, is awake!"

The guard peered in the room and nodded. Captain Gaspar quickly came and found Elisabeth holding his son's hand and the boy crying in pain. Dr. Stillingfleet lingered near the bed.

"Remille, Remille! I am here." He smothered the boy with words Elisabeth could not understand, but they seemed to calm the child down. "Anything for pain?" he pleaded in English.

"Sir, we can keep giving him spirits. But I am afraid these next few days will be difficult," explained Dr. Stillingfleet.

Elisabeth stepped back as the captain comforted his son. Her burden seemed a little lighter realizing her patient was conscious. Dr. Stillingfleet instructed her to tend to his wounds and distract him from pain. She would administer the laudanum the apothecary had given her. This nursing care kept thoughts and fears at bay.

As she looked at the father and son, she wondered about Remille's mother. How much she must worry about her young son on a war ship so far from home. Poor Remille should have his mother's comfort. And what about David? Did her husband long for her as she yearned for him?

When Captain Gaspar was about to leave, Elisabeth pleaded firmly, "Captain Gaspar, we need Mr. Richardson to translate. It would go so much better for Remille."

The captain nodded, and in a short while Elisabeth turned to see Mr. Richardson standing at the door. He motioned for her to come outside. This puzzled her, and she hesitated. The cabin seemed so much safer than bearing the stares of Captain Gaspar's men. But Mr. Richardson waved again more emphatically. She stepped outside and avoided everything except scrutinizing Mr. Richardson's bloodied and bruised face.

"They beat you!" she exclaimed, touching his jaw.

"Oh, these marks are nothing," Colin slurred the words through swollen lips and pulled away. "I have suffered much worse. But I see you appear better, Mrs. Allerton."

Did Mr. Richardson have to take their woes so lightly? She felt guilty about wanting to hit the man herself, simply for such cheerfulness.

He continued, "You have done it again, have you not, Mrs. Allerton? I hear your patient survives and is even awake!"

"Yes, thanks be to God!" She felt she could take little credit. She wished she knew how to convince Mr. Richardson the Lord was the true healer.

Elisabeth noticed the raw marks on Mr. Richardson's wrists. "You were shackled too!"

"Mrs. Allerton, never mind. Come over here by the deck and observe the horizon. Act casual. Keep your voice low. I believe the good captain decided a night's beating and imprisonment were enough to appease his men's sense of justice—at least for a while. The bloke who attacked you is already buried at sea. He was not a well-liked mate among the crew. Imagine that."

Elisabeth winced. She wished she could feel mercy, but she breathed better knowing the loathsome man's body was gone from the ship.

"Mr. Richardson, I am sorry my unfortunate plight caused you this pain. I realize more and more, sir, I am in your debt."

"That scum did not violate you, did he?"

His concern touched and embarrassed her. "No, I was able to—No, I was spared." She was not sure how to say it.

Colin did not wish to talk about the uncomfortable matter either. As he changed the subject, his voice lost its compassion.

"I am afraid my life is not worth much once we make port. I do not relish the thought of being snared as a slave for a French ship. I am going to prepare my escape, and I think it best, given these circumstances, that you come with me when the opportunity arises."

"Escape!" Elisabeth said it too loudly, and Mr. Richardson touched her arm and turned her again toward the ocean. He looked across the deck and saw Baptiste swing his head toward their direction.

"Mrs. Allerton, please!" he quietly gritted out the words. "I would like to advise you to trust Captain Gaspar, but he will have little power with the island's authorities. And after last night, I cannot entrust you to the charge of our Dr. Stillingfleet. Unfortunately, the trepanning of women is common in the new world."

Elisabeth shuddered that Dr. Stillingfleet could betray her to benefit himself. But the violent attack upon her made him suspect. Her face grew red. Mr. Richardson thought the doctor intentionally left her alone to bring favor to himself! He certainly was not as harmless as she thought.

Mr. Richardson slipped her a dagger, a good blade he had just pickpocketed from a distracted young sailor. "You need to hide this in your apron pocket. It might prove useful."

Elisabeth eyed the blade. It was too big for a pocket, but she could improvise. She sucked in her breath. The thought of using this weapon to take another person's life made her sick. Yet she was surprised how quickly she snatched it and tucked it away.

"Listen carefully, Mrs. Allerton. You must keep safe the sailor's clothes that were given to you."

"Mr. Richardson, why? What possible benefit are they to me?" She was very glad to be back in her plain green waistcoat.

"I am not sure yet. But when we get near to port, you must be prepared to impersonate a sailor."

"What are you talking about? I cannot pretend to be a man!"

"Yes, you can! And you must! Listen, woman, all we have are our wits and whatever we can scrounge up secretively from this ship. You do want to reunite with your Mr. Allerton, do you not?"

"Of course I want to reunite with my husband!" Elisabeth was indignant at his hint of disloyalty.

"Then you must do as I say, whether your Puritan mind thinks it is proper or not!"

Her feeble gaze was the only compliance Colin would get.

He continued, "Each day, come out of the cabin for some fresh air. Get acquainted with this ship. Watch the sailors and learn their ways—the manner in which they walk and talk, the ways they eat and work."

Elisabeth, speechless, thought how ridiculous this idea sounded. She wanted to protest. She should remain in the cabin, invisible to these men.

Then Mr. Richardson added, "There is something else." He hesitated and softly said, "You must be prepared to cut your hair."

"Oh, no! That is surely not necessary!" Elisabeth touched her head. So much of her identity was flying away from her.

"Think, Mrs. Allerton. I am trying to get you and that baby you are carrying onto English soil, but I cannot do it, and I will not do it, unless you are committed. Once we escape, they will be looking for an English woman with flaming red hair and a man, whose cheek scar marks him like a slave. They will not as readily be searching for a pair of cut and bait blokes. Can you understand that?"

It really was too much to comprehend, but she nodded. How confusing her world had grown. She needed time to think.

Mr. Richardson spoke of getting her to English soil! A chance remained to reunite with David. And he had mentioned her baby. So often during the trauma of the past few days she had pushed her thoughts of pregnancy aside. Yet, she knew without doubt she desired to protect her unborn child. This wee one growing within her pointed her to where she belonged.

Chapter 15

The Escape

With Remille on the mend, Dr. Stillingfleet took more interest in his patient and assumed full credit for recovery. He even played card games with the boy.

Elisabeth longed for the doctor to exhibit some humility and acknowledgement of God's favor in healing, but the man was full of self. She tried to challenge him on this subject, but he simply laughed and made her blush when he said, "I kiss no man's ass."

As the crew became more and more excited about reaching shore, Dr. Stillingfleet and Elisabeth became more and more apprehensive about what lay ahead. They did not speak of it; they did not have to.

Mr. Richardson kept his distance, except for his and Elisabeth's daily exchange of information at the guardrail. He told Elisabeth he could not stand to be in the same room as Stillingfleet, and he wanted to forge trust with the other sailors.

As for Remille, Elisabeth thought he was a heroic patient. The laudanum worked well, but only for a while. To ease the pain of a phantom leg, Remille would bite on a moistened rag. Sometimes, sweat broke out on his face, but he rarely cried out.

He did not want Elisabeth to hover over him. She dressed his wound and respected his efforts at manhood. There was one activity, however, they delighted in together.

Elisabeth started practicing with her dagger, throwing it at a wooden post from various points in the cabin. Remille found this amusing and asked to try it from his bed. Both became more and more accurate with their throws and enjoyed competing with each other. Their targets were anything they could think of to set around the room—a knot in the wood post, a piece of rope, and hard sea biscuits.

Captain Gaspar overlooked the fact his quarters suffered from these games. He simply seemed pleased Remille was distracted from his pain. The father even brought Remille a knife and whetting stone. Elisabeth wondered why the captain did not question her about her stolen dagger.

Elisabeth blessed First Mate Stone and his sailors for bringing her medical books and the chest aboard the *Xavier*. David had protested, but Stone did not listen, scooping up anything that would impress the French with bartering power.

Inadvertently, they also had brought Elisabeth's Bible and journal. This godsend mistake gave Elisabeth time for reading and writing. Fearing her journal was vulnerable to unwanted eyes, she kept remarks to mundane happenings of her captivity and Remille's progress. Occasionally, she wrote a coded phrase or word to trigger memories later.

The days were exhausting as she and Dr. Stillingfleet also tended the ship's wounded and sick. Although Remille was the main priority, Captain Gaspar commanded Elisabeth and Dr. Stillingfleet to treat the crew in the quarters of the French doctor who had died. Besides dressing wounds, they also treated abscess gums, boils, rashes, vermin bites, and consumption.

The French surgeon's dispensary was full of potions and vials that Dr. Stillingfleet readily used. He surprised Elisabeth by sharing his knowledge with her and treating her like an apprentice. She assumed he realized his survival depended on appeasing the French with medical abilities. To Elisabeth's relief, he eased up on his drinking.

The guardrail meetings made her extremely uncomfortable, especially when she noticed the leers of several French soldiers. She complained to Mr. Richardson.

"Mrs. Allerton, I am not fond of blubbering words with you either, but we must make appearances, so when I do have something important to tell you it will not look suspicious."

After that, they often stood wordless together, surveying the churning ocean with their backs to the sailors. Elisabeth tried conversation, asking about Mr. Richardson's family life. A scowl silenced any further prying.

"We shall make land tomorrow," Mr. Richardson stated quietly after they had done this ordeal for many days.

"Really? Land?" The word sounded hollow, far away, like heaven, like her husband.

Mr. Richardson sombered. "Mrs. Allerton, do you still want to attempt escape? If you say yes, you must fully commit to what I request."

She considered her options. Neither staying aboard the *Xavier* nor throwing her lot in with this strange man seemed appealing. She had little wisdom in this matter.

"Mr. Richardson, tell me truthfully. Do you think I should go with you?"

He sighed, and she sensed his doubt. "Maybe your prayers would give you a better answer than myself. But, aye, I think coming with me is the best chance of seeing your husband again."

"But how? I would like to know what is ahead of me—us. You tell me so little." These words, too, sounded foreign.

Colin didn't budge. "I think it is safer for both of us if you know only one step at a time."

Elisabeth chafed at being treated like a child, but she kept still.

"Do you still have the seaman's clothes?" Mr. Richardson asked.

"Of course. No one has asked for them. I think they have been forgotten."

"Good. Then tomorrow night, after we anchor, we wait until midnight to make our escape. I suspect the captain will go ashore by boat shortly after we arrive."

"Will he not take us with him?"

"No. He will gather as much information as he can before using us as bargaining chips. Most likely our fate will be decided the next morning when the tide is high and the ship can dock. Tomorrow night, after the sailors celebrate and drink themselves into oblivion, will be our best chance to swim to shore. You do know how to swim, Mrs. Allerton?" Mr. Richardson asked, suddenly alarmed.

"Yes, I do, a little. But I have never jumped from a ship before."

"No, and I do not want you to—too noisy. You put on the sailor's clothes tomorrow night after Dr. Stillingfleet and Remille are asleep. I will open the cabin door only a wedge, so you must watch for that signal. No sounds. We cannot afford any alarm. And, Mrs. Allerton, remember what I said you must do? Be prepared to have your hair cut before we get into the water, but not before then."

Elisabeth shuddered at the thought. "I still do not think it necessary, Mr. Richardson! I could hide my hair under a scarf, a hat."

"No! This must be done. Do you still not understand? Once we get to shore we will be two mariners out on the town, not two escapees from a ship. There could be eyes anywhere, watching us. We must look like two men—not a man and a woman."

"Mr. Richardson, it will be dark. Could we not sneak away in the shadows?" The thought of dressing like a man again seemed difficult enough, but to lose her hair was an additional humiliation.

"I hope we escape unnoticed. But we cannot take chances. It is safer for you to appear as a man."

Elisabeth knew what he meant and sighed. "I will watch the door for your signal and be ready."

"Bring your other clothes with you and tie them in a tight bundle, along with your dagger."

"You can be most certainly assured I will! Any chance I can bring my medicine chest—somehow?" asked Elisabeth, hoping for a miracle.

Mr. Richardson gave her a hard stare. Unbelievable! "No! That is impossible."

Not much later, as Colin predicted, the sailors took their soundings and were jubilant to know they were heading toward shore. Colin made it a point to engage the French captain about the possibility of serving under him. This pleased Captain Gaspar and probably spared Colin from spending the night shackled once they anchored. Under different circumstances, Colin honestly thought he might have enjoyed comradeship with this man.

The captain came to his cabin and asked Colin to translate a final message to Stillingfleet and Elisabeth. No shadow of emotion crossed his face, but he thanked them for saving his son. He said he intended to hand them over to Viceroy Phillipe de La Roche in the morning. He promised to put in a good word with the viceroy about their medical skills.

Perhaps, he added, Viceroy de la Roche would be sympathetic to their plight. They should not lose hope. With that said, he bowed and left.

In the evening, all aboard were served a feast: fresh bread, cheese, roasted pork, rice, and fruit. These foods came from the island through an enterprising, jovial merchant and his wife, who rowed out to greet them.

Elisabeth thought she would not eat. But once she started, she thanked God food tasted so good and gave her strength. Elisabeth gave her wine and rum portion, laced with a special sleeping potion, to Dr. Stillingfleet, the guard who had been assigned to them, and even a little to Remille.

Elisabeth began to think her potion was too weak when eventually the doctor, guard, and Remille drifted into a deep sleep. The lantern flickered on the slouched and snoring men. Remille breathed soundly, as Elisabeth straightened a blanket around him.

Satisfied she could put on the sailor's outfit uninterrupted, she slipped on the pantaloons without her petticoat. A rush of shame ran through her, but she shrugged it off. There was no other recourse except to stay and remain a prisoner. She touched her stomach and prayed for courage. Then she braided her hair, mourning its upcoming loss. The irony was not lost on her that she now grieved over hair she never appreciated.

After an unbearably long time, Elisabeth saw the dimly lit door open, ever so slightly. She slowly crept her way to the exit, carefully watching the snoring guard. Suddenly, Colin pulled her outside onto the darkened deck. She could barely see him, but she knew she must stay close and be as quiet as possible. She could hear the snoring of other sailors nearby. The crew obviously felt secure at port.

Mr. Richardson grabbed her bundled clothes and tied them with a rope onto his back. Then before Elisabeth could even squeak, he took out his knife. She only had time to catch her breath before one swift slice resulted in her braid dangling in his hand. Her hand trembled as she touched her head. Mr. Richardson knew flinging the braid into the water might make a strange sound, so he stuffed it inside his shirt.

Grabbing her hand, Mr. Richardson pulled Elisabeth to the edge of the ship and whispered, "I have attached a rope on the ship's side. You must shimmy down after me."

Elisabeth remembered her childhood days of taking a rope and jumping into a hay pile. Surely that child's play would help her now if only she could remember.

She whispered, "Yes, I understand." She told herself she could do this, for her David and their baby.

Immediately, Colin put his knife between his teeth and disappeared over the side of the ship, his hand waving for her to follow. She felt like she moved in slow motion; her heartbeats pounded inside her head as well as in her chest. Certainly someone was going to yell and grab her.

She scrambled over the side, stumbling and swaying slightly as her hands and legs clung to the rope. Her arm muscles burned from the pressure, and she knew she skinned her hands as she shimmied down. She squeezed her eyes shut, fearing she might let go and fall on Mr. Richardson.

When she finally reached bottom and slipped into the cold, dark water, she let out a whimper of surprise. The salt stung her hands, and her body recoiled from the cold.

Mr. Richardson put his hand over her mouth and gritted his teeth. "Shhh! You must swim quietly."

She shook her head acknowledging him, forcing herself not to think of the cold as her body quivered against the water's gentle laps.

Mr. Richardson pressed her arm and whispered, "Wait! Do not move!"

Above them, Elisabeth's breath caught as she saw a shadowed form peer out from the guardrail. He held a whip in his hand. Baptiste! Their rope dangled only a few feet from him. She and Colin clung to the ship's side.

Please, God, do not let him see the rope or us.

The figure looked around and then, apparently satisfied, disappeared. They waited a few minutes. Elisabeth feared her chattering teeth would bring Mr. Richardson's chastisement. Finally, he released his hand from her arm and beckoned her to follow.

She swam as quietly as she could, thinking, *I must do this for my baby. Lord God, help me. David! Our baby! Oh, Father, please give me strength.*

Her eyes stung from the ocean's salt, and she felt herself gulping water and suppressing coughs. Her clothes weighed her down. She grew tired. Her arms ached. Sinking, drowning? She panicked and flailed to stay afloat. Mr. Richardson grabbed her.

"Mrs. Allerton, easy landlubber. Quit struggling! Please! They might hear. Try to float."

"I am drowning," she sputtered.

She wanted to give up. Down, down, down her heavy body dragged her. The salt water made her sick. She suddenly felt a firm hand, lifting her up. For a little space of time, she looked up and saw a scattering of bright, little stars. She stopped fighting and found herself moving up and down in the water. She thought she heard music, voices, water slapping against wooden poles. She thought....

Chapter 16

Angelique's Refuge

After resting awhile on the sand, Colin rose and towered over the unconscious Elisabeth. He wanted to leave her. It would be so easy to walk away. He was tired of this ridiculous, confusing entanglement.

How had he, Colin Richardson, ended up caring for a pregnant woman whose husband was such an ass? Since Uncle Duff's death, he wasn't himself. He certainly never lived by any gentleman's code. He much desired spirits and a buxom woman to tend his needs. He hated playing nursemaid to this midwife.

Elisabeth's crumpled heap looked like a bunch of pathetic seaweed. Damn that Allerton man. How could such a man cast her off like some rejected fish? How could he have been so cowardly? Colin sighed. He bent down and heaved Elisabeth and her bundle over his shoulder. She moaned.

"Mrs. Allerton, you are worse than a drunken mate—almost as heavy I might add. Good lord, woman!"

He staggered up the beach away from tavern noise and the few flickering lights of town. He thought he made out a few shadowed figures slumped in doorways, but they didn't stir. A dog growled when they passed, but quickly settled down. Fortunately, no other boisterous soul harassed them.

He made it to the edge of town and veered off to a well-worn, rocky path that led uphill. At the top stood an intentionally isolated cottage. From its vantage point, one could see the entire community and the bay.

Colin took a deep breath and started the climb. Exhausted when he reached the top, he laid the unconscious Elisabeth down at the doorway as gently as he could. He quietly tapped on the door. When that brought no response, he pounded.

"Angelique, it's me, Colin. Let me in," he said in French. Soon, with candle in hand, a tall young woman with long black tresses wearing only her undergarments opened the door just a crack. She stuck the muzzle of a pistol in Colin's direction, and he heard a click. Colin knew Angelique carried at least two knives. He always admired her ability to defend herself.

When the candlelight silhouetted her visitor's face, she hissed, "Colin! You must be mad! You dare come to my house uninvited in the middle of the night!"

Although angry, she opened the door wider, and Colin quickly pressed in.

"Scoundrel, I should shoot you! I should scream for the viceroy's troops to take you away in shackles. What makes you think you can come to me after leaving without so much as a good-bye!"

"Angelique, I am sorry. I will explain, but I am a little desperate here. Please, I need your help."

"Ah, desperation. That does not get my forgiveness. Who is this pitiful friend?" Angelique held the candle lower and cried incredulously, "What! Is it a woman?"

"Look, I will explain everything later. But she needs care. She is with child."

"A pregnant woman! What kind of a man are you, Colin Richardson? Do you think I want to help you with this problem?" Angelique pointed her pistol at Elisabeth and then into Colin's ribs.

"Please, Angelique. Listen! The baby is not mine." He gently pushed the gun away. "I will explain; just let me get her inside somewhere. We are on the run."

"Oh, crazy fool, such polite words when you want something! Colin, I cannot allow you to jump in and out of my life!" Angelique waved the gun in his face. "And I will not let you put me in danger."

She paused and bit her bottom lip in thought. "I will let you stay tonight, and that is all! Make sure you understand. We are done! My heart cannot take it!"

Colin lifted Elisabeth and followed Angelique to a side room where there was a large bed. He gently laid Elisabeth on it. "Um, her clothes are soaked. Do you have anything she can wear?"

"Get out! Go make yourself useful and find some food and drink in the kitchen. You have a lot of explaining to do!"

Like a puppy under its mother's command, Colin obediently slipped away. How beautiful Angelique was, like her mother, more and more every time he saw her. Thank God, she did not remind him of her father!

In the morning, Elisabeth awoke to a gentle shake of her shoulder. Through blurred vision, she became aware of an ample-bosomed young woman hovering over her. The woman's large, dark eyes seemed to scrutinize Elisabeth's soul. Elisabeth smelled heavy perfume, so sweet it made her dizzy. Her stomach sent out an alarm. The beautiful woman with a heart-shaped face and wavy black hair spoke to Elisabeth in French. Her ruby-drop earrings glistened.

"Ah. Your coloring is a little better. Maybe you are not so sick, just tired from the pregnancy."

Elisabeth's blank stare made Angelique sigh and switch to English. "Mrs. Allerton, I am told that is your name. I am Mademoiselle Angelique Gervais. This is my home. Do not worry. You are safe here. How do you feel?"

"I am not sure. I cannot think. How did I get here?"

Elisabeth propped herself on her elbows but shakily fell back on the pillow. She then noticed she was dressed in a low-cut blue, satiny dress, threaded with pink ribbons and tiny pearls. Her stomach lurched because such finery convinced her she looked like a whore.

"Please, I need a basin," she said weakly.

"Ah." Angelique quickly grabbed a bowl from the end table.

Angelique thought this extravagant dress on her uninvited guest was just penance for a woman with awful looking hair who had disturbed her sleep and even slept in her bed. But Elisabeth's pitiful condition made her realize she probably had gone too far.

"Your clothes are being washed," she declared, as if that explained it. "Colin says you are pregnant, yes? Maybe a little broth will help settle your stomach."

Angelique tucked a blanket around Elisabeth and left the room. Elisabeth realized she was probably in her host's bed for there was an armoire with dresses and hats flowing from it—and that scent of sweet perfume lingered around her. A rocking chair, draped with a folded blanket, was positioned near shuttered windows. She could see slats of sunshine filtering through them, disrupted by bright green leaves blowing back and forth, casting shadows. Was that the ocean she heard? She wondered how far they were from the danger of the *Xavier*.

Angelique returned and put the wooden bowl of broth on the end table. She grabbed a blanket off the rocking chair, folded it and propped it firmly behind Elisabeth.

"Comfortable?" she inquired.

"Thank you," Elisabeth said. "You are very kind, and I am a stranger to you."

Angelique smiled and offered a spoonful of broth to Elisabeth. Elisabeth took it.

"I think I can manage this," she said and shakily took the bowl. "Am I really safe here, Mademoiselle Gervais?"

"Oui, for a little while you are very safe."

Angelique pulled the rocking chair close to the bed, sat down, and eyed her patient. She definitely did not seem like Colin's kind of woman. They were usually shallow creatures, good for only a few days of rowdy companionship. His interest in someone like this woman puzzled her.

Elisabeth knew she was being surveyed and broke the silence.

"Mademoiselle Gervais, where is Mr. Richardson?" Her last memory of him was their struggle in the cold ocean as they swam away from the *Xavier*.

"Oh, that wanderer! He is in the village trying to find a safer place for you to stay."

Angelique rambled off a few sentences in French that Elisabeth was glad she could not understand.

"Do you think the French soldiers will come here? I should get away." She started putting down the broth and tried to get up.

"No, Mrs. Allerton, not yet." Angelique pressed her gently on the shoulders. "There is time. Get some strength."

Elisabeth nodded weakly and blinked back a few tears. "You see; I must somehow find passage to Boston. My husband—he and I were on our way there when we became separated. Did Mr. Richardson tell you?"

"Colin mentioned you are married, and you both were taken by the French against your will. I am sorry." Angelique measured her words.

"Yes, I want to reunite with David as soon as possible. We were moving to New England to be with family, before the *Xavier* captured us. Mademoiselle Gervais, is it even possible to get off this island and get to Boston?" Her eyes pleaded for some hope.

Angelique softened a little. "It is not impossible, but it will take some delicate arrangements. You will need quite a bit of money, which Colin does not have. That sailor, scoundrel!"

More sentences flew out in French. Elisabeth ate her broth quietly and then in a steady voice said, "I am not afraid to work, Mademoiselle Gervais! I will find a way to Boston."

Angelique eyed her. "Are you willing to do any kind of work?" She chuckled as Elisabeth flushed, remembering the blue dress she wore.

"We will see. God knows," Angelique crossed herself. "You must rest while you can. But first, I must do something with your awful hair."

Elisabeth had forgotten about her chopped locks, made worse from the salt water. She touched her head. "Oh, my hair!"

Her hair, the despicable dress, this strange, new place! All of it felt so wrong. Tears again filled her eyes. She wanted to let them flow, but she could not—at least not now. If she let go, she might never return to sanity. She needed her wits to survive more than ever. She gritted her teeth.

"All is not lost," Angelique said as she took away the soup bowl and returned with a basin of water, a brush, and comb. She flicked a knife from her ruffled sleeve. "I think I will make an improvement. No?"

Wide-eyed Elisabeth gulped and forced a nod and the tiniest, pinched smile.

Chapter 17

Master of Disguises

Colin knew St. Paola from boyhood. That was both good and bad. It was good because he knew who to trust and what resources he could plunder if need be. It was bad because he broke a promise to himself. Only two years earlier, he vowed he would never return to this place again. Never! Now, here he was—albeit against his will.

Over the years, Angelique was the main reason he returned to St. Paola for brief, secret visits. Uncle Duff encouraged him to keep in touch with his half-sister. But the last time he came, it was nearly impossible to keep company with Angelique and avoid the rest of her family. Angelique thought—insisted—reconciliation was possible.

Colin knew better, but he refused to tell her his side of the story. What good would it do? He would not convince her that her adoring father would kill him if given the opportunity. He also knew his appearance would place Angelique in greater danger with her father, the unpredictable Louis Gervais.

Colin and Angelique, under Uncle Duff's counsel, had kept their meetings discreet. But every time he visited her, she pressed him to reconcile with her father and half brother. The siblings would argue and resolve nothing.

She was blinded by familial love to the truth of their unchangeable reality. Her father would always hate him and view his stepson as a threat. Colin grew tired of his and Angelique's tug of war. He finally decided it was best to break ties with the few people he cared about on St. Paola and leave the island for good.

So much for that great resolution! He was back on St. Paola, now in more danger than ever with a pregnant English woman. She was about as useful as a dolphin among sharks.

He did not feel guilty wondering if a quick death for her would be less painful than what might lie ahead. This island could be deadly quicksand.

He considered tipping off the officials to her whereabouts at Angelique's cottage. Angelique had the connections to survive the damage of harboring fugitives. Elisabeth would be housed in locked quarters until the viceroy decided what to do with her. Without Mrs. Allerton, his chances of getting off the island would be greatly improved.

But what would they do with this woman who had killed a French sailor, scum that he was? Colin tried to convince himself that betraying her made for a feasible plan.

It was probable she could be scurried from French ship to English ship under a gentleman's code of conduct. Colin rubbed the scar on his bearded cheek. A powerful French gentleman on the island had given him that mark. It was a constant reminder that gentlemen could not be trusted.

He sighed. He was stuck with Mrs. Allerton for a while. He admired her foolish loyalty and determination to reunite with that prissy husband in Boston—the ignoble coward who swam off without her. Definitely Allerton abandoned her. Colin imagined that man's face when Elisabeth appeared on his doorstep.

So master rescuer, Colin said to himself, *think, man. What is the plan? Who can you trust?*

Angelique, for sure, would help him. Their relationship frustrated her, but she had never betrayed him. They had a strange love for one another, this half-brother and half-sister who shared the same English mother. She loved her French father. He hated him.

How he wished fate had been different. Danger increased for her to harbor them at her cottage. Watchful eyes were always curious about her little place of independence. Another resource that could prove useful was Plantation Ross Hall. How well Colin knew it from boyhood days. If needed, he would secretly go there.

Then there was Berko. Colin did not want to jeopardize this man's safety, for he was his brother by an oath of blood. They had a protective understanding and would die for one another.

Colin also knew a few sordid drunks in town, sailors who had washed ashore and stayed for various reasons. Their help could be bought, but it was dicey to trust them. Fortunately, he had never revealed his boyhood connections to the Gervais household.

Thinking of mistrust, Colin considered the sorry Dr. Stillingfleet. No matter where the authorities placed him, that fool would have his ears attuned to useful information to save his ass. Dr. Stillingfleet was a sponge one could squeeze if necessary.

Colin realized he had a sorry summation of a miserable situation. These few allies were nothing compared to the French authorities wanting Elisabeth and him in custody.

Nevertheless, it cheered Colin to know his only present course was to contact Berko. He would be very surprised to know Colin was back. It would be a grand reunion.

As he entered Stubby's Tavern, Colin pulled down the hat Angelique had loaned him. At this early morning hour, there was one snoring sea dog with his head collapsed on a wooden table, his mouth hung open like a baby bird.

Colin ordered a drink from the black barmaid; her large gold earrings and necklace glistened against her smooth skin. She was new to him.

The wench moved flirtingly, swaying her hips, and her eyes and lips invited a proposal. He was tempted, but he had to think of safety.

When she set down the mug, he briskly whispered, "The Jungle King has an ocean friend."

Her eyes widened. Colin realized she probably never heard a white man speak of the Jungle King. But she recovered quickly and spoke softly. "And what is this ocean friend's name?"

Colin gave her a coin. "Tell him his scarred brother."

The woman nodded slightly and said, "I hope you return tomorrow, and we can talk more about this matter."

"Actually, I need him tonight. It's an urgent matter."

Her eyes squinted, and she whispered harshly, "The jungle is thick; the King has many duties!"

Colin nodded. "I know. I will wait in the jungle tonight at our usual place."

The barmaid eyed him skeptically. "The usual place?" Colin observed her irritation, but she conceded. "I will tell him."

Colin left the pub, pulled his hat lower as if to shade his eyes and walked along the wharf. It was coming to life with fishermen and boats, soldiers, and civilians. There were a number of French vessels in the harbor, actually more than usual—they were preparing to harbor for the stormy winter months.

It did not take him long to spot the *Xavier* slowly moving in to anchor. He did not stare at it directly but wandered around the market, inspecting wares in barrels and on tables. Occasionally, he glanced at its progress.

Any ship entering port was an exciting event, and people around him were curious about the *Xavier's* damage. They also wondered what news and useful cargo the ship carried. The soldiers were standing on board, exchanging greetings with the town's people.

Colin watched several soldiers gently carry Remille on a makeshift litter flanked by Captain Gaspar and the very attentive Dr. Stillingfleet. Captain Gaspar would probably meet with Viceroy de la

Roche in late morning after making his son more comfortable on land.

Colin imagined the two would dine together and exchange news, discuss the two escapees and calculate how much they were worth pursuing. Colin felt he and Elisabeth were at least safe until the next morning when a thorough door-to-door inquiry would be organized.

If they somehow discovered his connections and history to this island, his fate was more dangerous. But how could they? He was very glad he and Duff had kept their history secret.

With Berko's help, Colin knew he and Mrs. Allerton could lie low for a while. He quickly bought a loaf of bread and a fine yellow tail snapper before he headed back to Angelique's.

Chapter 18

Outside Angelique's Cottage

Angelique escorted the wobbly Elisabeth outside and led her to a wooden bench under the shade of a palm tree.

"Clare needs to clean the cottage and wash clothes," she announced. "Besides, the breeze and sunshine will do you good."

Clare, Angelique's slave, appeared from nowhere. The weathered woman eyed Elisabeth scornfully, shaking her head as she mumbled to herself. Obviously, Clare disapproved of her presence. She would gladly stay out of that one's affairs. Angelique went inside, and Elisabeth leaned against the bench, viewing the bluest water she had even seen.

Everything is so bright in this sunlight—the water, the plants, the birds, she thought. Then she swatted a pesky mosquito. She dipped a rag in the bucket of water Clare had plopped on the bench and cooled her sweaty face.

Angelique promised she would get all her clothing back after Clare had scrubbed them clean. Elisabeth noticed the garments hanging on a rope strung between two palm trees. There were her seaman's outfit and Puritan clothes, discreetly placed among the rest of the wash. Elisabeth longed to get out of Angelique's blue and abominable frills and into her sensible Puritan garments. Surely Mr. Richardson would not object to her wearing what belonged to her.

Clare moved slowly and deliberately. As she hung other clothes, she occasionally eyed Elisabeth, still shaking her head.

I confound her with my various fashions, Elisabeth thought, a little amused.

Searching the horizon, Elisabeth spotted Mr. Richardson climbing up the path carrying his fish and bread. Although he wore different attire, she recognized his quick gait.

Had he really carried her from the shore and up this hill to the cottage last night? Her face flushed. The man was stronger than he appeared.

"Good morning, Mrs. Allerton. Do you really need that attractive covering on such a lovely day?" He tried not to laugh at Elisabeth wrapping herself in a blanket, unsuccessfully covering Angelique's flowing dress.

Elisabeth adjusted the blanket, shading her eyes so she could look at Colin. "Good morning, Mr. Richardson. I am comfortable enough, thank you."

"Nice hair. And by the way, Angelique has your braid tucked away in one of her trunks. I suggest we bury it."

She touched her hair sadly. "I do not know how cutting off my hair helped our situation last night. This jagged mop will draw attention. What can I do with it?"

He moved past her and gave the snapper and bread to Clare, who fondly smiled at him and wobbled to the door. He sat down on the bench next to her. "It really is a becoming dress," he said, smirking.

She eyed him scornfully, as she pulled the blanket up around her. "My other clothes are drying."

"Ah yes, there they be."

Colin thought Uncle Duff would have been roaring in laughter at such comedy between Mrs. Allerton and himself! The thought of

Duff made Colin somber. He stared out at the harbor. "What, no word from Holy Scripture for our present predicament, Mrs. Allerton?"

"Not exactly, Mr. Richardson." She pushed out the words hesitantly. "I do feel that once again I am in your debt, this time for getting me away from the *Xavier*. I do not recall much from last night, but I do know you must have been God's hands in keeping me from drowning."

She paused humbly and added, "Please, once again, accept my gratitude. I do hope to repay you somehow."

Colin wanted to joke, but her sincerity made him uneasy. "Yes," he said, tapping his head. "I do believe my debt for your bump-on-the-head treatment is paid in full. Yet, here we are, invisibly shackled together in a godforsaken place. I guarantee you I would desire a different fate for each of us."

Elisabeth pursed her lips. "I would find no fault in you, sir, if you tried to save yourself. God willing, I will manage to get myself to New England. I still have faith it could happen." She sighed.

"Mrs. Allerton, neither of us is safe here. It is best we work together and find our way off this island."

"You have a plan to get me on a ship to Boston?" Elisabeth so much wanted a thread of hope.

"No, no plan yet—just a chance. I have a friend on St. Paola who will help us. We will meet him tonight. I am quite certain he will have a safer place for us to stay for a while. Then, we will have more time to think and plan."

He paused and added, "Sadly, you cannot wear such a becoming dress—or that blanket." Colin smirked again.

Elisabeth understood and asked resignedly, "I have to dress up like a man again?"

Colin got up and said, "Trust me, it will be the safest and most practical garb for where we are going." He could see her weariness and tried to lighten the mood. "Shall I call you Bert or Benny?"

Elisabeth refused to answer and turned her face to the amazing cobalt blue water and lush green palms swaying in the breeze. More conversation would probably just irritate them both, and she did not want to be the brunt of Mr. Richardson's humor.

Chapter 19

Meeting the Jungle King

By the time Colin and Elisabeth left Angelique's cottage, hostess and guests were more than ready to part company. The evening had started out well enough with Clare making a feast from the fish, rice, and bread. There were succulent fruits, too, that Elisabeth enjoyed. Then the dinner atmosphere spoiled.

Angelique and Colin drank too much rum, and soon they were arguing in French and English. Angelique grew angry that Colin refused to meet with her father and brother. Then she said Colin had abandoned her and now continued to insult her.

Elisabeth did not understand the crazy relationship. They obviously were fond of each other, and yet their drunkenness brought resentments to the surface. She was thankful she and David had never quarreled. Disagreements were always handled politely, respectfully.

Elisabeth finally excused herself to Angelique's bedroom. The couple did not seem to notice, but she could hear their voices through the thin walls. Eventually, the yelling stopped, and Elisabeth fell asleep. By the time Mr. Richardson shook her shoulder, the room was dark with only candlelight.

"Hurry and get ready. We have a long journey ahead of us," he said gruffly, leaving the room as quietly as he had entered.

She quickly used the chamber pot and put on her men's clothing and the wide-brimmed hat Angelique gave her. She took a longing look at her Puritan clothes. Mr. Richardson told her that Clare would destroy them in the morning. It was dangerous for Angelique to keep them around. Elisabeth knew he was right.

Taking one brief glance at Angelique's mirror, she touched her dress one final time and left the bedroom.

Colin was waiting and handed her a stick. "It will help in walking," he said. Then he turned to groggy Angelique. "I will repay you, my love."

Angelique threw her arms around him, "Be safe, mon chérie." She kissed him on both cheeks and put a cloth parcel into his hands.

"Here, take this for the journey. Give Berko my love. Tell him I miss him, and he should visit whenever he can."

Elisabeth was surprised to see the couple had made up so quickly. They were certainly the oddest of lovers. "Thank you, Angelique, for everything. I wish I had something to offer you in payment." Elisabeth felt uncomfortable in this woman's debt.

"Ah, there may yet be time to repay," Angelique responded, touching Elisabeth's hair.

Her smile did not reassure Elisabeth. But the woman embraced her and kissed both her cheeks. She then quickly pushed her out the door. "Godspeed. Go! Go!"

Elisabeth's eyes soon adjusted to the darkness, and the rocky path was not too difficult to navigate. A few of the town's lanterns lit the harbor, and one could hear faraway voices. A quarter moon peeked out among glittering stars.

As they descended nearer to the village, Elisabeth felt her stomach knot and her heart beat rapidly. Would she ever get over being frightened? She tried not to think of the dangerous possibilities and just to concentrate on Colin's dark form rapidly moving in front of her.

"Slow down, Mr. Richardson, please," she whispered. "I need to catch my breath."

"I am sorry, Mrs. Allerton," he quietly responded. "We need to move quickly."

"Where are we going? Can you not tell me something?"

Colin stopped on the trail. "We must get through the town to the other side. That is all. Try to walk like a man—huh, Benny?"

He continued his brisk walking. Elisabeth seethed at his manner, his rudeness. She gritted her teeth and determined to keep going. She only stumbled a little, and she had to admit the men's clothing made the journey easier.

At the edge of town, they crouched behind a boulder while a cart ambled past, its lantern swaying along the sideboard. "Throw your stick away, Benny. Try a swagger. I will show you."

Before she could open her mouth, Colin grabbed her arm and started singing a simple sailor's tune in French. The tune sounded familiar, so Elisabeth hummed along until she was sure she could mimic the words.

"Put more effort into it, Benny," Colin ordered through his teeth. "You can do it. Mates sing together."

Elisabeth swaggered the best she could, and it was not too difficult since Colin seemed to be leading her like they were doing some kind of English folk dance.

Singing the song in French took much concentration. Just when she felt she had it, a beefy hand startled her by squeezing her shoulder. She stopped singing and almost screamed.

Joining them was a large, barrel-chested man whose gold earrings caught the moonlight. His breath ranked of rum and rotted meat. Elisabeth's stomach lurched. She thought of the ogre on the *Xavier*.

"Good evening, men!" he said in French. "I do love that song. Come on! Let us all sing a round or two together."

His drunken head bobbed from one side to the other as his large body swayed toward them.

"Good evening, monsieur," Colin said evenly, as his hand slid quickly from Elisabeth's arm to his knife. "Me mate and I are off to an important engagement, but of course we can gladly oblige you one song. Come on, Benny, loosen your tongue."

Colin and the drunken sailor howled out the tune. Elisabeth froze in fear.

"What's wrong with you, mate?" The drunk swaggered in to peer at Elisabeth more closely. She forced herself to straighten and quietly spouted the ditty's chorus in her deepest voice.

At first, the drunk looked at her blankly, and Elisabeth thought she was undone. Then he wagged his thick finger in her face.

"Ah, young man, you need to crow louder than that; you need much practice."

He laughed, slapping her hard on the back. She nodded and chuckled gruffly.

"Hey, you want some good gambling? Let me take you to the White Whale. We can sing for everyone. What do you say, mates? I will buy the first round."

Colin disentangled himself from the man's grip and pried his other hand gently off of Elisabeth. "That is very generous of you, monsieur, but like I said, we cannot tonight. Another time perhaps."

"Hey, I am thinking you do not like my company? You said you wanted to gamble, and I wanna sing. I wanna sing!" He bellowed and drew forth his knife.

Colin grabbed Elisabeth's arm and backed away slowly, still all smiles. "Sorry, not tonight, monsieur. Like I said, perhaps another day." He grabbed Elisabeth's hand. They quickly walked away and then started running.

The drunken man yelled after them. "Come back here, and give me a song! I mean it! I will cut you both. I will rip those singing tongues right out of your heads!"

He stood there in the night, swaying like a palm tree. When Elisabeth and Colin turned the corner, they still could hear him yelling.

Elisabeth worried he would draw others, but Colin was chuckling, "Well, Benny, someone liked your singing, after all, even if it was a reeking beast."

Elisabeth's heartbeat was still thumping in her ears. She leaned against the wall. "Mr. Richardson, I do not think this plan of yours is working. Can you please just take me back to Angelique's? I feel faint. Surely there must be some other way."

"No, I cannot take you back to Angelique's!" Mr. Richardson mimicked her voice. "Listen, Mrs. Allerton, I would hate to prod you with a knife or leave you here for our singing friend to find. I guarantee you his bellowing will eventually draw somebody's attention. Right now, he is probably following our trail like a lonely mutt. We need to move."

"You would not dare use a knife on me, and I do not think you would leave me!" Elisabeth tried to sound like she believed it.

"You and I agreed my debt to you is paid. Do not put my life in unnecessary danger. We need to get to our rendezvous."

Elisabeth felt her distrust of this man surface once again, but she got up and Mr. Richardson put his arm on her shoulder. She cringed at his touch. No one else paid them any mind as Colin hummed and staggered and moved Elisabeth along. She was woozy, but her anger kept rising at this unpredictable, rude man and their plight.

She did not know how, but she vowed to disentangle herself from his company as soon as she could. Every time he made a slight gesture of decency, he followed it with twice as many insults. How could Angelique care about him? Love thy neighbor took on a whole new meaning.

Finally, they made it to the other side of town and left the dirt road where there was a large boulder. Colin leaned against it and offered a swig from his flask. She took it and regretted the swallow.

"Mr. Richardson, I need to rest," she said leaning against the rock and trying to keep from coughing.

"Only for a short while."

Elisabeth had barely caught her breath when Colin was back in motion again, offering his usual encouragement.

"It gets a little rougher, Mrs. Allerton."

With that, he brought out a rope from under his shirt and tied it snuggly around her waist.

"Just a security measure," he said.

Horrified, she protested. "No! No! This is crazy!"

"Just think of something nice, like your husband. Oh, sorry that may be a bad idea since we already know he has a tendency to fall. Maybe, think of God instead. He is, shall we say, uplifting?"

Colin chuckled at his joke, turned away from her, and tied the rope to his waist. He moved forward and started scrambling the cliff. Elisabeth hesitated as the rope pulled.

"Come on, Mrs. Allerton. My life is in your hands as certain as yours is in mine. You must do this. It is not as hard as it may appear."

He still taunted her, but she knew he spoke truth. Her stumbling could bring them both down. Elisabeth closed her eyes to find strength and clawed her hands into the rock. Surprisingly, she found footings to anchor herself.

Slowly they moved up by inches. In the partial moonlight, she could hardly see him. She felt her body giving into shakes of tiredness, but she gritted her teeth and forced herself to follow Colin's upward trail one step at a time.

"Good work, Mrs. Allerton. Keep coming. We are almost there." Colin said that about four times, but finally he grabbed her arm and pulled her up to a wider ledge. Elisabeth wanted to collapse, but he pulled her a few more feet. Then he quickly untied the rope.

"We are here," he announced.

"Where?" She was puzzled because it looked like a jutted cliff, high over the ocean and nothing more. Then Colin turned around and squeezed into a hidden crack between two boulders. Elisabeth followed, glad for the rock support on both sides.

She found herself entering a cave. Surprisingly, it was the size of a small cottage. A lamp on a table and a small campfire illuminated the craggy walls.

She stumbled to a bench to catch her breath and was startled to see a large muscular black man rising from a chair chiseled into the cave's side. A spotted fur skin was draped over his shoulder, and he held a stick with the skull of a monkey at its tip. She felt disoriented but not unsafe. The man exhibited an air of confidence and dignity.

Suddenly, his soberness broke. "Colin! My brother!" he yelled, grabbing Colin in a joyous embrace.

"Berko! My brother!" Colin responded.

Elisabeth was surprised by such a transformation of Colin's usually sour disposition. She realized this was the first time she had seen him truly happy.

"Berko, it is so good to see you! I cannot believe I am saying this, but you look even more like your father."

"Ah, Colin, my brother! Onyame has kept you safe and brought you here to me!" Berko touched Colin's cheek where the scar was, and Elisabeth wondered at its significance.

Berko glanced at Elisabeth, and she felt evaluated. She could read nothing from his face, but in the flickering light she noticed that Berko, too, had a scar on his cheek. This one, however, was shaped like the paw print of some animal.

"A white woman dressed like a man, Colin? This should not be. I do not even know what to think."

He seemed serious as he shook his head, sternly eyeing Elisabeth. She squirmed. But then Berko burst into deep laughter. Colin punched him on the arm.

"What mischief are you into, my brother, that you would come back to St. Paola? I think this is something different than your usual comings and goings." Berko gestured an invitation to the table where there lay food and drink.

Colin nodded. "Berko, I have much to discuss with you, but first some introductions. Berko, meet Mrs. Elisabeth Allerton, wayfarer from London to Boston. Mrs. Allerton, meet Chief Berko Kawawe, also known as William Richardson, the island's legendary Jungle King."

Berko gave a slight nod, and Elisabeth, quite overwhelmed by the strangeness of it all, stammered, "Thank you for your help, sir." Should she bow? No, that seemed wrong. It seemed she thanked a lot of unusual people lately.

She turned to Mr. Richardson. "Mr. Richardson, I am sorry, but I think I am not—" And with that, she collapsed into Colin's arms.

Lifting her up, he irritably said to Berko, "She has been fainting a lot lately. She is with child and double the trouble."

Elisabeth dreamt of home—back with her father, stepmother, and brothers. They were chasing one another and laughing. She smelled grass, but the homey scent was off. Her fingers reached out and felt palm leaves. She also smelled the musky animal scent of fur blanketing her. She recalled she was in a cave. She heard men talking quietly. She opened her eyes, making out the shadowy forms of Berko and Mr. Richardson sitting at the table sharing a jug.

"Berko, I am not comfortable putting you into danger like this, but I felt there was no other way."

"Ah my brother, you should know there is not much that causes me worry anymore. What good does it do? *Nsem nyina ne Onyame.* I trust Onyame with my affairs."

"Same old Berko! You know I prefer more safety nets than just relying on good ol' Onyame."

"Careful, my brother," Berko said as he stabbed a slice of meat with his knife. He paused before biting, shaking the chunk of pork at Colin.

"I do not understand this struggle you have to keep Onyame out of your life. You cannot outrun him. Some day you will know this, and that will be a good day."

Colin shook his head. "After all we've been though, Berko, I do not understand how you can believe and trust in Onyame."

Berko placed his hand over his chest. "Ah Colin, we still live, you and me. Onyame has brought you back again. I do not think this is any accident."

Berko got up and added twigs to the small fire. He said thoughtfully, "It is not difficult for me to believe, Colin. My father taught me well. There is only a thin veil between where he is and where we are. I know this with all my heart."

There was silence for a while. Then Berko prodded, "Brother, have you considered that Onyame brought you this red-haired woman to wake you up?" He snapped his fingers at Colin. "And I think she has. You are different."

Colin protested, "What nonsense! My interest is nothing more than paying back life for a life. Do not bring Onyame into it, Berko. I mean no disrespect, but what do you think I need to wake up to?" Colin took another swig from the jug. "Brother, you know me. My eyes are wide open, although right now some sleep is starting to look as good as a beautiful barmaid."

"Ah, Colin, you must quit running from yourself, from your past," said Berko. "That you have returned to this island with a woman, whom you say believes in Onyame—this must be Onyame's design. It is a great omen."

Berko grabbed the jug and took a swig. He pointed his finger at Colin. "Something big is going to happen because of her. You wait and watch." Berko lifted his hands. "Ah, the mysterious ways of Onyame."

Colin cut the air with his hand in reply. "Ah, whale guts! I do not intend to hold my breath. Trust me, that little Puritan midwife has been my longest and most agonizing toothache."

Elisabeth knew Mr. Richardson felt that way, but it stung to hear him say it. She bit her lip, determined to lie still and not catch their attention.

Mr. Richardson, she thought, *trust me, similar affections are returned.*

The Jungle King stood. "I must go. It will be dawn soon. May Onyame keep you safe until we meet again."

Colin got up, and the two men embraced.

Elisabeth marveled at their brotherly love. She closed her eyes, tearfully thinking of David, her father, stepmother, brothers, her home. She felt like she was trapped in an abyss, with no way of escape. Would God rescue her? She hoped David was praying for them as fervently as she was. Maybe, just maybe, through joint supplications, there would be a providential way for reunion, similar to what she just witnessed between the wretched Mr. Richardson and strange Berko.

Chapter 20

Life in the Jungle

After Berko left, Elisabeth slept fitfully. When she rose, stiffness and cold accompanied her. The fire was out, the table cleared, and the only light came from a slit between two rocks that protected the cave's entrance. Where did Mr. Richardson go?

She saw no chamber pot, so she grabbed some palm leaves from her bed and walked deeper into the cave, using a wall for guidance. What might lurk in the unknown crannies made her tense. She hurried to find relief.

As she returned to the entrance, Mr. Richardson reappeared with bananas and coconut. "Breakfast?" he offered.

"Yes, thank you, but is there any water nearby for personal needs?" She yearned for Angelique's cottage comforts.

He gave her an incredulous look. "Not this morning, Mrs. Allerton, but before nightfall you may bathe like a queen."

She wondered if he mocked her.

He whacked the coconut with his knife and offered her the broken half. Ravenously, she drank.

"Come see the view. It is warmer outside," Colin suggested.

They slid through the crack, and Colin squatted down by the boulder. She joined him, thankful now for the men's clothing that made it much easier to move. As she surveyed the world below her, she gasped. They were so much higher than she thought. The ships in the harbor were miniatures, and the villagers looked like fleas on a dog.

With the expanding horizon greeting her and the sun warming her body, Elisabeth felt strengthened and so grateful they had not broken their necks the night before. She unpeeled the banana Colin handed to her and bit off a large piece. They ate silently.

It now feels comfortable enough to gaze at this harbor together, Elisabeth thought, recalling their deck silence aboard the *Xavier*. "There is much beauty here," she finally commented.

"Yes, I have always thought so," Colin said quietly. His regretful tone puzzled Elisabeth.

"Mr. Richardson, would you please tell me the plan? I really must insist I know what involves me."

"On an island, too much knowledge is dangerous," he mumbled.

She waited, staring at him.

Finally, Colin continued, "You know we shall spend the winter months here. Look at all those ships. They anchor because it is becoming too dangerous for sea travel. We will use this season to work and gain passage money for Boston in the spring."

He cast his banana peel over the ledge. "Do not look so downcast, Mrs. Allerton. The land, the ocean, everything is always best in spring. Fortune will come our way." He offered his most lying cheerfulness because the last thing he needed was a panicky woman.

"I prayed this would not be—that there would be some way to avoid wintering here. I had hoped..." Her words drifted off. It alarmed her to think of having a baby without her family's support.

"Yes, no doubt, this is troubling to you." Colin was uncomfortable, too. "The baby complicates matters."

Elisabeth had many questions, but having Mr. Richardson so congenial to offer information was an opportunity she did not want to spoil. She quietly encouraged, "Please, tell me more."

"Berko keeps supplies in another cave deeper in the jungle. You and I will live there for a while. We will hunt the wild boar, which is prized in town for its meat and skins. Many buccaneers—um, decent sailors, too—earn money this way when they are landlocked. They work as partners. Disguised as a man, you can assist me as best you can."

Elisabeth scoffed at such a ridiculous idea. Share a cave with this man, impossible! But she asked, "How can I hide my growing girth like that?"

"I am sure you can make it work. You must. I heard of a woman buccaneer who disguised herself by dressing like a man and when she became pregnant, bound her stomach." He wished this woman did not expect him to solve every problem.

Her face frowned in distress, so he tried to comfort.

"Mrs. Allerton, you are pluckier than I thought. Back on the *Sea Venture*, if I were to bet on your survival, I would have wagered you would have been shark bait by now. Yet, here you are, God-believer that you are. Do those odds not speak something to you? Where is thy faith, Sister Allerton? Let us just get through this day and worry about the rest later."

Elisabeth felt anger that he would use God to justify this situation and pit her faith against conflicting emotions. Confused and fearful, she hated his mockery. She flung her banana peel over the ledge and indignantly took his hand. It turned out getting down the cliff required a different route during the day—one that guaranteed invisibility from any harbor telescope. Seeing her treacherous surroundings, hidden the night before, terrified Elisabeth. Colin again tethered the rope between them and effortlessly scrambled up, down, and around boulders. His moves were agile, hers hesitant.

She did her best to follow his instructions, but often she had to fight back tears, and words, clawing for her life. After an hour, she was filthy from loose dirt and reeked with sweat. She tried to concentrate on Mr. Richardson's sharp commands. She moved slowly, so slowly. She refused to look down, staring at her feet and hands.

Eventually, they reached level ground by the edge of jungle brush. The flies and mosquitoes started biting her as they walked quietly and slowly through thicker and thicker foliage.

"Is there no path?" she mumbled.

"This *is* the path," Colin retorted, slashing harder with his sword.

She wondered again if he joked. Why did the pests not bother him? Maybe they could not penetrate his stubborn hide! It irritated her that he was comfortable while she struggled, miserable. She bit her lip. All she could do was follow his sweaty ponytail, stumbling and swatting the bugs.

Several hours later, she heard a rushing sound. Colin lifted away some large leaves as if they were theater curtains revealing a stage. Elisabeth gasped at the wonder of a beautiful pond, complete with its own small waterfall. Her delight pleased him.

"I told you. Here is your water, your Highness."

With a yelp, he took off his boots, ran, and jumped in. Elisabeth walked to the edge and touched the water.

"Is it not grand, Mrs. Allerton? Come on. Jump in. Great way to wash soiled clothes." Mr. Richardson dove and popped up near her.

"I will not!" She sat down on a rock and scooped out water to refresh her face and neck. Then she took off her shoes and dangled her aching feet in the pond.

Colin found her mannerisms quite amusing. He dove and splashed around, enjoying himself immensely. Then he threw his clothing on the rocks. He would not let this priggish pregnant Puritan spoil his love of swimming. She stared at the waterfall, diverting her eyes from his bathing.

Then, he warned, "You better turn your head. No peeking!"

She flushed and quickly looked out at the thick, green jungle. After pulling on his britches, he towered above her, bare chested. She shaded her eyes to fix on his face; she dare not display any more discomfort to this impudent man.

"I am going to get us something to eat and scout out the area," Colin informed her, still dripping with water. You are safe here. If you want to wash your clothes, I promise I will not bother you. When the sun is halfway down, I will return."

She scrutinized his face. He seemed sincere. "Are you sure no one will come?" she said.

"Very unlikely. It is a big jungle, and most people do not travel in the heat of the day. "Do you still have your dagger?"

She nodded and pulled it out from her pantaloons. Clare had created a long pocket lined with leather just for her. He grunted his approval and quickly disappeared. For a while, she kept peering into the jungle feeling uneasy. She desired to feel cleaner. Her body ached. She took off her outer garments, set the knife on a rock, and stepped into the water. She cleaned her shirt and pantaloons the best she could and flattened them on the rocks.

Birds flitted through the trees. The waterfall's consistent sound reassured. She reasoned her choices were to wait anxiously for some unknown fear or to trust God and enjoy the blue sky and the jungle sanctuary, the cool water soothing her weary body. She knew if she wanted to bathe, she better do it quickly before Mr. Richardson returned.

Suddenly, she removed the last of her clothing and dragged them through the water as she swam. When she was satisfied they were as clean as possible, she rose from the water. More relaxed, she laid them carefully on the rocks with her other garments.

Work done, she floated and stretched her neck, massaging her small bulging tummy. Her muscles responded to the water as if they were receiving a healing balm. *At last,* she thought, *a pocketful of peace is all mine.*

Colin peered at her from the thicket, knowing she could not see him. God, he loved the form of a woman, even one a little pregnant, sun burned, and bug bit. Beautiful in the forest light, her fair skin and short red hair glowed and her curves moved in the rippling water.

Then, as if she sensed his gaze, she turned, peering in his direction. He sighed and pulled away to find some food. When he returned, Elisabeth was dressed, napping against a rock. The image of her nakedness in the water held him. He tried to push it aside. He would not—must not—trifle with her and cause them more trouble. He swore at himself.

"Your majesty, wake up," he said gruffly.

She stirred but did not awaken. He kicked her foot. She jerked up, grabbing her knife.

"Ah, I see the queen got some beauty rest."

Elisabeth gave him a dark look. Why did he have to be so ungentlemanly? He threw her a piece of light green fruit. When she bit into it, the sweet, pink flesh smelled musky. It was delicious, but before she took a second bite she exhorted, "Mr. Richardson, please do not call me royalty. I desire simply to be a servant to a much higher king in a better country."

He snorted. "Of course, you are servant of a higher power." Before she could respond he added, "We do not have much farther to go to reach the other cave. It should be a decent enough place to sleep, although I have not been there for a long time."

As they traveled even farther into the jungle, Elisabeth got used to the sounds and sights of birds, monkeys, and other creatures she had never seen before. She watched amazing feathered colors of red, blue, yellow, and green dart from branch to branch.

The new cave turned out to be much less accommodating than Berko's first one. It simply was a large hole in the cleft of a rock, cleverly covered with brush. Although small, it contained dried meat in a clay pot and a jug of rum.

Colin cut palm branches for sleeping. The sunset extinguished by the time they silently chewed on their roasted pork.

"I can light a fire, but it will be smoky. It does keep bugs away," he offered.

"No, thank you. I am fine." Elisabeth settled down, occasionally swatting bugs.

Neither of them felt like conversation, and Elisabeth sensed tension. "Good night, Mr. Richardson."

He said nothing but took a swig from the jug and lifted it toward her.

Chapter 21

The Scars

Unlike Elisabeth, Colin could not sleep. Instead, he rehashed his bitter, painful past. He cursed the fate that brought him to St. Paola once again, after vowing never to return to his boyhood home. Memories surfaced and swirled, revolving around his wretched stepfather.

After Colin's English father died from consumption when Colin was five, the Richardson family's French neighbor Louis Gervais charmed the vulnerable and grieving widow Katherine. Gervais and Katherine soon married and combined their two plantations. Then, Colin's safe world exploded.

Louis insisted the boy learn French, and he cruelly treated the newly acquired Richardson slaves—that included Berko and Berko's father, Sule Lumumba Kawawe.

Gervais gradually switched the crops from cotton to the more lucrative sugar cane. It came with a human price. Beloved family slaves were worked to death, some scalded and maimed by the harrowing process of turning cane into sugar. Others were whipped and pushed to their maximum strength. Colin's fear and dismay at the transformation grew to frustration and hate.

His mother seemed oblivious to Louis' iron hand. Her husband kept all gentleness with her. A year after their marriage, she took to bed rest, awaiting the birth of Angelique. She trusted Louis Gervais and his servant Adele with Colin's care.

What a nightmare shook the boy, except for the steady love and loyalty of Berko and Sule. When Louis drank or slept, Colin sneaked out of the house and found Berko and Sule deep in conversation at a small campfire near their slave shack. Occasionally, Berko's father took them to a secret cave.

There, undercover, Sule taught the boys the ways of his great village across the waters. The father pointed to his cheek and declared that the tattoo of a tiger's claws was evidence of who he was and where his heart belonged.

As boys, Berko and Colin pleaded for the tattoo initiation; they, too, wanted to be part of this invisible tribe across the great waters.

Sule would raise his hand and firmly say, "No! It is not yet time for Berko, and this is not your destiny, Master Colin. You must be strong for your momma and the baby who is coming. You will be their man."

Colin tried to accept this lot in life, but he hated Louis Gervais, his drunken binges, his fake charm, and his silky tongue around their friends. Qualities, to his bafflement, that had bewitched his mother and made them all slaves.

He knew Louis hated him. Louis even declared it once when their French lesson together went particularly wrong.

The stepfather threw the book at Colin and sneered, "You are so like your father, weak, addle-brained, English! You will never, never deserve a high position on this plantation. Never!"

Then he had strode out of the library, leaving Colin weeping, fully aware of his inadequacies, but determined he would never stop hating this man.

Colin knew his father had not been weak. He had been kind and evenhanded to all, even the slaves he reluctantly bought to make the plantation work. Among them were Sule and a motherless Berko.

Sule and Richardson had worked side by side on the cotton. It produced a living but not much. When Richardson died, all understood cotton would not be the crop that kept them going.

With Louis came the gradual transformation into a lucrative sugar cane business. Sule reluctantly led the slaves through this transition the best he could.

One night, Sule, Berko, and Colin sat around a campfire with some other slaves, laughing and talking about the old ways of their homelands. A drunken Louis stumbled upon them, led by a betraying slave trying to curry favor.

The slave had hinted to Louis that Sule and the others were planning insurrection. In a drunken stupor, Louis kicked the fire and ordered the group to get to bed.

Sule rose up, towering above them all. For a second, Colin thought Berko's father would end their miseries by snapping Louis' neck in two. But something changed.

The great man looked at his son and Colin and then did nothing. As an adult, Colin realized this protected the boys. But at the time, he despaired.

Louis seized his advantage and ordered Sule to be tied up. Nearby, Berko and Colin, frozen in fear, sobbed. Then in violent lust, he feasted on whipping Berko's father until the master's energy died. Louis threw down his bloody whip and staggered toward the house. As gently as they could, Berko and Colin lowered Sule.

With his dying breath, Sule spoke to Berko in a language Colin did not understand. He touched his son's cheek and died giving a blessing. Quietly, that night the grieving slave community buried this man who taught them so much.

When Louis came to breakfast the next morning, he said not a word about the event. Sule was an expendable casualty. The slave who had betrayed them all received a promotion. A few days later that betrayer lay in his bed with a knife in his heart.

Louis ignored this crime and placed a young French man named

Gerard as overseer of the slaves. Gervais knew he had crossed a line and relaxed the workload for a while.

Foreman Gerard demanded but not cruelly. Berko and Colin were almost invisible to them, which suited the boys. It gave them time to plan revenge.

Several years after the death of Sule, Berko begged Colin to do a hard thing. Would he burn the flesh of his cheek into the pattern Sule had carried? Finally, Colin agreed.

They went to the cave where Sule had created remnants of his African life. Together they made a little fire, and Colin took a knife he had stolen from the kitchen and laid its blade in the flames. Berko put a stick in his mouth while Colin seared the flesh on his cheek.

Then he begged Berko to do the same for him. These people were his family, not Louis, and if that madman chose to beat them all to death, so be it. But Berko shook his head, and, like his father, said this was not his destiny. Instead, they cut the inside of their palms, mixed their blood and drank it as blood brothers.

Later, when Louis saw Berko's tattoo he raged. He knew from Colin's defiant face that he had participated in this act. He grabbed his stepson and said, "So, you think you can do this to my slave, you wretched whelp! I will teach you that you belong to me. He dragged the boy into the kitchen and thrust his sword into the cook's hearth. With his blade hot, he slashed Colin's cheek recklessly in a zig-zag wound.

Pushing the sobbing boy down, he laughed, satisfied with the deed. Even in adulthood, Colin sometimes heard that evil mockery from his memory. It filled him with hatred.

Colin's mother was horrified when she saw her son's disfigured cheek. He refused to tell her what happened, fearing his stepfather would hurt the person he loved the most. Louis smoothly explained a drunken wayfaring sailor had done the awful deed and had been punished.

His mother's stunned expression told the silent Colin she finally realized the depth of her husband's lying and how her son suffered. She went into labor from the trauma and in sorrow bore Angelique—beautiful, little angel.

With this baby, Louis was all gentleness. She transformed him a little. He turned to making his plantations into something even more substantial for his family. He continued ignoring Berko and Colin, using Gerard to give them chores. Colin wanted to hate Angelique too. But she was so helpless and his mother loved her, and he loved his mother. When Colin turned nine and Angelique was one, his mother took to bed rest with another pregnancy. Shortly before this baby came, Colin's stepfather summoned him to his study and there was a good surprise—his Uncle Duff Richardson.

"Colin," his Uncle Duff uttered affectionately, touching the red, scarred cheek. "My lad, how you have grown! I have missed you."

"It is time for you to find your sea legs, Colin, like your Uncle Duff," Louis announced, briskly interrupting the reunion.

That very afternoon, Colin and Uncle Duff packed his small bag. The boy hugged his mother good-bye, not realizing he would never see her again. She died bearing Angelique's brother and his half-brother, Eduard Gervais.

When Colin reached adulthood, Duff told him his mother had written a letter pleading for him to come and rescue Colin. Duff believed she meant to save Colin's life by letting him go.

Eduard, now twenty years of age, helped Louis run the thriving Gervais/Richardson plantations. Colin expected nothing from this half-brother, who did not know him or their mother, and who was raised totally under the shadow of Louis.

Eduard drank like his father, though Angelique defended him. Dear, forgiving Angelique, who tried to embrace them all. Colin knew her demand for the cottage was partially for his benefit and partially to shut out her father's faults.

Angelique was true Caribbean-born—more independent than most women of her time, choosing to live fearlessly in a cottage within easy reach of Louis and Eduard's plantations. Why they allowed Angelique such freedom and did not force her to marry puzzled Colin, but he was glad for her!

Over the years, Berko had surprised Colin. He did not kill Gervais as he vowed as a child. Instead, one day Foreman Gerard told Berko he was a free man; Louis Gervais had released him.

Rather than leave the island, Berko quietly and covertly protected the other slaves the best he could, just as his father had done. He lived as their jungle king, appearing and disappearing like an angel. He became an island legend.

It was a mystery why Gervais did not kill Berko. Perhaps he knew he might have a rebellion on his hands if anything happened to the Jungle King. He symbolized freedom, albeit only a flickering hope.

Gervais' vanity assured him he could extinguish that light anytime he desired. It was a taciturn affair, but Gervais never doubted his control.

As seamen, Colin and Duff journeyed to Berko's homeland, but they never found the village Sule described. Colin did not have the heart to tell Berko he feared slave traders had wiped out his dream of someday returning home.

In the darkness of the small cave, Colin could hear the steady, deep breathing of Mrs. Allerton. He wondered how much more she could take of this cursed island. For such a long time it had given him only sorrow.

Somehow, he knew the protection he felt toward her connected to the pregnant mother he had said good-bye to so many years before. Maybe by saving Elisabeth he could purge some guilt about not being able to save his mother.

That sort of thinking confused him and made him angry. He might as well dive to the bottom of the ocean than figure out his motivation to get Elisabeth to her worthless husband. Finally, he pushed convoluted thoughts away and found restless sleep.

Chapter 22

The Wild Boar

The next day Colin asked Elisabeth if she felt fit for a long walk. He prepped his pistol and sharpened his knife.

"Yes, of course." She did not want to appear weak, although all her muscles cried out in protest.

"There are Arawaks, native islanders, as well as a few escaped slaves and pirates, secretly living in this jungle. I thought we could take on a girl servant from their tribe to stay with us. I think you would agree another pair of hands and eyes could be assets out here."

"Yes, a servant girl would be especially good!" Elisabeth was relieved to hear this possibility. She desired to be alone with this man as little as possible. All these circumstances would be so difficult to explain to David or anyone in her community. A servant girl's presence would add credibility.

"Don't be too enthusiastic or have high expectations about the help. Basically, an Arawak will do what pleases him or her and nothing more or less. You will be somewhat of a curiosity to them, but we can barter."

"With what?" Elisabeth could not imagine what they could scavenge to sell in this place.

"Mrs. Allerton, you have said you are not afraid of work to get to Boston. You will need that bravery and fortitude in the days ahead. Out here, wild boar and cows roam, even an occasional sheep or goat, left by the Spaniards from years past. Many sailors down on their luck hunt the animals for buckskins and meat. They make smoked meat, and sell it in town. This is what we need to do."

"How can I help?"

"Your job will be to flush out the sweet darlings. I'll kill them. Then we will tan the skins and dry the meat. The prices for our efforts will be greater in winter when the ships can no longer sail and supplies run low."

"I have not done butchering before, but I have watched, and I can learn."

"Good."

It was a difficult, hot walk that day. With his sword, Colin cut away branches for Elisabeth; nevertheless, she bore several scratches on her face as well as many bites. They stopped only to catch their breath, and then they were off again.

"You must learn to walk more quietly, Mrs. Allerton. This is not a promenade."

Elisabeth held back her tongue, but she felt Mr. Richardson should give her some mercy. She thought she moved along quietly in spite of the rough terrain, aching muscles, and dizziness.

When she was about to protest his pace, Colin raised his arm. She stopped and heard the heavy snorting of a boar, heaving and grunting, moving along just ahead of them. Colin eased his pistol out of his belt, loaded it with gunpowder, cocked, and aimed. Elisabeth held her breath.

The black boar stopped its grunting and smelled the air, aware of their scent. Elisabeth could see two long tusks smudged with dirt on a hulking male of about two hundred pounds. Just as the animal turned to run farther into the jungle, Colin fired.

He hit the boar in the stomach, but the animal did not topple.

Instead, it leaped as it let out an angry squeal and pivoted to face Colin and Elisabeth.

"Bloody hell, Mrs. Allerton. Turn around! Run!"

Elisabeth did not need the advice. She bolted, hearing beastly squeals of anger and pain behind her. By the time she stopped running to catch her breath, there were no sounds but the birds. She looked around and there was no boar, no Mr. Richardson. Her heart and head pounded and her chest heaved. She wiped away sweat from her eyes, pulled out her knife, and retraced the path.She feared the boar might be gorging on Mr. Richardson.

Instead, she found the man hunched over the bloody animal and whistling softly. She straightened herself and pushed her hair in place.

He turned around with a satisfied smile and lifted his bloody knife. "Now we have something to bargain with!"

Elisabeth felt anger that he took on such a beast and put them both in danger. But she resisted speaking and sat down. Mr. Richardson cheerfully dressed the boar. Already, insects were drawn to the feast.

"How do you plan to bargain with this?" She felt queasy. She needed water. She swatted flies.

"Oh, that will not be a problem, my dear lady. You will under-stand shortly."

His mood seemed much improved. Elisabeth's confusion lasted only a second, for out of the clearing came three half-naked brown men—one drawing a pistol, the other two holding bows. They tried to look ferocious, but Elisabeth could not help but find them comical. She had never seen such a sight! Half-naked men and wild pigs! This was all too much, and she laughed out loud.

Colin stopped dressing the boar and stared at her. Then he saw the men. He yelled a greeting in a language Elisabeth did not know.

They quickly lowered their weapons and ran to help him. They knew French. Soon Colin and they were pleasantly conversing. At one point, she felt they jested over her. She did pick out Berko's name in the conversation.

By the time Elisabeth's heartbeat returned to normal, the men had mounted the boar on a long pole. Soon out of nowhere came a half dozen giggling black and brown children.

"How safe are we, Mr. Richardson?" Colin looked at her a little annoyed, but her taunt face softened his reply.

"I trust them with my life," he said.

Given what she knew of Mr. Richardson, Elisabeth did not believe him. She tried to pick out landmarks should it be necessary to run away, but the tropical forest became a blur of twisted plants and trees. She gave up and felt as defeated as the boar swinging on poles carried by half-naked men.

Chapter 23

The Hideaway Village

When they reached a clearing, Elisabeth saw many paths leading to a central area where several women tended a fire pit. They wore shell necklaces and bits of colorful cloth. Feathers adorned one woman's hair.

The two men who carried the pig laid it on the ground and wrapped intertwining vines tightly around the boar's feet. A grey-haired woman bent down, sliced the boar open and removed what Elisabeth thought were the kidneys. The old lady put the bloody heart-shaped organs in a pottery bowl and hurried off.

Elisabeth had never seen people like this before, although she had heard stories of Indians in the New World. They did not seem the least bit interested in her. Mr. Richardson came and stood beside her. He had blood on his hands and arms.

"We will eat well tonight," he declared happily.

She then realized that despite observing this odd and bloody butchering, she was ravenous. "Do you know these people well, Mr. Richardson?"

"Only a few of them. Berko is a friend to their leader, Chief

Abasi. He has been told of our presence. Otherwise, I would not have dared to fire that shot in this area."

"Do these paths lead to their homes?"

"Well, yes and no. Some paths lead to dead ends. Only the villagers know how to get to their huts. They keep moving around to confuse enemies."

"Enemies?"

"Any damn marauder who tries to kill them. They are living on borrowed time, Mrs. Allerton. Many Arawaks already have been wiped out by foreigners. Others intermarried with town folks, doing the best they could to survive. These few remaining only exist because they live deep in the island's terrain, and the town folk welcome their barter. Unfortunately, with more and more land being cleared for plantations, the distance of safety shortens."

Elisabeth could not fathom such a fate, but she touched her stomach. What mother living here would want to bring a baby into such a dismal future? And yet there were children and old people existing around her. One woman with weathered brown skin approached Elisabeth and Colin.

"You come with Neesa," she said in English, which shocked Elisabeth because they had been speaking Carib and French to Colin. Neesa led them down one of the paths and came to a small thatched hut at the end.

"Rest. Eat," she ordered, motioning to the hut's entrance. Colin and Elisabeth found themselves again alone as Neesa went hobbling away.

"Not one of many words," Elisabeth commented.

Colin chuckled, and they went inside and found fruit and fresh water. They fell upon it with no conversation. Then Mr. Richardson said he would be back for her later and left. Elisabeth lay on the leafy bed and quickly fell asleep. She awoke to find him calling her name from the doorway. He had washed up and even his clothes looked cleaner.

"It's time to meet Chief Abasi," he explained. Elisabeth felt miffed that she only had time to brush her hair and smooth out her rumpled clothing.

Neesa also returned and took them to the campfire circle. Some forty people sat around the fire with children flitting about them like butterflies. Baskets of fruit, barrels of rum, and buckets of water were enjoyed. A short, slender man with small eyes, flat nose, and smooth ebony skin stood to receive them. Dressed in trousers he wore a simple shell necklace and carried a long knife pistol.

"Colin Richardson, we welcome you in peace because the Jungle King requested it. I am Abasi, leader of my people."

By the man's tone, Elisabeth sensed irritation. She wondered if Colin knew what he was doing.

"Thank you, Chief Abasi. We hope this gift of the boar shows you our good intentions." Mr. Richardson response in English surprised and gratified Elizabeth. At last, she could understand the conversation.

Abasi grunted and responded in English, too. "Gift? I know you are from the sea, sailor. You take from our land and give what's ours back as a gift?"

"No, Chief Abasi, I would not have taken this boar without permission except it attacked us. As the Jungle King told you, we come to you in good faith."

Elisabeth thought Mr. Richardson stretched the truth, but she remained silent.

"We could have taken the boar away and not shared. We could have used our knives and pistol against your men." Mr. Richardson could make their actions sound so reasonable.

"What? You would fight us with just this puny woman, who has parrot hair and looks like a boy?"

Abasi spoke Arawak to the people, and they laughed. Elisabeth stood up straighter. Her eyes flashed at the chief.

Abasi snorted, but at least he seemed less irritated. "What do you want, Colin Richardson? How do I know you are not a spy for the French?"

"As you stated truthfully, the Jungle King wants us to be friends. I know he is your great ally, as he is mine. Even more so, he is my blood brother."

"Berko told me this is true. But to allow strangers here is unsafe for my people. He asks much of me."

Colin persisted, "We understand and do not want to put you in harm's way. But we are in danger too. We will repay you when we are able."

Abasi grunted again and said, "For Berko's sake, we will help you. What do you need?"

Colin continued, "We desire your permission to hunt animals over the winter season, just enough time to earn money for ship's passage off the island. We will share the meat we take with your people."

"And what about the hides?"

Abasi missed nothing, but Colin was prepared. He looked amazed at the question. "The hides? Hmmm. It would be much work for just this parrot-head woman and me. Perhaps your people would help us with the labor? Then we would gladly give half the hides and share the meat."

While Abasi was considering the proposal, Colin threw in one more request. "As you can see, Mrs. Allerton is with child. We could use a servant girl to assist her."

"Yes, she has five full moons to wait," Abasi said.

Elisabeth did not think she was showing that much. She blushed and touched her stomach.

"What kind of servant girl does she desire?" Abasi asked.

Elisabeth surprised herself, speaking out quickly. "Chief Abasi, sir, I practice healing, using God's herbs and plants. Do you have a girl who could teach me something of your jungle's medicine? I want to learn."

Abasi looked pleased at this request. "Yes, that is good. Tana's family brings medicines to our people." He pointed to a family sitting nearby. Elisabeth briefly looked at the huddle, which included Neesa. She returned her attention to the chief.

He said, "Tana knows the ways of healing. But she does not work very hard, and she is young."

Elisabeth hesitated, but Colin quickly spoke, "Having Tana's help would be most generous!"

"Then we have a bargain, Colin Richardson. But I warn you, if you bring any others into our village, I will kill you first and then this woman. Berko would understand the danger!"

Abasi looked determined, but his tone quickly changed. He smiled. "Come, friends of the Jungle King, let us eat the fine boar you killed."

Soon, Elisabeth sat by a fire, holding a coconut shell filled with roasted pork and mashed root vegetables. Although she had to use her fingers as utensils, hunger made her grateful. The villagers also had rum, which Colin heartily drank. Elisabeth tried the burning spirit and dumped it as discreetly as she could.

The villagers merrily chattered as they ate, and the noise grew louder with the drinking. The children shyly touched Elisabeth's hair and ran away. Then they crept back and pressed in closer to examine her. Neesa shooed them with her stick. They would run away giggling but soon returned.

Elisabeth disliked this game of being the toy. The irritation made her long for family in England and friends aboard the *Sea Venture*. She reminded herself that survival depended on watching and listening.

Using French, Colin told tales of his sea journeys. Elisabeth noticed some villagers whispered and translated to their neighbors while he spoke. It seemed odd and amazing how they intermixed so many languages.

After the stories ended, Colin huddled with Abasi, sharing Berko's news of what happened on the plantations around him. Elisabeth tried to pick out words, but there were so many distractions her efforts yielded no information. She felt dizzy, overwhelmed by these people, their food, and languages. Jungle smells, bugs, and humidity did not comfort.

She wondered if this long nightmare killed her one piece at a time. Then she thought of her baby. Out of her dying, life grew.

During the evening, she noticed a girl of about fourteen staring at her. When Elisabeth glanced at her, she quickly turned away. This happened throughout the night, and Elisabeth realized the gawker must be Tana. Although Elisabeth did not understand the women's native chatter, she forced smiles and nodded politely. She attempted to converse with Neesa in English, but the wrinkled woman just grunted or nodded her head.

Finally, all that remained of the fire were glowing embers. Neesa suddenly grabbed Elisabeth's hand and led her down the dark path. Frightened, Elisabeth hoped Mr. Richardson would come too. She turned to see him half asleep in the circle of other drunken men. He had not acknowledged her once during the evening.

Elisabeth followed her hostess to a hut. Neesa pointed to the door and then dissolved into the night. Inside the dark dwelling, Elisabeth stumbled to her floor mat. For one brief moment, she wondered if she should worry about night creatures. But then, sleep came fast.

Chapter 24

Servant Tana

When Elisabeth awoke, she shot up disoriented. Her eyes adjusted to the light slanting through the hut's thatched roof. She heard the cacophony of jungle song —parakeets, monkeys, frogs, bugs.

Her foggy brain cleared, and she relaxed. Turning to lie back down, she noticed someone sitting cross-legged next to her bed.

Elisabeth jumped. "Who are you?"

The young girl blinked at her.

"Tana? Are you Tana?" The girl did not respond. Elisabeth wondered what thoughts were behind that blank face.

"We certainly are off to a fine beginning," Elisabeth said out loud. Yet she was relieved to have a female companion with her at last, even this Arawak girl.

Elisabeth got up and looked around for some water. There in a corner of the hut, flies buzzed around some fresh fruit, obviously brought in by Tana.

Elisabeth pantomimed with her hands and face that she wanted water to wash. Tana remained sitting and blinking at her. Elisabeth went to the hut's opening, and immediately, the girl bounced up and stood by her.

Ah, my shadow, Elisabeth thought. They went out together, and Elisabeth pantomimed again the signal for drinking and washing her hands. Tana nodded and grabbed Elisabeth's arm, pulling her down one of the paths. They came to a small stream. Elisabeth scooped water with her hands, washing her face and quenching her thirst, all under the attentive eyes of squatting Tana. When she finished, Tana led her back to the hut and pointed to the fruit. Elisabeth whisked the flies away and enjoyed the juicy flesh. She helped herself to some coconut meat too, wondering how to engage her silent companion.

Once again, Elisabeth blessed Angelique for giving the hairbrush. Tana watched as she brushed her short, red hair. It made her sad to know how ridiculous she must look, but she reassured herself and said out loud to Tana as well as herself, "It will grow back."

Ready to face the day, whatever it would involve, Elisabeth tied her scarf on and stood expectantly at the door waiting for Tana to get up and take her somewhere. Tana reluctantly came and beckoned her to follow down another path.

At the center campsite, they joined the tribal women busily working on hides. The women stopped jabbering and stared at Elisabeth. Neesa finally nodded to her.

Elisabeth responded with as much confidence as she could muster, motioning with her arms and saying, "I want to help. Please, will you teach me?"

Her offer was met by chortles and a buzz of chatter. But Elisabeth remained determined. She knelt down and said firmly, "No, really. I want to help."

They giggled and smiled.

Elisabeth reached out and touched Neesa's tool. "May I learn?" she asked.

Neesa grunted and gave a command. A young woman shyly smiled at Elisabeth and handed her a hand-sized scraper made from whalebone. She proceeded to show her how to push the scraper against the bristles of the boar's hide.

The women worked in a rhythmic motion, efficient, yet able to chat. Elisabeth, however, found herself scraping unevenly and clumsily. The labor hurt her fingers. Sweat dripped off her face, her sweaty clothes soon clung, and she developed a headache.

How she wished she were back home with her family, conversing and working together. These pangs of homesickness drove her insane. A few tears, mingled with sweat, dripped on the hide. She kept working, and gradually, the bumping motion became less.

By the time she handed back the tool to the young woman, she received another grunt from Neesa. She took it as a compliment. She had been so busy she hadn't noticed Tana had disappeared.

Abasi said the girl was lazy, but Elisabeth could not discipline her yet. When the women finished, they stretched the hides out under the hot tropical sun. Neesa offered her some berries, jerky, and water, which she gratefully accepted. Elisabeth's back ached, her hands were blistered, and she felt faint.

Just as she was about to motion for someone to take her to her hut, Tana appeared and led her there. Tana reached into her small pouch and pulled out some plump leaves. She broke one open, took Elisabeth's hand, and squeezed out a thick, cooling substance. Elisabeth smelled it, not familiar with the distinct pungency. As her blistered hands felt relief, she knew she must later ask Tana to show her this plant. She lay down on the palm leaves to rest, wondering what Mr. Richardson was doing. She thanked the Lord she did not have to hunt the wild boar with him.

Chapter 25

Snakebite

Elisabeth lost track of the days in Abasi's village. She rejoiced Mr. Richardson did not need her to hunt with him, nor did he tease her for not helping. Apparently, he had not counted on Abasi's generous hospitality or the readily available hunting partners among Abasi's men. They respected Colin's skills and allowed him to share their campfire and drink away the evenings.

Elisabeth noticed Mr. Richardson avoided her as much as possible. She presumed their unspoken rule kept their relationship as formal as circumstances allowed. This arrangement suited her, except she longed for English companionship. The villagers tolerated her as she helped the women dress the animals, dry the meat, and tan the hides. Sometimes, they invited her to join them in the rainforest to search for edible roots and fruit. Occasionally, Tana would show her an interesting plant and say, "medicine," but the girl could not or would not articulate how to use it.

Elisabeth noticed other foods, like fish and beans, appearing at some meals, but she did not know how such barter occurred with the town folk. She asked Colin about this connection, but he refused to tell her. She argued she preferred to know how she could reach the civilized world if the need arose. He shrugged.

No other strangers but themselves were allowed in this hidden village. Elisabeth realized Berko's influence in obtaining this sanctuary for them probably saved their lives.

As days passed and Elisabeth's pregnancy became more evident, the women not only tolerated her but included her. They patted her tummy and said words she did not understand. They wanted her to hold their babies and bless them with prayer. She knew they believed she offered good magic, and at first, she refused to bless. Neesa became very upset and shook her finger at her, scolding in the Arawak language.

Elisabeth tried to explain the humility of her faith, but Neesa retorted, "Jesus blessed children and you follow Jesus. You bless!"

Neesa always had the final word, and she dictated when the blessings occurred.

Elisabeth sat on a boulder, and the children scrambled and pushed to be first. One at a time she put them on her lap, gave them hugs, and touched each one with a prayer of blessing.

This action sent the mothers into hoots of delight, and the children usually grinned at the attention. There were some toddlers, however, who screamed in fear when their naked bottoms were plopped on Elisabeth's lap. Elisabeth thought they might be afraid of her red hair and pale face.

Neesa insisted Elisabeth bless the wriggly bawlers as best she could. There were some ailments Elisabeth desired to treat, like an eye infection or an open wound that refused to heal. Many times she wished for her medicine chest.

One day, Tana put Elisabeth's few belongings in a bag and announced, "Abasi says go. We meet Kidoh."

"Who is Kidoh?"

"Old, old man. Come. He teach you. He is a healer. You see."

Elisabeth balked.

"Is it just you and me going, Tana? Surely that cannot be safe! What is Mr. Richardson's mind on this matter?"

Tana stared at her. "It good. We go," she insisted.

Elisabeth stood still.

"Abasi say so. Kidoh wants to see woman with parrot hair."

"How far is it?" Elisabeth really wanted to have counsel with Mr. Richardson before taking this journey. She judged by her girth that she was about six months along. She definitely did not want to go into labor far away from a community that could help her with this baby.

"Not far," Tana said with her blank face.

Elisabeth had learned Tana's idea of not far could be completely different from hers.

"Here, you carry this." Tana handed her a boar skin bag, which had a rope tied around it. Elisabeth assumed from the bulkiness that it contained dried meat and fruit. Tana heaved a much heavier bag over her shoulders. Elisabeth did the same with her lighter one.

As they started down the path, Mr. Richardson met them.

"I hear you are off to meet the great Kidoh, Mrs. Allerton?" He panted and obviously had run to find her.

"Mr. Richardson, you know about this plan? Is it wise? Who is Kidoh?" She set her bag down and brushed sweat from her face.

Mr. Richardson squarely met her eyes, irritated that even as she got bigger with pregnancy, she had an attraction he could not shake. Why did pregnancy not make her uncomely?

"Oh, I think you will have a good time with Kidoh. He is a daffy old bloke, legendary to the islanders, a former slave who barters goods for his medicine. He lives alone." Colin paused, remembering something. "I do not think he is dangerous, but then again he is a sly old fox. He once gave me a sleeping potion in a cup of tea that knocked me out. No harm done, really. No worries. You will be fine."

"Your words are not reassuring, Mr. Richardson."

Colin smirked. "Ah, Mrs. Allerton, this is as safe as anything else we have done. Just make sure you wear your scarf and cover that belly of yours. From a distance, I wager you could still look like a bloke venturing around with his native woman, Tana. Can you do your Benny walk in your present condition?"

The man could still make her red-faced, insinuating she could look and walk like a man.

Colin asked, "Do you have your dagger? Have you kept it sharpened?"

Of course, she had her well-sharpened knife with her. She whipped it out, pointed it close to his neck, and startled him.

He backed off chuckling, "When you return from Kidoh's, we will discuss our next step in getting you to Boston."

Elisabeth called after him, "You have a ship to reach David?"

He shook his head no and disappeared, swearing under his breath, having been reminded of her loyalty to such a cuttlefish as David Allerton.

That man! Elisabeth thought. *It only takes moments for him to irritate me with his scornful humor!* She calmed down. "Forgive me, Lord—once again."

Tana stared at her, patiently waiting.

"I am ready, Tana," she said, straightening her shoulders. She wondered what Tana had in her heavy bag.

They trekked easily on the path Tana chose. Elisabeth guessed animals mainly used it, and she walked with much care.

Although her pregnant body was slowing her movements, Elisabeth found this outing pleasant in the cooler part of the morning. Her work in the tribe had made her stronger, and she was more acclimated to jungle heat.

She still marveled at the variety of different plants. Flowers of many colors unexpectedly popped up on the sides of trees, at her feet, and a few feet off the path. She continued to prod Tana with questions about healing plants, but the girl only shrugged. It frustrated Elisabeth that she learned precious little from this girl.

After walking for what seemed like a long time, they came to a little stream.

Tana threw down her pack and bent to drink. Elisabeth just

about followed, when Tana groaned and grabbed her hand. She quickly reached for a stone and brought it down on the head of a two-foot long, black snake.

This did not startle Elisabeth because snakes were common sightings, but Tana's face showed fear.

"Tana, what is wrong?"

The girl held out her hand with its tiny puncture wounds.

"No good, no good! Tana get sick."

"A snakebite. How sick?"

"It bad."

"How far is Kidoh's place from here?" Elisabeth quickly asked.

"Not far." Tana whispered, her eyes filled with fear.

"Good. We can make it. I am sure. Here, let me have your bag."

Elisabeth quickly drank some water and then heaved both bags on her back. They almost toppled her over.

"Leave bags," Tana said. Elisabeth gratefully put them down.

Tana then said, "Wait!" She frantically opened the bag, and Elisabeth gasped at the contents.

"My medicine chest! My books! How did you get these?" Elisabeth demanded.

Tana pleaded, pointing to the chest. "Good medicine?"

Elisabeth quickly opened her chest, delighted to see most of its contents in place. She grabbed some dried century flowers and crushed them. She made a cup out of a large leaf and mixed the powdered flowers with water from the stream.

"These are supposed to be mixed with wine, but we will make do," she said apologetically to Tana. The young girl quickly swallowed the mixture.

Then Elisabeth took some bruised leaves of marsh-mallows and mixed them with water into a plaster. "This always works well with bee and wasp bites. Maybe it would help," she explained to Tana as she applied the plaster.

Tana grimaced but seemed satisfied. Before Elisabeth could bind her hand with a rag, Tana plucked a few leaves from a nearby bush

She gently pressed them into the plaster and uttered some words in Arawak. Elisabeth bound the rag tight to keep the medicine in place.

"Can you walk?" Elisabeth asked.

"Yes."

Elisabeth was reluctant to leave her belongings behind, but she knew they must find Kidoh.

At first, the frantic Tana charged through the jungle, and Elisabeth could hardly keep up. But soon the girl slowed and her breathing became raspy. She perspired, and her eyes turned dull.

For a moment, Elisabeth panicked. They both could die in this jungle before anyone found them.

"Tana, tell me how to get to Kidoh's hut. How far?"

Tana staggered and stumbled, using her arm to point in one direction.

"Tana, you must rest now! Tell me how to get to Kidoh's hut. I will bring him back here. I promise."

"No!" she whispered. "We find water."

The girl struggled to her feet and pushed on. They finally came to another little stream. Tana propped herself against a rock and muttered, "Go. Kidoh. Stone like tree. Turn, sun."

Elisabeth looked around. How could she remember this place? By the stream, she spotted pebbles. She grabbed a handful, diligently keeping an eye out for snakes.

"Tana, I will come back. Stay here. Be brave and pray."

The girl heaved in pain but nodded.

How much farther was Kidoh's hut? Elisabeth had no idea, but she whispered, "Lord, please help us!"

She stumbled down the overgrown path, which seemed barely a path at all. Doubt flooded her sense of direction. The greenery looked the same no matter how she struggled to find a landmark.

Carefully, she marked her way with pebbles beside a tree trunk, near an exotic flower, atop a deformed rock—anything that would stand out when she retraced her steps.

With only two pebbles left, she saw a large, narrow boulder. It did not really look like the shape of a tree to her. Was this what Tana described? Her instincts said yes. She turned toward the sun; its light glistened through the foliage.

She started walking and calling out Kidoh's name. At first, she did it in a desperate voice, but as the way became more difficult, she stopped and yelled, "Kidoh! Kidoh! Help! Can you hear me? Tana needs you."

The jungle grew quiet with her yells.

Exhausted, she dared not go too far off course, losing her trail back to Tana. She slumped to the ground, discouraged, knowing she could only rest briefly before returning to Tana.

Through all her trials, she had submerged a primal desire to let go and rage over her situation. She wanted to scream, and scream, and scream. But she knew if she let go, she might not ever stop. Would she find death out here, alone, without having her baby and being reunited with David? It seemed so wrong. She had done everything she could to be God's servant, even in this wilderness. Did God will her and her baby to die here?

No! She could not accept that thought as truth, not until death took her. She bit her lip. She would not lose her mind to fear. She got up once again and yelled as loudly as she could, "Kidoh! Kidoh, please, show yourself! We need your help!"

It was quiet, as if the jungle waited for her next move. Sighing, Elisabeth turned around to follow the trail back to Tana. She gasped to see that only a few feet away from her stood a wizened, gray-haired black man, stooped over, carrying a stick and bag. He stared at her, his expression unreadable. Such a calm demeanor seemed so bizarre to Elisabeth's state of mind. She started laughing and crying at the same time.

"Mr. Kidoh. Abasi sent me. A snake bit my servant girl, Tana, and I think she is dying. We must hurry to her!"

She knew her ramblings were confusing, especially to a native. Then the man said in clear English, "Tana? What kind of a snake bit her?"

"I am not sure. It was black and this long. Tana killed it."

"Show me," he commanded.

She could hardly stand, but she struggled to get up. Kidoh cut off a piece of bamboo with his machete. "Use it as a walking stick," he said, and she chastised herself for not thinking of this earlier.

Elisabeth moved as quickly as she could, until she came to the tree rock and paused. She looked on the ground and saw her pebble.

Kidoh noticed. "Yes, you were wise to use stones. I can use them to find Tana faster than you. But will you be able to follow?"

Before she could even nod, he hobbled away. She strained to follow his path, but the jungle absorbed him. She stood to catch her breath, daring not to sit for fear of never getting up. She paused and prayed, searching the ground for the pebbles that directed her to Tana and Kidoh.

By the time she found them, Kidoh had Tana completely covered in mud, even her face. He had made a small fire and fanned smoke toward the sick girl. Tana was moaning, and her eyes were rolled back in her head; her breath came in short gasps.

At first, Elisabeth was horrified by Tana's mud-covered appearance, but she also felt helpless to offer a better treatment. *He must be trying to expunge the poison into the mud,* she thought.

"May I help?" she asked. "Please."

Without taking his eyes off Tana, he handed her one of the branches he was burning. "I need more, many more, but watch out for snakes!" Then he muttered something in his native tongue.

Chapter 26

Life or Death Treatment

For the long vigil, Kidoh and Elisabeth made a lean-to out of palms and bamboo against an old tree. Elisabeth thanked God for her knife. They sat by the fire, taking turns fanning the herbal smoke and reapplying cool mud to Tana's body. She went in and out of consciousness, and her breathing came in gasps and coughs.

Elisabeth held Tana's hand and tried to comfort her with soothing words. "It will be all right, Tana. Kidoh is here. God never leaves us. Never!" She reassured herself, too.

"Yes, Kidoh is here! Onyame is here!" The old man would yell as if Tana were deaf. Then he uttered words Elisabeth did not understand. The language was not Arawak, and that made Elisabeth wonder if Kidoh had been a former slave.

Tana stirred when they spoke to her and moved her withered lips, but there were no words. Elisabeth tore the flap off her carrying bag, dipped it in water, and used it to moisten Tana's lips. She and Kidoh shared jerky and berries while keeping vigil.

To break the silence, Elisabeth explained, "We were coming to visit you, Kidoh, to learn more about your medicine."

"I know," he said, putting more twigs on the smoky fire.

"Yes, of course, you did. I am sorry it turned out this way."

"God knows our days," he said, staring into the fire.

Elisabeth, surprised, sputtered, "Yes, he does."

"Tana is my granddaughter," the man said sadly.

"I did not know. I am sorry."

"She needs to be more careful. She has been taught since she could walk to look before taking. But she forgets. This time, her taking hurt her. Maybe she will remember from such a difficult lesson."

Elisabeth wanted to ask Kidoh if he believed Tana would live, but she could not find courage to do so. Tana's listless body and rasping breaths indicated the worst.

Elisabeth helped Kidoh the best she could, but he clearly wanted to be the vigilant physician. Eventually, she lay down in the lean-to for a short break.

To Elisabeth, it seemed her rest lasted only a few moments, but soon the morning's gentle beams shafted through the trees, and the jungle's animals noisily declared a new day. One particularly loud bird kept tweeting, "Look at me! Look at me!" Elisabeth lifted up and saw Kidoh holding Tana's head and serving her some liquid from a cupped leaf.

Kidoh glanced at Elisabeth with the slightest smile on his wrinkled, weary face. "Onyeme has been good to us through the night."

Elisabeth nodded, tears in her eyes.

Kidoh showed Elisabeth how to clean the mottled mud off of Tana. Then he hobbled away and brought back coconuts.

After eating, they half carried, half dragged the weak Tana to Kidoh's cave, hidden cleverly behind boulders and trees. Elisabeth knew she never would have found this secret place, even if she had walked directly past it.

The cave appeared as a palace by jungle standards. It was larger than the huts at Abasi's village. Light filtered through several wedged rocks, illuminating rows of unusual leaves and twigs hung upside down to dry. Herbal scents filled the room. Furniture included tables and chairs. Kidoh gently lifted Tana onto one of two bamboo beds, which set on slabs of wood.

Elisabeth noticed many shelves, wedged into the walls and lined with small clay pots. *These containers must hold Kidoh's medicines,* she assumed. Also on the shelves were feathers and shriveled animal bodies and bones.

A large table against the back wall bore piles of haphazard objects —pots, dishes, books, and clothing. Sitting next to it dominated an enormous hand-carved English chair, which seemed ridiculously out of place. It reassured Elisabeth that these pieces of familiarity had traveled over the ocean, much like her, and made their way undamaged into a jungle cave.

Taking in the view she suddenly remembered, "My medicine chest! My books!"

She had forgotten her precious belongings were now somewhere in the rainforest! She pleaded with Kidoh, "Will you help me find them?"

"I will find them," he declared. "You tend to Tana. Get her to drink this." He handed Elisabeth a small vial and then disappeared so quickly Elisabeth had no time to protest.

Elisabeth sat beside Tana, slightly amused she was servant to her servant. Without resentment, she thanked God this girl lived! Tana's coloring appeared slightly better, and she rested soundly. Elisabeth lifted the girl's head and gently shook her awake to offer a few drops of Kidoh's medicine mixed with coconut water. The exhausted Tana complied and then slid from Elisabeth's arm and slept.

While Tana rested, Elisabeth gravitated to the books on Kidoh's table and marveled to find a hefty copy of John Parkinson's *Theatrum Botanicum.* What a welcomed challenge to decipher the Latin and study the woodcut sketches of many plants. When Kidoh returned, he placed Elisabeth's medicine chest and books on his table of treasures.

"I cannot believe it!" she said tearfully. "My books and chest! This is another miracle!" She leaped up and touched her valuables.

Kidoh removed her hand from the books. "I am sorry, Mrs. Allerton, but Tana was bringing these belongings to me. If you lost them, they cannot be yours." He said it as if he had owned them always.

Elisabeth pursed her lips. She had to speak evenly. "Sir, these belong to me. I lost them when coming to this island."

"They were in the possession of another owner," Kidoh replied absently. He touched Tana's face and examined her hand.

Elisabeth clenched her teeth and tried again. "Sir, these books and this chest are very dear to me. How did you acquire them?"

Kidoh grunted again. He drank some water from a bucket. Then he sat in his English chair and lit his pipe. He motioned for Elisabeth to sit on a stool nearby.

"Kidoh understands your desires." A perfectly formed circle of smoke wobbled into the air.

Elisabeth resisted speaking and waited. Satisfied that his student learned some Carib patience, he said, "I sell medicines through a friend in the town. He said a fat Englishman offered these books and the chest in exchange for a little money and some of my potions."

"Dr. Stillingfleet!" Elisabeth said out loud. Would that man continue to try her, even in this place? Was he not a prisoner any longer? She would inquire of Mr. Richardson.

"Sir, is there any work I could do to get my—I mean—these books and the chest back? They are very dear to me."

Kidoh laughed. "When bartering, Mrs. Allerton, you should never let the person know that what he has is valuable. You have to learn this to survive here. I will think about what we can arrange."

More perfectly formed circles filled the air.

Elisabeth wanted to press, but she knew she must have patience. She asked with just a hint of sarcasm, "Do you mind if I read *your* books while I am here?"

"Of course not," Kidoh said. "You have helped with my Tana. I think she will recover, but she will be weak for a long time. It is best for you to stay here and watch over her."

Elisabeth was relieved to hear Tana would recover, but it concerned her a little to stay with this strange, old man. A sly old fox, Mr. Richardson had said. She must be careful.

"I hope you will teach me about your medicines, Kidoh. I have much to learn as you have said."

Kidoh gave a slight smile of approval, and Elisabeth smiled sweetly back.

She checked on Tana before she went to her books, touching them like long lost friends. She picked up her Bible and sighed. This offered strength to help her continue. What an amazing gift God had placed in her hands, just when she needed it the most.

Chapter 27

Kidoh's Hut

In the following weeks, Elisabeth's expectation of secluded rest shattered. Unexpectedly, but as regular as forest rain, someone called out for Kidoh. Then the old man sprang into action, grabbed his medicine bag, slipped through the cave's back entrance, circled around, and startled his searching visitor.

Sometimes, Kidoh treated the patient where he found him on the path. Other times, Kidoh blindfolded the guest and spun him around before they entered the cave. "Doctor" Kidoh pulled teeth, prescribed herbal powders, uttered incantations, offered counsel, and received island news in a language that still baffled Elisabeth. Grateful, bartering patients brought much to eat and drink as well as various English and French artifacts.

Elisabeth asked Kidoh if it were prudent for his guests to see her since she hid from the authorities. He grunted, "They would pay a heavier price than you if this hiding place was betrayed."

When Tana begged Elisabeth to brush "fire hair," Elisabeth knew her servant felt better. Elisabeth handed her the brush, secretly hoping the activity would make her hair grow faster. Tana tucked away any fallen red strands in a tiny pouch.

"What use are they, Tana?" inquired Elisabeth. The girl shrugged but touched the pouch as if she possessed gold coins.

Elisabeth managed to use rope and clothing from Kidoh's treasure table to cobble privacy around one of the bamboo beds. Her "wall" looked like a village clothesline. It displayed a guard's scarlet-lined blue coat, a peasant girl's speckled grey dress, a lady's green silk gown with yellow ribbons, a friar's brown robe, and a sailor's red breeches. Fortunately, Kidoh found Elisabeth's wall of clothing very amusing. Otherwise, she knew he would insist she return his belongings to the table. Kidoh and Tana sometimes popped their heads through the sailor's breeches to see what Elisabeth did and then laughed at her startled expression. The grandfather and granddaughter did not share her modesty, and Elisabeth knew it futile to insist on such matters. She learned to ignore them, and they lost interest teasing her.

Behind her cloth wall, she could rest and think. Stripped down to her linen nightgown—the only Puritan remnant she had secretly stuffed into her seaman's britches—she fanned herself with Kidoh's Spanish black-laced treasure. She definitely had better appreciation for cooler native garb.

Wearing her nightgown helped her in another way. It reminded Elisabeth who she was and where she belonged. This strange island offered no home! She vowed that once she got off St. Paola, no one would ever learn she donned men's apparel—even if the excuse to save her life was just. She doubted clucking Puritan women and crowing elders would ever declare nonconformity as a valid excuse.

Daily Bible reading and prayers also strengthened Elisabeth. Sometimes, it seemed as if the words were tailored just for her. She clung to Psalms 139 as a prayer for herself and her unborn child. She wrote the words carefully into her journal.

O Lord, thou hast tried me, and known me.
Thou knowest my sitting and my rising:
thou understandest my thought afar off.

Thou compassest my paths, and my lying down,
and art accustomed to all my ways.
For there is not a word in my tongue,
but lo, thou knowest it wholly, O Lord.
Thou holdest me strait behind and before,
and layest thine hand upon me.
Thy knowledge is too wonderful for me:
it is so high that I cannot attain unto it.
Whither shall I go from thy Spirit?
or whither shall I flee from thy presence?
If I ascend into heaven, thou art there:
if I lie down in hell, thou art there.
Let me take the wings of the morning,
and dwell in the uttermost parts of the sea:
Yet thither shall thine hand lead me,
and thy right hand hold me.
If I say, Yet the darkness shall hide me,
even the night shall be light about me.
Yea, the darkness hideth not from thee:
but the night shineth as the day:
the darkness and light are both alike.
For thou hast possessed my reins:
thou hast covered me in my mother's womb.
I will praise thee, for I am
fearfully and wondrously made:
marvelous are thy works, and my soul knoweth it well.
My bones are not hid from thee, though I was made in a secret place,
and fashioned beneath in the earth.
Thine eyes did see me, when I was without form:
for in thy book were all things written,
which in continuance were fashioned,
when there was none of them before.
How dear therefore are thy thoughts unto me,
O God! how great is the sum of them!

If I should count them, they are more than the sand:
when I awake, I am still with thee.

Elisabeth believed these words were as true for her and her baby as they had been for King David. God's hand lay on her and her days, in the past and in the future, no matter where she journeyed, no matter how difficult the surroundings. She believed the One, who "holdest me strait behind and before," would not abandon her or this baby, woven in secret. Most of the time her faith held because the unseen seemed as real to her as her hand and foot. She could not explain this peace, but she was grateful for it.

A few days of keeping her tongue finally led Kidoh to offer a bargain. He proposed he would give her any book from his "library," but only if she first read it out loud to him.

He declared, "Once I hear the words, I know a book and have no need of it anymore."

She almost laughed, but his stern expression stopped her. Then she felt compelled to chastise such arrogance and defend the Bible's uniqueness to be reread throughout one's life. She held back.

Elisabeth realized there would be no use in pointing out that earning back *her* books by reading every word was an unreasonable, if not impossible, undertaking. Kidoh had the advantage.

By candlelight each evening, she read out loud from Bible stories and medical receipts. Kidoh and Tana listened to everything. Elisabeth wondered how much they understood. Their blank expressions made her think they were not listening, but if she paused, Kidoh would order, "Go on. More."

Other times, he would interrupt with a wave of his hand. "Skip that part. I do not like all these tribal wars of people I do not know. I want stories tonight."

The sure signal she could stop reading came when Kidoh stood up and went outside to relieve himself. Then she closed the book, prepared for bed, and found lonely solace behind her wall.

Elisabeth continued to write in her journal, tracking what she learned, taking notes on plants Kidoh explained to her. She drew each plant the best she could and helped Kidoh find and dry them. He grunted approval rarely, even though she worked very hard to do his bidding. She knew any day Kidoh might ask her to read from the journal. If he did, she resolved to skip over the most private details. Her writing solace comforted almost as much as the reassuring kicks of her baby. She longed to place David's hand on her belly and have him feel the jabs that reminded her of a playful colt. She visualized her husband's pleased smile.

Occasionally, Colin came to visit. He brought delicious plantains with rice and beans prepared by Angelique's Clare. While eating together, he told them encouraging news that the boar hunts went well. They were making good money for passage to Boston, or so he reassured Elisabeth. She still could not discern when he lied.

If she pressed for details, he shut down and smoked a pipe with Kidoh. The two men conversed in French, which Elisabeth felt unfair. She pretended she did not care.

"You carry well, Mrs. Allerton," Colin commented.

She flushed, but she knew he tried to be polite. "Thank you, Mr. Richardson. I feel like a whale."

He laughed, tapping his pipe. "No, no, I know whales. You are not that big—yet."

Early in her stay with Kidoh, she implored, "Is there any way to get a letter to Mr. Allerton? Any way at all?"

Colin winced at the request. His voice strained out, "I suppose we could use some of our precious, hard-earned money to trust a seaman to move a letter along. But there are no guarantees."

He definitely was irritated, but Elisabeth pressed on.

"Sir, I feel I must try if there is any way—at least one letter." She whispered, "He might think I am dead because of my silence."

Colin softened and finally said, "By all means, pen a letter, if you must."

She happily asked Kidoh for paper. He said he had none. But he suggested he had already given her pen and ink to write in "his" journal. She tore out a page. Kidoh snorted protest. Elisabeth ignored him and began writing. When she finished and folded the paper, she handed the letter to Colin and prayed. She wondered how many hands would touch and read her message before it reached her husband. She did not even have a proper seal.

Later, Colin gave Angelique the folded letter and asked her to affix her waxed seal upon it. Angelique placed Elisabeth's letter and one from herself into a leather pouch. She handed this to her loyal confidante, Gerard, who took it to a French fisherman at Stubby's Tavern. The fisherman then sailed his skiff to a nearby English island where he traded and kept a mistress.

The mistress passed the pouch on to one of her sailor friends serving under a reckless captain who bucked winter advice and sailed to Boston with a load of sugar cane. After a harrowing time at sea, the ship reached Boston. The sailor inquired at his favorite tavern, The Pig's Whistle, about finding someone who traveled to Dorchester. As fate would have it, a merchant had a cousin who lived there, and he planned to visit him shortly. He even knew where the Allertons lived.

Thus, it happened Elisabeth's letter arrived in Dorchester the day before David was to marry widow Mary Rogers. Throughout the long months David convinced many Dorchester residents that he, too, as a widower, grieved. Indeed, he believed it himself until the good merchant presented David with a stained pouch. Taking it forebodingly, David dismissed the man with a chilly thank-you. Alone, he hesitated to open the contents.

"What is it?" his wife-to-be inquired as she carried little Isaac into their front room.

David shrugged and opened the pouch, finding two sealed

papers. He broke the seal on the larger one from a Mademoiselle Angelique Gervais and read the following:

Sir, enclosed is a message from your wife, Elisabeth Allerton. We bring you good news that she is not dead and is attempting to reunite with you. She is, however, hiding from officials here in St. Paola and is in great danger.

Monsieur Allerton, your immediate intervention could do much to secure her safety. I advise you to direct inquiries to our Viceroy, Jacques de la Roche. Please respond with the greatest expediency.

Mary broke into his reading, asking, "Is the letter bad news, David?" Her face was pinched and pale as she kept her distance from him and bounced little Isaac.

"I am not sure what to make of this, Mary. It appears it is a business prospect from the West Indies, of all places," he lied and shook his head. He needed to think. "Someone is making an inquiry to see if our family is interested in trading dried cod for sugar. Sounds unusual, but it is something I will have to sort out. Maybe the other paper in the pouch will bring more enlightenment."

He recovered so readily that Mary nodded her head and said, "I hoped it would be word about dear Elisabeth. If we only knew what happened to her...that would be so much better than imagining the many horrible ways she could have died."

David quickly folded the paper and put it back in the pouch. He moved to hug Mary and little Isaac.

"Mary, sweet Mary, concerned about Elisabeth after all these months. I know how difficult this is for you, too, but some fates are simply God's mysteries. We must accept them and press on in faith."

Mary nodded, sniffling, "I know, I know, and I try to push thimblefuls of doubt away from trusting in God's providence. Living in the past does us no good in this new land. I thank God for you, David Allerton! What would I have done without your help?"

She leaned into her future husband as he wiped away her tears. Smiling slightly, she patted his chest and sighed. "I will leave you to think on these matters. I have much to attend."

David took the pouch to his chair by the hearth. It was good Mary trusted him with marriage. He knew a few wagging tongues advised her against the matter—they said the couple should wait a while longer, just in case miraculous news of Mrs. Allerton came to bear. Others understood the pragmatic act to move on with life. David and Mary agreed God had brought them together to console one another after Elisabeth's kidnapping and after her Jonathan died of consumption on the *Sea Venture*. Most villagers seemed sympathetic of their plight.

And now David wondered if someone played a cruel trick on him by having these documents arrive the night before his wedding. He turned Elisabeth's letter over and surmised that the paper looked similar to her journal pages. Was it even possible she survived? He had not imagined such a miracle.

As he broke the seal and unfolded the letter, he braced himself. It was Elisabeth's handwriting.

My dear David, my dearest husband,

I must be brief, but there is so much in my heart I desire to share with you. Be assured God's mercies have kept me safe and well! I am in hiding on the French island of St. Paola, waiting for winter to pass with the hopes of finding a ship to Boston.

I have news that will surprise you. Please know with certainty that I wanted to tell you on the Sea Venture, *but the timing never seemed right with all our duties. Forgive me for that error, but you must know this truth. If God so wills that this letter be in your hands, I gladly tell you that I am great with child! Our baby, dear husband, will be born in March, Lord willing! God has protected us through much that I long to share with you. The seaman Colin Richardson has been a great assistance to me.*

David stopped reading, clenching his hand. Trickery! Colin Richardson! That scum sailor aided her! He had not counted on such a wretch serving anyone's purposes but his own. And why was Elisabeth in hiding? What deeds had she done with Richardson? David could not accept that Colin Richardson was a man of any honorable virtues. He read on:

My dear husband, keep faith and pray with me. I know God is going to reunite our family. Under his protection, I hope to arrive in the summer, when more ships sail. There is so much I want to write, but I must hurry. Pray and keep faith that I will be able to reunite with you.

Always, your loving wife,

Elisabeth.

Mary reappeared at the door. "David?" She could not make out the meaning of his grim expression.

David quickly folded the letter. "Mary, I just read another letter in this pouch, and there is news about Elisabeth! Prepare yourself, my dearest. It is not good."

"What? What is it?" Mary held her breath.

"It seems that Elisabeth was brought to the island of St. Paola. This letter writer, who calls herself Mademoiselle Angelique Gervais, reports Elisabeth died shortly after arriving there. This Gervais woman says poor Elisabeth had attentive care, but the tropical afflictions were too much for her."

David shook his head in faked sadness, and tears glistened in his eyes.

"Oh, David, I am so sorry! I know this news was what we presumed happened, but do you not think we should delay our wedding?" Mary played a role, too. She knew her future husband hid something, but she did not want to know. She refused to press and know more.

"No, no, postponing our wedding serves no purpose. Perhaps this has come at such a time as this so we can enter our marriage unhindered with doubts. Yes, I believe this letter's arrival is good and proper. It is a comfort to me that Elisabeth did not die without care."

David marveled that lying and pretending should be so easy for him. He could even convince himself that Elisabeth was as good as dead. Should her absence by hundreds of miles hinder his wellbeing?

She was penniless. How could she ever make it to Boston? He could not fathom such a selfish soul as Richardson allowing her to burden him for long. Then there were the rumors that France and England might go to war. Under such circumstances, David could safely wager Elisabeth would never make it back to him. How would he ever be certain this baby belonged to him? No, there would be no letter or money sent to St. Paola by his hand.

He turned to Mary and said what he truly believed. "We must live in the present, dear Mary. I thank God I have a sweet and understanding woman by my side. The good and cherished Elisabeth is in God's hands, and we will be comforted with that knowledge."

David folded the letter and put it in the pouch.

Mary rushed to comfort him. "Oh, David, this is such a trial for you, but I share your sentiments. May dear, sweet Elisabeth's soul rest in peace."

What most mattered to Mary was that in just one day David Allerton would be her husband and her son would have a father. She, too, could lay the first Mrs. Allerton to rest.

Chapter 28

The Move, The Plan

January came. At seven months along, Elisabeth fumed over clumsiness. She waddled like a duck and could not bend over on first attempts. Other than this awkwardness, she marveled at her jungle health. Perhaps Kidoh's teas helped. He reassured her no libation she drank would induce sleep. He even showed the herbal sleeping potion he used on Colin and gave her a sample wrapped in muslin cloth.

"Mr. Richardson may need it again," he chuckled, and Elisabeth burst out laughing.

One day, a young man from Abasi's village came and announced that Tana and Elisabeth must return to the village with him. The only one who seemed surprised by the news was Elisabeth. Tana, adequately recovered, readied her bag.

Elisabeth, however, needed time to pack. She did not want to damage any of the herbs and powders she and Kidoh prepared during the weeks of her stay. She knew the medicine man exercised patience with her as she tried to pry knowledge from him.

She asked Kidoh to teach her only about healing plants, even though he also wanted to teach her about his animal bones and medicine chants. That kind of knowledge made her uncomfortable. She had heard stories of dark magic from Africa, and she refused to give the devil this foothold. As she gathered her belongings and carefully put them into her bag, her eyes rested on her Bible, journal, the book of receipts, and other medical books.

"Kidoh, what about these books?" she asked cautiously.

"Did you finish reading any of them to me?" he retorted.

Reluctantly, she replied, "Only the book of receipts."

"Very well. Take that one. And, I give you your journal—I have no use for it. Take the quills and inkwell you used for I have enough," he declared. "I keep the medicine chest and other books. They are useful to me."

Her heart sank. That medicine chest and its contents were something she thought she might use as barter to get to Boston. Also, David's gift was one more tangible thread linking her to him. What were the chances of her ever returning to Kidoh's cave to retrieve the chest and her Bible? She resigned herself again to their loss.

"Thank you, Kidoh. You have been very kind to me, and I have learned much from you." She meant it and curtsied.

He grunted, and Elisabeth believed he did not think she had learned much at all.

She took one last look at her lost books and the chest. Then she grabbed the book of receipts, her journal, quills, and inkwell before the medicine man changed his mind.

"Goodbye, Mrs. Allerton. We will meet again," the old man said so assuredly that Elisabeth nodded in agreement.

When they returned to Abasi's village, there was much laughter and hugs. The village women made as much fuss over Elisabeth as they did Tana, touching her hair, giggling and patting her belly.

Colin translated, "They say you have become a real healer, Mrs. Allerton, because you have spent time with the great Kidoh. Kidoh shares his secrets with few; you should feel honored."

Elisabeth shrugged. "I do not think I learned enough from Kidoh. I hesitate to use what he taught me. An apprentice learns by spending months with a master, not weeks." She added helplessly, "Some of his herbs are poisonous in high doses. I tried to write down what I could, but Kidoh is not very patient with receipts. He taps his head and says, 'Keep in here. Keep in here.'"

"Given that bit of information, Mrs. Allerton, I change my mind about seeking your skills for an aching tooth."

Elisabeth could not tell if Colin jested as he quickly walked away. That man! She knew remedies for toothaches! That was basic!

In Tana's honor for overcoming death, the villagers celebrated with food and drink. There were beans and rice, roasted pork, fruit pudding, roasted squash and yams, ale and rum. Several times, Tana repeated her story of survival. There were many interruptions and teasing. Elisabeth was pleased her shy apprentice enjoyed this attention. She assumed Tana's gestures of pointing at her and cupping her hands in prayer meant that she and God were part of her story.

Long before the fires died, Elisabeth returned to her hut and massaged her back and belly. If this baby were a girl, she would name her Abigail, after her mother. If it were a boy, she would name him John David, after her father and husband. She was quite certain David would not object. It saddened her to make such decisions without him. But what else could she do?

Elisabeth determined Colin must find a proper place to deliver her baby when the time was near. She wondered if Angelique would help her. She felt uneasy about having this baby in the jungle. She must press Colin for a plan—when he was sober.

As it turned out, a scruffy, hung-over Colin appeared at her hut entrance the next morning.

"A little too much celebrating, Mr. Richardson?" she asked, already dressed and writing in her journal.

"No, I think just the right amount. I am fine," he yawned.

"Yes, I can see that," she replied with the thinnest smile.

"We need to discuss where you will have your baby, Mrs. Allerton." He stretched his arms before squatting beside her.

She was surprised he broached the subject, so she tried to overlook his tone of boredom. Her thoughts spilled out. "Oh yes, I agree. Is it possible Angelique could help me? Could I stay with her—in hiding, of course? I really would feel safer having my baby in a bed rather than on a mat."

She rambled. While he held one hand to his head, the other hand pressed for her to stop.

"Yes, yes, Angelique will help you, but a midwife she is not." He chuckled at the thought.

Elisabeth looked perplexed. What other options were there?

He paused, scratched his head, and knew he had to be persuasive. "Berko and I have a plan."

"Berko! How is he?"

"Oh, as good as he can be these days. His people, who work on the plantations, have knowledge that a ship is scheduled to anchor in early spring with much needed supplies. They also will carry servant hirelings and slaves. The plan is for us to slip you into the ship's queue as a servant and place you on Berko's former plantation. It will not be easy, but with a little luck, it is doable."

"What? This sounds impossible and foolhardy! Surely the authorities will notice an extra servant! They certainly have not forgotten about you and me in just a few months!"

"Hear me out, Mrs. Allerton. Berko has done this sort of thing before—actually just one time with a man—a slave—and he moved him out, not in, but it did work, so he thinks we can do it again. Angelique, too, believes this plan has a chance. With your nursing skills, you should be able to adapt to Ross Hall, and no one else from the ship will be serving inside the house."

Elisabeth felt panic gnawing her composure. "What will I do? How can I masquerade in such fashion? This is the best plan you can offer?"

"The plantation owner is Angelique's father—Louis Gervais, a man who is very ill."

Colin tried to keep his words even so Elisabeth would not notice his hatred for the name that felt like grit in his mouth. Elisabeth, now quite pale, seemed too intent on hearing his words to notice any unease.

Colin continued, "Gervais has an old faithful servant named Adele. Angelique says Adele is exhausted and needs extra help to care for Gervais. Your job will be to convince Adele that you are trustworthy and skilled in medicine."

Elisabeth could not speak. The plan sounded too preposterous, but Colin continued on as if it were no more difficult than rowing a boat.

"According to Angelique, Adele has placed full confidence in a slave named Zena to care for Gervais. But there is something about this arrangement that Angelique finds troubling. Gervais is getting worse."

To Colin, the thought of Gervais dying cheered him, but he kept his voice neutral. "Angelique wants to convince her family that she bargained for you at the dock so she could place you at Ross Hall."

"Bargained for me! Like a slave?" Elisabeth could barely squeak out this unbelievable idea.

"Angelique will have her people in place to make the transaction. With a little bit of luck—or as you say, 'miracle from your God'—we can do this without the Viceroy and his soldiers realizing anything suspicious. Then, you will be settled in a cozy Ross Hall bed when your baby comes."

Elisabeth found this plan very unsettling. Surely there should be a better way. "Sir, I do not know what to say. It sounds dangerous and crazy. There will be questions and suspicions about my pregnancy." Then the thought came to her. "And I speak so little French!"

"The Gervais family speaks English as well as French. Angelique thinks you should pretend to be the English widow of a Frenchman and—"

Her mind raced. She interrupted as she touched her hair. "My hair has not grown out to a proper length. Besides, I hate lies and deception! I doubt I can be convincing!"

Colin glared, his headache getting worse. "Mrs. Allerton, you must commit to this plan or risk getting captured by the authorities. Your baby should not be born in the jungle. This is the best offer you will get. Certainly, your hair is a problem—not so much the length as that blasted red robin color. You know it shouts, 'Here is Mrs. Allerton, the one the authorities have been searching for. And surely that sailor Colin Richardson, who helped her escape, must not be far from her side.' Listen to me, there are no safe plans! Besides, a servant's scarf will cover your flames, but you will have to hide that temper."

Colin was irritated with this woman's seeming inability to comprehend bigger dangers, not just for herself but also for others who risked much for her. He stood up to leave and scowled down at her.

"Mrs. Allerton, we are out of choices. Be ready. As soon as this ship approaches harbor, we will move you to Angelique's cottage, and at that time, we will have to act quickly."

He walked off, leaving Elisabeth restless as she worried over such a dubious plan.

Chapter 29

Hair Dye

As Colin predicted, Elisabeth's village stay came to an abrupt halt. She had just resumed helping the women smoke the meat when a guest appeared in the village.

A French man with grizzled hair and beard, he walked with a limp. From his waist hung a long sword that almost touched the ground, and a pistol handle stuck out of his trousers. Elisabeth could sense this outsider's presence raised tension among the villagers.

But Abasi knew him and greeted him. The man explained that Angelique had sent him to return Elisabeth to her cottage. Abasi beckoned to Elisabeth. She wiped her hands on her apron and stood before the two men.

"Madame Allerton, I am Gerard Lacoste. Mademoiselle Angelique requested I bring you to her." The man slightly bowed, but his voice bore no friendliness. He did not ask, but ordered, "Quickly gather your belongings so we can make it to Mademoiselle Angelique's cottage by sunset."

Because she had taken Colin's advice to be prepared, it only took her a few moments to throw last items into a sturdy bag that Neesa had taught her to weave. Neesa and the other women gathered around her, touching her and offering their blessings.

"Thank you. I will remember you always," she said, trying not to cry. They just chuckled and spoke soothingly in Carib.

Tana came with head bowed. Elisabeth doubted whether she had taught the lazy girl much, but in companionship, they had forged friendship.

"Tana. I will miss you. Thank you for helping me."

Tana looked up at Elisabeth and opened her hand to offer a shell necklace.

Elisabeth gasped, eyeing the speckled blue, purple, and pearl shells. "Oh, Tana! How beautiful! Thank you."

As the girl stood there awkwardly, Elisabeth understood something was expected of her in return. But what could she give? She hesitantly reached into her bag and pulled out Angelique's French hairbrush. She hated to let it go, but the beaming girl quickly grabbed it and ran off.

"Mrs. Allerton, you have been a useful guest in our village. You may come back if you wish," Abasi declared without emotion, his hands resting on his hips.

"Thank you, sir." She curtsied, knowing the chief gave her a generous invitation and would expect her to appreciate this honor. "Thank you for welcoming me."

Abasi raised his hand to her. "May Onyame guide you and your baby well in your journey to your husband."

Gerard Lacoste grew restless. He pushed his walking stick into Elisabeth's hand and took her bag. Before she knew it, she waddled after the limping man into jungle thickness. Any evidence of the village soon disappeared in a wall of greens.

Gerard retraced his path, cutting more branches with his sword and sending insects in all directions. Elisabeth attempted conversation, but this was met with deaf ears. The last rays of a beautiful sunset illuminated the quiet, blue bay as Elisabeth hugged a welcoming Angelique. Her cottage indeed was refuge.

The next day, Angelique watched with amusement as Elisabeth wolfed down eggs, cheese, bread, and fruit that Clare generously prepared.

As Elisabeth chewed the last bit of mango, Angelique declared, "Your hair is a problem."

Elisabeth touched her head and nodded.

"Ah, yes. Maybe, maybe, it can work." Angelique thought out loud. She quickly rose and grabbed a bowl, flask of wine, and some dark purple fruit that looked like plums.

"What are you doing?" Elisabeth found this woman's sudden enthusiasm unsettling.

"You will see! Trust me," Angelique said as she attacked the plums with much pummeling, and then added the dark red wine and indigo dye. She paused and examined her mix in disappointment, "Too purple."

"What?" Elisabeth feared to ask her outright if she meant to put that awful concoction on her head.

"Ah, I know the secret ingredient." She shouted to Clare in French, and Clare returned with a small bottle of ink. Angelique grabbed it and poured more than a few drops into her mix. As she stirred, she added more, declaring, "This will work! I imagine the King's royal court would buzz with envy. And my sister-in-law Isabella would love to get her hands on this. Yes?"

"Angelique, I do not think this idea of yours is the answer."

"We will see. Please come outside, Madame Elisabeth."

Angelique picked up her bowl, swished to the door, and expected Elisabeth to follow. "Come on, come on. This will take time. Sit!" she ordered, standing by a wooden bench. As Elisabeth obeyed, Angelique grabbed one of Clare's bed covers from the clothesline and swirled it around Elisabeth.

"Do not move a muscle. But do not worry, my friend. I have watched Isabella pamper her coiffure in many ways! This is no different." Angelique used her hands to massage the dye into Elisabeth's red hair.

Shocked by Angelique's enthusiasm, Elisabeth stiffened.

Angelique stopped. "Why resist? You know we need to try." And for emphasis, she boldly poured more dye on Elisabeth's head and vigorously scrubbed.

This preposterous situation and the ridiculous charade she soon would face overcame Elisabeth. She started chuckling, and Angelique scrubbed more seriously. She began laughing. Angelique paused and peered at her with hands thoroughly covered in black mess. Elisabeth pointed at her hands and laughed until tears started falling. She could not remember the last time she had laughed so hard.

Angelique chuckled, "You English women are crazy!" Then she kept massaging the dye into disappearing red hair.

When Elisabeth caught her breath, she asked, "Angelique, are you a miracle worker or a sorcerer? Wise beyond your years or just plain crazy?"

"Oui! I am all of those things," she said, shrugging and massaging. She finished and stared at her black hands. "Mon Dieu! How will I get this off?"

Elisabeth sweated under the baking sun for a very long time. Then, Angelique dipped numerous pitchers of water from a barrel and rinsed the plum pieces out of Elisabeth's hair. She held a small mirror to Elisabeth's face with an approving smile. The short, wet hair was raven black.

"We will find the appropriate servant's scarf for you, and no one will know you are a redhead. In fact, you will be a fashionable grieving widow."

Elisabeth stared at the mirror and did not recognize herself. She had always wondered what she would look like without her red hair. But it was not the only difference. She looked a little plumper from her pregnancy and, despite her best efforts, tanner, which actually blended the scattering of freckles across her nose. Her eyes projected a deeper blue within a frame of black hair.

But there was something else. The innocent girl's face she remembered as her own no longer existed. The one staring back at her looked only faintly familiar, like a fading memory.

After recovering from the shock of her image, she sighed, determined to accept the Elisabeth she was. In spite of all the changes to her body and mind, she knew her position, her destiny, was with David as his wife and mother to their child. Without that, who could she be? She felt a flicker of hope and fear. Could she really impersonate the widow of a Frenchman and become a servant on a French plantation as easily as one changed hair color?

Chapter 30

The Market Place

Angelique rehearsed the plan with Elisabeth over and over again, making her repeat answers about her fake husband's death, what he liked and disliked, how they met, what he died from, even how she felt about being married to a Frenchman. "If we fail, it will not be because you do not know your story," Angelique declared, finally satisfied with Elisabeth's answers.

The *St. Therese* had been spotted the day before on the horizon. The announcement came that the ship would unload its cargo that very morning. *St. Therese* had wintered at Nevis, but fair weather and a restless captain brought his ship to St. Paola for eager trading. Rumor was there were thirty servants and some twenty slaves aboard the *St. Therese*. The town's people, pent up with desires and tired of rationing supplies over winter, were eager for the ship's cargo of wine, cloth, spices, gunpowder, and other goods.

Thanks to Angelique, Elisabeth would be dressed in a fashionable blue cloak. Elisabeth thought the covering made no sense in such a warm climate, but Angelique shrugged, as she wriggled her hands into pink gloves with green lace. "Women do much for fashion, even on St. Paola. The servants will wear their best to be well placed. You will see."

Thanks to Clare, Elisabeth also had newly-acquired servant's clothing—a plain, loose brown dress with an apron. Tucked in one of the apron's pockets was a grey-colored headscarf that would go over her hair at the appropriate moment.

Elisabeth kept pressing Angelique. "How can people not notice me, a stranger, trying to line up as a servant? How can I change disguises in a crowd without drawing attention to myself?"

"Most eyes will be on the *St. Therese*. We only need to create an illusion. You will see. This plan will work," Angelique said, redirecting the conversation. "Fortunately, we have cooler weather this morning—at least for a little while."

"It is time," Clare announced, and Angelique gave one final approval to Elisabeth's hair and clothes.

"Oh, I almost forgot, one last addition," Angelique said as she handed Elisabeth a black silk pouch.

Elisabeth felt the coins inside. "Oh no, Angelique. I cannot take this."

"You must!" she commanded. "Servants from *St. Therese* could be a threat to you. They will know you are an impostor. You may need to silence them."

"Bribes!?"

"Oui, with a warning that they will find themselves cut down in their sleep if they say a word to anyone! My people will make that very clear, but you, too, may have to defend your position. You have your knife, do you not?"

Elisabeth faltered. She did not have Angelique's resolve, but she nodded weakly.

"Good." Angelique eyed her skeptically. "You must be on the alert at all times. Think of your baby. You must be strong, Elisabeth!"

Elisabeth sighed. When would this all end? Could she justify any of these actions? Were there any alternatives besides being an impostor or facing imprisonment or death? This insane world sunk her deeper into its follies.

Elisabeth vaguely recalled a Bible story about the Apostle Paul hiding himself in a basket to escape death. Certainly, the brilliant man must have wondered how he had come to such contrivances. His successful basket escape did not provide her much comfort. She also remembered he was whipped, stoned, shipwrecked, and bitten by a viper.

In her opinion, God's will seemed only to be known by God. The Sovereign Lord sometimes saved and sometimes did not. He had his reasons, but she wanted physical rescue, reassurance, and rest. Was asking for safety too much?

"Let us go," Angelique commanded, shaking Elisabeth out of her meditation. Angelique sounded happy as she called out, "Clare! Gerard!"

Elisabeth, trembling, realized this woman came more alive as danger drew nearer.

Gerard heaved Elisabeth's bag onto his back and gave her the faintest of smiles, which made Elisabeth wonder if he thought this a hopeless mission. His strength amazed her. He steadily moved under the load even as he limped, carrying his stick.

Angelique proudly led the group as Clare and Gerard flanked Elisabeth. They quickly made their way down the hill path toward the harbor. Many townspeople had already gathered for *St. Therese's* unloading.

Elisabeth kept her head low, but the busy marketplace had a thrill about it that caught her curiosity. People were excited and happy to have new wares landing on their island. She marveled that this buzzing place existed so closely to the jungle's different rhythm.

Her enthusiasm turned to sickening dismay when she saw the caged area of half-naked Africans, chained like animals. Many seemed defeated and damaged from their overseas ordeal. How different they were from Berko and Kidoh. Their faces were maps of sorrow. *Oh, Lord have mercy* was all she could pray.

Thoughts were interrupted by the approaching voice of a young Frenchman. "Angelique! Angelique!" Elisabeth turned her head away to view the ship's activity as the tall man rushed to greet Angelique.

"Eduard!" Angelique quickly embraced her dark-haired brother, kissing him on both cheeks. Clare and Gerard elbowed Elisabeth farther away from brother and sister, pointing to something near the ship. He must not notice her until she had gone through the *St. Therese's* servant queue.

Still within earshot, Elisabeth could not understand the siblings' rapid French, but she picked out "Poppa," "Adele," and "Isabella." Earlier, Angelique described her sister-in-law Isabella by saying the angels were so intent on fashioning her beauty that they forgot to give her any common sense. How different she would be from Angelique!

Eduard and Angelique nodded in sympathetic agreement about Adele. Elisabeth guessed Angelique softened him up for her proposal of an additional nurse.

Fortunately, Eduard's overseer approached him to consult on slave bidding. Angelique blew her brother a kiss and took the distraction to move her little group farther from him to the edge of the crowd. Near this area, a clerk gave directions and examined entrance papers of the disembarking servants.

Elisabeth whispered to Angelique, "I still do not understand how I can change—"

She was interrupted by a pistol shot. In a simultaneous wave, the crowd jolted and ducked and then craned their necks to watch two men fighting on the pier. They were knocking over barrels as they stumbled and fought.

"Mr. Richardson!" Elisabeth whispered, recognizing his form.

She started to move closer, but Angelique grabbed her arm, "Elisabeth, no! It is time!"

As the crowd gave its attention to the fight, Clare untied Elisabeth's cloak and put it in her bag. Angelique grabbed the servant scarf from Clare and with a few flicks of her hands secured it on Elisabeth's hair. She then placed fake identification papers in Elisabeth's hand. Gerard blocked this transformation with his body, pointing to the fight and yelling with the crowd. Elisabeth straightened her apron, adjusting her dagger and coin purse, as Angelique led her to the servants' line.

French soldiers pushed through the crowd to get to Colin and his adversary. Colin punched the man solidly across the jaw and ran down the dock, into the village.

Elisabeth knew Colin could outrun any French soldiers, whose drawn swords glistened in the sunlight and quickly parted the crowd. *God bless that man! Mr. Richardson has risked capture for my baby and me!* Elisabeth thought. The man certainly had his faults, but he continued to surprise her.

When the uproar quieted down, the servants resumed their queue. The last man in line turned around and eyed her, surprised and suspicious.

"Where did you come from?" he asked in French.

Angelique scowled at him and waved a gloved hand, flicking him away like a fly. Gerard enforced her displeasure by moving his hand to the handle of his sword while whispering into his ear. The servant quickly turned around and lowered his head.

When it was their turn to address the clerk, Elisabeth handed him her fake credentials. The clerk seemed impatient to get his work completed and head for a tavern. To Elisabeth's great relief, he quickly stamped the documents and handed them to her without even a glance. Angelique snatched them from her hand and nodded to Gerard, who disappeared into the crowd. She beckoned Elisabeth and Clare to follow her to where Eduard stood.

"Eduard, I want you to meet someone who I think can help us with Poppa," she said.

With a raised eyebrow, Eduard eyed the pregnant servant briefly and said, "What do you mean, Angelique?"

"She came on the *St. Therese*, and I have secured her for Poppa's well-being. It's a miracle!" Angelique waved the false documents in her hand.

Then she continued, "Madame Elisabeth Chauvin, this is Monsieur Eduard Gervais, my brother."

"Sir, it is a pleasure to meet you." Elisabeth lowered her head and gave her best curtsy.

"Madame Chauvin," he said, tipping his hat. Turning to Angelique, he quizzed, "English, sister?"

"Oui, Eduard, hear me out," Angelique said, speaking in English for Elisabeth's sake. "Madame Chauvin was married to a respected blacksmith, Monsieur Andre Chauvin, from Normandy. He, too, had been on the *St. Therese*. Alas, he took ill and died leaving poor Madame Chauvin in this manner." Angelique paused and pointed to Elisabeth, who tried to balance pity and grief with dignity.

She rushed on, "Eduard, she has much experience in nursing. I just know she could help Poppa."

"Yes, I am trained in midwifery, sir," said Elisabeth, as she sensed Eduard's skepticism of his sister's story. "In England, I was acquainted with the famous Dr. Nicholas Culpeper. My mother, a midwife, and I worked with him on several patients. Also, I attended to the health cares of our family estate and—"

"That is, before marrying Monsieur Chauvin," Angelique interjected to Eduard, who seemed bemused by the growing story.

Elisabeth hurriedly added, glad to be telling some truth, "Yes, love and grief have altered the course of my life to put me in these circumstances. Monsieur Gervais, I simply want to earn money to be reunited with my family. I would appreciate the opportunity to serve and help your father in any way I am able."

Eduard frowned skepticism during an excruciating long pause. He knew there was more to the story, but he loved his sister. Then he finally said, "Excuse us, Madame Chauvin."

He took Angelique by the elbow and pulled her aside, speaking in French. "Angelique, you should not have made such a decision without consulting Adele or me first."

"There was no time, Eduard. I did not want this nurse to be snatched up by someone else on the island. She is valuable."

Before Eduard could protest, she argued, "And you know Adele would not agree to this because it was not her idea. She cannot take proper care of Poppa. That crazy slave woman of hers is making matters worse. We need someone with a fresh perspective on Poppa's health."

"Yes, yes, Angelique, I agree. But this woman is much with child. We will end up taking care of her and a baby, too. We will be nursing the nurse as she nurses her baby!"

"She will not be pregnant for the entire five years, Eduard. I have a feeling she and her baby will not be a bother. Let us give this a try. If it does not work out, I will find another place for her to go, I promise."

Eduard shook his head in dismay but motioned to his slave to take Elisabeth's bag that Gerard had plopped at Clare's feet. "Bring Mademoiselle Chauvin to my carriage after the auction is over and we will go to Ross Hall."

Angelique grabbed her brother's arm. "Oh, Eduard, that is another small request. May I borrow the carriage? I want to see Poppa, and I can get Mademoiselle Chauvin settled at Ross Hall."

Eduard pondered this when Angelique said, "Thank you, dear brother!" and kissed him on both cheeks, hurrying Elisabeth away and beckoning Clare to follow.

Lifting his hands in surrender, Eduard smiled and called after the women, "You are brave to take on Adele, Angelique! Come have dinner with Isabella and me. Little Theophile misses his Auntie."

"Yes, very soon, I promise. Give them my love," she responded, blowing a kiss.

Quite pleased with herself, Angelique whispered to Elisabeth, "That went well, but let us not tempt fate. We need to get out of here before there is any more excitement."

Elisabeth heartily agreed. As they moved away from the bustling crowd, she thought she caught sight of Dr. Stillingfleet trying to move closer toward them. That man! He was free! She had forgotten about him, but she would recognize his bulbous head and egg-shaped body anywhere. She lowered her head and tried to keep up with Angelique's quick steps. Clare plodded behind them with her bag.

Chapter 31

Carriage Ride

"Good day, Samuel," Angelique said briskly to Eduard's coachman. The elderly black man with gray hair and slouching shoulders wore a suit of green serge with a feathered green hat.

Angelique commanded, "Master Eduard said you will take us to Ross Hall."

Eduard's slave hesitated, but he knew better than to cross any Gervais.

"Oui, Mademoiselle Angelique," he said as he bowed and grabbed the stool to help her, Elisabeth, and Clare into the carriage.

Elisabeth touched the gold satin cushions. "I forgot such luxury existed," she marveled.

"You have been through so much, my friend," said Angelique, as she smoothed out her dress and readjusted the ribbons on her sleeves. "I think Ross Hall may be an improvement for you. Although there are some who find it constraining."

Elisabeth knew Angelique referred to herself.

"Angelique, why do you have a cottage away from your family?"

The woman looked pained. "My heart is divided into two parts," she said quietly. "I am caught between warring factions. But at least by having my own cottage I can breathe freely, and my heart hopes for change. My father is good to tolerate this arrangement, although he knows there would be hell to pay if he did not." She sighed.

"I do not understand. Would you like to explain it to me?" Elisabeth asked gently.

"No, not today. Let's enjoy the first half of our victory. The real battle is ahead," Angelique said with a faint smile. Then she briskly changed the subject. "I hope you will be able to help Poppa. He suffered some kind of a seizure several months ago. Since then, he seems to be getting weaker. Adele, his mistress, does not admit how close to death he is."

"Oh!" Elisabeth was not sure how to absorb the information that Adele was a mistress. Angelique said it so casually.

Finally, Elisabeth asked, "How shall I address Adele?"

"She really is headmistress of Ross Hall, so Madame Adele will suit her. When my mother died birthing Eduard, it was Adele who took over our care. For years, she hoped to marry my father, but he never asked her. My mother remains the one and only love of his life. Although Adele was fair enough to Eduard and me as children, I always thought her main purpose was to win favor with Poppa. I cannot think of her as la mère. I still have a few wonderful memories of my real mama. She was an amazing woman. For Eduard, however, there are no such memories. He is devoted to Adele, who is the only la mère he has known."

Angelique sighed as she continued, "You have to expect that Adele will be suspicious of you and protective of Poppa. It will take some time, but I know you will win her over, especially if your ministrations help Poppa! Gerard told me you also have Kidoh's herbs. That gives me much hope."

Angelique's brightened face made Elisabeth wince. "Oh, Angelique, please do not expect too much. I promise I will try to help your father, but only the Lord can raise a person from the pallor of death. Please tell me more details of Monsieur Gervais' ailments."

"We think he suffers from some kind of apoplexy. When the attack first came, he could not move or speak for many days. Of course, the doctor used leeches to try and strengthen him, and there were many vials of medicines. Eventually, his movements and speech returned a little so we hope he is getting better. But he is still so very weak."

Elisabeth asked, "Has cupping been tried?"

"Cupping?"

"It is when glasses are heated and applied to afflicted parts of the body. They can draw out the sickness."

"No, I do not think our doctor even knows of such treatment," Angelique replied.

As they discussed Monsieur Gervais' medical condition, the carriage pulled up to a two-story stone house with manicured grounds.

Elisabeth marveled, "Why, it reminds me of a manor back in England!"

"Yes, my mother and her first husband were English. He was a close friend to Poppa. They fought the Spanish together when they first came to St. Paola, and the alliance sealed their friendship. When he died, Poppa and Momma married and had me, and later Eduard. I think Poppa continues to live in this house because it reminds him of my mother."

Elisabeth barely heard Angelique instructing Clare to find out the latest Ross Hall gossip. The house enchanted her, offering a familiar piece of home. She felt pangs of longing. A smiling, shirtless boy ran up to the carriage to greet Angelique. Clare directed him to carry Elisabeth's bag into the house.

"Remember, Elisabeth, you are my servant so I will treat you accordingly," Angelique whispered. "Be glad I have a reputation for a soft hand with my servants."

"I understand, Angelique."

From the front doorway, Elisabeth saw a woman emerging. She suddenly felt cold in spite of the warm sun. The woman was petite but sinewy, her black and gray hair knotted in a bun that made her face seem even more sharp and angular. She wore a green satin dress with lace at the collar and sleeves. Although she walked slowly with a cane, her posture was erect, and her harsh, black eyes zeroed in on both women.

"Angelique, welcome, my chérie," the older lady said in a passionless tone. Her lips barely moved when she spoke and her kiss to both of Angelique's cheeks was perfunctory.

"Adele, how is he?" Angelique asked.

Adele shook her head sadly. "No better, no worse. He just cannot get his strength back."

She raised her hands in helplessness that seemed genuine, but Elisabeth thought it did not fit the rest of the woman's demeanor.

Adele continued, "I am treating him with a potion Zena assures me will very much improve his condition. However, she says it takes many days to work."

"What kind of potion?" Elisabeth blurted out softly, and both women looked at her disapprovingly.

"Forgive me, Madame," said Elisabeth as she bent her head.

Angelique quickly spoke. "Adele, this is Madame Chauvin. She was a passenger on the *St. Therese*. I fortunately secured her as my servant. She has skills in medicine, and I am hoping she can assist us with Poppa."

Elisabeth was certain she felt a chill rise around her.

"Angelique, I really think we are doing all we can for your Poppa," the lady said tersely.

"Oh yes, I do not doubt your dedication, Adele! But Madame Chauvin has different medicines to try, and another pair of hands would ease your burden." Angelique oozed compassion. "You look very tired, Adele. Poppa's illness has been hard on you."

Elisabeth did not like the hostile scrutiny Adele gave.

"No!" Adele said. "Absolutely not! I am fine. We can manage without outsiders."

Angelique was not so easily dismissed. "We can discuss this later. I am hot and tired. I want to see Poppa and have something to drink."

"Very well," Adele sniffed. "Madame Chauvin can go around back to the kitchen."

"No, no, Adele. I want her by my side in case I need something."

Adele almost objected but reconsidered. She threw a haughty look at Elisabeth and briskly turned around to lead them into Ross Hall.

Chapter 32

Meeting Louis Gervais

As Elisabeth entered the house, she again marveled that Ross Hall, so far away from her homeland, had a surprising English touch. The heavy wooden furniture, woven rugs, and tranquil paintings of English pastures and people reassured her. She and Angelique followed Adele to a sitting room that even had a stone hearth. Elisabeth puzzled over how practical such a hearth was in this hot, humid climate. *Perhaps it was a sentimental touch,* she concluded.

Because Monsieur Gervais slept, Adele insisted they first have some food and drink before seeing him. "The servant has already brought the tray and even included some refreshments for you," she said dryly, pointing to the setting on the table.

To Elisabeth, the ale and bread, served with butter and fruit, were the best she had ever eaten. After jungle ways, she reminded herself to sit properly and pay attention. She thought of all those times she sat on the ground in Abasi's village. A good chair felt better for her body.

Madame Adele's eyes occasionally burrowed into Elisabeth,

taking in her pregnancy, but the headmistress of Ross Hall did not seem interested in prodding her with questions.

As Angelique and Adele chatted in French and forgot her, Elisabeth scrutinized the room more carefully. The sturdy furniture was old but polished and well maintained. Above the hearth was a portrait of a beautiful woman dressed in sweeping blue satin, pink ribbons, and white lace. Elisabeth assumed the subject must be Angelique and Eduard's mother. They each bore some resemblance to her, maybe in their noses and chins.

But something about the portrait bothered her. As she swallowed ale she tried to puzzle it out. She had seen those laughing eyes and slight smile before. When Elisabeth finally figured out the connection, she almost dropped her mug. The late Madame Gervais' penetrating gaze and teasing smile echoed the features of none other than Colin Richardson!

She recalled Angelique words, "When my mother's first husband died, Poppa and Momma married and had me, and later Eduard."

This startling revelation made her blush in surprise and embarrassment. Why had Colin and Angelique not told her? Their tumultuous relationship was not one of failed lovers, as she assumed, but of half brother and sister! Elisabeth felt foolish. She was grateful she had not tried to persuade Colin to try and win Angelique Gervais back again. Oh, how he would have enjoyed a bellyache of laughter over that!

But there was something else Elisabeth felt—maybe relief that Angelique and Colin were not involved intimately. Why should she feel that way? Nothing had really changed. She set her mug down and did what had become a habit when she needed comfort; she patted and massaged her stomach and said a prayer for David and her reunion. *Hasten it, Lord. Please, please hasten it!*

She studied the portrait with a different viewpoint and noticed more appreciatively how strong and beautiful Angelique's mother appeared. She obviously still held Louis Gervais' heart captive, even though she had been dead for many years. And to think this beautiful woman was Colin's mother. At one time, Ross Hall had been his home. She thought the ruffian came from more meager beginnings. There were so many secrets here.

She glanced at Angelique, who still tried to pry information about her father from the reluctant Adele. Indeed, Angelique had a heart broken in two—Colin was family; Eduard, Louis, and Adele were family. Angelique was caught in the middle.

"I will take you to Louis now," announced Adele abruptly in English, noticing Elisabeth's long interest in the painting.

"Good!" said Angelique, rising immediately and smoothing out her dress.

"Mademoiselle Gervais, excuse me," inquired a meek but curious Elisabeth. "May I inquire whether your mother is the subject of this lovely portrait?"

Angelique turned to the painting, and Adele glared at Elisabeth. "Yes, this was my mother," Angelique said reverently. "It was done before my parents were married. It reveals a lot about my mother's character, do you not agree?"

Adele interrupted briskly, "We have moved your poppa to the library, Angelique. Climbing the stairs became difficult for care, and I wanted Louis to be able to look out at the garden."

"Yes, that was a good idea." Angelique turned from the portrait and headed out of the room. "Let us go see Poppa."

They entered a back room with rows and rows of bookshelves. *What a wonderful reading treasure,* thought Elisabeth, noticing many volumes were in English.

The room's desk had been pushed into a corner, and Louis Gervais lay in a large poster bed facing the window. The elderly man's skin was sullen and yellow in color; his thin gray and black hair matted around a long oval face. Adele obviously had provided attentive care, for the frail man appeared bathed; his mustache and beard well-trimmed.

Angelique sat in a chair by the side of the bed and grabbed her father's hand. Cloudy and bloodshot green eyes opened.

"Angelique, ma chère fille," the patient whispered hoarsely in French.

Angelique kissed his hand and laid her head on the bed.

After a time, Gervais' eyes slowly turned to Elisabeth, and he weakly pointed a bony finger, "Who is this?"

"Poppa, I have acquired a new servant, Madame Elisabeth Chauvin."

At the mention of her name, Elisabeth curtsied.

Angelique continued, "She is trained as a midwife, but she also has studied with a great doctor in England."

"A midwife? Angelique, no, no, no." The elderly man tried to laugh, but it came out in a fitful cough.

Angelique poured some water in a cup and helped her father take a sip. "Poppa, Adele needs help. Please."

Adele interjected, "Louis, I told her we are doing all we can for you. But you know how stubborn she is."

The weak man did not have strength to debate these women. "I am dying, but I want to live. I want to live! We should try everything," he whispered hoarsely, addressing them as if it were a command they could fulfill. There was a long silence, and then, "She stays," he said firmly and closed his eyes.

"Poppa? Poppa?" Angelique tried to get the man to respond, but he did not acknowledge her.

"You see how weak he is, Angelique. Let your poppa rest," Adele said, nearly pushing them out of the room. She closed the door behind them.

Angelique stood in the hallway and whispered, "What do you think, Elisabeth? He is even worse since I visited a few days ago."

"I do not know, Angelique," Elisabeth softly answered. "I would have to examine him more closely. He obviously is very ill. The yellowing of his skin means something needs to be purged. I did not see a plaster on his chest for his cough, and I wonder if Adele gives him wine that has been soaked in iron. It could provide a little strength."

"Good, good. You have some treatments to try." Angelique nodded hopefully.

Elisabeth shook her head. "I do not know if there is much I can do. He is quite ill, and I very much doubt Adele will permit me near your father. We must simply pray that God will be merciful to Monsieur Gervais."

"Elisabeth, do not worry about Adele. I will deal with her. Poppa ordered his approval. That is good! She must listen."

Angelique moved down the hallway. "Come, Madame Chauvin. Let us get you settled in your room. I asked Clare to move the cook's helper upstairs to give you the small room off the kitchen. That way you can readily prepare potions, as you need them. It is good Adele moved Poppa to the library. You will be quite near him."

The white-washed room Angelique led her to seemed more like a large closet, but Elisabeth rejoiced that it had a small window, a bed with blanket, a chamber pot, a small wooden chair, and hooks for hanging clothes. A small table held pitcher, washbasin, and two candles. The travel bag Angelique gave her already perched on the bed. Elisabeth could hear the banging pots and chatter of kitchen servants as they worked. This noise mattered not. She almost cried for joy at such privacy and comfort. Her room had walls and a door!

My baby will be born here, she thought. And then she felt some panic. Who would deliver the child? The thought of Adele supervising her delivery horrified her. That just could not happen.

She turned to Angelique in fear, "I do not know if I can do this."

Elisabeth marveled at how Angelique's terse tone sounded like her father's commands: "Trust God, and heal my father."

Chapter 33

Colin's Plan

It energized Colin to create the disruption at the marketplace and have frantic French soldiers chasing him down narrow cobbled streets. His well-paid cohort performed nicely, buffing the air near his face and displaying convincing blows. They practiced their charade the night before, and Colin was quite pleased with the result.

As Colin zigzagged through alleys and squeezed between walls to confuse his pursuers, he found himself surprised he could not run as nimbly as he did as a boy. Some of the escape routes were much tighter. In childhood, Colin thought St. Paola was a vast kingdom; now as an adult, it seemed miniature. Catching his breath, he threw down his battered hat for the soldiers to find—all part of the ruse.

As he dodged around the corner of a cobbler's shop, he grabbed a red neck scarf, beige linen shirt, and blue vest that he earlier slipped on a hook. Fortunately, no one bothered the clothing since most of the town's residents were at the market welcoming the *St. Therese.*

On the street a small black girl played with seashells. Colin put his index finger to his mouth and threw a coin to encourage her silence. She caught the coin, examined it carefully, and slipped it into a shell. Flashing Colin a big smile, she went skipping down the street clutching her prize.

Ah, how quickly they learn, he thought.

He slipped on his new shirt and vest, stuffing the old ones under his shirt. He tied his neck scarf as he backtracked to Stubby's Tavern. After entering the pub, he tossed the old clothes to the bar maid, who hid them in an empty water bucket. She handed Colin a mug of ale, and he slid onto a bench to join two men playing cards.

"Good morning, Colin. Is that distant ruckus because of you, mate?"

"You know it is, sea devil. Now bring out your Shakespeare, and you will soon have a heavier pocket."

The two men handed him his cards, and the barmaid gave him his pistol. She then plopped a new brown hat on his head. By the time the door flew open and two soldiers tromped inside, the card group made a serene pose.

"Mademoiselle, have you seen a fellow wearing a brown vest and white shirt? He also lost this black hat," the breathless lieutenant inquired, having it in his hand.

"Not today, monsieur. What happened? What did this hatless man do?"

The lieutenant eyed the card players and ignored the barmaid. "And how about you men? Have you seen such a person today?"

One player thoughtfully stroked his long, brown beard and looked innocently at the officer. "I have seen no stranger today, sir. As you can see, we are playing cards, and unfortunately, I am losing."

The lieutenant drew closer to examine them. "Why are you men not down at the harbor with the other town folks?"

Colin responded, savoring a sip from his mug and wiping his mouth on his sleeve. "Sir, I have no interest in slaves, spices, and bolts of cloth. Give me my rum and these fine companions, who so willingly share their coins with me. When I am lucky, there is no better place to be." He raised his mug to the soldiers. "Could you not join us, fine sirs?"

The officer looked regretful. "Another time, perhaps."

"Monsieur, you would honor us." Colin tipped his hat.

The soldier returned his sword to his saber. "Come on, Denis. We will not find our brawler here among these gentlemen." The lieutenant bowed, and he and his companion left.

When Colin was certain they were gone, he clapped his hands. "Well done, gentlemen and my lady!"

From his pocket, he gave them each some coins and generously added, "Allow me to buy you fine actors some well-deserved drinks. Shall we continue our card game, and see if I can retrieve some of your earnings?"

The men bellowed merrily, and one said, "I believe that was the easiest money I ever made, Colin. So come on then! I smell fortune's sweet scent upon me."

Hours later, when Colin left the tavern, he had recovered a good deal of the money he had given out. He could have won it all—these men were not bright players and quite drunk—but Colin held back. He wanted their lips to remain sealed. One never knew when such services would be needed again.

He wondered how Elisabeth fared. It turned his stomach thinking of her in the house of the man he hated the most. He knew that even a very ill Louis Gervais could be dangerous. And that crazy Adele might do harm. When his mother lived, he remembered Adele covered up for Louis, lying to his mother! Adele witnessed the cruelty Louis inflicted upon him, a mere child, but refused to say a word of defense or offer any comfort. Adele was a poisonous adder. He wondered why his mother put up with her. Could it have been a fear he did not understand as a child? He doubted he would ever know.

Angelique and Eduard certainly tolerated, even loved, Adele as a surrogate mother. Perhaps she had changed. She had been part of the Gervais family fabric for so long that to rip her out would shake their world. She was one of the last links to their mother's memory. He well knew he was the intruder to the nest, and that made him resent Louis even more.

Colin had avoided his stepfather for twenty years—a lifetime. He wished he could put it behind him and forget. But that man ruined his life, murdered Berko's father, deceived his mother, took Colin's only home, and kept Colin's half brother and sister from him. Remembering such grievances fueled his anger.

If he could see Louis Gervais sick and dying in bed, if he could stand above him and smirk at his helplessness, maybe he would find some healing to childhood wounds. Maybe it would give him enough satisfaction that he would not feel compelled to thrust a knife into that cruel heart. Colin shook his head. He hated thinking of his stepfather because it filled him with such bitterness.

How could he have agreed to Angelique's plan for Elisabeth Allerton to stay at Ross Hall? The sooner he could secure a ship for Elisabeth and leave St. Paola once and for all, the sooner he could be free of the past, all of it.

Colin and Abasi's men had been busily hunting and curing meat. He figured he had about three-fourths of the money he needed to secure passage for Mrs. Allerton and her baby. He would need substantially more to pay someone to be a guardian for her.

Deep in his heart, Colin knew it was almost impossible to trust anyone with such a task. But he wanted to untangle himself from this Puritan distraction as soon as he could. Being responsible for her drove him crazy as well as kept him a pauper. He needed to get out on the sea and harpoon some whales, far away from women, babies, and memories.

How he missed the counsel of Duff! Yet he could hear his uncle's voice in his head, "Be patient, lad. That is the Richardson way, the wise way."

Yes, but patience came with a price. He could not act until the Allerton baby came and winter ended. He headed for the jungle to join Abasi's men. He needed to earn more money, lots of it.

Chapter 34

At Ross Hall

After Elisabeth said a regretful good-bye to Angelique, she found herself with nothing to do. Angelique advised her to wait until Adele sought her out and suggested she rest for night duty. She napped as long as she could and headed for the kitchen. Ross Hall's head cook Marie eyed Elisabeth and dismissively pointed her spoon to a seat at the kitchen table. Four bowls of steaming boiled fish and vegetables were set. Apparently, the slaves ate away from the house. Elisabeth overheard the little slave boy mutter, "Only lollie again for me." The servants ignored him as he sadly shuffled out the back door with a bowl of mush. Elisabeth took her seat, and the cook and two other servants sat down beside her. As Elisabeth's companions ate and conversed quietly in French, they occasionally glanced at her and each other.

Elisabeth tried to eat as if their stares did not bother her, but she felt nervous. "The stew is delicious," she said in English. The cook grunted. When the servants finished their meal, she helped the best she could, carrying dishes to a basin for washing. No one seemed the least bit curious about her. Her question "Does this pot go here?" was met with a slight turn of the head, pointing in what Elisabeth guessed was the right place. She finally decided she could be more useful by making herself available to Monsieur Gervais and Madame Adele.

She gently tapped on the half-opened library door. There was no answer, so she peeked inside. The sun peeked low on the horizon. Candle light illumined the room, creating shadows around Monsieur Gervais.

Elisabeth gasped. There were small gold goblets of what looked like blood placed at each corner of Gervais' bed. Feathers were scattered on his coverlet and a dead chicken with a broken neck lay on a towel over his stomach. A tall, willowy African woman stood beside the bed with long arms raised, her head thrown back and her eyes closed.

Elisabeth thought Monsieur Gervais saw her at the door and then reached out a feeble hand toward her. But Adele quickly blocked the view and rushed toward her.

"What are you doing here?" she hissed as flames flickered in her eyes.

"I came to ask how I could be of service, Madame," stuttered Elisabeth, confused over what she witnessed.

"Get out! Get out! This is no concern of yours, you spy! Louis is my responsibility. Mine! I will deal with you later. Go to bed! Leave us alone!"

With that, Elisabeth again found herself outside the room and heard a key turn in the latch. The darkening shadows and quiet of the house chilled her. Obviously, the servants had learned to make themselves scarce after supper.

There was nothing to do but go to her little room and prepare for bed. She lit a candle. Shaking, she put the chair up against the door. Then she undressed and curled up on the bed, hugging a blanket. During the night, she thought she heard screams, but she could not be sure if they were real or in her dreams. Her knife lay under her pillow. Her fingertips touched it for reassurance. How she wished she were back in Abasi's village! She felt safer there. Staying at Ross Hall was a huge mistake. What dark power corrupted this house? She recited Psalm 23, "Even though I walk through the valley of the shadow of death, I will fear no evil." Yet she trembled.

The next morning, after a fitful sleep, Elisabeth hurried into the kitchen where preparations were already underway for the day's meals. The room glowed with sunlight. Nothing seemed unusual or sinister like the night before, and Elisabeth relaxed—a little.

She offered to cut some fruit, but Cook Marie surprised her by speaking English. "No, no, Madame Chauvin! Madame Adele say no. My work."

The other servants shunned her, too, as they went about their chores. Elisabeth guessed Madame Adele's ironclad rules were behind such aloofness. At least little interaction kept her from saying or doing something that could be used against her.

Since Elisabeth had to wait until Madame Adele gave her instructions, she decided to walk out into the garden. She noticed the library's heavy drapes were still drawn. The kitchen garden bordered a stone courtyard with a three-tiered fountain at its center.

These spouting cupids seem an ironic touch for such a sad household, Elisabeth thought. *Perhaps the fountain was purchased during happier times.*

A leafy hedge shaded a nearby bench. Behind it, a stream trickled through the vegetation. To her delight, Elisabeth recognized many of the flourishing plants—pennyroyal, poppy, purslane, St. John's Wort, marigold, germander, and many more. She hoped Adele would give permission to use some of them in treating Monsieur Gervais.

Farther from the courtyard's fountain a trellised enclosure shaded a wooden table and benches for outdoor dining. Nearby a maze exhibited statues protruding from various corners. It had seen better days, apparently designed for long gone children's play and adult diversion.

Elisabeth walked through the maze, discovering moss-covered statues of the Virgin Mary and child, river nymphs, Hercules, and small busts of a boy and girl on pedestals. Eduard and Angelique perhaps? Elisabeth surmised the eclectic collection might be due to the limitations of island trade. People here were not as privy to European artisans as their wealthy counterparts in England and France. Or perhaps they did not care if the conventions of style bent due to personal taste. Beyond the maze, Elisabeth saw a fruit orchard tended by several slaves. And behind the orchard stood a tree-lined stone wall with a gate that led to slave shacks and livestock.

After satisfying her curiosity about the plantation's immediate layout, Elisabeth sat down on the garden bench. It was not long before Madame Adele appeared, walking slowly but determinedly with her cane. Elisabeth stood and curtsied, but Adele waved her cane in the direction of the bench. Her black eyes glared like two little daggers.

Elisabeth waited for the mistress to sit down first, and then she braced herself for an outburst.

Instead, Madame Adele surprised her. In a syrupy voice, she said, "Madame Chauvin, we did not have a very good beginning yesterday. I am sure you can imagine how unexpected your arrival was to me."

Elisabeth could not believe she heard pleasant words from this woman, who even attempted a feeble smile. Still, Adele's eyes remained dark and hard, and Elisabeth uneasily waited for true motives to emerge.

"Yes, Madame Adele, I agree," she cautiously replied.

"Then, let us come to an understanding. My wishes are that you pack up your belongings and tell Angelique you cannot do any more for Monsieur Gervais than what has already been done and is being done. That is simply the truth."

As Adele took a breath to say more, Elisabeth protested, "Madame Adele, I must respectfully disagree. I have some powders that would relieve Monsieur Gervais' cough and give him much needed strength. I would like to put compresses on his chest. Your kitchen garden is wonderful. I could make poultices and—"

"Madame Chauvin, do you not think we attempted using the best medicines and methods available and much, much more to little success?" The warm pretense disappeared, and an icy edge tinted Adele's voice.

Elisabeth tried diplomacy. "I am sure Monsieur Gervais would be worse off without your skills, Madame Adele. It is obvious even to a stranger like myself that you care for him very much. But I am in the employment of Mademoiselle Gervais, and she was quite insistent that I tend to her father. He, too, seemed to indicate yesterday that he desires me to stay and help."

The old woman squinted in a flash of acknowledgement and then erupted, "Angelique is a foolish young woman when it comes to her father! And Monsieur Gervais is not a well man with sound judgment. I am his caretaker in these matters. It has been that way for a very long time. I cannot possibly see how an Englishwoman so ripe with child can possibly be beneficial to the Gervais household!" The older woman calmed down and seemed to be thinking out loud. "Your appearance at this time to Ross Hall is most peculiar."

Elisabeth flushed. Would Adele soon connect the dots to the *Xavier* runaways? She knew she must now divert her thoughts. Maintaining an even voice, she said, "Madame Adele, please let me assist you. If Monsieur Gervais is not better in two weeks, I will tell Mademoiselle Gervais that I can do no more to help him and I will leave Ross Hall." She added, straining to be civil, "At least for this brief time, God willing, my condition will not hinder my service to you."

The woman pursed her lips and considered the benefits of such a plan. Finally, she spoke, "Madame Chauvin, I give you one week, with the condition that Louis is strictly my patient at night."

Elisabeth nodded resignedly. One week was not much time with such an ill man.

She gently asked, trying to keep accusation out of her voice, "Madame Adele, what were you doing last night to Monsieur Gervais? I have never seen such methods for healing."

Adele sighed. "It is a treatment my slave woman Zena said she used in her homeland with good results. For a while, Louis seemed to be getting better, stronger, but now he is the same again, maybe worse."

Her voice faded off in thought. "I need to tend to the household, and I am tired." Then she straightened up and ordered, "I give you permission to care for Monsieur Gervais with some of your treatments. Use any plants from our gardens, but I expect a full accounting every evening. Try to get Monsieur Gervais to take some broth today. I will tell Zena to assist you. She and I will tend to daily toiletry needs."

Elisabeth nodded and curtsied. She was glad to have some work. For her baby's sake, she needed to find a niche in this strange household. As Adele walked away, Elisabeth absentmindedly felt the knife under her apron. It gave her a little assurance, but she prayed, "Lord, may I never have to use this weapon."

Chapter 35

Zena's Ritual

It was not easy for Elisabeth to feel comfortable in the Gervais household. Besides bearing nervous guilt for deception, she quickly discovered Ross Hall operated quite differently from her family's manor in England. Elisabeth had assumed bustling chatter and an airy atmosphere would help her adjust. But Ross Hall held no joy. It was all whispering voices, tasks done gloomily, and draped windows permitting little sunlight. Here was a dying household as ill as its owner.

The servants often edged away and disappeared. Elisabeth wondered if their behavior was for the sake of their sick master or just a normal pattern established long ago. In spite of the heaviness of spirit, Elisabeth determined to help Monsieur Gervais. But to care for him, she had to work with Zena.

When Elisabeth first entered the library to meet Adele's slave, she was startled to see that the woman looked nothing like the powerful figure looming over Gervais' bed the night before. Although she was tall and strong, Zena by daylight hunched over and gave little eye contact or conversation. Her long flowing hair was braided and twisted under a work scarf. This Zena was dull and compliant. Elisa beth suggested they turn Louis in his bed. Zena nodded, and they wordlessly and efficiently completed the task. Then as Elisabeth tucked a blanket around their patient, the slave slipped out of the room.

Elisabeth soon realized Zena often disappeared, just like the rest of the working household. The tasks of removing dirty linens and meal trays became her work.

Maybe it is better this way, Elisabeth thought. She did not, however, want to cross Adele. She doubted the Madame would approve of Zena's lax approach to spying on her.

Adele insisted she personally would take care of most hygiene duties at night, and she made it very clear she wanted Elisabeth nowhere around. Elisabeth gladly retreated to her small room after she gave Adele her daily report.

During those first few days, Louis would awaken, perplexed over who she was. Her English voice, perhaps reminded him of his deceased wife and comforted the man enough to accept medicine and liquids. Eventually, he fell back into another bout of fitful sleep. When he was conscious, Elisabeth opened the drapes, and his watery eyes stared out the window. Adele made surprise visits as if she intended to catch Elisabeth disobeying her orders. Zena knew her mistress's whereabouts because she magically appeared, too. Indeed, she was extremely helpful when her mistress was present. The Zena of night and the Zena of day perplexed Elisabeth, but she decided to keep mum about the slave's daytime disappearances.

In tending to Gervais, Elisabeth applied cupping to his chest, followed by oatmeal compresses. These treatments seemed to relieve the coughing. She spoon-fed the weak man iron in wine. Cook Marie also assisted her in preparing herbal broths, teas, and coddled eggs. Gervais was too weak to do more than respond with groans and nods. She often wrung out and replaced the cloth on his feverish brow. He once whispered, "Angelique? Eduard?" He nodded when Elisabeth reassured him they would visit soon. Elisabeth sat next to him, read, and prayed for healing.

After three days of this routine, Angelique came quietly into the library and took her father's hand. He did not open his eyes. "Is he getting better, Madame Chauvin?" she tearfully whispered.

Elisabeth sighed. "Could we walk in the garden, Mademoiselle Gervais?"

Elisabeth was grateful Zena made herself available in the room just prior to Angelique's arrival. She could watch over Monsieur Gervais while Elisabeth and Angelique talked privately.

As they made their way to the garden bench, Elisabeth said carefully, "Angelique, I feel your father carries a burden that is affecting his health. Perhaps if he had someone who could attend to his soul during this affliction?"

Angelique frowned, but Elisabeth hurried on, "I have seen such misery before in my parish back home. Some people are not ready to die even though faced with its real possibility, and they fight it with fear. Is your father a practicing Papist?"

"Elisabeth, I do not like the way you are talking! I brought you here to heal my father not to suggest final confession!"

"Angelique, the mind, body, and spirit are intertwined like the blessed Holy Trinity. We must treat each part for the whole to function well. I am sorry if I am overstepping. You know I care."

Angelique's face softened. "Oui, I know you mean well, Elisabeth." The French woman sat back on the bench and sighed. "When Eduard and I were young, Poppa and Adele insisted we be baptized and confirmed, but otherwise, we did not attend Mass. There was always so much work. The local priest, Father Bénard, visited us, and I believe the priest and Poppa have some kind of understanding. But Elisabeth, I fear what Poppa would think in his condition if he saw Father Bénard's face hovering above him. No doubt he would think he is receiving last rites!"

"Would not your priest simply pay him a visit and say a prayer for him?" Elisabeth suggested.

"Maybe," Angelique said thoughtfully. "I do not think this would help..." Her voice trailed off and returned with more force. "Adele said she does not find Poppa any better under your care. I think, however, that at least she looks more rested since you are here. Have you won her confidence?"

"Not exactly. She has Zena spying on me. At night, she dismisses me and closes your father's door. And Angelique, there is another matter I must share with you. I am concerned about treatments your father is receiving from Adele and Zena at night."

"What kind of treatments?"

Elisabeth described the bizarre scene she had witnessed.

"Ah, it sounds like an African ritual. I am surprised Adele is trying that, but it shows our desperation to heal Poppa."

Angelique's passive response was not what Elisabeth expected.

"But what if these rituals are harming your father? I think he would improve without such dark practices. This is giving the devil his foothold into your father's soul, and I think you know the havoc it has caused." Elisabeth pressed her argument. "It would be prudent to get your priest's counsel if you do not believe me."

"Hmm. Maybe you are right, but I have a better plan. I think I know how we can get Adele and Zena away from Poppa for a few days. Maybe he could improve with just your treatments."

"Is that even possible, to get Adele away?" Elisabeth could not imagine Adele agreeing to a separation.

"Eduard could make it happen. He is the only one Adele really listens to besides Poppa. I will speak to him privately and perhaps, if I promise to stay here and bring Clare, we can get Adele to Eduard's plantation for a few days of rest. Give me a day to make arrangements."

Elisabeth agreed heartily. The thought of Adele being replaced by Angelique and Clare, even for a few days, lightened her soul. Their presence truly would benefit Monsieur Gervais and give her freedom on his treatment.

That night, Elisabeth stayed up instead of retiring at dusk as had been her practice. She left her door slightly ajar and sat on her bedside, trying to stay awake as darkness came.

She needed more knowledge on what Monsieur Gervais' nightly ritual meant. She had noticed that since witnessing Zena's treatment, the slave and Adele waited later in the evening to do this witchcraft, obviously suspicious of her interference.

Finally, Elisabeth's vigil was rewarded. Hearing hushed voices in the kitchen, she peeked through a crack in the door and saw from their candlelight that Zena and Adele were bent over a tray holding the four golden goblets. From her apron, Adele produced a small leather pouch. She took a spoon and carefully measured out some powder in each vessel.

What could this foul medicine be? Elisabeth wondered.

Then, Zena waved her hands over the goblets and spoke in a language Elisabeth did not recognize. Zena set a candle on the tray and carried it toward Gervais' room. Adele lifted a small basket. Elisabeth was sure she heard a clucking chicken. Elisabeth waited a few moments and very quietly opened her door and slipped down the dark hall.

When she got to Louis' room, she could see through the open door that Adele had placed the goblets at each corner of the sick man's bed. Meanwhile, Zena gently lifted the clucking bird above the bed and chanted in a soft, droning voice. In a blink, the sorceress wrung the bird's neck and took her knife out to make an incision in its throat.

Elisabeth held her breath. Carefully, the chanting Zena dripped blood into each goblet. Elisabeth gasped as she saw wisps of smoke rising from the vessels. Her stomach lurched. She covered her mouth and resisted fleeing from this repulsive sight.

Adele took one of the goblets and, with a spoon, tried to give Gervais the fresh blood. He moaned in protest and turned his head away. Adele coaxed him to take the medicine, but he refused. She finally forced his mouth open to take a few drops of the awful mixture. Then she moved to the other goblets and forced more drops into Gervais' mouth. All the while, Zena swayed and chanted, raising her long arms high above the bed.

When the final spoonful was given, Adele tenderly wiped Louis' face and kissed his forehead. Zena stood motionless in meditation.

Elisabeth withdrew from the cracked door and moved down the dark hallway to get back to her room. There, she ran to her basin and promptly threw up.

This was certainly the devil's magic! No wonder Monsieur Gervais' condition had not improved! The ritual had sickened and exhausted her. As her body shook, her baby protested with steady kicks to her stomach. She pushed her chair against the door and crumpled into bed. That night, she asked God to keep them safe, and she tried to block out the muffled moans that came through the walls. She clung to the thought that tomorrow Angelique and Clare would arrive at Ross Hall. She just needed to get through this night.

Chapter 36

Meeting in the Maze

Elisabeth awoke at dawn and gratefully used the chamber pot. She wanted to believe her experience the night before was just a bad dream. Yet the room smelled rancid from her basin. She opened her shutters and inhaled humid, but fresher, air. She could hear the servants bustling in the kitchen. She went outside and tended to her toiletries, finding some seclusion between the outhouse and the well.

When she returned to the kitchen, Cook Marie silently passed her a bowl of rice and beans. Elisabeth's kicking baby settled down as she ate. Cook Marie grabbed Elisabeth's bowl as soon as she finished her last bite, discouraging any help in the kitchen with a wave of her hand. Elisabeth peeked in on Monsieur Gervais. The scene appeared so tranquil. He rested, grey-faced with shallow breathing, while Adele snored in a nearby chair.

Elisabeth hesitated on what to do but decided a walk might steady her. She ventured to the very edge of the stone wall which separated the livestock area from the house.

At the gate, she discovered Colin Richardson quietly slipping in.

"Mr. Richardson! What are you doing here?"

He responded as if he were not surprised to see her. "I might ask you the same, Mrs. Allerton. I just happened to be in the neighborhood and considered taking board at Ross Hall." He chuckled at the irony. "Actually, I spotted you walking about and decided it was a good opportunity for us to talk."

"But how did you see me? Oh, it does not matter! I am just glad to see you!"

Before he could respond, Elisabeth gave him a big hug and clung to him. He could feel her trembling.

The man tried to pat the pregnant woman's back the best he could, but it felt awkward. Personal feelings, especially for Mrs. Allerton, could not get in the way of his duty. He owed that much to both of them.

"What happened? What is wrong?" he demanded, pushing her away to see her face. "Has someone at Ross Hall assaulted you?"

"No, nothing like that, but it is truly evil! The devil's foulest meddling!" she said, and proceeded to explain the night's events and her fears.

Colin relaxed. "Ah, Zena uses the power of Nzambi a Mpungu. It is something the Africans speak of, and it has the slaves' respect. As for myself, I do not believe in such gibberish. Trust me, her power lies more in her theatrical abilities."

Elisabeth shivered. "I wish I could be as sure as you. She was in a trance when she chanted, and I felt the air become chillier. Angelique is trying to persuade Adele to go to Eduard's, but I worry that Adele's absence will only give Zena more liberty over poor Monsieur Gervais."

Colin stiffened at her sympathy for his stepfather. It was hard for him to imagine his memory of this man matching up to what Elisabeth described as a sick, dying soul—one who was forced to drink chicken blood. He would not believe powerlessness until he saw it for himself.

He surveyed her intently. Maybe this Englishwoman was finally cracking under her ordeal?

"Please, may I go back to Abasi's village?" Elisabeth pleaded.

"No, that is not possible," Colin said. "There is talk the plantation farmers are rallying for another hunt like they did a few years ago."

"A hunt? What do you mean?"

"It is a wretched evil, far more dangerous than Zena's witchcraft. The local gents go out and hunt for runaway slaves and jungle people. They do it for sport and to put fear into their slaves."

"They hunt people, like hunting boar?" Elisabeth was alarmed.

"Aye—men, women, children. No one in the jungle is safe."

Elisabeth imagined old, hobbling Neesa trying to hide from plantation owners with guns and knives.

"Surely you have warned them; they must get away and hide!" Her concerns for herself seemed marginal compared to this news.

"St. Paola is their home, Mrs. Allerton," Colin said resignedly. "Abasi's people do have a few strategies to protect themselves, and the hunters are mostly lazy, not wanting to go anywhere their horses cannot journey. This sport is also an excuse to get together and drink. In the past, after finding a few wretches, they are satisfied."

"What about Berko's cave? Could the villagers hide there?"

"Maybe. Although Berko believes the cave is no longer secret. The point is you are safest at Ross Hall."

Elisabeth sighed. He was right.

Colin was already walking away. "I have to go. I will check on you again soon. You are safest at Ross Hall, Mrs. Allerton," he emphasized and added, "remember, it is only for a little while longer. By the way, you look quite full with babe."

He chuckled and tipped his hat as he unlatched the gate and disappeared.

She had not even asked him about his mother's portrait or about Angelique being his sister. His short visit, however, heartened her. Colin connected her to David and a family life she desperately needed. His confidence that they soon would have ship passage to Boston gave her hope. But did the man have to comment on her growing shape? He certainly kept insulting her and laughing at her expense!

Elisabeth walked back to her room and was surprised to see the door ajar! Someone had entered! Would Zena dare to meddle in her belongings? As she entered, she let out a gasp of joy and disbelief. There on the bed were her Bible, medical books, and medicine chest! Did Colin bring them? Elisabeth spotted a small paper and pouch wedged between the chest and books. She opened the note:

I am done with these books and have no use for them.
  I give them to you.
  Here is potion for Gervais.
  Mix two pinches in a cup of hot water.
  Swallow many times each day.

Kidoh! That crafty old man, Elisabeth thought.

She marveled at his abilities and wondered who in Gervais' household served as his ally. She scrutinized the note. Did that sly little man read and write? She blushed. He certainly fooled her. Or perhaps someone else wrote it for him? With Kidoh—with Colin—so much was not what it appeared to be.

She shrugged and opened the pouch and smelled its contents. Her finger dabbed the green powder, and she tasted the bittersweet mix. This herb-smelling blend resembled nothing Kidoh had shown her before. She could not decipher its ingredients.

She wished she could consult Kidoh about Adele and Zena's sorcery. Nevertheless, she would give Kidoh's medicine to Monsieur Gervais as soon as Adele and Zena left her alone to tend him. The poor man was so ill that anything was worth a try. She must be very careful. Madame Adele would throw her out of Ross Hall if she discovered any hint of treachery.

Chapter 37

Monsieur Gervais' Recovery

The patient's response to Kidoh's medicine was a miracle to Elisabeth. Several hours after giving the drink to him, Monsieur Gervais opened his eyes.

"Who are you?" he asked weakly.

"Monsieur, I am your day nurse, Madame Elisabeth A—Chauvin."

Foolish woman! Elisabeth said to herself, hoping the sick man would not piece the stumbled words together.

He gripped her arm, his face wincing with fear. "I have had terrible dreams."

"Monsieur, it is all right. You are safe. Please, take some more of this drink. It contains pleasant-tasting medicine."

In response, he opened his mouth.

Elisabeth helped the man sip Kidoh's special brew, and then she helped her charge lay back down on his pillow. He soon slept soundly.

Later, Elisabeth and a servant girl propped Louis into a sitting position. Although Gervais would not talk, Elisabeth noticed his eyes tracked her every movement. She straightened his blanket and offered more drink. That is how Adele found them.

"Louis! Oh, my God! You are sitting up!" The mistress rushed to him and grabbed his hand.

It pleased Elisabeth to witness her genuine concern, but she could not discern Gervais' feelings toward his mistress. The man just stared at Adele.

"You may leave us now, Madame Chauvin," Adele commanded crisply.

"No!" he voiced hoarsely. "She stays."

"Louis, you know you can trust me with all your needs! She is a stranger, a servant!" The mistress scowled at Elisabeth and gestured for her to leave.

Elisabeth froze, uncertain what she should do. Just then Angelique and Clare entered.

Elisabeth curtsied slightly and moved aside.

"Poppa! You are sitting!" Angelique grabbed his hand, and he smiled. He pointed to Elisabeth and weakly whispered, "She stays."

Adele stiffened and spewed a soft grunt of disapproval, but she could not dismiss her master's clear order. Her voice scratched sweetly, "Of course, Louis, whatever you want. She stays. Anything, anything to make you well again."

The man whispered, "I am tired," and closed his eyes. Adele adjusted his pillows and straightened his cover.

Angelique beckoned Adele and Elisabeth to follow her to the front room. There, under the portrait of Colin's mother, Angelique calmly declared, "Adele, Eduard and Isabella requested you come and spend time with little Theophile. You have neglected him too long, and he is asking for you. We all feel you need a rest from caring for Poppa."

Adele's surprise quickly shifted to anger. "Angelique, have you lost your mind? Eduard knows how sick your father is. Louis needs me more than ever! Can you not see he is finally getting better? I cannot abandon him now!"

Angelique pursed her lips. Her voice was gentle but firm. "No one questions your fine care, Adele. He is a little better. But you must rest, too, or soon we will be taking care of you! You should be comforted to know Clare will be staying to help Madame Chauvin."

Adele felt trapped, dazed. Although she was Gervais' mistress, Angelique trumped her in authority. She had been caught unaware, broadsided by Louis, Eduard, and Angelique. She needed time to think. She simply muttered, "Clare. Yes, that is good. But I think it best for Zena to take the night watch."

"We will work it out," Angelique said. "Do not worry. Poppa would agree with me that you must take care of yourself. Besides, little Theo pesters everyone to bring you to read to him. Imagine his delight and hugs when you surprise him."

Adele's face softened. Theophile, who looked so much like his grandfather and father, pleased her. "I have missed Theo," she murmured.

"Then it is settled. You can use the carriage Clare and I came in. I will be staying, too, for a few days, so you need not worry."

Adele let out a weary sigh. "Angelique, I do not like being ordered like this! However, it seems you and Eduard formed an alliance against my wishes. I will come back in two days, and you must promise me if your Poppa takes a turn for the worse, you will send for me immediately!"

"Absolutely! Thank you, Adele, for being so reasonable." Angelique smiled demurely at Elisabeth as the tiny, rigid woman limped off to pack.

Angelique whispered to Elisabeth, "You see how we handle Adele—at least for a little respite."

"And what about Zena?" Elisabeth asked, sighing.

"Oh, do not worry. I plan to deal with her, too," said Angelique, the new, temporary mistress of Ross Hall.

Chapter 38

Elisabeth and Zena's Fight

Midmorning, Adele left Ross Hall, still snapping orders at servants and slaves as her carriage rolled away. After her departure, the entire household's spirits lifted. Although Angelique exhibited a firm hand, the servants gladly obeyed her.

Elisabeth assumed Angelique ignored her throughout the day because she did not want to arouse suspicion of their friendship. The midwife busied herself in the kitchen garden, cutting and drying herbs and unsuccessfully trying to guess which plants were part of Kidoh's powder. She had the luxury of reading as she kept vigil at Monsieur Gervais' bedside. Elisabeth noticed his breathing improved, and although he slept fitfully, he did sleep.

At sunset, Louis stared out the window. Elisabeth marveled that Kidoh's medicine took effect so readily. His pallor was better, too. When Clare came to relieve her, there was a slight smile on the old woman's face. She whispered that Angelique wanted to see Madame Chauvin in the front room.

There, Angelique had already lit candles and beckoned Elisabeth to sit down beside a tray bearing fish, rice, and vegetables. As the young women drank wine and ate, Elisabeth told Angelique of finding Colin in the garden and then discovering the unexpected gifts in her room, including Kidoh's medicine.

"Did you know that Kidoh could read and write?" she whispered to Angelique.

"No," said Angelique. "I know very little about the mysterious medicine man from the jungle. Some people swear he is a ghost. You are one of few white people who have even seen him. Other people say he escaped slavery from another island. No one really knows his history."

"Oh, he is no ghost," Elisabeth assured, "and his healing knowledge is greater than anyone I have known! I never thought my jungle stay would teach me so much. I wish I could have stayed with him longer."

"There are many on this island who have benefited from his potions. They know his medicine secondhand in the black market. But, Madame Chauvin, I have never heard of him delivering a baby, so I am certain he was ready to say adieu to you," teased Angelique as she patted Elisabeth's stomach.

Elisabeth disregarded the joke. "Seriously, Angelique, do you think Eduard and others would really hunt down Kidoh and Abasi's people?"

"I had not heard of any such plans, Elisabeth, but Colin could be right. These atrocities have happened before. It is a disgusting island affair that I am ashamed of. However, let us not be alarmed by rumors floating on the breeze. I am more concerned about my poppa and you and your baby. How are you feeling?"

"Angelique, considering all that has happened I thank God and marvel he has given me such an easy waiting period. Only recently have I felt sharp back pains. Judging the fullness of my girth, I believe the baby should arrive within a month—God willing, of course."

The pregnant woman grabbed Angelique's hand and pursed her lips before speaking. "I have been meaning to ask you something, but the timing has never seemed right. And, I hesitate because you have done so much for me."

"What? What is it?" Angelique frowned.

Elisabeth took a deep breath and replied, "It would be such a comfort to me if Clare would be my midwife when the baby comes. Is that even possible?" The pregnant woman's face furrowed with distress.

Angelique chuckled and squeezed Elisabeth's hand. "Of course, mon chéri. I assumed you knew she would help. In fact, I doubt you could keep her away. Clare has delivered many babies on this island, including my nephew Theo. I wager you will find her a better midwife than yourself!"

"Oh, thank you, Angelique! This is such a relief. I know Clare did not like me at first, but we seem to have a decent respect for each other now." Elisabeth relaxed, hugging her friend. "Thank you, thank you, for permitting her to help me."

Angelique laughed. "Oh, Elisabeth, Clare decides who she helps and who she does not. I know she likes you, and she loves babies. Rest assured, Clare will be with you when your time comes, and maybe, just maybe, your mistress Mademoiselle Gervais, too."

Elisabeth smiled and changed the subject. "I have been wondering where Zena is. I have not seen her since this morning. I am quite sure Adele would disapprove of her spy not watching me more closely."

"Zena! I am so angry with that one! You were correct about her, Elisabeth. She proudly told me she practices black magic, finding our medicines lacking in power. Even if that is her belief, she should not say such words to a Gervais in such a manner! After her insolence, I turned her over to Gerard and said, 'Find any kind of work for her— just get her away from Ross Hall.' I assume he put her in the cane fields. Trust me, her body will need her magic tonight! I warned her if she causes any more trouble, I am selling her to the next slave master that sails into the harbor. She stood there with her head bowed, but I sensed her rage. That one is bad. I should have dealt with her sooner."

"Adele will not be upset with your decision?"

"Adele will be glad Poppa is better. His welfare is most important to her. She would do anything for Poppa."

"I have noticed her dedication and love. But how does your father feel toward her?"

"Hmm, that is a good question. I think he cares more for her than he will admit. He would probably say she is useful to him. And, he values loyalty above most qualities. I think he would be quite lost without her admiration and care."

Angelique straightened her dress and stood up. "Elisabeth, get some rest tonight. Clare and I will stay with Poppa. We will make sure he sips Kidoh's miracle tea that you have so faithfully given him throughout the day."

Elisabeth rose and received an unexpected kiss on both cheeks. With a soft, "Thank you, my friend," Angelique hurried toward the library.

When Elisabeth stood up, she realized she ached. She blew out the candles, except for one, placing it on the tray with the dishes. Her candle offered only a sliver of light in the dark house. How long had she and Angelique visited?

She picked up the tray and ambled down the hallway, noticing how her pregnancy slowed her movements. After placing the tray on the kitchen table, she took the candle and returned to her room, heartened to know sweet rest awaited. But then, just as she set down the candle, someone grabbed her from behind and pressed a knife tip to her ribs.

The intruder hissed, "You ruin everything. You make Babalu-Aye angry. Bad medicine! Now, you will offer gift to Yemaja and make balance."

"Zena!" Elisabeth gasped in fear. She felt the knife prodding into her more deeply as Zena pushed her to the bed. Elisabeth resisted by moving awkwardly, trying to think. If she yelled, she knew Zena would kill her instantly as well as her baby.

Stall, she thought.

"Zena, wait! Please, do not hurt me," she pleaded. "I am sorry. I just wanted to help Monsieur Gervais. I do not understand your medicines."

"You bring Zena much pain. You turn her fortunes! You must sacrifice! I must make balance between the darkness and the light."

Zena poked Elisabeth harder with her knife, and her hot breath pressed her ear. Elisabeth flinched, which brought her to the edge of the bed. Zena pushed her down. The knife's poking brought on sharp pains from her baby.

By candlelight, Elisabeth made out the shadowy outline of Zena, her twisted face and blazing eyes. With her free hand, Zena pulled a rope from the folds of her dress.

She plans to tie me to this bed! Elisabeth thought. *And then what will happen? Am I going to end up murdered in this bed, so far from all I held dear?* She remembered Zena's bloody chickens. *No! No! It could not end this way.*

Like a rushing wave came the memory of the *Xavier* ogre charging to overpower her. His face and Zena's face blended into one. Suddenly, instead of fear, Elisabeth discovered a burst of angry energy. Quickly, she jerked her arms away from Zena's grasp and jabbed her feet into the woman's stomach. This action caught the slave by surprise and with a heavy thrust Elisabeth sent her attacker flying across the room, arms flailing to keep balance.

Elisabeth felt another jolt of pain from the baby. She ignored it and fumbled for the knife inside her apron pocket. As Zena rushed toward her, Elisabeth grasped the knife and slashed wildly in Zena's direction.

Zena let out a yelp of pain and surprise. She dropped her knife to the floor as she grabbed her bloodied arm. The slave cursed in a foreign language and bent down, frantically scrambling to find her weapon. Elisabeth did not hesitate. She grabbed the water pitcher off the nightstand and brought it crashing down on Zena's head. The crockery shattered and water cascaded over Zena's head. The woman moaned and crumpled to the floor.

Clare came rushing into the room with a candle. "What is going on, Madame Elisabeth? Did you fall?" Clare's flickering light illumined Elisabeth's half-collapsed body on the bed. The glowing candle captured the horror on Elisabeth's face and her shaking hand and knife.

Bringing her candle closer to the huddled form on the floor, Clare cried out, "Zena! You witch!"

"Clare, be careful! She has a knife somewhere near her, and she is out of her head! I cut her arm! The pitcher! I cracked it over her head!" Elisabeth could hear her words but the tense, frantic voice from her lips was not familiar.

"Oh, Holy Joseph," Clare said as she found the knife and plopped it into her apron.

"Madame Elisabeth, I go get Madame Angelique! I be back!"

Elisabeth cried out, "No, Clare! Please, do not leave me! My baby is coming."

But Clare was already gone. Elisabeth could do nothing but lie there and take short breaths, holding her knife shakily in the direction of Zena. She prayed the woman would not rise from the floor and choke her.

Chapter 39

The Birth

The long night languished in physical and emotional pain. Nothing separated endless waves pushing on the inside of Elisabeth's core and her painful thoughts of fear and abandonment. She could not even catch her breath to think clearly. She bore this child without family support, without her David.

She witnessed many women screaming out their plight, but she could not surrender herself to cursing. Instead, her crying came out in gurgles as her body shook in uncontrollable spasms. She tried to concentrate on Clare, who firmly took charge and comforted her, encouraging, "It will not be long, Madame Elisabeth. The baby's head is down. Good. You are strong. You doing just fine, just fine."

To Elisabeth's relief, a half-conscious, groaning Zena was dragged away by Gerard and another servant. Angelique came rushing in and held Elisabeth's hand. Speaking half the time in French and half the time in English, she tearfully assured Elisabeth that Gerard locked up the witch, and they would get Zena off the island as soon as they could.

Although Elisabeth mentally knew how each step of child birthing went, she clung to Clare and Angelique for directions. They wiped her brow. They told her when to bear down and when not to. They promised to keep her safe.

When she concentrated on their voices, she could block out Zena's hissing jumble—the strange names of her gods and the idea that one of those gods wanted her baby as a sacrifice. Did such a nightmare really happen? Where was her knife? The surreal memories and birth pain swirled with confusion.

Eventually, exhaustion claimed most of her. She gave up on life itself, prepared to let the darkness swallow up her and her child. Yet, somehow, pain kept moving mother and baby forward.

When all seemed hopeless, Clare commanded her to push. With one final resolve and one primal yell, it was enough. Her little daughter emerged, slippery and bloodied. Exhausted, Elisabeth waited for the choking cry of life, and seconds later, it came. Quickly, Clare cleared the baby's mouth with her finger and wrapped her in a blanket. Assisted by Angelique, Clare cut and tied the cord and handed this tiny bit of humanity to her mother.

Angelique cried out, "A girl! C'est une Fille! And what a pretty one she is!"

Elisabeth always believed and even experienced how every successful delivery contained some fragment of holy space within the suffering. Heaven and earth intersected during the birth of a fragile soul. Her mother taught her to pay attention to this. It was one of the midwife's greatest blessings to be aware of sacred space, whether it occurred readily at birth or thankfully at death.

Yet not one of the births and deaths Elisabeth participated in as a practitioner of medicine prepared her for the birth of her daughter. After all the sorrow and work, here lay her beautiful baby, her Abigail Angelique Clare Allerton. A miracle evidenced in her arms.

As she heard the first birdsong of a new day, the Psalmist's truth meant more to her than ever before: "Weeping may abide at evening, but joy *cometh* in the morning." Overwhelmed with joy and relief, she wept and kissed her daughter's downy head.

Chapter 40

Vows Declared

After Gerard tied up the moaning Zena and left her in a shed, Angelique asked him to find Colin. Gerard knew the adult Colin Richardson only through Angelique's words and actions. The half-brother's island visits came too infrequently to size up the man. Gerard did not understand Angelique's consistent protectiveness of this disgraced family member, but he honored her pleas to keep Richardson's visits secret from Gervais.

Excluding Angelique's association with the mysterious half-brother, the rest of the Gervais family presumed Richardson had died at sea years before. All of this mattered little except Gerard resented Richardson's hold on Angelique. After every sibling goodbye, Gerard and Clare restored their mistress's damaged spirit. How many times would this half-brother wound and abandon her? Yet, if Colin remained important to Angelique, then he remained important to Gerard.

Gerard had loved Angelique ever since she was a young girl. For many years, he believed his affection was more like a protective uncle. He assumed Gervais would marry off his beautiful daughter to a wealthy plantation owner. There had been many suitors, even from other islands, and Gerard silently suffered knowing none of them were good enough for her. But he should not have worried. Angelique was like a cat playing with mice. Eventually she would declare,

"You bore me!"

"You are a Cabbage Head!"

"Find a woman fit for your talents. I am not she!"

When a suitor left rejected, it amused and relieved Gerard. He even told her she reminded him of a cat. She laughed and playfully hissed at him.

It also surprised Gerard that Gervais allowed his daughter the freedoms she had. He did not understand why Angelique gained permission to have her own cottage, but this arrangement kept her independent and unmarried. Gervais instructed him to keep a watchful eye on her, and because of that order, he enjoyed much delightful contact with her. Of course, Gervais demanded reports on his daughter. But Gerard kept Angelique's closest secrets protected. He knew if Gervais ever discovered Angelique's fealty to Colin Richardson and his foreman's part in protecting the relationship, it would mean the end of his position at Ross Hall. Angelique was worth every risk.

When Angelique rejected a third suitor Gerard finally comprehended what his relief meant. It shocked him to admit he harbored adult affection for his master's daughter. At first, this realization almost sent him fleeing to another island. But he knew he could never leave Angelique until she ordered him away.

At times, he sensed Angelique felt the same for him—impossible as that seemed. He could swear she challenged him with a quick touch on his shoulder. But he dared not be mistaken. He could not bear her rejection, even though she reigned supreme to him in every way.

Gerard determined to keep his love unprofessed. After all, he was 20 years her senior. The age difference might be overcome if they were equals, but Gerard's status remained hired help. Professing his love to her would mean rejection and heartbreak. And what would Gervais do to him? At least as a servant and friend, he could love and protect Angelique. He resolved to stay content with that.

At the present moment, that meant obeying Angelique and seeking out Colin Richardson. Gerard entered Stubby's Tavern and found the seaman playing cards. Catching Colin's eye, he casually gave a nod, figuring if the man were half as wise as his sister, he would know Gerard wanted to confer. Gerard settled down with a mug of ale at another table and waited. Colin took his time, winning a little money and then excusing himself from his companions.

One of them yelled at him as he stood up. "Aye, Colin, as always, you are the scoundrel leaving the games when we just begin to draw better cards! Stay longer, man."

"Sorry, gents. The night has been long, and I have other duties. But as always, thank you for such honorable playing and for gaining me a little allowance. Do not fret. I will return to find out if you blokes were just unlucky tonight or simply unskilled."

Colin grabbed his mug and moved to Gerard's table.

Gerard slowly sipped his ale, measuring Colin's temperament as he waited for his news. The seaman patiently endured the silence, so Gerard finally plunged in. "Well, Richardson, I thought you would like to hear what is happening at Ross Hall. Madame Chauvin, that woman who has kept you landlocked on St. Paola, is bearing her baby."

"Mrs. Allerton, I mean Madame Chauvin? Tonight? This morning?" Colin found himself stuffing emotions under Gerard's watchful scrutiny. He thought the foreman brought a different message from Angelique.

"Oui, as we speak."

Colin said his words softly, as if thinking out loud. "I thought we had more time, but aye, this day will do. Who is tending her?"

"Mademoiselle Gervais and Clare."

"Good, good." He thoughtfully nodded.

"But there was trouble, Colin." Gerard hesitated to share this news.

"What trouble?" Colin became agitated when Gerard explained the details of Zena and Elisabeth's fight, which apparently triggered her labor.

"No worries, my friend," Gerard said. "I daresay Mrs. Allerton got the better of that crazy slave. Zena's arm bears a respectable knife wound, and she has a large bump on the head. I wager her noggin will ache for several days. She is tied up in the shed."

"Really? It cheers me to hear such news," Colin said steadily and raised his mug to take a final, quick swallow.

He left a chuckling Gerard and walked out into the darkness. It was near dawn. He had lodged the past few nights at Angelique's cottage, concerned about Elisabeth's stay at Ross Hall. His instincts had proven correct; she was not safe in Gervais' house even though Angelique kept reassuring him that she was.

He preferred to stay away from that plantation. It triggered longing for his parents and brought back searing memories of his abusive stepfather. Yet he could not abandon Elisabeth. She certainly turned out to be pluckier than he thought. And he found himself conjuring up her smile at the oddest moments. She had generosity of spirit—a very unusual virtue in his world.

My God, man, he said to himself, *If you keep thinking about her, she will turn you into a "gentle man," and that will cause you nothing but trouble. Sink mad thoughts, sailor, to save yourself.*

He kept arguing with conscience as he trudged along the shadowy path. In the end, he sighed, knowing it did no good to resist. He turned in the direction of Ross Hall.

Angelique told him Elisabeth lodged in the room off of the kitchen. This location made it easier for him to enter the house unnoticed. As he quietly made his way to the back entrance along the hedgerow, he could not help but peer through a crack in the library's drapes. He could make out Angelique bending over someone in a bed. He stuffed down rising fears of childhood memories until

Angelique moved from the bedside, and he saw his stepfather. He grunted in disbelief.

By candlelight, the sickly old man looked nothing like what Colin remembered of his stepfather. Could this be the same person who gave him nightmares of humiliation and beatings? No, that adversary of his dreams was robust and twenty years younger. This man appeared so needy, an invalid. Colin shook his head. He would have to sort out this mind-blowing incongruity later.

Entering the dark and quiet house, he crept easily into the kitchen and slowly pushed open the door to Elisabeth's room. She was propped against a pillow, cradling her baby. At first, she was alarmed by his presence. Clare jumped from the chair next to her bed with a knife in her hand.

The women relaxed as Colin put his finger to his lips.

"Oh, Mr. Richardson. It is you. Come meet baby Abigail. Come see," Elisabeth whispered, as she discreetly removed the sleeping baby from her chest and covered herself.

Colin found that Elisabeth's warmth and radiance undid his cold resolve. He felt out of place, but he moved in closer. New life cast its enchantment.

Elisabeth laughed. "You remind me of the many fathers I have seen at the births of their firstborns. Men! They can be so capable in many ways, but wee ones slay their hearts. Do not worry, Mr. Richardson." She added, whispering, "A baby's power cannot harm you while she sleeps."

Colin moved in and peered down at the fuzzy red head. She was a marvel, but he did not think the wrinkled creature very pretty.

"Is she not the most beautiful baby?" Elisabeth asked.

"Aye, yes she is," he lied awkwardly, and muttered, "Red hair, like her mother's."

"It does appear that way," she proudly claimed. "Here, Clare, help Mr. Richardson hold her."

"No! No! No! I can admire from a distance." He backed away to the door.

Clare grunted and rose from the chair, grabbing Colin's arm. "Sit down here, Monsieur Richardson." She chuckled as he awkwardly complied.

Clare gently took Abigail from Elisabeth and placed the baby in Colin's stiff arms.

"Loosen your arms a bit, Mr. Richardson. It will be easier," Elisabeth said, relishing the moment.

He nodded and then looked down at the peaceful babe with puckered lips. Aye, she was a little pretty, in some homely kind of way.

He did not know if he uttered these words in his head or under his breath, but they caught him by surprise: *Ah, wee one, may all your waters be calm. May God bless you day and night!*

To break the silence, Elisabeth whispered, "Mr. Richardson, thank you. Without your help, I do not think Abigail would have been born."

Colin looked at Elisabeth, whose face was weary but happy. He knew he had to say it, but it felt like sand in his mouth.

He whispered truthfully, "Mrs. Allerton, I swear it! I swear I will get you and this wee one to Boston! You have my word."

Teary-eyed, she lifted her hands in gratefulness, then clasped them and said, "Thank you, Mr. Richardson! Oh, thank you, kind sir! You cannot know how much that means to us."

Chapter 41

Madame Chauvin's Dilemma

At breakfast, a baffled Gerard came into the kitchen, holding ropes in clenched fists. He reported to Angelique that Zena had done the impossible.

"Angelique, you know I would have tied these ropes extra tight!" he said. He was angry and mystified as to how the witch had broken free of his knots.

Angelique spewed French words Elisabeth did not understand and was glad of it. The new mother placed sleeping Abby in a nearby basket and thanked God her baby could not know of Zena's present danger. Observing Gerard and Angelique's anger made her fears rise, but glancing at her innocent child fortified her. She renewed her determination to handle Zena and any other danger that dared to cross her.

After Angelique calmed down, the French woman rubbed her hands together as if to remove dustings of flour. "No matter, Gerard. I doubt she will come back to Ross Hall!" She emphasized these words for Elisabeth's sake. "I wager Zena has run off into the jungle to hide. May a poisonous snake bite her!" Her fist punched the air, and then in a softer voice, she ordered, "Gerard, you must go and tell Eduard and alert Abasi's people about this crazy woman."

Gerard nodded and limped off, muttering to himself.

"He will find her," Angelique said confidently as she picked up the breakfast tray Elisabeth had assembled for Gervais. It bore Kidoh's miracle drink and a broken egg floating in a bowl of chicken broth.

Later, Elisabeth planned for Louis to sip Culpeper's "Drink a Julep," a mix of white-wine vinegar, rose water, spring water and much sugar, steeped together and cooled.

The Ross Hall kitchen was well equipped for anything Elisabeth desired, and Angelique instructed the servants to do what Madame Chauvin requested. Without Adele's presence, the kitchen help was friendlier and much more accommodating. Even the head cook admired the newborn.

Then, Angelique beckoned Elisabeth to the hallway and whispered, "Elisabeth, Poppa knows you bore your baby last night. He wants to see her. Maybe this afternoon, all right? New life will cheer him." Angelique smiled toward the basket, but Elisabeth shivered. Her masquerade could be so easily undone, especially with a red-haired infant, but she did not want to dampen her friend's cheerfulness.

"Certainly, Angelique. When do you think Adele will be returning?" The thought made her even more wary.

"It could be anytime. When Gerard tells Eduard about Zena, she will be begging Eduard to allow her return. He will not be able to keep her beyond tomorrow."

Elisabeth picked up a grunting Abby from the basket, and Angelique continued. "Adele will be pleased with Poppa's progress but suspicious of your miracle healing. Elisabeth, it may be difficult, but you must be as accommodating as you can. I am sure Adele would not hesitate to deliver you to the authorities if she knew your secret. Which reminds me, I brought more hair dye and some leather gloves for my hands!"

"Angelique, how long will you be staying?" The thought of Angelique leaving her brought fear. So much for the bravado she felt at breakfast.

"Clare and I will leave when Adele returns. If we were to stay longer, she would be suspicious. And my friend, I am sorry, but I feel like a caged bird in this house. Even though my cottage is so much smaller, I am restless here. Ross Hall was the house of my childhood and not my womanhood. Oh, chérie, do not look so downcast. We will come often to see Poppa and baby Abigail."

Elisabeth did not dare protest, but she realized this might be the best time to request something else.

"Angelique, forgive me, but I must speak out. Since I saw the portrait of your mother, I have known you and Mr. Richardson are brother and sister. I have observed how this family discord lies heavy on your heart. So, I must ask, is there any way reconciliation is possible? Cannot the memory of your beautiful mother be common ground?" Elisabeth spoke cautiously. She knew she intruded.

Angelique sighed. "I wondered when you would put our sad family pieces together. This one subject neither Poppa nor Colin will even discuss with me. Poppa says, 'Let the past stay dead. Leave it alone.' Colin says, 'Angelique, I will not drag you into this matter.' With both of them I have begged, thrown tantrums, refused to speak with them. Nothing works. Stubborn fools! They do not realize how their secret feelings affect Eduard and me, too!"

She shrugged. "I wish with all my heart that reconciliation was possible between these two men. But, Elisabeth, it would take a miracle greater than Kidoh's medicine to change what is." The young woman closed her eyes. "Do you have a receipt to take away bitter regrets and lingering memories?" She opened her eyes and smiled resignedly. "I better get breakfast to Poppa." Pointing to a squirming Abigail, she said, "I think your baby wants to eat!"

Elisabeth went to her room and gently placed Abby on her bed. She loved looking at her. She so wished David could be there to know his daughter from her beginning days. Why God had allowed this separation grieved her so, but she would not allow herself to doubt his wisdom. Her fate could be so much worse. And she had a daughter! A heart of gratitude is what she desired to nurture.

She trembled, remembering Zena's twisted intentions to appease her gods by killing her and sacrificing Abigail in some kind of pagan ritual. She knew God desired forgiveness of one's enemies. After all, he had forgiven her. But forgiving Zena seemed like an impossible task.

She prayed, confessing, "Help me to forgive. I have hatred in my heart for this enemy."

That afternoon, Elisabeth took Abby to visit Monsieur Gervais. He was propped up in a chair and staring out the window.

"Ah, the one who saved me," he said hoarsely. Elisabeth marveled at his remarkable improvement—a miracle! His eyes and skin coloring appeared brighter, and his movements showed a little strength.

"Sir, I did very little. Our God cures you!" Elisabeth wished she could give Kidoh a little credit as well, but that would be too dangerous for him and her.

Gervais snorted and waved his hand as if shooing a fly. "I do not believe it has anything to do with Providence, Madame, but I gladly admit feeling better and stronger." After coughing a little, he added, "I finally am hopeful I will recover. Madame Chauvin, come closer. Let me see your infant."

Elisabeth was surprised by the commanding voice of her patient. She drew nearer and pulled back the blanket, proudly showing Abigail.

"Ah yes, red hair, like yours," he whispered smoothly.

The way he stared intently for her reaction caught Elisabeth off guard. *How did this feeble man know?* She wanted to pull her scarf over all her hair. Was her hair's true color peeking through so much that a sick man noticed or was he fishing out his suspicions? She did not know how to behave, but she slowly pulled Abigail toward her.

"Is it Madame Chauvin, or is it Madame Allerton?" he taunted, watching her face for any reaction. He seemed to be drawing strength from her fear.

Elisabeth froze for only a moment and then looked steadily into his eyes. For her baby's sake, she had to be convincing, fearless, at least in appearance. *God help me!* "Monsieur, I am Madame Chauvin. Who is this Madame Allerton?"

"Sit, Madame Chauvin." He sighed but seemed to savor having some power, even in his weakened state.

Elisabeth sat on the chair next to his, trying to suppress fear and a great desire to flee.

"Do not be frightened, Madame. I am grateful to you for my remarkable recovery after lying helpless in that damn bed for so many days. You should not underestimate how news swirls like tidal waves around this island. It always settles at my door, even if most people are convinced it is a dead man's door. We will surprise them, will we not?"

He chuckled at his joke and observed her reaction. Elisabeth determined to feed him no information. She would sort out Gervais' comments later.

He pressed, "Please tell me, how have you managed to stay out of the authorities' sight these many months? That puzzles me a little."

Gervais coughed, and his shaky hand took a sip of tea. "They are not looking for a pregnant Madame as you recently were, but they are on watch for a sailor and a redheaded woman. English spies, the authorities say. You are English, are you not, Madame Chauvin?"

"Sir, I do not understand these inquiries, but I assure you I am no spy. I am here at the request of Mademoiselle Angelique to help you get well."

Elisabeth knew she was no good at deception, but she hoped Gervais was not as confident as he sounded.

"Ah, secrets, Madame Chauvin. Those challenge me. It really does not matter what you say because I have theories to test and prove." The man coughed, wiped his hand on his mouth, and continued. "If you are lying, I will find out the truth. But have no fear. You keep restoring me back to health, and I think you will discover I am a worthy ally to you and your newborn."

Elisabeth silently grasped for something to say, but fortunately Gervais seemed satisfied with his inquisition.

"Madame Chauvin, would you please refill my cup with your marvelous receipt and ring the bell for Clare? This has been an enlightening diversion, but I need to rest. And you, Madame, you just bore a baby. Surely you need to rest and tend to your little redheaded one."

As Elisabeth tried to pour the drink steadily, she felt his penetrating eyes upon her. He really enjoyed his power. She gave him the cup, curtsied, and wanted to rush out of the room. Yet she refused to give him any more satisfaction of feeding her fear. She forced herself to move slowly away, but she could hear him chuckling behind her. What kind of man was Angelique's Poppa? He chilled her soul.

In early evening, Adele returned, and the house seemed dismal once again despite the tropical light. Adele acknowledged Elisabeth with a nod and barely glanced at her baby.

"I know this child will not deter you from fulfilling your duties, Madame Chauvin," she sniffed. Then she rushed into Louis's study and closed the door.

Elisabeth could hear Adele's voice, chirping about the change of health in her master. Angelique, too, joined in this joyful chatter.

Elisabeth felt cold and held her baby tightly. She knew Angelique and Clare would leave soon and return to their cottage. She so wished she could go with them or run off to Abasi's encampment.

Her conversation with Monsieur Gervais kept her edgy and puzzled. He was, indeed, a complicated man with a dark soul. How she wished she could go search for Colin. Perhaps she could find him at one of St. Paola's bawdy taverns. But if she ran to find him, then what would happen? He would be very displeased. She knew that although it was dangerous to stay at Ross Hall, it was even more foolish to leave.

Elisabeth resolved she must wait until Colin came to her. She must pray they find passage to leave this island as soon as possible. She would force herself to believe that someday she would be safe again in David's arms. Last night, Colin reassured her and vowed again he would help her and Abigail reunite with her husband. She must cling to that promise. It remained a shaft of light in this dark house.

Chapter 42

Party Plans

During the next week, Elisabeth saw no sign of either Colin, or Zena. Adele slept in Louis' room and took care of him at night. The mistress of the house hovered during the day, too, scowling disapproval at Elisabeth. To Elisabeth's relief, as Gervais grew stronger, he seemed less interested in her and Abby.

Adele enlisted slave boy Peppy to help with most tasks. She instructed Elisabeth to sit on a chair outside Gervais' room and come when the bell summoned her. Fortunately, Clare had given her a large, hand-woven basket for Abigail to lie in as Elisabeth sat by the door. She read when she could or sang quietly to Abby.

Daily, Elisabeth rushed from kitchen to library at Adele's bell-bidding for egg, soup, tea, and strong drink. She persuaded Adele and the cook to try Dr. Alexander Read's receipt for cock ale, although they were skeptical. It took Elisabeth and the grumbling cook much of a day to make and bottle the chicken brew. Then Elisabeth emphasized the mixture had to set for a month before it could be used. Cook Marie tasted it and scrunched her face, adding black pepper to her sample.

Louis said little, but Elisabeth sensed he savored his power to threaten her. After all, he could summon soldiers to arrest her at any time. Obviously, that deed would put him in greater favor with Viceroy de la Roche. Elisabeth suppressed fears of what would happen if she were arrested. Officially, she still could be charged for killing that French soldier aboard the *Xavier*. The guilty were hung for less.

Gervais now regularly sat up in bed. With Adele's help and the use of a stick, he shuffled around the library. Eduard visited often to discuss plantation business. The son acknowledged Elisabeth with a nod, but said little. One day while Elisabeth poured tea, Louis declared in English, "I want to have a dinner party."

Eduard looked puzzled, glancing at Elisabeth, but he also answered in English, "Poppa, are you strong enough?"

"I eat and talk, do I not? I want to have the island leaders over, lots of people. I want to know what everyone is thinking. I also want them to see for themselves that Louis Gervais is back from the grave!"

"Are you sure, Poppa, it is not too soon? You know I tell you everything I hear. In fact, I wanted to tell you I spoke with the Viceroy de la Rouche yesterday, and he is nervous. Ships carry rumors that France and England may go to war again, and he fears we will come under attack."

"Not surprising, Eduard. We must anticipate war as regularly as we expect ships to visit our harbor. Fickle royalty! All the more reason to make sure Ross Hall is prepared for anything. We strengthen our survival with local allies. This is even more reason to host a dinner as soon as possible," said Gervais.

The men sat in comfortable silence. Adele bustled in and smoothed Louis's bed coverings. Elisabeth stood awkwardly, awaiting new instructions. As she listened, she concentrated on revealing no emotions and puzzled over why she was privy to this conversation in English.

Then Eduard slowly spoke as if he were thinking out loud. "Some plantation owners have been talking about a hunt of Abasi's people, breaking the black market once and for all. They grumble of dealing with runaway slaves, too, and picking up some free labor. A hunting party would build unity among the owners as well as improve local shooting skills."

He then proposed, "Poppa, would you like to host a grand dinner and hunt? I could bring some of my slaves over to help with preparations. Or, Isabella and I could host if you would need more time to convalesce."

"Ah, Eduard! What an excellent suggestion. If war is brewing, the island owners must maintain fearful compliance among their slaves before they face an external enemy. A hunt would serve all of us well. The musket practice and camaraderie would be good, and we could wipe out the jungle pests permanently. Trust me, I am quite healthy enough to host guests at Ross Hall and enjoy a meal."

He stared at Elisabeth when he said this. She busied herself with the tray.

Gervais continued, "As an added benefit, we can find that wretched Zena. You would like to have Zena back, would you not, Adele?"

Adele nodded and smiled stiffly. Zena was a sore topic. "I certainly would desire a chance to whip her for bringing added harm to you, Louis."

Louis chuckled. "You were deceived by her charade, Adele. I understand, but never allow feelings to snuff out your good judgment."

"Poppa, the commoners will not favor us if we bother their jungle suppliers too much."

"I do not concern myself with commoners, Eduard. They will become agreeable at the first sign of any threat, and we can toss them some bones when we have to."

Gervais became more enthused. "Eduard, you must speak with Viceroy de la Roche and involve him to select the day. Adele, I expect you to begin working on a menu. We will invite the usual guests, but I want to meet new people, too. Let us bring out our best wine and rum. We will get them all so drunk that before the night is over, they will be spilling every secret. Knowledge is power, Eduard."

"Ah, Poppa, you are feeling more like yourself!" The son glowed with admiration.

The older man smiled coldly as he waved Elisabeth away. Officially dismissed, she could hear the father and son conversing in French again and her heart sank. She realized more and more that with Louis Gervais there were so many layers of intentions. She must be careful, but somehow she also must warn Abasi and his people.

The next day after morning duties were fulfilled, Adele instructed Elisabeth to tend the kitchen garden. Then the mistress latched the library door to be alone with Gervais. The winter noontime sun was warming and Adele's order gave Elisabeth and Abby welcomed solitude in the garden. Elisabeth routinely included strolls through the maze and along the hedge, hoping Colin would bring her news. This day, Elisabeth walked in the maze and came upon a gardener in a wide brim straw hat trimming a hedge next to the Hercules statue.

"Ah, Mrs. Allerton, sit down on the bench and tend to your baby so no one suspects you are acquainted with me."

"Mr. Richardson! Are you not concerned someone will recognize you?"

"No, not really. I used to play hide and seek in this maze as a boy and go for hours undisturbed, especially at this time of day. Hercules provides fairly good coverage from watching eyes at the house. Although I remember old Herc being much bigger back then."

Elisabeth burst with her news, but she realized she must be cautious. She sat down on the bench, peering into Abby's face as she spoke. "Mr. Richardson, I have the most terrible news."

"Well, this will be no fair exchange then. My news is good," Colin said as he clipped.

"You have a ship for us!" Elisabeth exclaimed.

"Bad news first. Let me hear."

Elisabeth's words rushed out, "Monsieur Gervais is planning a party, and a jungle hunt of the kind you told me about! They want to clear the island of spies and runaway slaves. I fear they want to destroy Chief Abasi's village permanently."

Colin stopped trimming and spit. "That old snake has not changed! He bites whenever he gets a chance! I told you, Mrs. Allerton, you should have let him die!"

Colin's anger distressed Elisabeth. His accusing words spoke truth and they hurt, but she simply asked, "What can we do?"

"You must leave," he said firmly.

"Leave now?"

"Aye, your presence is little consequence in this matter, but it could place you in greater danger. I have made contact with an old acquaintance. He is English and trades on St. Paola. He has a small boat hidden from the authorities that he occasionally sails to St. Kitts. That island has an English community where his wife and children live. He always needs money, so he is willing to take you and Abigail with him. From St. Kitts, it will only be a matter of time before you book passage to Boston."

"Mr. Richardson, this plan sounds dangerous. Is your colleague a trustworthy man?"

"Aye, Richard Gates is a good seaman and more honest than most. To guarantee his loyalty, I told him that if Angelique does not receive a Boston letter from his passenger within a year, I would come after him and his family. He knows better than to double-cross me."

This threat alarmed Elisabeth, but she appreciated the seaman's protective nature. "What about you, Mr. Richardson? I thought you were coming with us."

Colin finished his trimming and took off his hat to wipe his brow. "Mrs. Allerton, I need to move on. The sea is my home. There is nothing for me in New England." He said it more firmly than he felt. He wanted her to believe he thought of her as a burden.

"I understand. I do," Elisabeth said, biting her lip. How could she expect more from him? But her conscience pricked. "This hunt

Gervais is planning is so evil. How can I leave, knowing people who helped me are in such danger?"

"What could you possibly do to prevent this, Mrs. Allerton? Abasi and his people will do what they must to survive. They knew this day was coming. It is really their fight, not yours."

Mr. Richardson gave a convincing argument. Elisabeth knew it, but she felt so torn.

"Mrs. Allerton, you must think of baby Abigail. And your husband." Adding that last part was difficult, but he had to be persuasive. "Listen carefully. I will pick you up tomorrow evening when the household is settled. You will hear a rooster's crow that sounds like this." He demonstrated softly, cupping his hands to his mouth. "Understand?"

She nodded. She had heard alarmed roosters infrequently crowing at night. It would not draw suspicion.

Colin asked, "Do you have any medicine that will keep little Abby from crying? A baby's cry could bring us ruin."

"Oh, Abigail!" Elisabeth did not like the suggestion of drugging her. She said hesitantly, "Kidoh gave me some dried leaves that he says makes a good sleeping drink. I believe you are familiar with it. I suppose I could give her a little."

"Do it," he said firmly and mused, "Kidoh's brew had me sleeping like a baby. You won't need much." As Colin slipped away into the hedge, he added, "This is our best hope, Mrs. Allerton. You must be prepared for anything."

Elisabeth reluctantly agreed. He was right. Finally, here was her chance to get off the island and make it to Boston! As she walked back into Ross Hall, she could not ease her thoughts about escape. Had she not longed for this news? Now that it was time, she shivered with fear and hesitation.

Chapter 43

Choices

The next day Elisabeth went about her duties hoping no one would pick up on her nervousness. Then she spilled Monsieur Gervais' medicine. His eyes bore into hers.

"Pardon, Monsieur," she said humbly, wiping the spill with her apron and tucking a blanket around her master. He allowed the mistake to pass without comment.

With Adele, he wanted details on party preparations. The guest list was altered numerous times. It seemed to Elisabeth the entire household wished her and Abby invisible. With Adele around, no one dared to converse with her. As for Gervais' knowledge of her true identity, Elisabeth assumed he felt confident she had nowhere to go and would be readily available when he needed leverage against her. She knew his presumptions and the staff's neglect would make her escape easier.

Elisabeth thanked God that Abigail slept often and experienced little colic. Her daughter nursed well and was healthy and strong. Despite her mother's tumultuous feelings, Abigail in an infant cocoon remained oblivious to danger.

As for Zena, Gerard did not find her, and this greatly agitated the man. Elisabeth knew the foreman prided himself on tracking abilities, but crazy Zena left no trace. Gerard and Angelique assured Elisabeth the runaway must be hiding in the jungle and would not dare step foot in Ross Hall.

It gave Elisabeth chills thinking Zena might pop out of nowhere and take revenge on her and Abby. She put the chair in front of her door when she went to bed, reciting the Twenty-third Psalm to calm her nerves. "Yea, though I should walk through the valley of the shadow of death, I will fear no evil; for thou art with me: thy rod and thy staff, they comfort me. Thou dost prepare a table before me in the sight of mine adversaries...."

Colin had warned Elisabeth not to tell anyone of their plans, not even Angelique. Everyone's safety depended on it, he had emphasized, and she understood. Yet her conscience struggled with how she could abandon Abasi and his people. They welcomed her into their village and kept her protected even though they were at risk. Was it really God's will for her to leave in such a cowardly manner while they faced being hunted like wild boar?

Elisabeth spent as much time as possible kneeling in prayer by her bed. She paged through her Bible, marveling that it and her belongings were still with her. Surely their preservation was a sign of God's faithfulness. Reluctantly, she knew she would have to leave them behind once again, but she prepared herself to do it.

God had protected her thus far and would provide all she and baby Abby needed. She pleaded for his mercy on Abasi and his people. Finally, when she said her last prayers, she resolved to do whatever it took to reunite her family. Still, there remained a nagging tug at her conscience.

Far into the night, Elisabeth heard Colin's rooster call and gently grabbed sleeping Abby. Fortunately, she had walked the grounds so often she knew the path well even with little moonlight. Gingerly she stepped her way to Hercules's bench where she and Colin agreed to meet. Elisabeth barely made out his shadowy form moving in the darkness when he saw her approach.

"It is a long walk," he whispered, "but we should get to the rendezvous point before dawn. You and Abigail will be able to rest then before taking the boat."

Elisabeth took a deep breath. "Wait, Mr. Richardson," she said softly, grabbing his arm. "I must tell you something." She felt him stiffen, and she hurried on. "I am sorry, but Abigail and I are staying here for now."

He was tempted to curse but gritted out the words quietly. "What do you mean, Mrs. Allerton? Not go now?"

She quickly explained. "I have prayed earnestly about these circumstances, and I cannot leave! I have no peace in the matter. This jungle hunt! There may be something I can do to stop this awful injustice. I do not know what, but I must try and I will."

She knew she sounded crazy, but she grew more confident with the saying of it. Her decision was simply the right course of action to take.

"Woman!" Colin grabbed her shoulders and wanted to shake her. "Do you realize you put yourself and little Abby in greater harm by staying? Dammit, this is your chance for escape! I cannot promise another opportunity like this."

"I know, I know, Mr. Richardson. Please, hear me. I am grateful for all you have done for us these many months, and I know how much trouble we have been," Elisabeth whispered tearfully. "I owe you my life, sir, but I cannot leave and suffer a pricked conscience the rest of my days. What kind of Christian would I be then? You have no need to bear any responsibility for Abby and me. You have done more than enough. God has kept us safe thus far, and I trust him, no matter what lies ahead."

"Oh, you trust in the invisible, do you?" Colin mocked her bitterly. "I guarantee, Mrs. Allerton, that if you stay, you will see more hell than heaven on this island. You do realize you and Abby will almost certainly die!"

Colin knew it was unsafe for them to whisper in the maze, and he was tired of this insanity. He turned and moved slightly away from Elisabeth. The thought slipped through his mind that he could meet Gates at the rendezvous point and take passage himself to get off this cursed island. He finally could get away from her.

He threw up his hands, and looked back to her. "So be it, Mrs. Allerton. I wash my hands of you. It is goodnight and goodbye."

"Mr. Richardson, are you able to leave this island while your friends and Angelique face such evil?" She asked the question more out of puzzlement than accusation.

"Dammit, woman, I have been saying goodbye to St. Paola all my life. It is simply survival. Live or be killed." He added, "You with your Puritan code of right and wrong have no idea about the troubles that prick my conscience."

Elisabeth really did not understand. But she was resolved. She moved to him and touched his shoulder once again. "Well then, it truly is goodbye. God bless you, Mr. Richardson, and thank you for all you have done. You have been a true gentleman. Someday, I will tell Abby about how you saved her and her mother."

Colin's heart lurched for one brief pause as he touched Abby's head in the shadows. "I will get money to you somehow through Angelique." Then, before Elisabeth could protest, he was gone.

She felt strangely empty and yet at peace. She took in a deep breath. She realized she had turned her back on the greatest opportunity for freedom. Yet her decision to stay went to the core of who she was. Through all her troubles, she knew God had been with her in suffering and loneliness. He still could provide another way of escape. She believed that, but she could not fathom how such a miracle would occur without Colin's help. No matter, she told herself. Colin had left, but God was near. Like the Old Testament men thrown into the fiery furnace, she resolved to believe that God would save. And like those men, she was willing to die for her convictions if he did not intervene.

Not far from Elisabeth, hiding in the maze, a twitching Zena watched Elisabeth return to the house. Her fingers pumped her knife, her chest heaved, and her eyes blinked wildly. She wanted to charge this wretched woman and stab her over and over again. But, an invisible barrier restrained her.

She painfully whispered, "Not yet, not yet. Yemoja says wait. Wait."

Zena reluctantly put her knife back into her sheath, muttered a chant, and slipped quietly into the nearby storage shed where Gerard had tied her up many nights before.

Colin made it to the rendezvous point in time to rest and eat. At dawn, a rowboat appeared with Richard Gates in it.

Colin signaled him. "Ahoy mate, I see once again the authorities did not net an old slippery eel like yourself."

"Damn right about that, Colin," said Gates, jumping out of his boat. He was in a hurry to get on with their bargain. Searching about, he asked, "Where are the woman and baby?"

"She bailed on us, Gates. Women! This one is particularly irksome, so count your blessings you do not have to take her on as a passenger."

"Ah, Colin, then will you be coming with me? I much prefer your company."

Gates took a swig from a jug and wiped his mouth on his sleeve. He offered it to Colin. "We should hurry though—the tide is good. If you do not object, I would like my payment upfront before we take off."

"Right, mate. No worries. I have your money, just let me get my bag."

Throughout the long walk from Ross Hall, the idea of leaving with Gates had tumbled in Colin's mind. Colin wanted more than anything to get on this boat and put physical distance between himself and cursed St. Paola—all the people who were driving him insane.

Fleeing St. Paola consistently kept him from being overwhelmed by a past he felt powerless to change, but this time leaving conflicted him. Elisabeth Allerton's words and example hit their mark.

Could he really abandon Berko, Abasi, and Angelique without a fight? Was he such a coward? Did old and weak Louis Gervais still have the power to push him away from everything that meant anything to him? Still, what could he or any of them really do? They would be ridiculously overpowered by Gervais' control of the island.

Suddenly, somewhere within himself, he distinctly heard two commanding words: *Finish it!* Could the decision really be that simple? Was it time for Colin the man to stop running like Colin the boy had been forced to do?

He sighed and reached into his bag, giving Gates his payment in a pouch of coins.

"Thank you, Colin. I need this," the sailor said, saluting with the pouch and then knotting it to his belt. "We best be going."

"Ah, Gates, I guess you will not be taking any passengers this time. I have changed my mind."

Gates looked surprised, then broke into laughter. "Oh, Colin, if I did not know you better, I would say a certain little mother has bewitched you."

Colin laughed. "You know me better! She is a Puritan, Gates, and married, too."

Gates laughed harder. "Be careful then, or you might find God's eye upon you, and you will discover it unfavorable. I learned long ago not to mess with religion or married women." He crossed himself and whispered, "No sense in tempting fate."

"Get out of here, you old sea devil," Colin said. "Godspeed."

"And to you, mate. You know how to reach me if you need my services again."

As the sunrise radiated pink and orange against its blues, Colin helped Gates push his rowboat into the water. Then he sat on the beach, watching the boat bob on the waves until it became a small speck and disappeared. He shook sand off his clothing and headed for Abasi's village.

Chapter 44

Berko's Plan for Escape

When Colin told Abasi news of the hunt, it only confirmed what the chief's black market contacts were already saying. Abasi called for a village meeting, and he invited Colin. To be included to council meant the tribe respected Colin as an advisor, or so he thought.

That night, as the campfire lit the somber faces, he wondered what this group of outcasts would do. Throughout the years, they heard stories from other islands of terrible bloodshed. Although there had been sporadic violence on St. Paola, the plantation owners' actions had been more a symbolic gesture rather than full-scale assault. The settlers valued trading with Abasi's people and usually overlooked the occasional runaway slave who joined them. But this time something seemed different. Colin could sense their fear.

"I say we strike first and kill as many as we can! The hunted will be the hunters!" shouted one young man, shaking a spear with one hand and a pistol with the other. "We have friends working on the plantations who will fight with us!"

Others muttered their approval.

"We cannot take them all down. They are too many with too

many weapons," snorted an older man. "Gervais and the others are no fools. And, trusting our plantation friends is unwise. If just one slave betrays, we all die!"

"I would rather die than become a slave again!" retorted the man.

"You are brave, but what about our children?" asked a mother tightly holding a little boy. "How can we protect them if we die? They will die, too, or become slaves without us. This happened to me when I was a child until Abasi's people took me in."

People broke into conversations, muttering in anger and fear. Colin knew their options were few, but they were struggling to grasp at any lifeline.

When some of their passion subsided, Berko stood up. He waited for them to notice him and become silent so he could speak.

"My brothers and sisters, I tell you a hard truth. We no longer can live on this island as we have lived for many years. More and more strangers come, and there are more and more slaves. We know it is becoming impossible to hide because our jungle is being cleared for plantations."

Several nodded, and there were murmurs of agreement. Others shifted their bodies nervously. If Berko, the master of staying invisible, said it was impossible, what hope did they have? The gathering quieted down again, but Berko remained silent.

It feels like a funeral, thought Colin.

Finally, Berko spoke. "We have two choices. If we stay, we die or become slaves—all of us."

"Then we fight to the death!" spat the young man.

"No!" said Berko, raising his hand. "I am not afraid to die, but I want to live! I want all of us to live! There have been far too many deaths already."

Abasi asked, "Berko, do you see another path?"

"Yes, Chief Abasi, I think there is a better way. My brothers and sisters, my father often spoke of his dream to take me to his homeland. I have had visions of this place many times, and I have seen myself living there with others."

"Berko, dreaming is for sleepers. Wake up! Our past is gone!" muttered an old woman. Several snorted and shook their heads in dismay.

Berko held up his hand. "You may find it foolish, but I do not. Hear me out. I have a blood brother who sits among us tonight. He has sailed the waters to many places including my homeland. My brother Colin Richardson could lead us off this island and to my homeland in Africa."

Colin choked on the spirits he was drinking as all eyes turned toward him. Clever Abasi, the fox! Now he knew why he had been invited.

Colin stood up, sputtering protest. "Berko, hold on there! You cannot be serious!"

"You are a great seaman, Colin. And you know the way to our homeland."

"Well, yes, it is true I am a seaman, but I have no ship, no crew, no money—"

Berko interrupted, "You can teach us, Colin! We can steal a ship! You journeyed on the *Xavier*, and she sits in our harbor right now, waiting to be snatched. We can take her while everyone is busy hunting us!"

The people buzzed with excitement. Hope fired in their eyes. Colin wished he had a bucket of water to douse such impossible flames.

He protested loudly, "Hold on! This is crazy! I cannot lead you into such danger. You would all be killed before we even left the harbor. Or worse, out at sea without any seamen among you to navigate the storms, you would drift endlessly and end up a ghost ship. No, this idea is impossible! I am sorry, my friends, but you must choose a different course of action without my help."

Colin spilled his spirits on the ground and walked away.

Berko followed him, and Colin finally stopped and leaned against a boulder far from the campfires. "Berko, you should have not tricked me like this and offered these people a hopeless plan."

Berko leaned against the boulder next to him. "Ah, Colin, my brother. Hope is better than death. My people need this. We cannot survive here. You know that. We will try to take a ship without you if you do not help us."

Colin scoffed. "You are all landlubbers. Is there even one sailor among you? Maybe we could get word to Richard Gates to make some trips to ferry you to another island. You could hide for a while and then return when circumstances are better. That plan is more hopeful than getting you to Africa. Trust me, it is no paradise."

Berko sighed. "Colin, I am tired of running and hiding. I want my freedom and my homeland. Do you think I should hide in a cave all my life? You know I have saved many gold coins. Listen to me. We can bribe a few seamen, but we need a captain we can trust. That would be you. My brother, have I ever asked anything of you since you gave me this?" Berko pointed to the tattoo on his cheek.

Colin stared long at Berko. He had never seen his friend more serious. It was true. Berko had never asked him for anything. He understood his dream, his longing for freedom, but this idea held no good ending. Colin's head spun with impossible logistics and the odds of betrayal.

Saying yes would mean suicide or hanging. Yet was his self-preservation really so important anymore? There was a long silence as Berko kept his eyes and mouth closed in prayer.

Finally, Colin shrugged and simply said, "Dammit, Berko. I guess if we are to die, dying with you makes some kind of foolhardy sense."

Berko opened his eyes, laughed, and embraced Colin. "We can do this, my brother! Do not look so sad. It will be Onyame's special gift to us. You will see."

"You and Mrs. Allerton and your God talk! It bears on me worse than a toothache. I will make you a deal, Berko. If we do not die through this venture and live to sail the *Xavier* on open sea, I will swear there is a powerful God watching over us. But my better judgment advises you to prepare for our deaths. And, please, when we die together, you must grant me a little peace before the rope tightens."

"Ah, brother, then your conversion is another reason for Onyame to grant us favor." Berko grinned broadly.

Colin shook his head. "Come down from the heavens, you fool, so we can make plans to steal a ship. I know Captain Gaspar has kept his men busy fitting the *Xavier* all winter. That ship should be well supplied and in tip-top shape by the time we take it."

Berko chuckled. "How hopeful that sounds to me."

The two men went to counsel with Abasi. The three of them huddled long into the night making plans. They agreed few would know details until the time was ripe.

Chapter 45

Elisabeth's Opportunity with Gervais

A few days later, the dinner party preparations were in full swing at Ross Hall. Elisabeth was downcast and anxious. Colin came to mind often enough, but it did her no good. She knew she must forget him. She determined to bend her thoughts on rescue plans for her island friends as well as for herself and little Abby. What they needed was a miracle. Her twisted plans became pleading prayers.

At times, Elisabeth dwelt on how foolish she had been to refuse Colin's final offer of escape. When she told Angelique, the French woman's surprised look confirmed she had made the wrong decision. Fortunately, her friend refrained from comment and simply took her hand and squeezed it hard while shaking her head. Elisabeth's head and heart hurt thinking on how her decision jeopardized Abby's life. She made Angelique promise to care for her daughter if something happened to her.

Elisabeth thought Angelique would protest, but she simply said, "I still hope we can find a way to get you both off the island. But if that is not possible, I promise you I will do all I can for Abby."

This pledge was an enormous relief to the young mother, and it catapulted her to boldness. Elisabeth determined she would approach Gervais and attempt to plead with him to cancel the wicked hunt. Surely even he could be persuaded to recognize such evil. But there never seemed to be a good opportunity to speak to him. Adele constantly hovered over her master, and she eyed Elisabeth with suspicion and contempt. When Adele once caught Elisabeth wiping tears from her eyes, she sneered, "An eagle does not concern itself with a fly. Which are you, Madame Chauvin, bird or insect?"

Gervais walked better, albeit weakly, with a cane. Elisabeth often found him resting in front of the portrait of Colin's mother. He seemed unaware his attention to his dead wife made Adele extremely cross. The servants and slaves suffered her displeasure for his lack of attention to her.

As Adele chewed out the cook one afternoon, she ordered Elisabeth to take Louis an herbal drink. While he stared at the portrait of his deceased wife, he dreamily asked her, "Do you have regrets, Madame Chauvin?"

His question caught her off guard because he frequently had ignored her. The question also chilled her, but she sensed an opportunity to speak out. "Monsieur Gervais, I suppose everyone has regrets. We are sinners, after all."

"Ah, yes, sinners. But do you wish you could have changed your destiny?"

Elisabeth thought about her marriage to David. Would it have been better if she had refused to go with him and stayed in England with her family? Then St. Paola would have been nonexistent to her, and she would be with loved ones, safe. The thought surprised her, and she blushed.

Louis laughed. "I tell you, Madame Chauvin, I would have done it all the same. Everything! No regrets. I have wealth, a fine son and daughter, even a grandson. And for a season, I loved one of the most beautiful women in the entire world."

Elisabeth could not resist. "Sir, did she not also have a son, your stepson?

Louis's surprise quickly turned to bemusement. "Ah, my stepson. I am intrigued you have heard of him, Madame Chauvin. I suppose Angelique mentioned him." He took a sip of his drink and said thoughtfully, "Maybe my only regret is I did not allow his foolishness to destroy him before he left the island alive."

Elisabeth's shocked expression made him snort. "His mother loved him way too much, spoiled him. Even as a child, he manipulated her, and he was not worth it! She eventually came around to understand his weak nature. But that is all in the past. He is of little concern to me now. Do this household a favor and persuade Angelique to forget him as I have."

Suddenly Elisabeth realized her conversation might hurt Angelique. She said hastily, "Oh, Monsieur Gervais, your daughter only mentioned her half-brother the first day I arrived, after I admired this portrait of your beautiful wife. It was a comment I should not have said. Forgive me for bringing up the past." She curtsied.

"Angelique is a lot like her mother, too tenderhearted. But it would be wise for you not to mention him ever again. You may leave me now." He dismissed her by returning his gaze to the portrait.

Elisabeth wondered if he ever connected the resemblance between his beloved and the rejected stepson. Slowly, she picked up the tray and left the room. Her face burned, and she scolded herself for using this conversation to plead for Colin, now long gone, when she should have tried to persuade Gervais to cancel the hunt. She shook her head at her terrible mistake. Here was the opportunity she had prayed for, and she had squandered it. Elisabeth could not imagine feeling any worse about this error in judgment.

Chapter 46

Colin Enlists Angelique

Through Colin's regular tavern visits, he kept tabs on Gervais' plans. He knew many guests would arrive at Ross Hall for dinner and some would stay overnight. Hunters would then gather at Ross Hall the following morning to root out jungle people.

To guarantee a grand affair, Viceroy de la Roche promised to have as many officers and local merchants there as possible. The finale for the night's festivities would be fireworks, something many had heard about but never seen.

For Abasi's people, the fireworks' attraction would leave the town and the *Xavier* vulnerable with only minimum security. The *Xavier*, indeed, floated in the bay, primed to sail soon. It had ample supplies aboard as well as a cargo of sugar. Colin planned to sell the wares in Boston and buy provisions for Berko's long, African journey. The seaman still hoped he could persuade Berko against an Atlantic voyage. He wanted to suggest another place for resettlement, but that conversation would have to wait. There were still too many details to worry about first.

Colin started thinking they might have a slim chance of success after all. They, however, needed inside help. He knew he had to let Angelique in on the plans.

"You are planning to do what? Colin, such craziness! You will all be killed!" Angelique fanned herself rapidly, thinking of the possibilities.

"Angelique, would you rather these people bleed slowly in the sugar cane fields or burn in those blasted mills? If they do not die in this damn hunt, they will certainly die as slaves. They want hope and freedom. Can you blame them?" Colin thought he was starting to sound like Berko.

"But, Colin, if your plan does not work, it will be a massacre. Survivors will be hung. You will be hung! Surely the hunt will kill some, but not all. You are talking insurrection! There would be so much bloodshed!"

"I know. This could be the end for all of us. And Angelique, believe me, I hate placing you in the middle of this. I do not want anything to happen to you."

Angelique's face softened, and she hugged her brother. "Oh dear, dear Colin. I am glad this time you have not vanished without a good-bye. You have taken up a noble cause, so of course I will help you. Do not worry about me. I am a survivor!"

Colin looked at his young sister's face and saw something in her that reminded him of his mother from long ago. She definitely was Gervais' daughter with her black curls and eyes, but her good, strong spirit was all from their mother.

"Angelique, you must promise to do exactly as I say so you will be in less danger."

She nodded, but they both knew she would do exactly what she wanted.

"It really will be glorious if you succeed!" Angelique's eyes brightened with the thought. "How can Clare, Gerard, and I help?"

Chapter 47

Dinner Party

The day of the dinner arrived. Elisabeth helped the slaves with food preparations under the watchful eyes of Adele. She felt the heavy fog of sadness that blanketed servants and slaves alike. Even if none of them wore shackles, they helplessly remained chained to fulfilling the orders of their mistress. Their survival depended on it.

Elisabeth decided she must do what she could to prevent more death. She hoped God would forgive her for doing something she thought she was never capable of doing—abusing the administration of her medicines.

She decided to offer beverages to select dinner guests laced with Kidoh's sleeping potion. They would sleep long, she reasoned, and not participate skillfully in the hunt. As she mingled among the guests, she picked out ones who boasted most about their excellent reputation for marksmanship. She whispered a prayer that God would forgive her for using medicines in this deceitful manner.

While Elisabeth busily served her drinks, Dr. Stillingfleet, one of Isabella's attending guests, spotted her. He inched close and grabbed her wrist.

"Well, well, what a surprise to find you here. I thought you and Mr. Richardson had somehow escaped this wretched island without me. Pity, to see you stuck here as am I. By the way, it is a lovely hair color."

The doctor reeked of alcohol and swayed as he tightly held her wrist. Elisabeth remained composed and replied in the little French she knew, "Monsieur, you are mistaken. Please, let go of me. Here, have this last drink on my tray."

"Ah, ah, it is you, Mrs. Allerton. Your French is terrible. Where is Richardson? Maybe you and I could use him as a bargaining chip with my friend, Viceroy de la Roche. He has found me quite useful these days."

Elisabeth forced a smile and pressed the drink into Stillingfleet's free hand. "I am sorry, monsieur. You are mistaken. Please, let go of me before I call out to my friend, Captain Renault."

Dr. Stillingfleet did not release his grip, as he took a sip of the drink. Elisabeth could smell his sour breath. "We will have words later, Mrs. Allerton. I am sure we can come to a fair agreement that will benefit us both on this wretched island. You have yourself set up pretty nicely here. Oh, and didn't I see you with a baby? Think of your child when you so easily disregard me. Monsieur Gervais' beautiful daughter-in-law Isabella and I are also quite friendly. You do not want to tangle with this family without an ally."

Elisabeth noticed Isabella frowning at them from across the room, and then the young Gervais elbowed her way toward them. Elisabeth quickly twisted her arm loose from Stillingfleet's grip and moved away. "Excuse me, I have to get more drinks," she muttered as she headed toward the kitchen.

"Hey, come back here. Where do you think you are going to run, my dear?" Dr. Stillingfleet swaggered after her, but he could not match her pace. He gave up the pursuit as he held his wobbling head and took another swallow.

"Do you know our servant, Madame Chauvin, Monsieur Stillingfleet?" inquired Isabella of the dizzy man.

"Ah, Madame Gervais, I thought I did, but perhaps I was mistaken. She looks like someone I knew when I visited King Louis' court."

"Her?" Isabelle laughed. "Oh Dr. Stillingfleet, you would not find the likes of her in King Louis' court. She is much too plain and simple. These matters I know, trust me."

"Indeed, you do, Madame," replied the doctor, looking around for a chair.

Elisabeth had no idea what Dr. Stillingfleet would say or do in his drunken state, but she knew she could not stay visible. She must get word to Angelique. She rushed to her room, where a little slave girl tended Abby.

"Petite, I want you to find Mademoiselle Gervais. Tell her I need to speak with her in my room as soon as possible."

Angelique flirted with an officer of the *Xavier* when Petite tugged on her sleeve. She bent down to the girl, heard her whispered message, and then said to the officer, "Excuse me, my good sir. There are some problems in the kitchen. I hope to be back shortly. Please, enjoy more food and drink."

She burst into Elisabeth's room. "What is it? You are so pale!"

Elisabeth wrung her hands and paced the floor. "It is that horrible Dr. Stillingfleet! I should have been more cautious, but he recognized me."

"Are you sure? That foolish drunk is barely standing."

"He rallied enough strength to grab my arm, but I fled here. I fear what he might do."

Angelique pressed her lips, thinking, and then ordered, "You must stay here. I doubt Dr. Stillingfleet plans to expose you immediately. He will wait for timing that benefits him most. But we cannot take chances. It is good Colin already has a way to get you off the island during the fireworks this evening."

"Mr. Richardson! What do you mean? Does he remain on the island?"

Angelique nodded, still pondering their next moves.

"Why did you not tell me?" Elisabeth's feelings were so mixed she felt dizzy. "We are leaving tonight with Mr. Richardson?"

"Oui, my friend, you are indeed. We thought it safest not to tell you until it was time."

"But how? Is Mr. Gates returning with a boat?" Elisabeth could not sort it out.

"Trust me, it is safer you do not know. I think, however, it is best if you stay in your room this evening until someone comes for you. I will make excuses for you if Adele notices your absence. If you need anything, have Petite get it for you. I will have her keep an eye on our drunk doctor."

"Angelique, wait. Will I see you again? Is this goodbye?" Elisabeth was dazed at the rapid turn of events.

"What is this? Tears?" Angelique took her lacey hanky from her bosom and wiped Elisabeth's eyes. She cooed softly, "Ah, my brave friend, Elisabeth Allerton. I learned long ago from Colin that goodbyes never mean goodbyes. Who knows what God has in mind? We will meet again." Her face glowed with confidence.

Elisabeth sniffed and nodded. "Angelique, thank you for all you have done for Abby and me. I know hiding us put you in great danger with the authorities. I will never forget your kindness. Please tell Clare thank you, too, and give her our blessings and goodbyes."

"Ah, chérie, you helped heal my father, and brought my brother Colin to my doorstep. I am grateful to you, too. Write me when you are secured in Boston. Godspeed, Madame Chauvin."

Angelique winked and kissed Elisabeth on both cheeks. She then bent down to kiss Abby and quickly swished out the door, the scent of her perfume trailing behind.

Elisabeth could not piece together what was happening. She did not know anything, except that she and Abby must be ready to leave with whomever came to get her. Would it be Colin?

Her thoughts whirled over why he had stayed. Could it be that rescue of Abasi and his people happened in conjunction with her rescue, too? How was that even possible? She did not have enough information to puzzle it out. If David only knew the kind of gentleman Colin Richardson had turned out to be! Would David ever believe her story?

A short while later, Petite brought her a satchel with some food in it. Angelique thought of everything. Elisabeth packed her journal, Bible, clothing, and sadly touched her medicine chest. She needed to travel as lightly as possible with Abby. If necessary, she prepared to drop her few belongings and run with Abby. But the chest had been with her through so much. If she brought it back to David, maybe it would help their reunion be easier. Maybe that was crazy. She reached under her bed for the bag she had brought out of the jungle. She stuffed in the medicine chest and determined to persuade whoever came to get her to carry it for her.

She left a note of instructions for continuing treatment of Monsieur Louis, but she was not optimistic. Kidoh's medicine ran out the day before, and Louis Gervais' pallor already appeared grayer. Elisabeth suspected his illness would return worse than ever. How ironic Monsieur Gervais destroyed himself as he set out to destroy the ones who could save him.

She tucked her knife into her waist pouch and nursed Abby as she restlessly lay on her bed, waiting until it was time for the fireworks.

Chapter 48

Sneaking Around

Out of the seventy members of Abasi's tribe, fifty decided they would risk freedom with the *Xavier*. Colin sent word to boatman Richard Gates and arranged for him to ferry and hide eighteen people on another island. That left two stragglers, Kidoh and Neesa. They refused to leave.

"This is our home. We will not go," they declared to various pleas.

"But it has become too dangerous to stay," Colin insisted.

Berko and Abasi pressured the old couple.

"We need you with us," Berko pleaded.

"I can order you," warned Abasi.

To that, the couple broke out into fits of laughter.

"Do not worry," Kidoh told the three men. "We will hide in the caves and pray good medicine over your departure. Neesa and I know this island better than anyone. We have no desire to leave. St. Paola is where we will die. We are old. It will be soon."

"If you change your mind, Kidoh, there is always room for you and Neesa on the *Xavier*," Colin said, knowing the possibility of that happening was as great as a snowball falling from the sky.

The escape plan was simple but dangerous. For two days, Gerard, with Colin's assistance, lugged a donkey and wagon with building materials through the village to the stony hill that led up to Angelique's cottage. Impulsively, Mademoiselle Angelique Gervais decided she needed an extension on her small home. Gerard's tavern talk guaranteed town folk knew all about it.

Among the wood, inside the water barrels, and within a false wagon floor, Gerard created space for Kidoh's people to stow away. Making numerous trips without drawing suspicion, Gerard and Colin moved Abasi's group through town. The passengers dressed in slave and servant clothing provided by Angelique and Clare.

At the bottom of the hill, Gerard and Colin unloaded supplies while the hidden passengers dropped down and out. These so-called plantation workers then helped carry the materials and (hidden children) up the hill. Only the lazy one with a telescope might observe that less plantation workers came down the hill. Angelique wagered her remodeling appeared harmless and even boring.

A watchful Clare supervised everyone. She hoed in the garden, hung up laundry, and signaled the stowaways to enter the cottage only when she decided the time was right.

Inside, Angelique and Clare demanded order and quiet from their guests. Cranky babies and children were given small doses of Kidoh's sleeping potions that made them lethargic with barely a whimper. "When they are safely on the ship, they can jabber all they want," Clare reassured the mothers.

The hosts kept their stowaways busy. They fitted them with French uniforms and villagers' apparel, courtesy of Kidoh's cave supplies and Colin's resources. They counted on night's darkness to help with their ruse. Clare chastised her guests to quit giggling and teasing each other about how they looked. She pleaded, "S'il vous plaît! You must be serious and walk like a French person. Try, try, try!"

But even she could not help but smile at those who marched

around the room in comical fashion. The atmosphere charged with tension and hope.

At dawn before the hunt, Colin hid and waited in an old mango tree near Ross Hall. Exhausted, he fell asleep and dreamed of his mother walking out of her portrait with her arms reaching toward him. When she stood next to him, her face bent close to his, she whispered, "Do you not remember, Colin? Do you not remember what I whispered to you the day you left home with Uncle Duff? Think and remember!"

With a jerk, he awoke and almost fell out of the tree.

He remembered!

For years, he tried to forget that painful goodbye with his mother when Uncle Duff came for him. She tightly embraced him and whispered tearfully, "Your treasure lies behind me; remember, my Colin, your treasure lies behind me."

At the time, he stiffened at her words, interpreting them to mean she was abandoning him to her past with his father, selfishly claiming a life with Louis Gervais and their children. With anger and disbelief, he jerked away from her and moved to Duff's side, grabbed his bag, and walked away.

Later, he talked with his uncle about why his mother would banish him to the sea under those cruel words, "Your treasure lies behind me."

Uncle Duff assured him she meant his treasure was the family life he experienced with his father and mother before Louis entered the scene. "I guarantee you, Colin," Duff insisted, "Your mother had me take you away, because she wanted to protect you from your stepfather!" Colin found some comfort that his uncle knew his mother's character better than he did as a boy.

And now as an adult so near his childhood home, this dream needled him. He felt there must be more to his mother's odd wording. This day, he determined to find out for certain at Ross Hall.

If he and Berko accomplished their escape, he doubted he would ever return to the island. Now would be his last opportunity to look behind his mother's portrait. Thanks to Gervais' fireworks, he would have the distraction he needed to retrieve Elisabeth and Abby and discover if his mother's haunting words meant anything beyond a dream.

The cliff on Louis' plantation offered perfect viewing for the fireworks when they were to be launched at twilight in the harbor. The carpenters had completed a miniature wooden castle. On a boat sacrificed for the cause, the castle would flame, spin, and spout white and orange fireworks.

To further impress the crowd, Viceroy de la Roche and Louis Gervais ordered the construction of two wooden dragons, pulled by rowboats. The dragons would fight it out on the water in an array of fireworks and smoke. For safety, Viceroy de la Roche ordered the harbored ships to unfurl their sails and anchor farther out of the harbor.

While Gervais' grand event astounded drunken partiers, Berko and his men would exploit the distraction to dispose of harbor guards. Then they would row Kidoh's people to the *Xavier*, overtake the skeleton crew, raise anchor, and sail away. The fireworks' smoke would be great cover. Once the alarm sounded, Colin wagered the other vessel captains would not pursue the larger *Xavier*.

Still, anything could happen.

Colin yawned in his tree, occasionally catching glimpses of Gervais and Adele talking and laughing among their guests. He still could not look upon them without feeling resentment and a desire for revenge. From his perch he surmised his old stepfather was once again healthy enough to do treachery.

As the day passed, more and more hunters returned to Ross Hall, laughing off their lack of success. They reasoned someone had warned Kidoh's people because not one native or runaway could be found. They vowed to find the jungle rats another day. Then they dove heavily into Gervais' hospitality.

Colin spotted Angelique flitting like a butterfly from one person to another. Her guests were so vulnerable to that Gervais ability to coax out secrets, private matters they thought would never leave their lips. He smiled, knowing the next day they would wonder if they really had spilled so much information to the enticing Angelique. His sister was more than a survivor. That comforted him.

Chapter 49

Zena

From a crack in the wall of the cooling shed, Zena watched slaves come and go, loaded with food and drink for Gervais' guests. They carried pipes of wine and barrels of rum and beer. Imported foods like sweetmeats, capers, olives, and anchovies overcrowded the kitchen. Feast edibles included hams and dried fish, as well as suckling pork, fresh fish, and poultry. Garden vegetables, fruit, and breads completed the fare.

Earlier, Zena slipped out from a hidden door, grabbed dried fish and a loaf of bread, and gobbled up the food in her secret, dusty hole. She doubted anyone missed these small items during the servants' rushing back and forth. How she relished being so close to her enemies! She savored the power to choose her timing for a surprise attack.

When her first attempt to kill Madame Chauvin failed, Gerard dragged and tied her up in this shed. Although her head pounded from the white woman's blow, Zena struggled for hours against Gerard's ropes. Finally exhausted, she rested, sobbed, and then saw it. In the moonlight, just several feet from her chair, a pile of broken barrels and mud-plastered patches concealed most of a hidden door.

Only someone like herself, tied up, would ever pause to notice the subtle cracked patches.

Zena thanked her gods for this salvation. She summoned all her deities' powers to get out of Gerard's ropes. She mumbled into a trance, and although her wrists were raw from the effort, she finally wriggled free.

Then, she carefully crawled among the barrel pieces like a snake. Finding a meat hook, she picked at the bottom half of the cracked doorway and moved it with some effort. She only opened it slightly, just wide enough to squeeze her lean body through the crack. Then she pulled the door behind her and stood upright. The passage led along the shed's wall to a sloped tunnel under the courtyard. Pinholes of light from splintered wood and stones helped her eyes adjust to the darkness. The passage trailed to a small door adjoining Ross Hall. After opening this entrance as quietly as she could, Zena soon found her way along the front room's wall. There, she discovered one could exit through the hearth. This passageway obviously had not been used for a long time. *Perhaps*, thought Zena, *original owners designed the hideaway as a possible escape route from invading sea enemies.*

Indeed, if she were extra careful, her secret place could protect her. She would have time to make escape plans with plenty of food and drink to steal. Zena's deepest desire was to create balance between her invisible and visible worlds. By her way of thinking, she must kill Madame Chauvin and drink her blood to restore the life power she somehow lost to this white medicine woman.

Zena knew her plan kept her in danger, but she feared nothing. However, it puzzled her that Babalu-Aye restrained her from quick action. She felt his invisible ropes around her wrists. She did not like his whisperings of patience. Through her thoughts, he reassured she would find the path to balance, and her life would make sense once again. Zena must prove her allegiance by waiting. At night, it took all her strength to refrain from rushing into Madame Chauvin's room and stabbing that sleeping woman over and over again.

If Zena succeeded in killing Madame Chauvin, she knew Gerard would soon be hot on her trail. She planned to kill him too. Several times, he came into the cooling room like a bloodhound puzzling out her whereabouts. But Babalu-Aye shielded and restrained her.

Finally, the foolish Gervais party gave her the perfect opportunity. It would be this night while everyone slept, drunk and exhausted, that she would take out Elisabeth's heart and offer it to Yemaja.

She was uncertain if she would kill the Chauvin infant, too. The baby might prove useful as a slave for trade to get her off the island. Zena felt certain she would decide its fate later. Meanwhile, in the dark shed she waited, savoring the thought of her new life that soon would be bright as the sun. She sharpened her blade over and over again.

Chapter 50

Fireworks

As she did Angelique's bidding and flitted among guests with a tray too big for her, wide-eyed Petite proved a fair spy for Elisabeth. The little slave popped into Elisabeth's room and reported such details as how several hunters snored outside in the garden. Others arrived with their families to party around food and drink. Petite reassured Elisabeth that although many soldiers brought arms, they acted merry, not warlike. Madame Isabella de La Roche dressed like a queen, she reported, in sparkling pink, white, and gold satin. "And, oh, Madame Chauvin, little Theophile and the children play such wonderful games: quoits and queek, tug 'o war, stick combat, hide and seek. I am sorry you miss the party, Madame," she concluded breathlessly.

"Have you seen Dr. Stillingfleet, the man with the big head who Madame Isabella enjoys?" Elisabeth asked.

"No, Madame, no big heads," answered a puzzled Petite.

"Keep watch for him," said Elisabeth. "And report to me when you see him."

Petite said Monsieur Louis boasted he knew where the natives and runaway slaves hid, deep in the jungle in a secret cave. He boasted he would send hunters to flush them out the next day. Petite quoted him, "Messieurs, it is quite a distance away. So do not worry about it today. Let us just enjoy ourselves. Come, eat, drink, play cards and games."

Elisabeth once again felt such sinking grief. Louis knew of Berko's hideaway, and he probably guessed correctly the natives hid there. Or, did he possibly know of Kidoh's cave? What wickedness!

The thought plagued Elisabeth that she had played an important role in these forthcoming murders. After all, it was her nursing and Kidoh's medicine that had brought the dying man back to life. How different life would be now if Gervais would have died. Colin had warned her, and she did not listen.

"God, what have I done? How can your good triumph over such evil?" Throughout the afternoon, she prayed and wrestled with remorse. She searched hard for at least a mustard seed of faith to offer some confidence in her God.

Meanwhile, Colin drifted in and out of sleep in his tree. He finally shook himself awake as the dimming sunset gave way to twilight. He ached from his vigil. He watched slaves light torches and escort guests to the cliff where they would soon watch the fireworks. Ross Hall emptied and even the slaves and servants were given a reprieve to witness this amazing sight. He knew he could slip into Ross Hall undetected.

Colin had seen fireworks on his journeys to the Far East. He knew the crowd would be astounded if only the Viceroy stored the fireworks well enough to keep the powder dry. This entertainment offered the critical elements of distraction and surprise. Colin stiffly climbed down from his tree. After relieving himself, he retrieved his sword and pouch from a nearby hedge, where Clare had gifted him with a fine French officer's uniform. He did not plan on encountering anyone, but just in case, she had insisted on this disguise.

Meanwhile, Louis Gervais enjoyed garnering information he needed to feel empowered about the Viceroy's concerns as well as those of St. Paola's genteel leadership. Throughout the day, he ignored occasional streams of pain shooting through his left arm. Mentally, he willed them to be gone, as if they could be ordered about like slaves. They obeyed it seemed, but as darkness came and he and Adele headed out to the cliff, he felt a thrusting pain through his arm and chest.

"No!" he gasped as he bent over.

Adele grabbed his arm. "Louis, what is it?"

"I, I think I am having another attack," he whispered. "Where is Madame Chauvin?"

Adele had been so busy with guests she had not thought of Elisabeth all day. By torchlight, she frantically searched the crowd.

"Poppa! Poppa!" Angelique said as she and Eduard ran up to them and saw the stress on their father's drained face.

"Where is Madame Chauvin?" Adele demanded of Angelique.

"She was not well, so I sent her to her room to rest with her baby," Angelique said, anxiously eyeing her father.

Louis tried to straighten up and take command. He gasped, "Do not alarm our guests. Adele and I will go back to the house. Angelique and Eduard, you must stay and take care of everyone. I just need to lie down and drink that medicine."

"Poppa, are you sure? Should we find the doctor?" Eduard asked.

"No, no. I will be fine. Adele will summon Madame Chauvin. Please, honor my request. If I lie down for a while, I am sure I will revive." Gervais faked a smile and stood straighter, raising his hand to Viceroy de la Roche to signal his guards to start the fireworks.

Eduard and Angelique watched as a slave holding a torch led their father and Adele slowly to the house. A burst of shooting flames rose in the sky, and the crowd shouted and cheered.

Chapter 51

Under the Portrait

Colin waited for the guests and servants to empty the house. Only a few torches remained lit. He easily slipped into the kitchen and knocked on Elisabeth's door.

She opened it a crack and, at first, gasped at the French uniform. Then she recognized Colin and flung open the door. Forgetting herself, she hugged him. "Mr. Richardson! You did not leave!"

He held her briefly and then pushed her away.

"No time for chatting, but this is finally our night, Mrs. Allerton. Are you ready to get off St. Paola?"

"Are we going with Mr. Gates?" Elisabeth asked as she grabbed the satchel and scooped up a sleeping Abby.

"Ah, change of plans. But I am certain you will like this idea better—that is, if we do not die in the attempt. Give me your bag."

Elisabeth held onto the satchel. "I can take this and Abby, if you can take that," pointing to her chest.

"Woman! What are you thinking! Your damn medicine chest!"

"It has been useful a number of times, and I think it will be useful again."

He really wanted to swear, but there was no time. He picked up the chest, tightening the bag around it. "We need to make a stop in the front room before we leave."

Elisabeth resisted asking any questions and quietly followed Colin. As they entered the front room, they heard the crowd cheer as the first bursts of fireworks popped and illuminated the cliff area. Its uniqueness made Elisabeth pause in wonder.

Then she noticed Colin had pushed a chair to the hearth.

"Mr. Richardson, what are you doing?"

He stepped on the chair and struggled to lift the portrait off the wall.

"Mrs. Allerton, put Abby down and help me! Hurry!" he gasped as he started budging the portrait with stretched fingers.

As the painting wobbled and finally lifted off, Elisabeth reached up to help Colin steady the frame. They tottered under its size and weight but were able to lower the portrait to the floor. Then they pushed it against the hearth wall. More fireworks illumined the bemused face of the late Mrs. Gervais.

Colin moved his hand behind the portrait. "Oh, dear mother," he whispered reverently as his fingers touched something. He took out his knife and carefully pulled away a flattened cloth pouch. He was about to open it when Elisabeth gasped in horror.

"I kill you, evil white woman. You are mine!" crowed Zena, who emerged from the hearth with a knife in her hand.

Just as Zena wildly lunged at her, Elisabeth dodged and ran behind the sofa, grabbing Abby from it.

"You crazy witch!" Colin said as he drew his cutlass. Elisabeth pulled out her dagger.

Zena glared at them and holding her knife high hissed, "I have the power of Babalu-Aye to protect me. See, he even lights the sky with his magic."

Just then, Adele, supporting Louis, came into the room accompanied by a slave. "What is going on in here?" she demanded. Seeing her former slave, Adele yelled, "Zena, how dare you return to us!"

Louis stumbled to his chair and weakly pointed at Colin.

"Madame Gervais' painting! You moved it! I promised her it would remain there until I died."

As they stared at the gasping Louis, Zena bolted toward the stairway.

"Get her!" Adele ordered the slave, who ran in pursuit with his torch.

Colin pointed his sword at Louis. "Monsieur Gervais, do you not even recognize your stepson? I have the right to remove my mother's painting. She told me when I left Ross Hall to return and claim what was behind it. Today, I honored her wishes." He raised the pouch.

Louis grunted a weak scoff and found strength to speak. "I knew you would show up eventually, pitiful boy. But I never suspected your mother had a secret intention for her portrait's permanent placement. That surprises me, but it does not matter now."

"You and Madame Chauvin have made it so much easier for Viceroy de la Roche to arrest you and be hung. You should not have come back. Your mother died as my wife and, therefore, what you hold in your hand belongs to me. Give it to Adele."

Adele walked toward Colin, and he tilted his sword.

Louis started coughing. "Your mother belonged to me, not you. She was mine! I loved her far more than you ever could, such a small, weak child!"

Colin stared at the sick, demanding man he had feared all his life. He looked at the terrified Elisabeth clutching Abby and the loyal Adele, whose hand reached out for the pouch. Suddenly, he laughed and lowered his sword. It was crystal clear. Lies that clouded his thinking disintegrated. He had never been a weak boy, only a boy threatened and abused by a greedy man.

He shook his head in disbelief. "Louis, you are the obsessed, deceived fool, dying before my eyes. You still do not fathom the capacity of my mother's heart. Her love could have encircled all of us as a family, but you did not allow it. Instead, you broke her, making her choose between her son and her husband. You suffocated and killed her with selfishness. You took advantage of your best friend's family and his land. I see that clearly now. I should hate you for all of it, but no, I just pity you."

He raised the pouch. "I do not know what is in this pouch, but my mother left it for me. I am taking it, and you cannot stop me. Adele, I think you better hurry and get the doctor."

Louis slumped further into the chair and through his coughs scoffed, "I hate you, Colin Richardson! This is not over! I will hunt you down, even from my grave!"

Suddenly above them, they heard terrible screams. Zena yelled in her native language.

The slave came running into the room, holding his side. "She is mad, Madame Adele! She stabbed me and grabbed the torch. I could not stop her. She is setting the top rooms on fire! We need help!"

As soon as he finished speaking, they smelled the smoke.

Adele yelled frantically, "Go! Go! Quickly get the others! Show them where we keep the water pails!" Part of her wanted to leave and take charge, but Louis gasped for air.

She addressed Colin and Elisabeth, pleading, "Please! Help me get him out of the house!"

"No! Do not let them touch me!" Louis hoarsely commanded and then more softly said to Adele, "It is no use. I cannot move my arms."

"They can carry you!" Adele pleaded.

"No! Not them!" he whispered.

"I want help, but I cannot leave you, Louis!"

The man looked firmly into the eyes of his faithful mistress. She understood. She collapsed at his feet and grabbed his hand.

Gervais' coal black eyes blazed at Colin and Elisabeth. "Get out!" he said with hostile gasps. "Get out of my house!"

He then turned to the portrait. Colin and Elisabeth heard roaring flames. Smoke cloaked the room.

Elisabeth, clutching Abby more tightly, put her dagger back in her pocket, and Colin snatched both bags. Looking out the window, Elisabeth saw guests running toward the house.

"Mr. Richardson, there are so many people coming! What shall we do?"

"Quick, into the hearth—there is a passageway." He moved into the hearth and turned. "Adele, are you coming? You still can save yourself?"

The woman paid them no attention. Her cheek was pressed against the dying hand of Gervais.

Colin and Elisabeth squeezed into the passageway and followed the dark tunnel to the cooling house. As Colin readjusted the bags to fit better on his back, Elisabeth peeked out the door and watched Ross Hall erupting in flames.

"We need to go," he ordered and led her and Abby once again into the jungle.

On the roof, a wild Zena jumped up and down, swinging her torch and making war whoops. Out of the garden emerged a bulbous-headed man with a haughty strut carrying a musket. Dr. Stillingfleet took careful aim. His one shot sent Zena falling to the ground.

The inferno provided an even greater diversion for hijacking the *Xavier*. Soldiers abandoned their posts to help fight the fire. When Berko and his men slipped aboard the ship, they easily surprised and overcame a handful of sailors. Berko ordered them gagged, tied, and thrown into the belly of the ship. Abasi's people climbed aboard in wonder, whispering their victory.

Meanwhile, Elisabeth and Colin slowly moved through the jungle. She missed her men's clothing as she struggled to keep up with Colin. At least this time, however, they traveled on a path that had been used by others. Abby squirmed but remained drowsy from her sleeping medicine.

They walked silently, trying to piece together all that had happened. Colin thought about Louis, his obsessed stepfather, who surely must have died by now in burning Ross Hall. How could any man facing death be so vile? Colin never foresaw how quickly his quest for revenge would move from hatred to pity, but oh, how freeing it felt. He wondered how badly his hatred of Gervais had crippled him for years without impacting Gervais at all. Gervais' self-centered life worked fine as a twisted delusion, but it hurt so many people.

And what about Adele? She dedicated her life to loving someone who did not love her. How could she be so blind to his indifference? It seemed her kind of love, even though not returned, slowly turned her into the reflection of her master. It baffled him, but Colin vowed never to be deluded by hatred again. He also determined not to love someone who loved another. He glanced at Elisabeth.

She interrupted his thoughts. "Mr. Richardson, where is our rescue?"

"Mrs. Allerton, do you not believe the good Lord will provide?" He had to lighten the tension. They both needed a little humor to keep them going.

"Yes, of course, I believe that more than ever! But, sir, a few more details would be helpful."

"You know we might have to swim all the way to Boston. But then there is little Abby. Have you taught her to swim yet?"

Elisabeth did not reply. She was too overwhelmed with no answers. She desperately wanted off this island.

They reached a shoreline Elisabeth had not been to before. Colin pointed to a rowboat tied to some brush and quickly put their bags into the vessel. "I guess your medicine chest gets one more journey," he joked, rubbing his back.

"A rowboat? Mr. Richardson, I am surprised."

"It is a sturdy boat. It will see us there."

Elisabeth was not sure about "there," but she was too spent to ask any more questions. There was no turning back.

Colin dragged the rowboat to the water's edge and gestured for her to get in. She gave him Abby and climbed aboard. It was not quite dawn yet, but the sky had turned from black to milky gray.

"There is our ship, little Abby." Colin pointed to the horizon where a vessel lay anchored for them. Elisabeth turned from Colin's face to look out over the water.

Even by those first few glimmers of sunrise, Elisabeth thought the ship's outline appeared to be the *Xavier*. Her heart jumped as she realized the ship that once was her prison would now be her rescuer. She determined to hold onto faith. She reached out for Abby and then clung to her as Colin pushed the boat into the water and rowed toward the *Xavier*.

Elisabeth marveled she and Abby still lived. They were no longer captives on St. Paola, and they soon would be heading closer to David. How God had protected them! Tears filled her eyes when grinning Berko, in sailor attire, helped her aboard the *Xavier*. His presence, too, was a miracle. Then, there were more miracles as she gazed upon Abasi and the others who greeted her. She had no words. This was crazy joy. Even if they did not make it to Boston, presently they were safe and free. Miracles!

A little later as they sailed north, Elisabeth observed Berko, laughing and pushing Colin aside to the railing. The big man tried to get Colin to admit to something, but Elisabeth could not hear their conversation. She only saw a reluctant Colin finally raise his arms and speak something that satisfied Berko. He patted Colin on the back and gave him a big hug.

Chapter 52

On the Xavier, Once Again

The days on the *Xavier* rolled by quickly for Elisabeth. Colin assigned her the captain's cabin where not long before, she and Dr. Stillingfleet, as prisoners, had treated Remille. This time around she shared the quarters with Tana and several other women and children.

As they journeyed north, Colin trained man and woman alike in handling ship tasks and using weapons. Even the children learned how to do multiple jobs.

No one questioned the plan to head first to Boston before finding Berko's homeland. It humbled Elisabeth, and she tried to thank Abasi and Berko for this sacrifice. Berko replied, "We all need practice before sailing to Africa. Do you not witness our sea legs growing, Mrs. Allerton? I hope you have good medicine for our new body parts." He laughed at her puzzlement as she chuckled a little.

Colin's persuasive skills won over the French sailors Abasi's people had captured. They were not a bad lot. Berko and Abasi promised the young men they could have the ship once it got their people to a new home.

"We will have no need of it then," Berko declared. And the others agreed.

But the leaders took no chances. They had each sailor assigned a watchman who spoke French. These young men were not allowed to fraternize with each other except when the islanders were beside them. This arrangement broke down cultural barriers. The sailors even taught the islanders to fish from the ship. Berko and Abasi declared they enjoyed this challenge as much as hunting wild boar.

Elisabeth marveled at the crew's ingenuity. The ship possessed flags from France, Spain, the Netherlands, and England. Several times, they spotted ships on the horizon and would fly the most appropriate colors. Colin had a polished ability to discern the ship's country. No one pursued them.

Elisabeth tended to various injuries as "ship's doctor." The women and children fussed over Abby, who appreciated the attention as much as Elisabeth did.

Elisabeth understood the formal distance Colin kept from her. They had gone through so much together. She still owed the man more than she could ever repay. Yet she was a married woman with a child who needed a father. If she felt too much fondness for Colin, she knew it was inappropriate and wrong. She checked herself on this affection. She knew with whom she belonged, and she knew this was God's will. It could be no other way.

As for Colin, he foresaw his obligation as almost completed and that brought him relief. Finally, he could get this woman to where she needed to be. Entanglement with her had been a heavy burden, although he admitted he felt gratitude too. She really had been God's instrument in helping him jettison past bitterness.

The idea of God's existence did not seem such a distant reality to him as it had been before. In fact, he sensed a presence he could not dismiss. He did not understand this spiritual aspect to life, but it no longer frightened or angered him. He did not want to lose such peace and hope. After delivering Mrs. Allerton to her husband, he felt confident he could explore faith further, on his terms.

It took a while for Colin to find courage to look in the pouch his mother left for him. The contents contained a will from his father that laid out a plan for Colin to take over Ross Hall. In the papers, Louis had been designated his godfather and estate overseer until Colin reached the age of eighteen.

Of course, Louis had no intention of giving Ross Hall to Colin. But it gave him solace to know his father had tried to make provision for him. Also, his mother had left him a beautiful necklace of gold and rubies folded into a letter. The ink was smeared—he assumed with tears.

In it, she wrote,

Colin, my dear little man, I want you to know I love you more than you will ever know. My heart broke when your father died, and it has broken again, now that I am sending you away with Uncle Duff. Please know without any doubt I did this for your safety. May you forgive me for any errors in judgment. Although the scar you bear on your cheek came from hatred, I want you to know the scar I carry in my heart from sending you away is one of pure love. You always will be my beloved son.

Colin wept. His poor mother! He wished he could comfort her. What she silently bore! She did not have many choices, but she did the best she could out of love for her child. She really had not abandoned him but saved him. This was the Katherine Ross Richardson he would remember. He visualized her smile restored, free from Gervais' grip. Colin's past no longer haunted him in jagged pieces. He felt loved and whole.

Chapter 53

Boston Arrival

Tension built for crew and passengers as the *Xavier* sailed into Boston's harbor and anchored a safe distance from the main wharf. One mistake would raise suspicions, yet the ship needed to resupply. Most of the villagers remained below deck while Colin, Berko, the French sailors, and their guards performed duties topside.

The plan played out just long enough to satisfy the curiosity of wharf venders who rowed out and offered their wares to Captain Richardson. Colin and the others decided to anchor only one or two days—just long enough for Colin to get Elisabeth to David and for the *Xavier* to resupply and sail away. The time had come again for goodbyes. Elisabeth knew she would never see these people, who soon would cross an ocean.

"I still have nothing to give you," she said tearfully, "but I will never forget you. I will keep you in my heart and my prayers."

Tana grunted and soberly declared, "That is enough." Elisabeth marveled how much she sounded like her grandmother Neesa.

Abasi added, "We will not forget you either, Parrot Head. But I have a small request. May I cut a little of your hair?"

Her hair shone bright red with some black undertones. She hesitated to lose hair once again, but she nodded and removed her work cap.

Abasi quickly brought out his knife, and Elisabeth winced. He took only a small piece. Raising it in his fingers and shaking it, he offered a high compliment, "You are a good omen, Mrs. Allerton."

In the early morning, she hugged her friends goodbye as they patted Abby's head, speaking words Elisabeth did not know. It felt like a dream. With tears in her eyes, she climbed into the rowboat, and took Abby from Mr. Richardson. Soon, she and her baby would be where they belonged. Colin and Berko rowed them to the bustling Boston wharf.

After securing a room at the Pig and Whistle for Elisabeth and Abby, the hungry travelers ordered a breakfast meal of corn mush with maple syrup and ale. Colin spoke privately to inn proprietor Anne, placing a few extra coins into her hand to guarantee Elisabeth's safety and comfort. He also asked her to find some clothing for a Puritan woman.

She raised her eyebrows and laughed, "I might have to steal them, ye know," and then seeing his surprise, added, "No worries. I know some religious folk."

Finally, he and Berko headed to the merchants on Conduit Street to inquire if anyone knew of the *Sea Venture* and the fate of its passengers.

As they walked, Berko asked carefully, "Are you sure Mrs. Allerton belongs with this David Allerton? I have my doubts from the little you have said of him."

This truth irritated Colin. "Berko, I cannot unwind Mrs. Allerton's reasons. I do not understand how she can love such a foxy coward."

"Like Louis Gervais?"

"No, not that bad. But I know Allerton for a coward. He is one who uses others and their convictions to get what he desires. He is the wolf in the sheep pen! Foolish are they who suffer him!"

"Ah, Colin, I think your love is an open wound that will not quickly heal," Berko said sympathetically.

"No, Berko, I am fine!" he lied. "I just want to reunite a family that has been broken apart. That is all, and I will dance a little jig when Mrs. Allerton and Abby are where they are meant to be. The same goes for you, my brother."

"Colin, you know we must leave in the morning. We cannot afford to stay here once we sell our cargo. The longer we stay, the more we place ourselves in danger."

"I know, Berko. I plan to make it back to travel with you. But I must say, you have become a fine seaman, and there is enough talent among your people to get you to your land— with Onyame's help, of course."

"Yes, my brother, like Mrs. Allerton needing to get to where she belongs, I know my place lies across this water. I sense my father and his father watching over me on this journey."

"I hope Onyame will fulfill your heart's desire, Berko."

Berko grinned and clasped Colin with both arms. "It is good to hear you say so."

Colin still did not have the heart to tell Berko his suspicions about the extinction of the African village. He knew he must, but not right then.

Colin and Berko entered the mercantile house, not the first one from the wharf, but one that appeared prosperous. The red-nose clerk possessed squinty eyes and greasy brown hair. He raised his head from his papers, looked briefly at the men, sniffed, and returned to his writing.

Colin put his hand on the papers. "We have a cargo of sugar and cotton we want to sell, but before we discuss the price, I want to inquire about a vessel called the *Sea Venture*. Do you recall her coming into port sometime last year?"

The clerk sniffed. "Maybe, maybe not. Why do you need to know?"

"We carry some cargo for a Mr. Allerton, a passenger on that ship."

"Cargo, you say? What kind of cargo?" The man had some curiosity after all.

"Sir, this is between Mr. Allerton and myself. Can you help or not? I am sure there are more accommodating places where I can sell my fine Carib cotton and sugar. I am not in the business to dally with fools."

The clerk squinted at Colin, and for a second Colin thought his impatience might draw unnecessary suspicion. But then the man relaxed. He smelled profit.

"No need to worry, mate. I do remember the *Sea Venture*. She arrived damaged, but her passengers seemed well enough. I remember they also unloaded two fine horses."

"That would be the ship. I thank you, sir, for this information. Now about our cotton and sugar...."

Colin knew the man haggled the cargo for less than a fair price, but Colin wanted to get the money into Berko's hands quickly so supplies could be purchased for their journey. The mercantile agent agreed he would arrange for them to unload and resupply the ship that very day.

Elisabeth told Colin she felt certain David would be with his Uncle Tobias in Dorchester. It only took two tavern stops for Colin to find merchant Mathias Clark, who that afternoon was returning to Dorchester. Indeed, the friendly gent knew the respected Allertons, and, yes, he would be glad to take this Allerton cousin and her baby there. Colin thought it best to keep Elisabeth's true identity private.

Colin sent Berko back to the ship, while he bought some woman's clothing that he thought might work for Elisabeth. When Colin got back to the Pig and Whistle, he found Elisabeth and Abby sleeping. He hated to wake them. If only certain moments could be frozen like a portrait. He wanted to keep them like this—safe and peaceful.

He shook Elisabeth's shoulder. She bounced up. "Mr. Richardson, did you find David?" Her face lit up with hope.

Colin's heart sank at her glow.

"Aye, and even better," he said, forcing a smile. "There is a merchant willing to drive you there as soon as you are ready. He is anxious to travel while there is good light."

Elisabeth quickly moved out of bed, and Abby awoke and whimpered. "Mr. Richardson, will you hold her in the hallway while I do my toiletries? I will hurry."

She handed him the baby, and Colin took Abby outside. *There is nothing as innocent as a baby,* he thought. He just hoped she would be more like her mother than her father.

Soon, they hurried down the stairs, and the smiling Mathias Clark waited at the door.

"Good day, ma'am. I hear you are related to the Allerton family. Fine family in our parts—I am pleased to give you passage and welcome your company."

Mr. Clark, indeed, appeared amiable, and Elisabeth doubted she would have to drum up much conversation as he rambled on and on.

Elisabeth did not see the need for pretending to be an Allerton cousin, but she decided not to argue with Mr. Richardson. Let them depart in an agreeable manner.

"Here, let me help you with your bag, Mrs. Allerton," said Mr. Clark. "Mr. Richardson told me you have a wee one. I made a nice warm spot for her in the wagon. You two will be quite comfortable there."

"Thank you, Mr. Clark. That is very kind." Elisabeth smiled, but her feelings ached with regret, knowing the moment had come to say goodbye. She adjusted her cap in the chilly air and bounced Abby to keep her from crying. The good Mr. Clark put her bags aboard his wagon.

This is happening too quickly! Elisabeth thought. What could she say to her rescuer? Tears filled her eyes. She leaned in closely to him.

"Mr. Richardson, I have no words," she whispered.

His heart could not bear this. He wanted to crush her to him and never let her go, but he steeled himself for her sake. "Mrs. Allerton, no words are needed," he whispered back and then said more loudly as Mr. Clark watched them, "But I have a song for you."

"A song? Here?"

"We better get going, daylight is waning," Mr. Clark said as he climbed up to his seat.

"Of course, Mr. Clark. Straight away."

Then Colin took Abby from Elisabeth. He kissed the baby's downy red hair and handed her to Mr. Clark. As he lifted Elisabeth into the back of the wagon he added, "I will sing to you all as you head down the road. It will be a fitting goodbye. Trust me."

Elisabeth tried to suppress tears, as Colin handed Abby from Mr. Clark back to her mother. "God bless you, Mr. Richardson, wherever you travel. Thank you, kind sir. I cannot forget you and will keep you in my prayers."

Colin took off his hat and in a surprisingly good voice, sang a song Elisabeth had not heard before. Mr. Clark nodded approvingly and joined in as he took the reins and the horses began to trot down the road. Long after she could no longer see or hear Mr. Richardson, her driver belted out the song until he had sung all the verses to the very popular "Love Will Find Out the Way."

> *Over the mountains*
> *And over the waves,*
> *Under the fountains*
> *And under the graves,*
> *Under floods that are deepest,*
> *Which Neptune obey*
> *Over rocks which are the steepest,*
> *Love will find out the way.*
>
> *You may esteem him*
> *A child for his might,*

Or you may deem him
A coward from his flight.
But if she, whom Love doth honour,
Be concealed from the day
Set a thousand guards upon her,
Love will find out the way.

Some think to lose him
By having him confined.
Some do suppose him,
Poor thing, to be blind;
But if ne'er so close ye wall him,
Do the best that you may,
Blind Love, if so ye call him,
Will find out his way.

You may train the eagle
To stoop to your fist.
You may train, inveigle
The Phoenix of the east.
The lioness, you may move her
To give o'er her prey;
But you'll ne'er stop a lover;
He will find out his way.

When Mr. Clark's wagon disappeared, Colin breathed heavily and wiped away a few tears. Passersby stared at him. He had not cried for a woman since he had said goodbye to his mother as a boy. The loss felt similar—almost too much for him to bear. But bear it he would; he had done it before, and the sea had been his salvation. He headed back to the *Xavier*.

Chapter 54

The Welcome at Dorchester

Elisabeth, too, cried. She snuggled with Abby, stifling her sobs. After finishing the many verses of "Love Will Find a Way," Mr. Clark said, "Aye, a most excellent song. But, my dear, you must be exhausted from your travels. Take heart, you will feel much better when you are with your family."

"Oh, yes, I pray so," Elisabeth managed to say. "I am sorry, Mr. Clark. I fear I will not be good company on this journey."

"Do not worry, my dear. You and that little one settle in and just rest. I will make haste to the Allertons; you will be with family before the candle lighting."

He cracked his whip to show his determination, humming as they traveled. Elisabeth did not have to say another word until they made it to the Allerton home at sunset.

A pleased Mr. Clark jumped from the wagon and offered his arms to hold baby Abigail. Then Elisabeth forced her tired limbs to move. The rutted road still challenged her legs after so many days at sea.

Abby remained the good baby she consistently proved to be, quiet and with eyes wide open. Elisabeth anxiously steadied herself. She assumed the delightful infant would ease this reunion.

Mr. Clark grabbed Elisabeth's bags off the wagon. As he knocked on the front door, he chatted how the Allerton name was much respected in the community. "They brought good fishing commerce to our area and have helped Dorchester prosper."

But Elisabeth barely heard him. Uneasy, she stared at the square two-story clapboard house, quite elegant by Dorchester standards. What kind of greeting would she receive? How should she even begin to tell her story?

When the servant opened the door, Mr. Clark introduced the Allerton cousin and instructed the servant woman to take her bags.

Mr. Clark tipped his hat to Elisabeth and said, "I will see you in a few days, my dear. I will bring Mrs. Clark by when you are settled. Tell the Allertons I am sorry I must hurry off. The wife is waiting, and I still must milk my cows."

The perplexed servant escorted Elisabeth into the parlor where Mary sat embroidering. The two women froze as recognition settled in.

Elisabeth broke the silence with warmth and tears. "Mary! It is I, Elisabeth! Thanks be to the Lord! I am so glad to look upon a familiar face!"

Mary stared at little Abby in Elisabeth's arms. She tried to stand up but could not. "Elisabeth!" she whispered, turning white. "We thought you were dead!" With that, she collapsed to the floor where Isaac played.

The servant rushed over to the fainted woman. Elisabeth sat Abby on the floor next to Isaac and helped get Mary back up on the sofa.

Then David walked in. "Mary! Oh, Mary, what has happened?"

Elisabeth turned her face to him.

He blinked in surprise and stood frozen. "Elisabeth!"

"David!" she responded with reserved affection, puzzled by his reaction.

He recovered and instructed, "Wait here. Let me carry Mary to the bed. Alice, you bring Isaac."

Elisabeth tried to comprehend Mary's presence, and it left her feeling uneasy. Where was her husband Jonathan? Why was she here? She picked up Abby and held her tightly as she examined the room.

David returned quickly and flatly asked, "Elisabeth, how did you get here?"

Indeed, this cold beginning caught her off guard. "David, are those the only words you have for your wife who has been lost but now is found? For months, I have thought of nothing else but getting back to you, reuniting with you, and presenting our daughter to you," she said softly.

David looked at Abby and winced. "Elisabeth, how could she be mine?"

His words felt like a slap in the face, a jolt that shook scales from her eyes. Was this the man she had loved for so long?

Anger crept into her voice. "Excuse me, my husband. But I think if you look closely at this child, you will see she bears a strong resemblance to the Allerton line."

David stared at Abby and scrunched his face. He could not or would not admit it. "I am sorry, Elisabeth. I do not see it." He sighed.

Elisabeth remembered that sound when he chastised a servant who had done shoddy work. *David wants to blame me,* she thought.

"Let us sit down. This is quite overwhelming," he suggested coolly.

Elisabeth did not want to sit; she wanted to run from this man and have time to think.

"Would you like something to eat and drink?" he asked, also needing time to think.

"Yes, thank you. I have had a long journey."

David rose and instructed the servant to bring some food.

He returned. "Elisabeth, your sudden appearance is unsettling.

After so many months, we thought you were dead. You must understand how difficult this is for me."

"For you? Did you not get my letter, David?"

David's eyes flickered with recognition, but he asked innocently, "What letter?"

She could not believe his level of deceit. "I think Mr. Richardson sized you up correctly, but I defended you at every turn."

"Mr. Richardson! That sailor you fraternized with aboard the *Sea Venture*? He has been your companion all these months!" David saw his opportunity. "Is he the father of this child?"

Elisabeth's face grew red. "Husband, how dare you! I have been faithful to you. You have no idea what I have been through, but believe this, it is only by God's providence that your daughter and wife have been brought to you. And, Mr. Richardson turned out to be his instrument of good. We kept our family obligations, but what about you?"

She felt like a ship in a storm about to be defeated by the forces around her.

David perceived her differently, and it shook his confidence. This woman bore some resemblance to the same Elisabeth, and yet she threw a larger shadow. She was more mature, more confident, and more disrespectful. He did not like her at all. She could cause trouble. He had to proceed carefully.

David sat down and tried to appear relaxed. "I am sorry, Elisabeth. You ask a fair question. You must understand we thought you were dead. Jonathan Rogers died en route to Boston. It seemed providential for Mary Rogers and I to grieve the loss of our companions together. Mary and little Isaac needed a husband and father. I believed I was widowed. We felt God's hand directed us. We were married months ago, and Mary is bearing our child."

Elisabeth let out a breath. She certainly had been a fool. This man cared nothing for her anymore. He had moved on without giving her much thought.

David needed time to find a way forward. He suggested, "Elisabeth, we both need to sleep on this matter. Look, you and the baby can lodge in my uncle and aunt's room. They are presently in London. In the morning, I will fetch Reverend Richard Mather. He will help us sort this matter out with wise counsel."

Elisabeth wanted to run back to the *Xavier*, but she knew she could not. There was no way to get to Boston before the ship sailed. And running away could not possibly be God's will, could it? She needed time to think.

"Yes, David. Abby and I are tired. Please show me the room."

"Of course. Get some rest and eat some food. We will talk in the morning."

Elisabeth heart sank as she noticed David did not even care to look at Abby. *What a fool I have been!*

Chapter 55

Decisions in the Night

That night, for a long while, Elisabeth heard the muffled sobs of Mary weeping and David soothingly trying to comfort her. Her husband bedded with his new wife! Where did that leave her and Abby? *I am not an adulterer! They are!* Yet, she felt unsafe in their territory. Who would believe her?

When the household quieted down, she still tossed and turned in a fine English bed. What should she do? She lit a candle from the hearth's embers and tiptoed into the main room. She did not know what compelled her. Was it fear, anger, self-preservation, or all the emotions that had fueled her for many months?

She spotted the Allerton desk, so similar to her husband's from long ago. She knew where the Allertons traditionally kept their money. And, yes, this desk also had a secret drawer. Her hands grasped a heavy pouch—enough coins to keep her and Abby secure for a long while—at least until she figured out a better way. Perhaps they could get passage back to England, to her father and stepmother.

She reached for a piece of valuable parchment paper. Dipping the feathered pen in the ink well, she paused. Was her mind really telling her to steal and preserve herself? No, she wanted to do this for

Abby's sake. Was not an innocent child's future reason enough for an unjust deed?

Then she felt a twinge of doubt. Did little Abby inherit a thief for a mother as well as a liar and adulterer for a father? How would David use this act of stealing against her? She would not be free of him.

Elisabeth looked out the window and saw the smiling moon. They could flee this place by its light. She could take a wagon and one of David's precious horses and disappear.

She really did not hate David as much as feel pity and frustration toward him. She felt she had outgrown him somehow. The man's deceit ensnared him. She knew this flaw would not serve him or Mary well in their lives together. At least she and Abby would be spared from that hypocrisy.

Elisabeth bowed her head. "Lord, I do not know how you will rescue Abby and me from this shame and danger, but you have been faithful to me always. I have tried to be faithful to you. Forgive me for what I almost did here. I will not commit this sin against you."

She put the pouch back in the hidden drawer and then noticed the letters. By candlelight she read Angelique's plea for help. She held up her letter to David, torn from her journal in Kidoh's cave. Her husband received them after all! Her hands clutched this evidence. Then, she shook her head. No, she did not need these to prove anything.

She declared, "Neither by an army nor strength, but by my Spirit, saith the Lord of hosts." She put the letters back and crawled into bed, holding her daughter close. She slept a few hours and awoke at dawn.

Chapter 56

Rev. Richard Mather's Decision

Elisabeth imagined a merry crew, Colin, and Berko, on the *Xavier* sailing out of Boston harbor. They would fire the cannon in farewell. Their freedom made her glad, but her heart beat heavy. She felt like Hagar with Ishmael, out in the desert alone with her Abby. How would God provide? She did not know, but she had to believe he would.

Servant Alice brought her a breakfast tray. Elisabeth sensed condemnation, but she did not care. She knew her innocence. She ate for strength and took her daughter to the main room to wait.

When David finally came, he brought with him the Rev. Richard Mather. Elisabeth knew of his fine reputation in London. The elderly man helped write the *Bay Psalm Book*, and she once held a copy in her hands.

David made introductions and explained, "I have told our situation to Reverend Mather."

Elisabeth looked alarmed. How had David spun their story?

The Rev. Mather took command. "Sister Elisabeth, it is an interesting story Brother Allerton has told me. I would like to hear your words. Brother David, please leave the room and let me converse with Sister Elisabeth."

David did not expect to be excluded from the conversation. Elisabeth let out a sigh of relief.

"Certainly." David bowed and left.

The Reverend Mather stared intently at Elisabeth and motioned for her to sit down. He smoothed his black cloak comfortably over the chair. "Please, daughter, tell me your story."

"Reverend Mather, I tell you truthfully that my baby and I should be dead, but God's mercy and providence spared us and brought us to where we thought we belonged. I know it is almost unbelievable, but these are truths."

She then relayed the details the best she could. She even ended by admitting to almost stealing from David in desperation but deciding instead to trust in God's providence.

The minister remained silent for a long while. Elisabeth wondered which part of her story he found questionable.

Finally, he spoke. "Daughter, I know Providence's hand. Long ago, when I was brought to these shores, I was in a severe storm, and God's hand was evident to all for our physical salvation. Indeed, he has been with you through most difficult trials."

The Reverend set his clear eyes on Abigail and said evenly, "She is a lovely child. Hair like yours, and I do believe that nose is exactly like her father's, David Allerton."

Elisabeth wanted to hug him for believing her! Tears trickled, but she desired to keep composure.

Rev. Mather continued, "It seems the father should bear the consequences of this problem. I regret I believed him when he told me you had been lost at sea. I am guilty of witnessing his marriage contract to Mary Rogers. They should be severely punished for lies and adultery. By law, you and Mr. Allerton are still married."

Elisabeth imagined a future whipping and possible expulsion from the community for David and Mary. For Elisabeth, as David's true wife, at best, she would endure a life of humiliation, knowing he did not want her or Abby.

"Reverend Mather, God bless you for believing me. You do not know how grateful I am for your confidence in my character. All I spoke has been the truth, but I fear there is much sorrow for everyone in these circumstances. I must tell you plainly I do not believe I could ever go back to a man who does not want me, and who has another woman and two other children to think upon."

"Daughter, by law, he is your husband!"

Elisabeth sucked in her breath. She did not want to be married to that man. Let Mary have him.

"Reverend Mather, my affections for him are slight at best, and I know he and Mary have made a good start together."

"Mrs. Allerton, we do not do God's will by relying on our affections!" Rev. Mather firmly stood on this point.

"I know, but I beg you to find a way to release me from this contract of marriage, and yet allow it to be done as quietly as possible. I am learning that mercy is God's good and pleasing will. Is it not?"

The Rev. Mather sighed. He did not want to bend the rules for the sake of convenience. God's law must reign supreme in all they did. Yet, his law did offer latitude.

"I have a suggestion, daughter, but I do not know if it will be much comfort to you and the child. By law, you may divorce Mr. Allerton for adultery. I can witness the papers and file them with the magistrate. Then, David and Mary could marry legally, in a private civil ceremony."

Elisabeth nodded in relief. This plan resulted in the least amount of pain for all.

The Rev. Mather arose. He summoned David and Mary back into the room. He told the anxious couple the plan, adding that given the circumstances and for the sake of all, it would be done quietly so David and Mary would not have to suffer punishment for adultery.

As the couple held onto each other, he pointed his finger at them, exhorting, "David, Elisabeth could rightfully demand much justice from your irresponsible actions. I think you need to provide generously for her and Abigail."

David nodded puzzled. "All right. Certainly. What do you need, Elisabeth? Where are you going?"

"I am not certain, but I will return to Boston and most likely secure passage for England. Rest assured, I will not bother you two again. You have my word."

She waited for her husband to offer something. He just clung to Mary, so she stated the obvious. "I would like to have a wagon and Bountiful and Blessing to take me to Boston. And, I will need some money."

The Rev. Mather suggested, "David, perhaps you could give an offering to Elisabeth while Mary and I bear witness."

David trudged over to the desk and pulled out the pouch. He hesitated, not knowing how much to give? With all eyes watching, he then handed Elisabeth the entire bag.

The Rev. Mather nodded his approval. "I will go see the magistrate now and discreetly make arrangements."

He touched Elisabeth with a fatherly hand on her shoulder. "Daughter, God bless you and Abigail. May his face shine upon you and be gracious unto you."

He left, and Mary followed, not looking at her former midwife but mumbling, "I must attend to the household. Thank you, Elisabeth."

That left David and Elisabeth awkwardly alone with Abby.

Elisabeth broke the silence. "David, you have not asked me one question about all these months apart and how I got back to you. For Abby's sake, I want you to know it was for love, David, and our covenant vows, and our child."

David shrugged uncomfortably.

Elisabeth fought back tears. "Honestly, tell me one thing if you can. Did you jump off the *Xavier*, or did those guards push you?"

"You mean Mr. Richardson did not tell you what happened?" David assumed the seaman placed him in the worse light.

"No, he said he was uncertain what happened."

"Elisabeth, you deserve to know the truth." He looked directly into her eyes. "Those French ruffians pushed me and truly, I grieved deeply, thinking I had lost you forever."

"I see," Elisabeth answered, and she really did.

David instructed a servant to prepare the wagon and horses, while Elisabeth readied her and Abby for another journey.

When the wagon pulled up in front of the house, Elisabeth placed Abby safely on the wagon's floorboard in her basket. David secured the bags and exclaimed, "Oh! Is that your medicine chest! It is a miracle you still have it!"

"Yes, indeed. A miracle," was all Elisabeth said.

David assisted Elisabeth up onto the seat and handed her the whip.

There seemed nothing else left to say. David shuffled anxiously for her to go

"Good bye, Elisabeth."

"Goodbye, David. I hope we meet in heaven someday."

"Oh, most certainly," he said hurriedly. "God bless."

She cracked the whip, and Blessing and Bountiful took off down the road. They were spirited animals, but Elisabeth knew she could handle them. They would travel fast to Boston and as far away from David Allerton as they could get. She swallowed hard. Life spun crazily, and she welcomed the concentration and solitude of the rutted road. She headed for the only place she knew—the Pig and Whistle. There, she would regroup and make plans for Abby and herself to travel home to England.

Chapter 57

The Pig and Whistle

Colin spent the afternoon drinking at the Pig and Whistle, but it did not relieve his emptiness. Earlier Berko insisted Colin stay in Boston, talking nonsense that Onyame commanded it.

Even though Colin protested, Berko gave him a bag of coins, his portion of the booty. In return, Colin finally told Berko he believed his friend's African village had been completely wiped out by slave traders. He told him that among the *Xavier's* maps was one of the New World's coastlines. If Africa became impossible, he advised Berko to head for an unsettled place—*La Louisiane.*

Neither man could suffer a long goodbye. They hugged and quickly parted. "Until we meet again, my brother," Colin said. Berko smiled and pointed upward with both arms raised as he left the tavern.

Colin's way of handling goodbyes was to get rip-roaring drunk. Foolhardy with a devil-be-damned spirit, he drank and drank, trying to numb the pain that both Mrs. Allerton and the *Xavier* were gone forever. He shook his head, muttering to himself, *Elisabeth Allerton put a spell on me. No, that sounds wrong, you fool. It really is her God who opened your heart to love and look what it has gotten you? Nothing, once again.*

He slumped on the table, barely aware two nearby sailors murmured their plan to rob him. *To hell with them!* Maybe a beating would knock some sense into him. He cared nothing about survival. Let them rob him. Let them beat him or stab him to death.

He felt a hand reaching for his moneybag, and he prepared for a fight. Then, he thought he heard a woman's voice.

"I would not do that if I were you," Elisabeth warned, hardly believing her eyes. Colin still remained in Boston! What a sorry mess of a man, but he was real!

"And who will stop me, little missy?" snickered the smaller thief, his withered hand on Colin's pouch. Elisabeth could not bear one more fool. She whipped out her knife and landed it on the table, stabbing the man's sleeve and pinning it to the wood. His startled companion rose from his table.

Quickly, Elisabeth grabbed the thief's knife from his sheath and held it to his throat. "My friend Mr. Richardson and I do not have a quarrel with you or your mate. But unless you take your dirty paws off of his money pouch, I will be forced to cut your throat."

The man released his grip on the pouch and smiled with his broken, black teeth. "No misunderstandings, missus. Mr. Richardson and us have been companions all night."

Elisabeth loosened her grip on the man's knife. "You were blessed with such sweet fellowship then. Now be off with you!" She pulled her knife out of the table and handed the seaman his own.

He bowed slightly and sauntered away, rubbing his neck.

She shook Colin's shoulder. He recognized her and thought he dreamt. "Mrs. Allerton! Care for a drink? Where is Abby?"

"Abby is safe in my room. You, sir, have drunk way too much!"

Colin put his head back on the table. "Ah, get out of my head and let me be."

"Will you help me get this man to bed?" Elisabeth asked tavern mistress Anne, who grabbed one of Colin's arms. Together, they half dragged the amiable drunk up the stairs, into the room, and onto the bed.

Colin tried to get up. "You, woman, have caused me so much pain. And, now you are back in my head? This is a dream, a nightmare! Please, I cannot take anymore. I am tired of you, Mrs. Allerton. Go away. Please, dammit, go away." He laughed exhaustedly.

"I know, sir," Elisabeth said, choking back tears.

"Where is your weasel husband?"

"In Dorchester with his...second wife. You were right. He is a weasel."

"Oh, this news is too much. I am dreaming—sorry, I cannot take anymore," Colin said. He rolled away from Elisabeth, and began to snore.

Elisabeth looked down at him and saw the scar bumped up below his beard. It saddened her to know such cruelty was done when he was a child. She touched it. May Abby never know such cruelty. She had no regrets that she had taken Abby away from her father. What daily scorn would he have heaped upon their daughter and her if they had stayed with him?

She did not know why Colin remained in Boston, but she prayed, *Thank you, Father! Maybe there is hope.*

She grabbed Abby out of the basket and went downstairs to eat at Anne's table. She was famished. The two seamen respectfully nodded to her, and she nodded back. When she finished and went upstairs, Colin still snored. She crawled into bed, pushing him away from her side. Before she could even think about how inappropriate this arrangement appeared, she succumbed to an exhausted sleep.

And that is how Colin woke up, remembering a dream of Elisabeth telling him she had left the weasel. Did she really call David Allerton a weasel? It was dark in the room as he stumbled to the water basin and washed his face. Then he heard a baby's cooing. It sounded like Abby. As his eyes adjusted to the darkness, he saw two silhouettes in his bed. One was a baby! Abby cooed.

"Mrs. Allerton? Abby? What are you two doing here?" His head hurt.

Elisabeth's voice sounded contrite. "Mr. Richardson, I was a fool. You were right."

Colin's heart thumped quickly. "About what?"

"David has married. His wife, the former Mary Rogers, is pregnant." Saying it out loud brought sobs from Elisabeth. She felt so lost and humiliated.

"Just wait here. I do not want to talk to you in the dark."

Colin went into the hallway to find light for his candle and brought it into the room so he could see Elisabeth. She really existed there before him. She looked brokenhearted. He awkwardly sat on the edge of the bed, and he immediately reached for the wiggling Abby.

"Hello there, little Abby," he said placing the candle on the end table and then cuddling her to his chest. He laid a hand around Elisabeth's shoulder. "Abby, it looks like you and me are going to have to take care of your momma some more."

"Oh, Mr. Richardson. This entire journey came to nothing! You sacrificed so much. I am such a fool, and here I am troubling you again!" Elisabeth's heart burst for this man.

Colin smiled. "Trouble? Maybe some aggravation, but please, Mrs. Allerton, do not call all that happened to us 'nothing.' Let me tell you this: throughout my life I have never experienced such unexpected riches. They are beyond any of my dreams!"

Elisabeth chuckled as she wiped her tears. "You really feel that way? I know what you mean. I feel the same about—about you."

Colin held Elisabeth and Abby tighter. "Elisabeth, we are going to be fine. The Lord willing, we are going to be just fine."

Author's Afterword

Dear Reader,

Thank you for your interest in Elisabeth Allerton's adventure from London to St. Paola to Dorchester, Massachusetts. My curiosity for Puritans began while acquiring a M.A. degree in Christian studies over three decades ago (Calvin University).

From many readings I concluded Puritans often received unfair press, reduced to the bizarre Salem witch trials. In reality, how successful Puritans acted out their faith depended on individual hearts and the leadership of communal life. It was a mixed bag, but they were a brighter light than most during that period. I hope Elisabeth displays some of the good heart described in *Worldly Saints* by Leland Ryken and *The Puritans: Their Origins and Successors* by D.M. Lloyd Jones.

St. Paola is a fictitious island drawing on historical touch points from several Caribbean islands including Nevis, St. Kitts, Haiti, and Jamaica. For example, voodoo has roots in the history of Rose Hall in Jamaica where the story is told of a serial killer white woman influenced by African superstitions. In this book a mentally traumatized slave uses voodoo to aid her survival.

Europeans who settled in the Caribbean carried out Carib hunts that were done to remind slaves and free islanders what happened if they stepped out of line. My sentimental tendencies would wish that all enslaved people could hijack ships and find peaceful shores. We know reality was and is far from that happiness. The plantation history of slavery brims with an ocean of tears, and I am not qualified to write about this. Yet to set my protagonist in the 17th century Caribbean meant some attention to slavery.

In 1666, Caribbean farming was still in formative stages of turning from cotton to sugar cane, which needed inexpensive labor. The book *Sugar and Slaves: The Rise of the Planter Class in the English West Indies, 1624-1713* by Richard S. Dunn helped me understand how slavery, the sugar cane production, and the colonization of the New World moved all its people toward our present context.

Elisabeth's interest in her favorite London apothecary Nicholas Culpeper is a straight line to Americans' keen interest today in alternative medicines. Culpeper's book *Complete Herbal* was a bestseller in America for many years and is still available (*The English Physician*). Another medical contemporary during Elisabeth's era was midwife Jane Sharp, who wrote a valuable resource for her colleagues, *The Midwives Book* (1671).

The Rev. Richard Mathers (1596-1669) in *Unexpected Riches* is the only dialoguing character who existed, but his words and actions are fiction. From his journal, one reads he lived through the turbulent sea experience he mentions. Colin's motto *Antes Muerto que Mudado* (sooner dead than changed) comes from a youthful motto of poet and pastor John Donne prior to his conversion. The quote on marriage by Rev. Richard Baxter (1615-1691) was delivered in one of his sermons.

The song Colin sings, "Love Will Find Out The Way," was a popular 17th century tune and is performed even today. You may find various versions of the song on the internet. English musician Sarah

Garrard graciously granted me permission to use her adaptation on my website: csboyll@q.com (see the *Unexpected Riches* tab).

Some readers may wish for more Shakespearean language in the novel, but I hope the reformed hymn "Sing Praise to God Who Reigns Above" (Johann Jakob Schütz, 1675); Colin's 1600s song "Love Will Find Out the Way"; the English tale, *Babes in the Wood*; and scriptures using the *Geneva Bible* satisfy how Elisabeth and company spoke. These sources exist in public domain.

Thank you for reading this adventurous historical tale. My prayer is you will discover unexpected riches in your life, even when your world turns up-side-down.

Sincerely,
   C. S. Boyll, 2022